## HER FACES IN THE MIRROR

Enid Tregaron was a sheltered innocent, ignorant of the violence of the world.

Enid Tregaron was the brutal murderess of her own mother and father.

Enid Tregaron was the victimized bride of a husband who used her as his helpless pawn.

Enid Tregaron was a sensually ravenous creature seeking satisfaction in shameless adultery.

*Enid was everything that was good. Enid was all that was evil. Enid did not know the maddeningly elusive answer—and had every reason in a sulfurously stifling Victorian world to be afraid to find out. . . .*

## THIS BAND OF SPIRITS

# Big Bestsellers from SIGNET

# This Band of Spirits

## Noël Vreeland Carter

Ⓞ

**A SIGNET BOOK**

**NEW AMERICAN LIBRARY**

TIMES MIRROR

NAL BOOKS ARE AVAILABLE AT QUANTITY DISCOUNTS
WHEN USED TO PROMOTE PRODUCTS OR SERVICES. FOR
INFORMATION PLEASE WRITE TO PREMIUM MARKETING DIVISION,
THE NEW AMERICAN LIBRARY, INC., 1633 BROADWAY,
NEW YORK, NEW YORK 10019.

Ⓞ

SIGNET TRADEMARK REG. U.S. PAT. OFF. AND FOREIGN COUNTRIES
REGISTERED TRADEMARK—MARCA REGISTRADA
HECHO EN CHICAGO, U.S.A.

SIGNET, SIGNET CLASSICS, MENTOR, PLUME AND MERIDIAN BOOKS
are published by The New American Library, Inc.,
1633 Broadway, New York, New York 10019

First Printing, February, 1980

1 2 3 4 5 6 7 8 9

PRINTED IN THE UNITED STATES OF AMERICA

This book is for
Seon Manley,
a lady who loves the
dark mysteries
of
Victorian murder,
as a thank-you for
her many kindnesses.

And in those days shall men seek death,
and shall not find it; and shall desire to die,
and death shall flee from them.
       —*The Revelation of*
       *St. John the Divine, 9:6*

... seek, and ye shall find ...
       —*St. Matthew, 7:7*

# 1

# THE MAN
# CALLED DE'ATH

My name is Death: the last best friend am I.
 —Robert Southey

And the worst friend and enemy is but Death.
 —Rupert Brooke

It was cold in London during that dark winter of 1849—colder and danker even than usual—and the chill wind, moving a solid, sodden blanket of steel-gray cloud aloft above our heads, brought along as well the nightmare stench of the great city that sprawled, ugly even then, at our hunched backs as we stood on the brow of that naked hill, a huddled cluster of black-clad, funereal figures. Yet, had I known what was to follow, what the ensuing months were to bring as a result of the happenings on that grim hill in that grim cemetery on that windswept and darkening day—how irrevocably all our lives were to be changed for good or ill, depending on our several dispositions—I might well have found comfort even in that scene, safety even in the familiarity of that gray life of mine, and I might never, never have left.

But I did leave, and that, after all, is whereby hangs this tale—my tale, Augusta Tregaron's tale, and that of those others who entered our bleak lives on that particular morning and on that particular hill. It is even, in some respects, the tale of the man whose body we had thought to leave in the earth of that hill, for as it happened, we really did not leave him there at all. Rather, he came away with us to share in our tale of bitterness and fear, of love and forgiveness; our tale, ultimately, of Death and of life itself.

The name on the ornate granite marker by which we stood, one of hundreds in that grim orchard of mournful stones, read TREGARON in large, deeply incised Gothic letters. Below, pale and chaste, the very etching almost as timid as the woman commemorated thus, was the further legend: "Amelia, lamented wife of Llewellyn, 1794–1830."

It was that Llewellyn, supposed lamenter of his long-dead wife, whom we had gathered to mourn and to bury on that December day of 1849; that Llewellyn Tregaron, who had been my uncle and the last remaining brother to the forbidding, crepe-enshrouded woman who stood beside me with set mouth and unseeing eyes—eyes that burned with a kind of furious intensity, unfathomable and fearful to behold; eyes that might, of old, have characterized Medea, the Cumaean Sibyl, or the very Medusa herself.

I remember now, even as if it were yesterday, how, though her arm rested upon mine, the touch was light; the old white fingers, like bones already, protruding rigidly from the black mitts that covered her hands to the knuckles. She put no weight upon me on that terrible day, nor had she before— and on only *one* since that time. Augusta Tregaron, as far as was known, had put no weight of hers upon anyone in her long, cold life. Even the loss of her last and best-loved brother could not weaken the rigid discipline of that spare, hard body or that self-contained and unbending soul. I remember thinking that she might, one day, fracture and splinter into crystalline fragments like stone, but never would she, like a flower, sway and wilt and wither on the stalk. Though when the day actually came, to my surprise and hers as well, she actually did neither. But that was a day as yet unborn, and need not concern me now.

After the service was over—cheerless, comfortless, empty words with no meaning in them but the meaning of a myth; no truth in them save hollow platitude—we stood, the two of us, and stared down at the massive black coffin with its heavy bars of bronze along the sides and at the ends. One by one, the tall, solemn elderly men who had been the friends, companions, and business associates of Llewellyn Tregaron paid us their respects and stretched their long, bony, angular old men's legs over the brow of the hill and down through the orchard of tombstones to their waiting carriages. The sound of wheels rattling on cobblestones swelled and faded on the soggy air until at last we were alone, we two grim women, dressed like carrion crows and perhaps as merciless—at least to each other—standing by that casket and that stone on that bare hill.

Below, our own carriage waited, tended by our man, his liveried arm banded in black, his tall hat trailing sable ribbons and his very whip bound with black rosettes, as were the blinders of the horses. Behind it sat a hackney coach hired for the occasion and crowded with the house servants, looking uncomfortable in their Sabbath best and insecure in their futures now the master had departed for other worlds.

A tremendous gust of cold wind slashed across the hill just then, setting the dark, brittle ivy on each grave to rattling like so many dry bones and wafting aloft great masses of the last brown leaves of the autumn just passing. A shiver went through my frame and I longed to be away from that horrible, melancholy place.

"Shall we return, Aunt?" I asked stiffly, lest any note of eagerness sound in my voice. If it had, she would have noticed it and delayed all the more. Augusta Tregaron was that kind of woman and I had cause to know it well.

"Someone approaches. It seems not all the mourners have left." Her voice, old and dry, imitated the crisp rustling of the ivy on the graves around us.

I looked down the hill to my left, away from our own equipages, and saw that far at the bottom was a large, old-fashioned closed carriage, immaculately black and as shiny as new patent leather, with gleaming brass lamps and jetty horses in funereal harness, as plumed and bedecked with crepe as any pulling a mortician's finest hearse. Beside it stood a man in deepest mourning, so tall and slender and pale of face that he might just have been taken from his casket and propped, corpse-stiff, against the side of the bulky carriage. That he was well and truly alive was made apparent to me by the gradual turning of his head as he followed the progress of his manservant up the granite-studded hill to where my Aunt Augusta and I waited to receive him.

"Name of Tregaron, Ma'am?" he called out to us with a want of breeding and manners that made me wince and caused my aunt to utter an audible gasp of disapproval and grow even more rigid with dignity than was her wont. His accent was of the London streets—cockney—though, as he continued to speak, it became very clear that he made a constant effort to imitate his betters by affectations of accent and vocabulary, and to ingratiate himself with an obsequiousness that only made his inferior origins all the more apparent to me. In short, I took an instant dislike—and, as I thought then, an abiding one—to this man.

He came toward us with a determined stride, and regardless of the paths, set his black-booted feet upon grave after grave until he stood before us, whipped off his tall hat, and with an ostentatious bow slapped it against his black-clad chest.

"Jemmy Burkers at your service, Miss Tregaron—both the elder and younger Misses Tregaron . . ." he amended deferentially, smiling toward me with a great show of wide, square, white teeth. "My master, Mr. Ambrose De'Ath, Esquire"—and here I could not help but wince again, for surely Mr. De'Ath himself hardly felt it necessary to affect such a title—"extends 'is condolences to you at the loss of your nearest and dearest and, no' wishin' to intrude upon your grief at this time, desires to present 'is card"—here he bowed again and offered a black-bordered *carte de visite* with a broad hand tightly encased in black kid—"and begs leave to call upon you at any time in the immediate future wha' is most convenient to yourselfs."

Aunt Augusta took the proffered card, glanced at the name thereon, and turned it over. On the back, written in a fine copperplate script, was one sentence: "I knew your brother."

She looked up sharply, first to the servant before her and then down the hill toward his master. The tall man nodded slightly and with great dignity. My aunt looked at the card again and after some seconds of consideration raised her own eyes levelly into the dark, crafty eyes of Jemmy Burkers.

"You may tell your master that I shall receive him tomorrow morning at ten."

"Oh, fank you, ma'am. I—"

"You may go," she cut him off and turned at once toward our own equipage, which waited at the foot of the hill to our right.

"My master would wish me, ladies, to escort you to your—" the creature persisted.

"Your master's wishes in your regard are, I assure you, Mr. Burkers"—she said the name with an eloquent sniff of disdain—"no concern of mine."

Together we descended the path toward our carriage, leaving Mr. Burkers to make his opposite way down the hill to his waiting master. The chill wind blew the stench of London toward us, rattling the ivy like dry bones on the graves even as the wheels of our vehicles and the hooves of our horses rattled on the cobbles of the road. Dry bones . . . dry bones . . .

Aunt Augusta set me to letter-writing after breakfast the next morning; to the tedious work of replying in her name to the many letters of condolence which my uncle's death had precipitated. I sensed that this was, in part at least, busywork, calculated to keep me out of her company and away from the drawing room, where I knew that she awaited the visit of Mr. Ambrose De'Ath, "Esquire." I should have felt far less sulky over this, and harbored far fewer feelings of pique in my breast had she merely asked me to absent myself upon the arrival of her visitor.

This, however, was not my aunt's way with me—or, for that matter, with anyone else I suppose, for whilst she could be painfully direct when directness was sure to cause hurt and indignity, in small matters of no real consequence she was obnoxiously obscure and circumspect, with the result that one could not help but feel resentment at the insult to the sensibilities and intelligence that such slighting treatment implied. One might think that I, at twenty-seven, and after more than thirteen years in my uncle's household with her, should have been inured to such treatment, but I assure you that it was not so. Over the years I had hardened my heart to her, but my deepest, innermost feelings were as liable to hurt as ever they had been when I was a child. There seemed to be no help for this, and my only consolation was that as a general rule I was able to hide my pain as well as I did. This hiding of my deep feelings was perhaps unwise in the long run of things, for the toll upon my nerves and personality as a result had made me, as I can see now, appear to be even as rigid— as cold—and as hard as was my Aunt Augusta herself. Yet, no matter how it was I appeared to the world at large, within I was soft and a prey to the constant assaults of my Aunt Augusta, whose way was never sparing, never kind, never gentle.

Mr. De'Ath had arrived, as expected, upon the stroke of ten. It was nearly the noon hour when I was sent for at last, and I must confess it was with as much curiosity as surprise that I obeyed her unexpected summons and entered the drawing room to meet her guest.

"Come, dear," she said in a coaxing tone, as if talking to an idiot child. "My guest has expressed an interest in meeting you," she stated, as if rather surprised that anyone should actually entertain such a desire.

"Miss Tregaron, it is indeed a pleasure."

Of a sudden, and without any more formal introduction than that I have just described, I found my own warm hand grasped in the slender, cold white one of a tall, extremely pale, and gaunt man of indeterminate years whom I knew at once to be that Ambrose De'Ath whose card the servant Jemmy Burkers had presented to Aunt Augusta on the previous afternoon. He raised my hand to his thin, straight lips and touched it to them lightly.

My first impulse was to draw back in surprise at his impetuosity, if not in actual revulsion at the touch of his cold skin, but I was a young woman of breeding and so I suffered in silence—or nearly so.

"I do not believe we are acquainted, sir," I replied coolly as I withdrew my hand from his and sat upon a chair across the room from both him and my aunt, who was seated rigidly on the edge of a sofa by the long windows which overlooked Park Lane.

"Through the good offices of your Aunt Augusta I hope, surely, to amend that lack." His words had the sound of presumption and impulse about them, and yet his manner of speaking and his very stance itself were coldly severe and remote.

"Do you, sir? I cannot think why!" Turning to my aunt, who, all the while, had watched our exchange with an enigmatic expression that I was at a loss to fathom, I addressed her thus: "Who is this person, Aunt?" with the deliberate intention of being rude, the which was my defense in a situation which I did not understand and which troubled me vaguely.

"He is," she drawled slowly with a shrewd look about the eyes that I did not like, "Mr. Ambrose De'Ath of the Cornwall De'Aths and descended from Huguenot nobility who fled the St. Bartholomew's Night Massacre. He says that he has been long in France and is only just returned from there."

She looked then with hooded eyes at the portrait on the wall behind me—a portrait of her late brother, Morgan Tregaron—and burst her bombshell with no more warning than that: "Mr. De'Ath claims to have known your parents."

"Say to have met them, rather. . . ."

"Claims to . . . ?" I could say no more, but was completely overcome. I scarcely heard the words of his own emendation of my aunt's statement. She, noting my discomfiture with satisfaction, pressed her advantage: "You know, then, Mr. De'Ath, not only the names of my lamented brother, Morgan Tregaron, and his poor wife, Caroline"—and even then, after all those years, the note of loathing crept into her passionless voice at the mere mention of my mother's name—"but you must, of necessity, know as well the name of Enid Tregaron, to whom I introduce you now."

"Once again, Miss Tregaron, it is a pleasure." Ambrose De'Ath inclined his gaunt, pale head in my direction. I still could make no reply, the old sick feeling knotting the pit of my stomach with dread once more. I knew what was coming next—what always came next—and I awaited the words the way a condemned man awaits the dropping of the planks beneath his feet.

"The name of Enid Tregaron, Mr. De'Ath, obtained some unfortunate notoriety coincident with the deaths of my brother and his wife. It was thought at the time—and with some logic, I will admit—that Enid had been responsible in some way for their demise." She paused, having chosen her words carefully as always, like an executioner testing the tautness of the rope around my neck; pressing her toe on the boards beneath my feet.

Ambrose De'Ath stood motionless between us with a reserve every bit as rigid as Aunt Augusta's own. If she had said no more, I doubt he should have pressed her, for he seemed to be a man who waited more upon other people's revelations, making, I suspected even then, very few of his own. As for myself, I only sat and waited for the dropping of the trap and the last, inevitable, sickening thud.

"It cannot have escaped your attention even in France, Mr. De'Ath. In fact, I believe that the French papers, with their grotesque love of sensation, made even more of our little family tragedy than did the hawkers of such horrors on the streets of London."

"Surely, Miss Tregaron, it is unnecessary to revive sorrows that are . . ." Ambrose De'Ath broke in stiffly and evidently on my behalf, for he cast me a glance which, though not actually warm, seemed to indicate a desire to spare my feelings. I felt a small twinge of gratitude and shame for my own rather unpleasant behavior toward him.

"Nonsense, Mr. De'Ath! We are all adults here, and are capable of facing the ugly realities of our lives. My niece Enid must live with the fact of the murder of her parents even as surely as I must live with the fact that I perhaps shelter their murderess; that I myself may one night be murdered in my bed even as was my brother Morgan—"

"Aunt Augusta . . ." I could bear no more.

"My brother Morgan," she went on relentlessly, "was beaten about the head with a poker, Mr. De'Ath, and his wife, Caroline, had more than twenty stab wounds upon her body. The only servant in the house that night, the old cook, was stabbed six times and did not die at once, but rather bled to death crawling to the kitchen door in a vain attempt to summon help."

And then came the dreadful final pause in her tale. Her guest stood his ground, unmoved, revealing not the slightest emotion; not the twitching of an eye nor the curl of a lip. I sat in torture, unable to move had my life depended upon such an action, as my knotted stomach rose to meet the burning lump in my throat.

Augusta Tregaron spoke again, the cold, dry tone of irony intensifying the significance of her words. "My niece Enid, who was just fourteen at the time, was the only other occupant of the house on that particular night. Miraculously, she not only escaped the murderer's blade, but had the good fortune to sleep through the whole nightmarish episode."

"That was one fortunate occurrence at least, Miss Enid," Ambrose De'Ath remarked to me in his austere manner. "The world could not have afforded to lose so young such a pretty face as yours."

I looked up at him in confusion. His cold manner so belied the warmth of his words, and yet, the words must be kindly meant or else why say them? After all, he must have grasped the true intent of my aunt's words and realized that by passing any compliment to me, he greatly displeased her. But then, why desire to please either of us? What, pray, were we to him? He must have seen the small look of gratitude that I dared to cast his way, but if he did, he made no acknowledgment. Instead, he turned to my aunt and remarked with carefully chosen words (or so I sensed) that he had indeed heard news of the triple murder while on the Continent and had, in fact, written a letter of condolence at the time which had no doubt gone astray, since no member of the Tregaron family had ever made reply.

The implication of such a breach of etiquette—lapses in etiquette being numbered amongst the cardinal sins by my aunt—brought Augusta Tregaron up with a sniff. She pretended not to notice the remark, but got quickly off the subject by a counterimplication of her own that breeding demanded Mr. De'Ath bring his visit to a swift conclusion. Mate, checkmate! The interview was at an end, and I, excusing myself to my aunt and her guest, left the drawing room and mounted the stairs to my own rooms, where I lay in a near-stupor with a sick headache until, at last, I fell into a deep and troubled sleep.

How many such headaches I had suffered; how many such troubled sleeps I had endured over those long, blighted years, I could not begin to count. No more than I could count the endless times since my childhood that Augusta Tregaron had put me through just such a scene as that enacted before Mr. Ambrose De'Ath.

Yet this time it had been different—he had checked her in the telling of her tale; had not responded as she would have wished and as I had expected, given all the times I had been exposed thus to her friends, acquaintances, and even the most casual of visitors to her lair. He had almost seemed to protect me in his rather austere way.

How very odd. Until that moment, no one—not even my uncle—and nothing had ever protected me from the cruelties of my Aunt Augusta; no one save myself, of course, and nothing save that wall of ice that I had learnt I must build up around myself.

How odd, I mused thoughtfully as I fell at last into my uneasy slumbers, a protector.

For some days after this visit, my Aunt Augusta remained aloof, secluded within the dark recesses of her suite of rooms on the second story of the great, grim house in Park Lane. Though I usually found her occasional seclusions a relief from the otherwise nearly constant constraint of her company, this time, it was not a relief but an annoyance, the magnitude of which grew with each passing day.

I have ever been a curious person—one whom riddles annoy until they are solved; one impatient with puzzles and frustrated to fury by situations which I do not understand. In short, confusion unsettles my equilibrium whilst understanding and enlightenment are to me as the soothing balm of Gilead. This was true of me in all things, save, oddly perhaps, the riddle of the one greatest mystery of my own troubled life; that riddle I never sought to unravel. That puzzle remained untouched by my thoughts and unprobed by my otherwise ever-curious brain. The reason that that was so is obvious to me now, though it was not then: I was afraid.

But it was not the mystery of my own dark past that concerned me then. It was, rather, the mystery of Ambrose De'Ath and the as yet unknown reason for his visit. How irritating I found it not to know the reason for it! (I did not for a minute believe it to be merely a call of condolence, though at the time I could not for the life of me have said why.) How frustrating Aunt Augusta's unaccustomed seclusion when I, with as much cunning and subtlety as I might muster, longed to worm from her all that I could of him and especially of the contents of the mysterious packet which arrived on the next day following his visit.

I had taken a tray in my room on that night after awaking from my fitful slumbers, and so it was not until I entered the breakfast room the next morning that I leaned that Aunt Augusta too had taken dinner in her rooms and was breaking her fast there as well.

I had an errand in the shops which kept me away from Park Lane most of the morning, and so it was quite fortuitous that I chanced to arrive back at the house in time to be greeted by the obsequious Mr. Jemmy Burkers, still in his mourning livery, as he leaped down from the box of Ambrose De'Ath's hearselike coach and landed, light as a thief, on the pavement before me.

"Greetin's, Miss Tregaron. I'm the better for seein' yer fair face and desire herewith to place in your lily-whites this packet meant fer the old lady Tregaron, knowin' that it shall not be long in arrivin' at its ultimate destination."

With that, he bowed low, sweeping his tall, beribboned black hat off his dark head and smacking it hard against his heart. Upright once more, he slipped a thick envelope of stout vellum tied round with a black ribbon and seal of black wax into my hands and leaped back up onto the box. He cocked his head, winked impudently, and cracked his whip over the ears of the great, sleek black horses. Their plumes bobbed, their breaths puffed on the chill air, and they were off in an instant, leaving me with only the packet in my hands and the fading sound of hooves in my ears as proof that such a person as Jemmy Burkers had ever been nigh.

When I entered the hall, Aunt Augusta was at the head of the stairs. "Bring that packet to me at once, Enid." Clearly, whatever it contained, she had been expecting it.

"Yes, Aunt Augusta," I replied stiffly, and stopped at the mirror in the hall to remove my hat and gloves.

"At once."

"At once," I echoed, and giving my mantle to the maid, smoothed my hair and attended to a crease in my skirt. Then, packet in hand, I climbed the stairs slowly and carefully. Time, I had always known, was on my side, and my aunt was never a patient woman. Such minutes wasted were far more valuable to her than to me, or so I thought, and so I cost her dearly in minutes such as these whenever I was able, a fact about myself that I do not now like, but then—all those years ago—there was such pain and bitterness between us in that dark, unhappy house, and I fought her hatred of me in the only way I knew, never then realizing how dearly that fight cost *me* as well as Augusta Tregaron.

"Your packet, Aunt." I smiled when at last I reached her, and her old black-mitted hands grasped at it like an owl seizes a mouse in its talons. She retired at once to her rooms without another word. Her seclusion continued and my long wait began. What was in the packet?

It was on the third morning after the packet arrived that my aunt finally descended the stairs and entered the breakfast room.

"Enid, I wish you to speak to Mr. De'Ath for me." She spoke, though we had not seen each other for days, without any further ceremony than that. Her abruptness, though so characteristic, still caught me by surprise.

"I, Aunt! Speak to Mr. De'Ath? Whatever for?"

"Because of this," and she placed that mysterious object of such great conjecture and curiosity on my part—the black-beribboned vellum packet—beside my plate. She hesitated only a moment beside me, as if she were about to speak further, but evidently thinking better of it, she then made her way to the sideboard, where she took her breakfast from the covered silver dishes set out, as they were every morning, with faithful, unchanging, endlessly boring regularity.

Something in the set of her shoulders and the rigidity of her neck told me that she was waiting—for what? The triumph she would feel if I eagerly grabbed up the envelope and betrayed to her the agony of my curiosity? If so, she would be disappointed, for I sat to my meal with straight back and bowed head, biding as always my quiet time. But no, there was something different in her manner. She was waiting for my reaction to the contents of the envelope. Again, why? Was there something in it that she knew would hurt me? Some dart from that terrible past of mine with which to wound me the more? If so, again she would be disappointed, for my reaction to her remarks in front of Mr. De'Ath was a rare one for me. I had been unprepared and had betrayed my feelings too easily. I was stronger now, and more wary.

Again I looked at that rigid back. She dawdled over the trays, almost clanging one of the covers against another—so unlike her. So unlike. Why? And then I realized that it was *she* who was nervous; anxious for *my* reaction. Something in that packet struck a cord of fear and anxiety in *her*. For once it was not to hurt *me*, to gauge *my* pain, but to see my reaction to something that wounded *her*. Something in that envelope touched a vulnerability of hers, and how strange it made me feel to sense it. "Is this a dagger which I see before me,/ The handle toward my hand?" Was I, so long unarmed, being given a weapon at last with which to fight? I could not believe it!

I arose from the table even as she sat down to it. "I shall see to this in the morning room, Aunt, after I have answered my letters." I did not wait for a reply, but walked calmly to the door, the packet in my hand.

"It is rather important, Enid."

"Is it indeed, Aunt?"

"I should like you to read over the contents. You are a clever young woman in your way, and I should like your comments. . . ." Her voice trailed off tentatively, but there was a plea for urgency implied in her every word and even in every small gesture of her fluttery old hands.

Yes, I thought maliciously, which is exactly why I shall make you wait. I left the room without another word. It must be important to her. It filled her with such trepidations that she had not even given me her favorite order: "At once," as she had in the hall those few mornings before. But then, on that other morning she had not yet known what the packet contained and was not yet *afraid!*

The Antiquarians
December 14, 1849

Dear Miss Tregaron,

Needless to say, I am sensible that the topic of our discussion this morning was a painful one to you. Save for your niece, you are now alone in the world, cut off from your once numerous family by that great Unseen Wall whose name is—like my own—Death.

As it is with you, only one living being of mine yet lives, and she, I fear, must leave ere long. It is a subject of great pain to me, and the knowledge that I must be cut off for good and all from her hardly bears thinking upon. Think upon it I have, however, deeply and often, and such contemplations have resulted in what has now become my lifelong study. Yes, now, after what I humbly admit has been an aimless and luxurious life of travel and indolent waste, I have begun a pursuit which, hopefully, will result in discoveries of the greatest benefit to mankind. To that pursuit I have pledged my life and bent my fortunes, confiding in none but a few trusted servants, confidants, and she who is my only family—until this day, when I opened my heart and spoke to you.

In the hours since leaving you, I have thought much upon our meeting and have decided to take you into my confidence the more and to ask you to consider joining me in my work. That I should ever have contemplated making such a request of anyone is a revelation to me—so secretive and lonely have been my studies until this moment. Yet, what seems to me to be incontrovertible proof of our ultimate mutual destiny lies before me as I write, and how can I deny its import? After you have examined it, how indeed can you?

And so I come to entrust the enclosed sheets to your care and beg you to peruse them at your leisure. Their content indicates to me that you and I are destined to join forces in further pursuit of this study of mine, and once having met you, I cannot but think that it is indeed meant to be. You are a strong and single-minded woman of great character, intelligence, and vision, and you have suffered—even as have I. Perhaps it is fitting that two such as we should strike out together on a course uncharted in the history of mankind and touch together upon the greatest mystery of Life—Death itself.

Until I hear from you, Miss Tregaron, I remain your obedient servant

Ambrose De'Ath
Thanatologist

I let drop the last sheet of the black-bordered vellum on which Mr. De'Ath's letter was written in his neat, tight copperplate hand.

Thanatologist. In Greek mythology, Thanatos was Death, twin brother of Hypnos, who was Sleep, the two being sons of Night. Mr. De'Ath called himself a student of Death. I looked closely at the black wax seal that dangled unbroken from the ribbons that had held the envelope closed. The impression was that of a skull between two reversed torches, these last being the emblem of Thanatos if I remembered my mythology aright.

I did not know quite what to think—that the man was mad perhaps. But then, who was I, in this house of madness, to call others mad? I unfolded the bundle of enclosed sheets to which the letter referred and looked at them in blank stupefaction. Here was madness indeed!

The paper was the same fine quality, heavy black-bordered vellum as that of the letter, but the writing at the top of the paper was very old-fashioned and un-English in style; the hand that had held the lead pencil must have been very frail. The name Henriette De'Ath was repeated over and over again on the page, the signature hardly varying from top to bottom. The second page appeared to be much the same at first glance, until one noticed that some three-quarters of the way down the page, the writing took on a more and more careless, scrawled quality. The writer, one might think, was tiring, but such was not the case. The same hand, scrawling feebly from the last "t" in Henriette, had begun to form another word, and the letters, though clumsy, were firmer. The new word thus formed was "Hentittreg" followed by "De'Ath" written in the frailest of hands. By the time the signature had been repeated half a dozen more times on the page, it was no longer the name Henriette De'Ath, but rather simply the lone surname Tregaron. By the bottom, it had become a scrawled but recognizable imitation of my late uncle's own distinctive hand, and read: Llewellyn Tregaron.

By the bottom of the third page, the hand was firm and masculine, the script English in style, and the signature the most perfect replica of my uncle's own hand that it would be possible to imagine. The fourth page was another dozen renderings of my uncle's signature, now scrawling more and more, until the name of Henriette De'Ath had become the predominant one again, and finally—by the fifth page—the only one.

I sat back in my chair, the stiff sheets of vellum unfolded before me on the desk in the morning room, and took in my hand the last page, reading over and over the legend that had been added at the bottom in Ambrose De'Ath's own by now familiar copperplate script:

The foregoing signatures were written solely by the hand of Madame Henriette De'Ath from ten o'clock to quarter past eleven on the night of December 9, 1849, at

—⋇{14}⋇—

Thanatos Abbey, Cornwall, in the presence of the undersigned.

> The Reverend Enoch Pond
> Mrs. Peggy Pond
> Jemmy Burkers
> Ambrose De'Ath

I thought long and hard on the contents of that envelope before I returned the pages to their place, and so it was some time before I actually left the morning room and, packet in hand, began to mount the stairs to my rooms. My step was arrested by the sharp voice of my aunt behind me.

"Enid, a word with you." She stood in the doorway of the drawing room, stiff and cold in the stark black of her mourning. The silk of her skirts rustled like the brittle ivy on a grave as she turned, preceding me back into the darkened, drape-shrouded room from whence she had come. As I entered, I could barely make her out in the dim, flickering light that came from the small fire in the grate. The room was overheated, airless, and rank with the mingled scents of her rice powder, her lavender-scented clothing, and her bitter, old woman's breath. She, always so rigid and controlled, actually sat twisting a black-edged linen handkerchief in just such a nervous manner as might once have been induced in me by her cold and heartless presence.

I crossed to the mantel and, ignoring the heat of the fire, stood looking down at her. She seemed so old and frail now, her grotesque powdered face the only thing about her visible in the flickering gloom; that, and her bony white fingers twisting the small black-and-white square of linen.

I ran my own fingers deliberately across the long cut-crystal drops that hung from one of the pair of candlesticks at either end of the mantelpiece. She started at the cold, tinkling sound but said nothing, not wishing to give me the satisfaction of a protest. Her reaction had pleased me well enough, however, and so I relented and spoke at last.

"Mr. De'Ath is a thanatologist. It is a word the parts of which I understand quite well, coming from the Greek 'Thanatos,' meaning 'death,' and the suffix '-ology,' meaning 'to discourse upon.' I daresay Mr. De'Ath must have coined the word himself."

"I daresay, Enid, but that is neither here nor there. What do you make of his letter; of his enclosure?" Her impatience was altogether too spirited even yet. I must break her.

"I make nothing of it."

"Nothing?" She was astonished and disappointed, though she hid it well.

"Nothing, Aunt. What is there to make? Some lady unknown, presumably a relation of Mr. De'Ath's, has written her name and the name of Uncle Llewellyn a tiringly repetitive number of times on several sheets of good-quality vellum and before a number of witnesses. To what end, I do not know, but surely to have been witness to such a futile exercise must rank high among the most boring occupations known to man. I realize that there must be precious little to do on a cold winter's evening in Cornwall but—"

"Enid, do stop playing at words," she said, striking to the heart of the matter. "Henriette De'Ath is an old—elderly—woman, Mr. De'Ath's own mother. At the very time of her beginning to write, your Uncle Llewellyn was dying. He died even as she was reproducing with her own unconscious hand the perfect facsimiles of his signature that you have seen. Does that not indicate anything to you?"

"What, pray, should it indicate to me, Aunt? That Madame De'Ath is a consummate forger?"

"Why, that Llewellyn wishes to communicate with us; that he is not dead—not *really* dead."

She had said it. She had made a fool of herself at last with her deep fears and her futile hopes. I gave no quarter.

"Aunt Augusta, we saw him die. We saw that waxy, embalmed mummy into which those carrion birds of prey called undertakers translated him before they dropped him into the ground for us. Uncle Llewellyn *is* dead."

"Enid, he has a spirit, an immortal soul, and that soul is trying to reach us." She spoke hotly now, insisting on her point. God, but she was strong.

"Immortal soul be damned! He was a piece of flesh and bone like you, like me, and like the saddle of mutton that the cook is preparing for our dinner tonight." I had not meant it to, but my temper flared in spite of itself, unwise, for by waxing hot, I risked the loss of my advantage.

"Is that what you were doing on that night thirteen years ago? Dressing a bit of flesh and bone for dinner?" Her voice cracked shrilly as she cried out. And then the horror of what she had said came home even to her, and she snapped her jaws shut like a trap.

I said not another word myself, but with every nerve in my body quivering in bitter rage, I quietly took the packet from the mantel beside me and dropped it carefully, deliberately into the very middle of the flames in the grate. There was a deadly edge to my voice when I finally spoke.

"So much for thanatology and so much for you, one day soon, Aunt, for if you do have an immortal soul, it's going to be a long, hot eternity."

I left the room even as she shrieked in dismay and knelt down before the fire, trying to wrest the burning envelope from the middle of the flames with a poker. The maid, Mary, ran past me to see what the trouble was as I went into my uncle's library and locked the doors behind me. I had much to think about. Suddenly, life was taking an interesting turn, and I remember how wickedly I smiled to think upon it, for I was, then, as consumed with bitterness and a desire for revenge against my tormentor as she was consumed with hatred for me. She had punished me these nearly fourteen years past for the events of one long-ago nightmare night of murder, and now, at last, fate had seemed to put a weapon in my hand, and that weapon was Augusta Tregaron's own *fear.*

# 2

# PRISONED YET

> ... and through the chinks and breaches
> of our prison we see such glimmerings of light,
> and feel such refreshing airs of liberty,
> as daily raise our ardour for more.
> —Edmund Burke

> Prison'd in a parlour snug and small,
> Like bottled wasps upon a southern wall.
> —William Cowper

Events, like sorrows, when they come, come not as single spies but in battalions. So, beginning with my uncle's sudden death, the defiant striding of Jemmy Burkers into our lives, followed close upon by the solemn, dead-march entry of Mr. Ambrose De'Ath himself, events trooped in their battalions, and I, prisoner for so long in that dead house in Park Lane, saw at last the possibility of being freed; of the lock breaking, the bars bending, the dead and dying past slipping from my wrists like rusted shackles, leaving me free at last to enter the world of living—happy—human beings.

My reasons, enumerated, were thus: Llewellyn Tregaron had been, like all the men in our family, a quiet and austere man, but there had always been a certain warmth and charitable kindness in his attitude toward me; a certain unspoken but quite palpable sensitivity to the pain of my peculiar position in his household. It had led me to believe in him as a silent but well-disposed friend in addition to his role as guardian and controller of my inheritance.

With his death, his management of my parents' estate must needs dissolve—or so I had every reason to suppose. It was, in fact, that quite reasonable supposition which had bred in me, since my uncle's death, a heady sense of my own approaching freedom and destiny; that had caused, despite my genuine sorrow at his loss, the beginnings of my sudden high spirits and my renewed defiance of my aunt.

In short, so sure was I of the inevitable turning of events in my favor, that I came to feel, in that cold month of December 1849, a reawakening of my confidence; my sense of my own destiny and power over my own life growing far beyond any bounds I had ever known. I played the old cat-and-mouse game with my aunt in my very best form. My spirits were high and I came alive with such a fire and passion of my true nature as had long lay banked unnaturally within me. There was even a spring in my step that far more befitted the young and lively girl I might have been than the unlovely and unloved spinster that I had become over so many long years in that grim dead house that I believed was at last behind me.

Behind me! Yes, my Uncle Llewellyn's house in Park Lane was nearly behind me; would be out of my life forever in a matter of days or weeks only. I believed that with my whole heart and reveled in the knowledge of it. And it was in such a frame of mind as that, that I took to my carriage and rode through the gray streets of London on a particular late December morning, my eyes alight with pleasure at the decorated windows of the fine shops, the wreaths of holly and greens, the carts of evergreen trees being delivered to the homes of those who had adopted the Prince Consort's Germanic notion of Christmas trees. The pleasant, pungent aroma of roasting chestnuts overwhelmed even the usual smell of horses, and the happy cries of holiday greetings drowned out the shrills of street hawkers and the whining of street boys as they swept the crosswalks free of offal for pedestrians, dodging carriages and begging coppers all the while.

It was just then, on one of those busy streets, amongst all those bustling people, that I spied the long, spare frame of Ambrose De'Ath as he strode with a placid, detached air of superiority through the holiday crowds, his deep mourning giving to him the aspect of an undertaker as he passed along the crowded sidewalks. He carried in the crook of his arm a bulky and oddly shaped parcel, which he shifted from time to time, as if somewhat troubled by the inconvenience of carrying it.

Upon what impulse I know not, I ordered my driver to the

side of the curb as we passed him by, and when he caught up to us, I called out with a smile, "Mr. De'Ath, I bid you good morning."

He looked about him in some bewilderment before he saw me in the carriage at the curb, but when he caught sight of me at last, he smiled at once in recognition and came across the walk toward me with alacrity.

"Good morning, Miss Tregaron," he greeted me. "I cannot think of a more pleasant surprise. You are looking especially bright and saucy this pleasant, sunny day." It was the most voluble speech I think I had heard from him until then, and its lightness and cheerful flattery quite surprised my sensibilities and expectations.

"Have you been in the shops?" I asked with a nod toward his parcel and for want of anything else to say in the face of his compliment, which had rather embarrassed me.

"I have been buying treasures, Miss Tregaron, and am finding that even a treasure may be an unpleasant burden when wrapped up in an ill-tied bundle. At this time of the year, the help in the shops is quite lamentable—even more so than usual, I fear." He spoke so amiably that I was charmed entirely. It seemed, despite his mild upbraiding of holiday shop clerks, that he was really in quite as fine a mood as I, and so I responded with an impulsive warmth that rarely showed in the personality of the blighted woman that I was then.

"At the risk, Mr. De'Ath, of sounding too much like a knight in armor to the rescue, may I offer you some aid in your distress? A lift, perhaps, to wherever it is you are bound?" I suggested with a glibness that surprised even myself, let alone my driver, I am sure, who was witnessing behavior he had never before seen in his solemn, friendless young mistress.

"If you can go so far out of your way as the Antiquarians, I should be much obliged, Miss Tregaron," he answered with another of his austere but by no means unpleasant smiles.

By way of reply, I unlatched the carriage door and nodded with a smile for him to enter. He did so at once, giving order to my driver where to take us as he climbed in and took the seat opposite me, his back to the horses.

"Now," he exclaimed, "see what I have purchased," and with that most enthusiastic order, whipped the brown paper and string from around what was perhaps the most ugly and grotesque curiosity that I had heretofore seen in my life.

I drew back instinctively at first, but then, my interest overwhelming my distaste, I leaned forward and examined the thing he held out to me in his black-gloved hands. It was a skull, or rather—since so much of skin and hair yet clung to its face and cranium—say a *head* with a small portion of neck still attached and, owing to the presence of so much desiccated skin over the face, an expression upon the remaining features that was extremely lifelike.

The eyelids, still fringed with delicate bands of lashes, were closed down upon the cheeks and seemed, though dry as last autumn's fall of leaves, as if shut in a sleep from which they might awaken even yet. Above the eyes, coppery red brows still arched high toward what remained of a once full head of wavy copper hair, in an attitude of surprise. What little brittle skin and bone remained of the nose was pathetic to behold and belied the lifelike expression of the rest of the features, but most grotesque of all was the mouth, for the teeth, firm and strong and turned golden brown with age like unto antique ivory, were clenched together in an obvious and immediate agony that was harrowing to behold.

The skin and musculature of the cheeks was taut with pain, the lips laid back from over the teeth in such a grimace that conjured up in my mind images of hot tongs and racks such as the barbaric Spanish Catholics had been wont to use upon their hapless intellectual and philosophical (to say nothing of moral!) superiors in the days of the Inquisition.

"Well, what do you think?" Ambrose De'Ath asked almost eagerly.

"A . . . a most fascinating object, indeed," I countered diplomatically. "I have never seen its like."

"Indeed you have not, outside of a museum, I expect!" he agreed with feeling and a certain pride. "It is the head of a martyr."

"A martyr," I exclaimed, rather interested now, for I could see that my intuition about torture and inquisitions was not far from the mark.

"The head," he went on, "of a Coptic Christian martyr of the first century A.D., dug up in Egypt."

"A mummy, then?" I asked.

"No, not a mummy exactly, but *mummified* by the natural effect of having been buried in the hot sands of the desert before it had had a chance to decay in the air. See, here, where the rope of the garrote was drawn around the throat from behind," he instructed, tipping the head so that I could see, on the dried flap of skin and bone of the neck, the traces of ancient cord even yet embedded in what was left of the martyr's throat.

"Fascinating," I agreed with mingled curiosity, distaste, and outright revulsion. "Tell me, why does one wish to own such a thing as that, I wonder?"

"The most puerile and common reasons would be for the remoteness of its antiquity, its historical significance, its value as a mere curiosity . . ." Ambrose De'Ath explained.

"But your reason is not so puerile as those," I suggested with a hint of flattery in my tone.

"Exactly," he answered solemnly. "All those reasons interest me on the face of it, but beyond that . . . thanatology."

"Thanatology," I repeated uncertainly. Could he really be sincere? And if he was, what would he think if he knew I had burned up his letter on the subject to my aunt?

"This man, look you, died in agony and torment for his faith—and indeed his faith must have been strong for him to submit to torture and death for it. Now, suppose enough remains of that strong character and spirit, contained in this head or in its vicinity, for me to reach it?" His eyes were alight with a fire, as he spoke, that I should never have thought they could possess.

"I do not understand," I said flatly.

"Suppose the spirit and life force of this martyr has not yet been entirely vitiated with the passage of time, what then?"

"I cannot guess. *You* must tell *me*," I answered dryly.

"Why, then, it should be possible to reach that soul, to make contact with this martyr from beyond the grave and speak to him," he said in a tone of wonder, as if the implication should be self-evident.

"In Coptic Egyptian or in plain English?" I asked with somewhat impolitic practicality.

"Never mind," he snapped precisely. "You would not understand," and with that he whisked the head out of my sight and back into the parcel, as if to protect it from my impious gaze, which was quite all right with me, since I found it detestable to view at all.

We talked then, somewhat stiffly, of minor pleasantries until our arrival at the marble-columned facade of his club, the Antiquarians, where the doorman helped him to exit my carriage. At the curb he turned and smiled again, his affability (such as it was) restored.

"Thank you again, Miss Tregaron, and I bid you good day. My regards to your aunt."

We smiled our farewell, and my carriage rolled away from

the club with some speed, for I had not long before I was due at my solicitors' offices in Bedford Row. What a strange man, I thought to myself, looking back over our peculiar ride and remembering that ghastly head of his. And then, I laughed out loud to think of myself like that—being driven on the London streets with a gentleman antiquarian in my carriage, dropping him at his exclusive and very well-thought-of club, going on from there about my own business—all new, free, rather dashing things in my life, smacking of that new life I felt was so soon to come.

Yes, as I left the Antiquarians, my feelings of hope and joy made even grimy old Londontown seem more enchanting to me than it had been since I was a child coming in from Wales for a visit. Suddenly everything seemed alive and beautiful, the people good and kindly and benevolent. Faces smiled out of the crowd, and I returned those smiles with joy in my own glowing demeanor. And I did glow! I felt it in myself. It even sounded in the click of my heels on the pavement as, at last, I alighted from my carriage and strode briskly across the walk and up the narrow, dark stairs that led to the upper chambers—ancient and smelling of the Middle Ages, as did all the precincts of law in that district—of my solicitors, Pepper and Pepper. The clerk, as old, it seemed, as the offices themselves, announced my arrival and admitted me to the room of a junior partner, whose news I awaited with great expectations and high good hopes. How I left that room was another matter entirely. . . .

"Enid, I have sent word around to Mr. De'Ath at his club, and he has agreed to call. We shall have tea in the drawing room." Aunt Augusta's voice was itself once more; full of haughty command. I had no spirit in me to fight her, nor even to be surprised at seeing Ambrose De'Ath twice in one day.

"Yes, Aunt. You need not worry. I shall absent myself."

"I do not wish you to be absent. Moreover, Mr. De'Ath has asked specifically that you join us. He expects it."

Still I had no spirit to challenge her or this near-stranger's expectations of me. "As you wish, Aunt." She smiled triumphantly, as if she knew where I had been and what it was I had learned. Perhaps she did. I would not have put it past her to know.

Once in my rooms, I had all I could do to keep from breaking down and weeping my eyes out. Only the knowledge that in a short time I would have to present myself before

Aunt Augusta and her guest prevented me from losing all control; it would never have done for me to have appeared with red, splotched face and swollen, puffy-lidded eyes before the scrutiny of those two souls, the one so cold and forbidding and implacable, the other austere, enigmatic, and maybe even slightly mad. Rather, I had perforce to control my emotions, summon up my courage, assess my situation as passionlessly as possible, and try to make what little I could of my life.

My life! My situation! What irony was implicit in those words! What future had I now, having learned from my solicitor the devious and constricting ways in which I was bound up and imprisoned even yet, despite my high hopes? My uncle's death had done nothing to free me. All I knew now was the confines of my prison—the length of the sentence which I yet must serve.

I was seven-and-twenty, spinsterish and virginal, embittered once more and bound in by the ugliness of my days in that grim, dark Park Lane mansion, kept by my warden—Augusta Tregaron—and, so I had believed until but an hour earlier, about to be freed from my terrible past and even more terrible present by the sad fact of my uncle's undeniably convenient death. But such was not to be! In those few brief minutes this very morning, my solicitor's words had dashed utterly my high hopes.

Uncle Llewellyn's seeming goodwill toward me was a sham, and he had, it seemed, included neither love nor trust in the catalog of his feelings toward me. The money coming to me from the estate of my dead parents eluded me yet, for he had ordered in his own will (which excluded me entirely) that control of my inheritance not be put into my own hands until my fortieth year unless I were to marry, in which case it would come to me as early as my thirtieth year. Until then, it was to be administered by my solicitors and continue being doled to me at the present rate—forty pounds per annum, payable quarterly. In short, I had enough pocket money to keep me in reasonable comfort as long as I remained under the Tregaron roof, but not nearly enough to escape that roof unless I chose to live in abject penury, as alone and friendless as some poor orphaned governess out of a ladies' novel.

How could Uncle Llewellyn have treated me thus? I asked myself over and over again. But then why ask! I *knew!* This was not his doing, but the fine workings of Augusta Tregaron's devious mind. This was her continued punishment of me! I had even challenged Mortimer Pepper, the head of the firm, and with some cunning calculation laid the deed solely to my poor uncle, reviling his memory in a particularly cruel manner, deliberately meant to arouse the indignation of such an old family friend as the elderly solicitor had always been to the Tregarons, and to elicit an unguarded response from him.

"Enough, enough, Enid," he had protested at last. "You do not know what you are saying. I can appreciate your disappointment, but your uncle Llewellyn took advice before he drew up this will."

"From you?" I snapped sharply.

"From me," he acknowledged with dignity, "and from . . . others. *Others*, as you know, Enid, have had very great influence on him over the years."

"Others! Others! Oh, my prophetic soul, my aunt," I raved dramatically, in a gesture I had seen the great Macready make in his celebrated version of *Hamlet*. I had got just the reaction I had been looking for. Yes, I could see in Mortimer Pepper's face what he could not say, but also could not deny. I was bound to that house even yet, despite my potential wealth, by the machinations of my own mortal enemy, the nemesis of my life, Augusta Tregaron.

How I could, at that moment, have gladly wished her dead—yet even her death would have availed me nothing. Control of my inheritance was not (thank God!) in her wicked hands, but rather in those of the law—for which I think I have Mr. Pepper to thank, for I am sure Aunt Augusta had wished my uncle to pass control of my money to her after his death. In that, at least, she had been foiled.

But being the woman I was, I could not really have wished anyone dead—even Augusta Tregaron. Moreover, since unlike Hamlet, I did not believe in Heaven, I thought it best, upon consideration, to leave her to Life. As long as she yet lived, I might have the satisfaction of seeing her eventual punishment. Again, that ugly theme—revenge—crept into my bitter heart, and though it shames me now, I cannot deny it: *then* I did truly want revenge.

Yet, by the time I had arrived back in Park Lane, my first flush of anger and hatred had abated and in their place was only a deep despair. I had seen realistically, as I thought then, the utter hopelessness of my situation, and so, as I entered the front hall of that dark old house, my spirits had been dampened beyond rekindling.

"Enid, Mr. De'Ath is coming to call," she had said.

"Yes, Aunt," I had replied. She had won. There was, it

seemed, no freedom for me. Would I live, I wondered, till forty? Or would Augusta Tregaron live to bury me?

"It pains me to see you looking so suddenly peaked, Miss Enid. The damp of the city this morning and your recent loss are working upon your accustomed good looks, although, I vow, I had not thought so this morning." Ambrose De'Ath, alone with me momentarily in the drawing room, spoke with an odd softness in his voice. I was not used to being spoken to with soft words, and had I not hardened myself, I think I should almost have cried. Instead, I reacted with that cold civility which had heretofore served me so well against the cruelties of my small world and its unhappy inhabitants.

"You have seen me thrice now, Mr. De'Ath. Pray what makes you assume that I am normally in any better looks than you now see?" I could not make out this strange man's attitude toward me. His pale haughty face was nearly always virtually expressionless, yet his words were usually solicitous and attentive—and this morning he had actually *smiled*— though more, I suspected, at his satisfaction with the martyr's head than with mine! Nevertheless, he was undeniably a most enigmatic man. But perhaps I should not have been surprised at that, after all. Was not my life bound round by enigma?

"You are a handsome young woman, Miss Enid. Any eye can see that. I expect men of my manservant Burker's class would term you an ' 'eartbreaker'! Having been reared as a gentleman," he added rather haughtily, almost as if reassuring himself of his own superior origins, "I am forced by my education, breeding, and natural conservatism to use less colorful, though surely no less heartfelt, terminology in describing you.

"I find you a woman of natural good looks, at this time somewhat out of looks due to the general inclemency of the weather, though today has been a good day all around, and the troubles which you have so recently endured. My own sympathetic inclination toward you causes me to be concerned on your behalf."

Inclemency be damned, is what I felt like replying. It is the long years of torment in this prison of a house; it is the horror of that night long ago that I bury in the back, shadowy places of my poor mind and heart that have worked their havoc on what good looks I might ever have expected to have. But I could not dare say such things to him—to anyone, for that matter—and so I went on playing at words with this odd man.

"You unsettle me, sir. I cannot think why, given all of the little you know of me, you should have any sympathy or inclination toward me at all."

"Yet, Miss Enid, I do." He said no more, for at that moment my Aunt Augusta returned from the morning room with a small parcel in hand.

"I am not a woman to fluster easily, Mr. De'Ath," she remarked, as if she were continuing a conversation already started, instead of interrupting one that had gone on in her absence (who, after all, would wish to converse with the notorious Enid Tregaron!), "but I am nonetheless mortified at the condition in which I am forced to return to you this packet of vitally important papers which you so graciously entrusted to my care." She unfolded the parcel into his hands and exposed the burned and scorched remnants of vellum which I had dropped into the fire on the previous afternoon.

"I can only blame myself," she shrilled with the air of a martyr. "I was foolish enough to entrust it to Enid; to seek her opinion of your mother's 'automatic writing,' as you call it, and to inform her of dear Llewellyn's attempt to communicate with us. *This* was her repayment of my trust." She flashed a look of blazing fury at me and muttered, "Willful girl, you are too bold." How many times I had heard *that* before!

"Pray be reassured, Miss Tregaron. I see that only the envelope and my covering letter have been destroyed. The inner pages, though damaged, are still legible. Think no more of it." Ambrose De'Ath exhibited no more surprise or pique than if he were looking at a burned tallow candle. He merely refolded the scorched pages in the outer paper again, and wrapping the whole in his large, black-bordered pocket handkerchief, placed it in the inner breast pocket of his coat.

"You are too kind and tolerant of my niece, Mr. De'Ath," Aunt Augusta remarked stiffly. Clearly she wished him to berate and humiliate me as she had attempted to herself. He, evidently, would have none of it.

"Your niece, Miss Tregaron, is a young lady of high spirits. She is, moreover, intelligent, and being so, she is a natural skeptic." This last with a glance at me which told me he was thinking of the morning's conversation about the head, of which my aunt knew nothing. "I can only think that she sensed some ruse and wished to spare your feelings. I was, by the way, about to beg Miss Enid's company for an hour's ride tomorrow, when your return broke my thought." And then, turning to me, he asked, "You do ride, Miss Enid?"

"I do indeed, Mr. De'Ath," I blurted out without a thought, so completely was I taken aback by his abrupt change of subject. Once again I felt as if he were somehow my ally, dared I say it, my protector, as it were.

"Splendid! I shall call for you in the morning and we shall ride before breakfast."

"Mr. De'Ath, my niece rarely rides out in the park; and never has she done so in the company of a man. There has been quite enough talk about her in past years . . ."

"And shall being seen in the company of a gentleman cause talk? I strongly doubt it, but if talk there is, it can only be the most natural and pleasantest of gossip; speculations on the wedding date and what the bridesmaids will wear—that sort of thing, what?" Here Ambrose De'Ath gave my aunt a mirthless smirk, and half-turning his gaunt, pale skull in my direction, twinkled his cold, colorless eyes at me almost merrily. Aunt Augusta was speechless with mingled dismay and shock.

As for myself, a strange sense of unreality gripped me. This peculiar man, so recent an intruder into my small, cold world, defending me from my aunt, seeking my company as if he really desired it! Why?

But what did the why of it matter? This last exchange with my aunt ended his visit. Hardly had he left when I ran up to my rooms to look over my riding habit. Whether Aunt Augusta approved or not (and she did not!), I had an engagement to ride out with a gentleman on the morrow—and willed she or nilled she, I *would* ride out!

Ambrose De'Ath and I were married by special license on the first day of January 1850 in the town of Portsmouth, and set sail immediately for Cherbourg and a honeymoon trip across France to Paris.

What consternation we left behind us, neither of us ever mentioned. We had simply done the deed without consultation; neither I with my Aunt Augusta nor Ambrose with his mother and household. For my part, I felt that I would have no cause to regret my sudden marriage. I felt that I knew exactly what I was doing with my life. If my heart was not actually engaged by this pale, gaunt, and somber husband of mine, my mind was in perfect, clearheaded order. This marriage, doing what my uncle's will had not, freed me from that house in Park Lane, from the clutches of Augusta Tregaron, and from the poverty I would have had to endure had I taken courage and left alone. Moreover, Ambrose was kind, attentive, and gentlemanly. If I did not actually love him, I was not really aware of it then, for I was grateful and in awe of his kindness; amazed by his defense of me—however mild it may have been; and protected by his solicitous manner. Being in some ways incredibly naive even at the advanced age of twenty-seven, I honestly think that I confused those feelings of gratitude, awe, and safety with love. And, after all, given the blighted existence I had led for so many years, what did I actually know of love? Especially the love of a woman for a man? Suffice to say that I married Ambrose De'Ath for many well-meaning if misguided reasons, and I meant indeed to be his good and grateful wife.

What reasons Ambrose might have had for marrying me, I gave no thought at all, oddly enough. Never once did I ask myself why such a man, having reached his early-middle years without a wife, might suddenly, and with the impulsiveness ordinarily associated with youth, have taken to wife a poor and plain young spinster of no great education or accomplishments and with the added disadvantage of having been accused of the foulest of crimes—that of parricide. He had seemed happy enough at the alacrity of my acceptance of his impulsive proposal, and after the marriage itself said nothing to make me think that he was other than as contented with our deed as was I. We were both taciturn and private people by nature, and it seemed that we suited each other well. What more, therefore, could either of us have asked? It was, it seemed then, a well-made bargain indeed.

At the end of January, happy and satisfied with our pleasant travels, we returned to England, and after a few days in Plymouth, began our trip overland to the great wild, cliff-bound moors of Cornwall, to the home that was my husband's and was also now to be mine—to the place Ambrose called Thanatos Abbey.

# 3

# THANATOS ABBEY

Hope springs eternal in the human breast.
—*Alexander Pope*

All hope abandon, ye who enter here.
—*Dante Alighieri*

It is possible that in thinking of Ambrose's home, there had lurked in the back of my mind descriptions of Fonthill Abbey, that romantic eighteenth-century folly which James Wyatt designed and executed for William Beckford; of Horace Walpole's Strawberry Hill; and of the house in Jane Austen's deliciously satirical novel, *Northanger Abbey*. Certainly, aside from those eccentric, delightful, and rather tongue-in-cheek concepts of a habitable "abbey," I had no idea of what to expect of the home to which I was being taken as bride and wife. And nothing—not even Ambrose's own natural solemnity and avowed vocation in life—could have prepared me for my first view of Thanatos Abbey sitting on that bleak promontory overlooking the gray, cold waters of St. George's Channel.

We had crossed Cornwall by coach from Plymouth, driven through the Cornish Hills, and begun a slow descent toward the northern coast. We had passed through Wadebridge, the only town of any size in the area, and come to the abbey by way of a little-used highway skirting the coast. At a sudden turning of the road, in the midst of an isolated and barren wilderness, Ambrose had ordered the coach to stop, and leaning past me, he slid down the windowpane and pointed a long bony finger down to the promontory below us.

"The abbey, my dear."

I looked, following his extended finger, and saw a group of huddled buildings, low and gray and almost invisible, gripping as if for dear life the edge of the cliffs overlooking the dark waters beyond. They, as well as the bleak, flat landscape surrounding them, were dusted over with a light coating of snow that only served to intensify the chill feeling of repulsion that overwhelmed me at my first sight of Thanatos Abbey. The effect of dun-colored earth, winter-deadened grasses and gorse, the gray stone of the low buildings, and the steely waters below were magnified by the clean, sharp white of the powdery snow and only made me realize more quickly how ugly and barren that landscape would be when that frosting of snow had disappeared.

"Well, what do you think, Enid?"

"Give me time, Ambrose." I smiled bleakly. "It is all so new to me." And secretly, the heart within my breast grew cold as a lump of coal with some nameless dread. All hope abandon . . .

It had been argued by Ambrose with the utmost vehemence that my Aunt Augusta belonged at the abbey with us, her only relatives, as he was wont to put it. His insistence on that point had been the only mar to my pleasure during the wedding trip to France, but I, adamant to the end, had won out. I had refused absolutely to have her under the same roof with me again as long as I had the breath in my body to resist.

Finally Ambrose had given in, although I had the wit to sense even then that at some future date the subject would be brought up again. After all, he had contacted her with some motive other than meeting me, although exactly what that motive was still eluded me. That they had in common a morbid fascination with death was obvious. What was to come of that common bond I had no idea, for while Ambrose surrounded himself with the aura of mourning out of some bizarre attraction to death, Aunt Augusta's equal obsession was based on fear and revulsion. My uncle's death, followed close upon by Ambrose's entry into our lives, had acted strangely upon her, and that fear of death which heretofore had caused her to avoid the subject completely, had now become a constant presence, appearing suddenly as a broad crack in that brittle soul of hers. It was the first time that I had seen Augusta Tregaron weak and afraid. It had, I admit now with no little shame, given me great pleasure to observe, for my heart was hard against her and had been so for more years than I could count.

Now, free of my hated Aunt Augusta, I had no intention of having her intrude upon my new life and in my new home—if such a place could rightly be called a home. How sad it was! I had arrived at Thanatos Abbey only to find that I was even yet forced to use those abilities of survival which my life with Augusta Tregaron had refined in me over the long, lonely years under her roof: to steel myself, to draw in my feelings and wall them around, to adapt to that which I must perforce endure.

In short, I bore up under my first tour of the abbey with a heart deadened and a mind controlled. I observed noncommittally the grim gray stone buildings, the gray slate roofs, the crumbled ruins of the original little chapel, the byres and stables and coach houses, all adapted from the ancient original buildings which had been built in those remote ages before the Conqueror and his Normans had invaded and begun the civilization of England. The place was aptly named both on the score of actually having been an abbey in the dim past, abandoned long before our good King Henry VIII drove popery from our shores, and on the score of the grim, gray, deathlike mood of the place. Indeed, one could hardly imagine a fitter hell, a more punishing afterlife than one spent amongst those granite buildings on that narrow, rocky promontory overlooking that gray cold sea. Thanatos Abbey indeed!

Within, the long public rooms of the main buildings were low-ceilinged and dark; warm only if one remained near the great ovenlike fireplaces, but otherwise cold as ice as one moved from room to room down the long, chilly halls. The windows were few and of the casement type, given as much to drafts as the chimneys were to smoke.

The walls were plastered in the smaller rooms, hung with arras and draperies in the larger ones. Black oak furniture and chests of austere Jacobean design abounded, as did huge brass and wrought-iron candlesticks, suits of armor, and all manner of grim, death-oriented religious paintings, carvings, and statues.

The tapestries portrayed such subjects as the Crucifixion, the raising of Lazarus, the Ascension of Christ, the Four Horsemen of the Apocalypse, and countless famous death scenes of history, myth, and legend. The oil paintings, mostly dark and medieval-looking, depicted similar unpleasant subjects. There was a multitude of statues—mostly of demons, warriors, skeletal figures of death, and a variety of saints in writhing death agony. There was, as well, a seemingly endless collection of human skulls in various sizes, either nature's own work or her counterfeits, carved or cast in many stones, woods, and metals. They rested in groups—almost in heaps actually—on every surface, gaping from shelves on the walls or peeping, hollow-eyed and gaunt, from cabinets and cupboards that in any other house would contain silver, china, and other attractive household wares. That ghastly head which Ambrose had shown me in London should, perhaps, have warned me, but how was I to know that the one in hand represented scores of others in the bush, so to speak?

In short, Thanatos Abbey was one long, dark, miserable dirge on the subject of death and dying, and the tour of those low, mournful abbey buildings, connected, as they were, into one long, single-story house, was to me like the tour of a catacomb or the ancient tombs of some medieval crypt. As Ambrose showed me about, I remained silent and noncommittal, reminding myself that outside, once spring had arrived, all would be green and alive and that I need not remain within this place of living death forever. At least, I hoped not. Finally, after having seen all—or almost all, as I later learned—Ambrose led me back into the front hall, which was long, low, dark, and furnished as a sitting room, with clusters of carved straight-backed chairs huddled close to the two fireplaces that gaped from opposite walls like caverns.

"Well, Enid, my dear, what do you think of your new home?"

"I think, dear Ambrose, that you have been right all along, and that I have been a selfish beast. Pray send for my Aunt Augusta. My conscience will not rest till she is here with us; till she shares our home." Was I wrong, or did a look of relief actually pass over his normally passive countenence?

"Enid, that's wonderful!" he exclaimed. "I shall wire Jemmy Burkers at once and have him escort her here from London as soon as possible."

"Do that, Ambrose. I think that Thanatos Abbey is exactly where my Aunt Augusta should be. It is exactly what she deserves." And with that, I smiled quietly to myself, knowing that I should not sleep happily in my bed until Augusta Tregaron should herself be under the death-shrouded roofs of Thanatos Abbey. It was indeed *exactly* what she deserved.

I had been but three days at the abbey, seeing no one but Ambrose and a few of the house servants, spending my time in unpacking the fruits of my Paris shopping, and dispersing my personal things in as attractive and comfortable an arrangement as was possible, given the cold, low-ceilinged suite of rooms that had been given me. That they had once been monks' cells was evident from their size and shape, but they had been connected and made habitable by reason of some plaster and paneling added in the seventeenth century. The furniture was dark, spare, and far too large for the size of the rooms, but I did not despair. Indeed I had realized on my first day at the abbey that I dared not for a second give in to despair. Had I done so, I should have been destroyed in a moment of time. Rather, I set to thinking of how I could make these unpleasant little rooms more comfortable and less somber. I began by banishing every painting and statue in sight and by removing every one of the many crucifixes with their agony-wrenched Christs. It left walls bare and furniture denuded, but at least there was nothing ugly or depressing in view. Come spring, I would find some vases and fill them with spring flowers; and if there was no garden, then I would pick wild ones until I should plant one. Yes, if I must live here in this isolated place, in this stark, cold abbey, I would do my damnedest to make my corner of it, at least, bearable. There was, after all, as I kept telling myself, more than one way to skin a cat!

I thought at one point during my unpacking and rearranging that I heard some commotion without, but gave it no particular mind. Now, some minutes later, I chanced to hear voices as I came down the long passage leading from the bedroom wing to the main hall. Something in the tone of those voices caused me to slow my pace and stand behind the door, where I could not be seen, and listen unabashedly. The first words to reach my ear were spoken by Jemmy Burkers.

". . . fink you've been about?"

The old panels were thick, and not every word came to me above the pacing of booted feet and scraping of newly arriving baggage being set about on the flagstone floors.

" 'Ow far do you fink 'er forty pounds a year will get us?" There was ill-contained fury in his tone.

Ambrose interrupted momentarily, cold and dispassionate as ever.

" 'Ear me out . . ." Jemmy Burkers persisted. Something scraped across the stone floor. ". . . so now, damn me, you've blown it for . . ."

"Jemmy, now you hear *me* out. She hates her, I tell you. It won't make any difference. . . ."

"Blood's thicker'n any water."

"And I tell you it won't make any difference. She's already asked me to send for the old lady, you fool," Ambrose insisted.

" 'As she?" Some surprise registered in his strident, angry voice.

"She has, and I think I know why. She's probably after the . . ." More noise; the words were lost.

"Does *she* know yet? 'Ave *they* met?"

"No." Ambrose's voice was deadly.

"You're afraid ta tell 'er, ain't you?" Burkers' voice was crafty with insight. Getting no reply, he went on, "Ambrose, why in God's name did you do it?"

"Jemmy, I wanted her from the first sight. I don't know why. I wish I did," he added softly.

"Did you 'ave ta marry 'er, then?" he asked contemptuously.

Silence.

"Do you actually love 'er?" There was disbelief in his voice now.

"I suppose I must."

We dined together, Ambrose and I, before a fire in the main hall that night, with Jemmy Burkers—obsequious as ever—waiting upon us. He played his part perfectly—the overly abject servant—and Ambrose was the detached, cold master to equal perfection.

Had I not heard that hurried, savage little argument earlier in the day, I should never have believed that there was anything to the relationship between these two men other than man and master. Now that I knew it was more complex than that, I realized that Ambrose, by impulsively entering into an elopement and marriage, had somehow upset some plan that the two had worked out. What plan it was, I had no idea, but that it evidently involved my aunt was apparent. I could not help but think that it must be sinister in nature. Somehow that thought did not frighten me. I merely resolved that I should be on my guard at all times. Needless to say, none of what I had heard—especially reference to my humble forty pounds per year—made the repulsive Mr. Burkers any dearer to my heart. And Ambrose, defending me in that curious, halfhearted way of his, had lost respect, if not trust, in my eyes. He was a gentleman, high-bred and cultured. What possessed him to allow himself to be spoken to in such a manner and by such a one as this supposed servant of his? What hold had this lowly and—as I thought then—utterly detestable Jemmy Burkers over my husband Ambrose? I felt the beginnings of grave misgivings on that day, and nothing that happened in the next few days did much to reassure me either about Jemmy Burkers or—more especially—about my husband Ambrose himself.

On the morning after Jemmy Burkers' unexpected arrival from London, the two were closeted for a time in the New Hall, one of the few rooms in the abbey that I had not yet seen. There was no way that I could have approached the doors unseen by servants, and so, unable to eavesdrop on their conversation, I busied myself as best I could in my own rooms and waited.

Finally Ambrose, who had absented himself from my bed the previous night, came knocking and entered looking rather stern, as if he had steeled himself to follow some course of action not his own, and all unwilling into the bargain. I said not a word, but listened, gratefully forearmed by my new and inadvertent awareness of the unseen layers of relationship between my husband and his purported servant.

"Enid, my dear, I have been thinking and have decided that it is best if I return to London myself and fetch your Aunt Augusta. Since Jemmy has returned, there is no sense in sending him back for her when I am sure she would prefer my company to his anyway. His coarseness makes him something of a burden as it is, and besides, it will show a greater courtesy to her if I go myself." He looked almost embarrassed as he spoke.

"And we must ever be courteous to Aunt Augusta, mustn't we?" I purred sweetly.

He ignored me—or did not hear—but went on, speaking more brightly as he did, warming to his subject no doubt, and allowing arguments meant for me to convince his own reluctant self.

"But of course, my darling," I agreed helpfully. "And it will give you a chance to know Aunt Augusta all the better. By all means go, and with my blessing." I smiled warmly. Yes, go and give me time to sound out the cunning Mr. Burkers, who does not seem, like all good servants, to know his place.

"Jemmy will be in charge in my absence, Enid."

"But of course." I nodded agreeably, wondering the more if he weren't in charge in spite of Ambrose's presence.

"You shan't mind, then, if I go?"

"Of course not."

At this he looked a bit surprised and even hurt.

"Darling," I added hastily, "of course I shall *miss* you, but I agree it is best that you fetch her yourself. Go at once, and I shall make the best of my time acquainting myself with the abbey in your absence. The sooner you go, the sooner you return to me."

"I'll leave in the morning," he said, coming closer, putting his bony fingers around my shoulders. He held me hard and kissed me rather passionately with those cold, thin lips of his. I could not help the shiver of revulsion that passed like a chill through my frame.

Ambrose De'Ath was not the man I had thought him to be—strong, detached, and masterful. Ambrose De'Ath was not even his own master. How, then, in God's name, could he be *mine*?

My husband's coach had not been gone an hour when that sudden rush of solitude which I was finding so pleasant and welcome was rudely interrupted by a single knock upon my sitting-room door, followed immediately by the unceremonious entry of Jemmy Burkers.

"Enter, by all means," I said dryly. He ignored my sarcasm, striding across the tiny room to take a stance against a small, heavy Baroque secretaire.

"Makin' yourself right at 'ome, ain't ya?"

"I assumed that as wife of the master, I had not only the right but the duty to do so."

"Stiff, cold, and ladylike. An 'aughty bitch, after all." He crossed to the single small window and looked out frowningly.

"Does Mr. De'Ath allow all his servants the privilege of assessing their betters?" He didn't answer my question, but stood staring out the window, his coarse, thick black hair shining in the strong sunlight; his crooked nose—no doubt broken several times—heavy jaw, and full, sensual mouth in sharp relief against the blue of the distant sky beyond him. His was a coarse face, sulky and crafty by turns, but with much expression. I found myself regarding him with interest.

Finally he spoke. "When I first laid me . . . my . . . eyes on you, lady, I fought, 'Now, there's a real looker. She's got class.' And my first reaction 'eld for the second viewin' as well."

His tone, like his words, was not harsh. I should almost have liked to answer him kindly, but could not. He was too far beneath me and too little to be trusted with kindness. Instead:

"And, Mr. Burkers"—I said his name, as always, with undisguised distaste for its commonness—"am I to be flattered that my husband's servant" (this to bait him into revealing his true position, if I but could) "considers me a 'looker,' as you so eloquently put it?"

He spoke hotly now, through clenched teeth. "I could even bear, as I always 'ave from others of 'igher station than me, the insults of your attitude and demeanor. After all, Enid Tregaron, what do you know of me or my kind? But you—you—wi' your airs of superiority, fill me with nothin' but contempt and disgust. I 'ate the very sight of you, lady, an' I come 'ere this mornin' ta tell you so. I'm not one ta let somethin' stick in my craw fer long if I can 'elp it, and so I want it settled now, once and fer all." He stopped suddenly, as if to master his own anger, which even he seemed to realize had got quite out of hand, and to control the obvious contempt he had for me. It seethed from him like poison.

I was shocked; completely taken aback by his whole manner. His loathing of me was so genuine and sincere, and I was so at a loss to understand its origins, that I realized I must perforce hear the man out—if only to satisfy my curiosity.

"Go on," I whispered. My cold civility to him might have engendered dislike of me in his heart, but what had I done to earn his deep contempt?

"Go on? Am I allowed? Does the great lady permit ' 'er 'usband's servant' as you so nicely put it . . ." His voice oozed with irony.

"Nicely, perhaps, but not accurately. You are *not* his servant, are you, Jemmy Burkers?" I interrupted hotly.

"That's neither 'ere nor there, lady. You're allowin' me ta 'ave my say, man ta woman?" he persisted.

"I think perhaps that I must. I too like things said directly. I have lived too long in the shadows of unspoken words; too many things left unsaid in my past. I am beginning a new life here at Thanatos Abbey, here with Ambrose. I prefer it to start well."

"And 'as it?"

"No, no it has not," I said frankly, and turned quickly

away, for my face, upon my answering that unexpectedly soft and honest question, crumpled in pain and I dared not let this lowborn, hot-tempered beast of a man see my vulnerability. I composed myself and turned, haughty again behind the cool mask I had made of my features.

"Well, I'm sorry for it then," he mumbled gently, with pity in his voice.

"Say what you have to say directly and get out, Mr. Burkers. The one thing I will not tolerate from you or any of your ilk is pity," I retorted.

"Of course, I forgot for the moment. I'm not permitted the privilege of pitying my betters, am I?" Here he snickered. "Ya know, the funny thing is, I fought when I first laid eyes on you that you were class, a real lady. Finely bred, intelligent and beautiful—"

"Beautiful?"

"Yes, does that surprise you?"

"I have always felt so . . . so plain."

"Well, you ain't," he said savagely, and went on, "You found out you 'ad only your miserable forty pounds per, which'd never be enough for the likes of a lady like you, and so you married Ambrose De'Ath for 'is money. You sold yourself, like any poor poxy whore on the streets, for what you could get."

"That's not true," I cried with a sinking sensation in the pit of my stomach. Had I?

"Ain't it?" He sneered nastily. "Well, Enid Tregaron, you got yourself Mr. Ambrose De'Ath, Esquire, and you're welcome to 'im. 'E's just wot you deserve."

"Indeed, sir, he is!" I came back at him in fury. "He, at least, is a gentleman. He, at least, is well-bred, educated, and of a station equal to my own. He is not the ill-bred, coarse-speaking, diseased, and nameless scum of the London stree . . ." I broke off, realizing that I was screaming like a fishwife and that Jemmy Burker's dark face was growing more ugly and furious with my every word. His looks actually frightened me.

"No, he's not nameless scum," he said with a voice that had a deadly edge to it.

"He's a man—" I began weakly.

"Is 'e? Is 'e a man? You've been in 'is bed, so you'd be in a position to know, I suppose. And no, as you say, 'e's not ill-bred and diseased. Leastwise, 'is body's not diseased."

"What do you mean by that?"

"Don't you know?" His tone was crafty again, his dark

eyes sharp with cunning. "No, I'm wrong," he went on, as if correcting himself. "Beggin' your pardon, miss. *'E's* been in *your* bed. Am I right?"

"Don't you dare to speak to me like this." I was frightened now in earnest.

"I *am* right," he insisted. " 'E's come to you in there, 'asn't 'e?" he asked, gesturing toward my bedroom door.

"What . . . what of it?"

"Nothin' . . . nothin'.'" He smiled malevolently. "Only I think it's time that you see where your 'ighborn, well-bred 'usband sleeps when 'e ain't wi' you. I want the privilege of showin' you the man you married as 'e really is."

He grabbed me by the wrist and began pulling me toward the door.

"No," I cried. "Don't you dare. Let me go." My struggles were useless and feeble against his wiry strength.

"Damn me if I will. I want you ta see the bargain you've made, you bitch. You're no better'n a whore, and I want you ta see what manner of gentleman you've sold yourself to."

And so, struggling, wrestling, half-dragged and half-carried, I was forced by Jemmy Burkers out of my rooms and down the long cold halls of Thanatos Abbey toward Ambrose's own suite of rooms.

By the time we had reached the threshold of his book-lined study, I was exhausted; spent and actually bruised from my fruitless struggle. My pulses pounded from the excitement of this terrible ordeal, and my spirits, though fearful, were high. It was evident that Jemmy Burkers, though of no great height as was my Ambrose, was strong and powerful. I would not win, no matter what I did, and so at last I submitted with seeming meekness and walked beside him obediently to the narrow black oak door that led to Ambrose De'Ath's bedroom.

"Now, my dear, I think it only fittin' that you see where 'e sleeps, that fine gent of yours."

I drew in my breath and glared at him as defiantly as my quaking heart would permit. "I shall submit to your will in this, Mr. Burkers, for you can force me by sheer strength alone, and I am undefended with Ambrose gone; but he shall, I assure you, hear of this the moment he returns."

"That, lady, leaves me quakin' in me very boots." He smiled, and sneering at me in the most ugly manner, said something that left my spirits sunk within me. "You'd be un-defended, as you put it, even wi' Ambrose 'ere."

I could not but feel the rightness of his boast. I did not

doubt his words for a moment. My only course lay in ignoring his remark and endeavoring to regain some shred of my personal dignity at least.

"I have always paid you the courtesy of correctly addressing you, Mr. Burkers. Pray at least pay me the like courtesy, if only as a matter of form. People of my class, as you may have observed, practice the small niceties of life and are ever civil to each other regardless of how intolerable each may find the other one to be. Is that fair enough?"

"Oh, fair enough, fair lady," he replied with a low, mocking bow. "And now for a peep at the *sanctum sanctorum*," he said, unlocking the door with a great brass key and pushing me into the darkened cell beyond.

"After you, Mrs. De'Ath," he said, mimicking Ambrose's cultured voice, and followed me in, laughing the wickedest, most vulgar laugh I had ever heard.

I looked about me as defiantly as I could while what was left of my heart shriveled, like some dead thing, within me.

# 4

# THE OLD
# LADY DE'ATH

She walks in beauty, like the night
Of cloudless climes and starry skies;
And all that's best of dark and bright
Meet in her aspect and her eyes.
—Lord Byron

How now, you secret, black and midnight hags!
What is't you do?
—Shakespeare

Jemmy Burkers and I remained at daggers drawn for some
few days after this incident, passing each other occasionally
in the halls with only the barest civility. I was attended by
house servants, taking my meals alone, either in my own
rooms or before the fire in the great, dark front hall of the
abbey. There was no pretense anymore that he himself was a
servant in that house; indeed he moved about it with far
more authority in his manner than did Ambrose De'Ath, its
nominal master.

I do not remember much of those first few days alone in
that house with Jemmy Burkers, other than the fact I was
afraid of him and wondered if I would be less so once Ambrose had returned. I think I must have conveniently blotted
from my memory the heartrending turmoil and despair that
must have tormented my days and made sleepless those solitary nights.

I do know that I busied myself with an almost compulsive
fury in making bouquets and garlands of silk flowers with
remnants of some exquisite old fabrics that a maid found for
me in a storeroom. For days, my dressing table and every

available surface was strewn with swatches of the brightest materials I could find. Paper patterns and green silk leaves and stems, bits of wire, scissors, and paste—all the necessaries of my craft—lay scattered about. I was determined to make those blank little cells habitable and homelike if here I must live on those bleak cliffs overlooking that cold sea, with only Ambrose, Jemmy Burkers, and Augusta Tregaron for companionship. I was, in fact, determined as well to make the best I could of my marriage.

I did not fool myself that my love for Ambrose was deep or passionate, but I did care for him. Our minds meshed well, our backgrounds were not so disparate as to preclude marital harmony, and he had, after all, come into my life at an opportune time. He had, in fact, been virtually my rescuer and had cared for me enough to contract this impulsive marriage in the first place. Moreover, ever since, he had been both courtly and courteous of my sensibilities at all times. What more dared I ask? Given my life as it had been for the previous decade or more; given my foreseeable future under Aunt Augusta's roof in Park Lane, had I any alternative? No, I thought not. Now at least when Augusta Tregaron arrived at Thanatos Abbey, the roof would be mine to offer, the hell mine to create and control.

I smiled as I worked on my little silk roses at the thought of Augusta Tregaron sleeping—if she could—under the gray roof of Thanatos Abbey, under *my* roof for a change.


On the third evening, as I stood before the fire in the great hall, Jemmy Burkers came up to me. I had a glass of sherry in my hand, and at his approach I toyed in my mind with the idea of dashing its contents into his coarse, insolent face. His first words, however, made me glad that I had resisted the impulse.

"Your maid tells me you've done wonders wi' your rooms. She says they're almost cheerful." He spoke softly, a serious, almost tentative look on his face.

I did not speak, but turned my head slightly, raising my eyebrows haughtily as if I questioned him.

"That's not an easy task, is it? Makin' this mausoleum cheerful. I'm glad that you're the sort what . . . that . . . would try. It's an admirable trait ta have, spreadin' cheer." He smiled slightly at me, whether slyly or shyly I could not tell.

"Why are you speaking to me like this? Is it a trick? If it is, be warned, I am on my guard."

"Oh, yes, Mrs. De'Ath, I can see that. I can see you're on

you're guard. And I can see why. I know I've treated you 'arsh. A lady such as you ain't used ta men treatin' 'er that way. It comes, I think, from the vast differences in our background and experiences, don't ya know. You've 'ad it easy and 'appy, arter all." He spoke slowly and with care, trying to be both gentlemanly and grammatical; modulating his harsh, rough tones as if by doing so he would tame himself as well as his words. It was hard for him, I sensed, and it almost made me pity him for his efforts. Ultimately those efforts were not entirely in vain, for I found myself relaxing my wariness a bit and actually listening to him.

"I, bein' the lowly person I am—I'm not used ta the company of ladies . . . although I do admire their more sterlin' qualities, you see, from afar as it were. And you, you're not used ta any but the company of gents and swells. Now, beggin' your pardon, but from what I've seen of your average common an' garden swell, 'e may be a gent and ta the manner born, as they say, but 'e ain't much of a man arter all."

"Oh, I see, and you are?" I sniffed.

"Yes, ma'am. I am that. I am a man, though you'd no more recognize me as one than I'd ever be able ta detect if you was a real woman underneath the stiff lady part o' you which is all I ever see." He was so soft and earnest; his dignified self-defense so nearly poignant, that the implied insult to me seemed but the gentlest of slaps, not vindictive at all. It stung me deeply nonetheless.

"I am, I assure you, a 'real woman,' Mr. Burkers," I retorted, a little stab of pain going through my woman's heart.

"That, I suppose, I shall never know, ma'am, but forgive me if I do 'ave my doubts."

"Must this fruitless converse go on forever?" I snapped, waving my glass impatiently.

"No, no need ta go on, Mrs. De'Ath. I'm 'ere ta extend an invitation ta you on be'alf of my mistress, Madame 'Enriette De'Ath." He bowed low with all the formality and civility of a well-trained butler.

"Ambrose's mother?" I broke in, startled. He smiled craftily, perhaps at my surprise.

"Ambrose's mother." His tone was snide.

"Where is she?"

"She's in the New 'All awaiting dinner. She dines at this time every evening."

"I see. When, pray, did she arrive?"

"Arrive, Mrs. De'Ath?"

"Don't be stupid, Jemmy Burkers. I'm asking you when she arrived at the abbey."

"I'm not stupid, Mrs. De'Ath," he whispered with almost deadly patience, "but I think per'aps you are. She never left. She's been 'ere all the while."

"Since before my arrival?" I was incredulous.

"Long before. Months before."

"Why did I not know? Why did not Ambrose intro—?"

"That, Mrs. De'Ath, you'd 'ave to ask your 'usband."

"Am I to dine with her?"

"No, ma'am." He smiled almost serenely. "She takes dinner wi' other company this evening. You must come at nine."

"Very well, then, at nine. Now, for heaven's sake, Jemmy, leave me. My own dinner is sent for, and I wish to eat it in peace."

"By all means, Mrs. De'Ath." He smirked, and bowing in that insolent, mocking way of his, withdrew.

This, I thought as I savored the last of the thick, creamy sherry in my glass, is an interesting turn. I am about to meet the authoress of those very pages of signatures that began this whole bizarre turn in my life. Now I would see for myself: Henriette De'Ath, crazy old lady, obsessed, like her son Ambrose, with death and dying? Madame De'Ath, liar extraordinaire, forger unsurpassed? Which was it to be?

Somewhere a clock struck eight. I had not long to wait.


The room was long and wide, the ceiling much higher than those of the other rooms in the abbey, and lost in shadows, giving an impression of vastness to the eye. Everywhere was the golden glow of candlelight. The very air, hazy as an illuminated mist, was warm and scented with the heat of those hundreds of tall white tapers. They stood at every level—on tables, in tall candelabra, affixed to sconces on the paneled and painted walls, in clusters of small candlesticks on low desks and chests—everywhere. And in their subtle, breathtaking light, they caught the rich, burnished gleam of delicate gilded furniture, of ormolu and rare, polished woods, of fine porcelain and marquetry. Bowls of flowers—fresh flowers—abounded, adding their exotic perfumes to the candle-scented air.

I had stepped across the threshold onto an Aubusson carpet, and stopped at once, my eyes blinking at the brilliant and unaccustomed glow, adjusting to the wonderful light. I stood, not in another of the many bleak, cold rooms of Thanatos Abbey, but rather in such a grand salon as might have been possessed by a courtier of Louis XVI. Marie Antoinette herself might have sipped chocolate from Sevres cups in such a room as this.

I scarcely noticed that Jemmy Burkers had approached me until I found him grasping my arm to escort me farther into that wondrous salon.

It was crowded with furniture, set about in little groups of chairs and tables conducive to amiable conversation. We threaded our way through this engaging and eye-pleasing, eye-dazzling maze, until suddenly my attention was arrested by a brighter point of light far down that long room. A huge *bronze-d'oré* candelabrum, rococo in style, its tapers glowing brilliantly despite the tiny, elegant shades that covered each flame, stood upon a magnificent table desk of rare inlaid woods, the colors of which glistened like jewels from its polished surface. Across the top of this desk was arranged a deck of large, ornate playing cards of such peculiar and varied designs as I had never seen before.

Out of the shadows just beyond the reach of the candlelight came a pair of frail old hands, mitted like those of my Aunt Augusta, but not in somber black wool as were hers. Rather, these hands were encased in pale lavender lace, the bare fingers laden with flashing gems—amythysts, rubies, emeralds, and canary-yellow diamonds. The burden of those stones, I remember thinking, should have rendered those ancient fingers immobile, but instead they moved with quick, agile gestures, flicking those bizarre cards onto the table before them with great purpose.

I slowed my pace, fascinated, feeling somehow as if I were approaching something—someone—awful and mystical and wonderful. Hecate herself perhaps.

And out of the shadows, into the warm light of those many tapers, came a pair of eyes, a brow, a face whose impression I shall, to my dying day, neither forget nor desire to forget. Such majesty rested on that brow, such power in those great brown eyes, such haughty nobility in that exquisite profile, such strength in that firm chin that I was virtually aghast! And to see such things in so old a face as well! But somehow, whether by a trick of the light or the effect of all that unexpected splendor on my senses, beneath the wrinkled skin, heavily layered with white powder—arsenic and white lead, I suspected—the garish, red-rouged cheeks, the old-fashioned black patches beside the painted mouth and kohl-shadowed eyes and the monstrous, fantastically dressed silver wig, I could yet see the remnants of such beauty on that ancient face as must once have dazzled kings and kept even the gods themselves in thrall. I looked at that face, awestruck and amazed. Beside me, as if interpreting the inarticulate thoughts that raced pell-mell through my reeling brain, Jemmy Burkers muttered a line of Byron:

> She walks in beauty, like the night
> Of cloudless climes and starry skies.

Such was my state of mind at that moment, that even such words and the sensitivity that they betokened in him, coming from the lips of the lowly, ill-spoken Jemmy Burkers, failed to surprise me. I could only breathe a heartfelt, "Indeed, indeed," in response to his remark, my eyes still fixed on the old woman before me in the candlelight. It was, I felt then, the most magic and mysterious moment of my life—and nothing since has ever changed that long-ago evaluation.

Ever in my mind's eye that old woman will walk in the beauty that her ancient face held for me on that strange winter night in Cornwall so many ages past. Magic!

She looked up at me with those huge, dark, heavy-lidded eyes, as brilliant, despite her age, as if she were yet a girl, and smiled a small smile in the corners of her closed lips. She had the look of evaluating me in that expression, but only for a moment. Then her eyes, softening visibly, slid over to the face of Jemmy Burkers, who still stood beside me, his hand on my arm at the elbow to guide me. I had not even noticed that he had been touching me until that very second, and when I did, I pulled away instinctively with, I must suppose, a look of disdain. The old woman's face froze for an instant at my action, but changed at once to an expression of serenity. Her eyes sought out Jemmy's once more, and a signal seemed to pass between them.

"Madame De'Ath, may I present Enid Tregaron, the lady Ambrose 'as taken to wife, and who now bears the name o' De'Ath 'erself." It was a curious, cold introduction and betokened still further his dislike of me.

"And I, my dear, am Henriette De'Ath."

"I am pleased to meet you, madame," I stammered, curtsying deeply. "I wish to assure you that I shall do all in my power to make your son happy. Ambrose is a very kind and good man."

"Nothing, my dear, can make my son Ambrose happy." The old woman spoke simply, her French accent not so much apparent in the pronunciation of the words themselves as in the actual rhythm of her speech, which was very cultured and spoken in a honeyed, well-modulated voice that showed little sign of her great age.

"Madame, that is a terrible thing to say. Everyone is capable of happiness, surely?" I protested in dismay. "Else why continue to bear the troubles of this world, if not in the hope of happiness?"

"Why indeed? But *are* they?" She smiled. "Are *you* happy?"

"I . . . I expect to be, madame."

*"Bien,"* she said, clapping her hands together abruptly with a sound that startled me. "Perhaps then you will be, one day. I pray it will be so. But for now, Jemmy, pour our young friend a glass of wine, if you will, please."

Jemmy Burkers walked across to a gilded side table and poured a glass of port from a dazzling crystal decanter. I watched him intently, noticing that he wore the evening clothes of a gentleman rather than the black livery of a manservant, and that he wore those neat, elegant, uncustomary clothes quite well. There was a smooth, catlike grace to him as he approached, presenting me my wine with a gracious nod of his head. Turning back again to the sideboard, he picked up his own glass, already poured and evidently begun before my arrival. Madame De'Ath raised her own already tasted glass and made a toast.

"To the young Madame De'Ath. May she find that happiness she yet expects." Her voice held that trace of mockery a parent has when patronizing the silly whim of a child.

"To happiness for us all, madame," I countered with dignity.

"That is what I shall drink to as well: 'appiness for all of us," Jemmy Burkers echoed me solemnly.

"Well, then, children, I shall join you: happiness for all of us," Madame De'Ath amended as we each sipped our wine. How odd that moment was! We actually toasted as if that toast had power, and by it we might really charm our futures.

There was a long silence then as we each were lost briefly in our own thoughts. Perhaps each of us was thinking then of what it was that would ensure that hoped-for happiness of ours.

"It is a wise man who knows what it is will make 'im 'appy," Jemmy Burkers whispered, looking deeply into his glass, a furrow across his broad brow and a look of wincing pain in his whole aspect. His expression embarrassed me and

I looked away in confusion, my eyes straying to the large, oddly marked cards on the table before Madame De'Ath. I studied them with curiosity.

"Yes, my dear, these cards could indeed tell you the answers to the questions you are so afraid to ask. The stars," she whispered, gesturing in a dramatic, typically Gallic motion of her hand, "could answer as well."

"I have no questions to ask."

"No?" She smiled questioningly. "No, you do not!" she went on, speaking definitely, emphatically, and again in that kindly, patronizingly parental tone that she had used earlier. "I can see now you do not. Pardon! I have been wrong. Presumptuous."

"Beg no pardon of me, Madame. You have only meant to be kind," I replied with stubborn dignity.

"Indeed."

The matter dropped and again there was silence.

What more can I say of that bewildering evening, the first of many such evenings spent in the company of Madame Henriette De'Ath—the remarkable Madame De'Ath? That she puzzled me? She did. That she frightened me? Most certainly. That she charmed me? Yes, beyond words. I was utterly fascinated and could have studied her, her gestures, the expressions, passing like so many flower petals, each differently and subtly shaded, across her ancient painted face, unendingly.

Sometimes, as if she knew I needed to watch her, to study her silently and alone within the privacy of my mind, she let me. She would ignore me for long minutes on end, and for that I was grateful. Then, conversely, she would suddenly pry and meddle and try, though I resisted her efforts willfully, to penetrate the very secrets of my mind, the workings of my heart and soul. It was then that *I* would ignore *her*, or barring, by virtue of her persistence, the possibility of that, I would bid her *adieu* and retire to my own chambers.

At other times, she would speak on, rattling endlessly of France, of the lost Louis and his beheaded queen; prattling like an old lady who had lost her wits and found them again only in the memory of her long-gone youth. It was at such times that she seemed just a crazy old woman whose poor body was cruelly outliving her mind. Then I was patient and kindly and pitying. Sometimes, though, I suspected my kindliness and pity were a waste, for suddenly that crazy, prattling old lady gave way to the witty, spoiled, sophisticated *grande dame* that one associates with France before the Terror. She was then in what I came to call in my own mind her *salon* mood.

Jemmy Burkers—the ever-present Mr. Burkers—dressed in the finest evening clothes, jeweled studs and cufflinks, gold watch and chain, presided each evening, taking his dinner, like a gentleman, with the old Madame De'Ath; pouring her wine, escorting her, as she leaned her light, graceful old body on his arm almost lovingly, from a chair by the fire to a chair at that table of strangely figured cards; from there to a settee on which she sat, graceful as a dove, presiding over the chocolate cups, pouring for us as if we were children at a tea party.

At other times, she bent over a marquetry and Sevres porcelain secretaire, drawing charts and casting horoscopes with the aid of a dozen old leatherbound books and ephemerides. Charts of the heavens and the figures of the zodiac hung in gilded frames on the walls above and around her. An astrolabe and great globe of the world stood in their mahogany and ormolu bases to either side of the desk, and to these she would make frequent reference, speaking to herself aloud in French and Latin, forgetting even that we were present.

At such times Jemmy would read or play at patience and I would wander unrestricted amongst the treasures of the room, studying the *objets d'art*, the *bijoux* and *bibelots* arranged in the *étagères* or scattered across the tables and cabinet tops amidst the many bowls of ever-fresh, ever-fragrant flowers that perfumed the air. Sometimes I would linger long over the books, old and rare, cheap and new, a profusion of which squeezed indiscriminately, cheek by jowl, onto every available shelf of every likely breakfront and commode. These were in many languages, though English, French, and Latin predominated. Only Madame's rare old astrological volumes was I forbidden to peruse, and having no interest in such matters to begin with, considered the prohibition no hardship. What piqued me was that Jemmy Burkers had free access to all the books, a fact the more remarkable to me since in the beginning I had doubted even his ability to read at all. That he could do so in the first place had come as a great surprise, and the quality and catholicity of his reading was an even greater one.

I suppose I must have resented him more than ever on those first evenings spent in the company of Henriette De'Ath. He was greatly my inferior, I felt, and hers even more so. He did not belong in our company, and yet, lowly as he was, he came near to dominating it by virtue of the kindness, respect, and almost loving deference which she paid him. Who was he to receive such treatment at the hands of a lady; of someone I suspected of being more than a lady, if the truth were known. Henriette De'Ath was surely one of the old aristocracy of France, descended from generations of noblemen and courtiers! I looked shrewdly at that ancient face. Might she not conceivably be of the blood royal? Who, then, was Jemmy Burkers to hold her with his dubious, affected charms; his pretentious, imperfect imitation of the manners and speech of his betters? Yes, I suppose that I must actually have been jealous of the knave, and it shames me even now to admit it. I had grown jealous of such a thing as Jemmy Burkers! My resentment and seething hatred knew no bounds.

Feeling as I did about that lowborn creature, I began to long for Ambrose's return as if he were indeed my savior. And he was mine! Him I would treat as the gentleman and the husband that he was. Let Jemmy Burkers be petted and spoiled by the old woman if he would. I was young and a bride; a wife with a fine, highborn husband to look to, to care for and to love. So much for the coarse and ugly and vile Mr. Burkers.

It was on an afternoon in early March that the messenger came with a note from Ambrose. He and my aunt were but a day's journey from the abbey. The following night they would sleep under its roof.

That same night I had a dream of Ambrose and of Ambrose's room, the room that Jemmy Burkers had forced me to view nearly three weeks earlier, and the memory of which I had somehow put from my mind, so unbearable had I found it to think upon. Now, with Ambrose but a few hours away, the remembrance of that bizarre place returned to haunt my dreams and make me wonder, when I finally awoke, cold and wet with perspiration, which were worse—the nightmares of my sleep or the waking nightmare yet to come?

# 5

# ENID IMPLACABLE

Blessed are the merciful; for they shall obtain mercy.
—*St. Matthew 5:3*

Charity and Mercy. Not unholy names, I hope?
—*Charles Dickens*

It was long after the mid of night and the abbey slept in the light of a great full moon—the abbey slept, and all within her, save the single exception of myself. I had lain awake till I could bear the lying no more and so I had crept from my bed and crossed the small cell to its only window. Taking a vase of my newly made artificial flowers from its place before the casement and setting it aside, I slid onto the wide sill in its place and huddled, my back against the wall and my knees drawn up toward me, feeling for all the world like a lost little child.

It would not work, I realized sadly, painfully. All the hopes I had fostered, all the plans I had made in his absence had come to naught in the few short hours since Ambrose's return to Thanatos Abbey. I was no bride; no wife. There would be no pride in being his love, in caring for him; there would be no children. There would be nothing. There was far more joy in old Madame De'Ath's misplaced affection for Jemmy Burkers than ever I could spark in the emptiness of my relationship with Ambrose—my husband Ambrose. I looked up into that bright, benighted heaven and sighed.

For a long time I sat gazing out onto the moon-bleached and somber landscape: grass and coarse ground cover, still more winter-yellowed than spring green, ran in a nearly colorless expanse to the dark, rock-bound cliffs. The still, black sea beyond hardly rippled at all in the white beams of the cold silver moon.

I was a prisoner still, I realized ironically, lonely, isolated; only saved from the utter fearful desolation of my plight by the newness of my surroundings and the fascinating eccentricity of these few strange people who now populated my life in this mournful abbey. Once I had accustomed myself to this place and to this new life, the deadness of it all would become unendurable. And yet, as I reflected further, I realized that there was actually more to the situation than that. True! There was a deadness to this place I now perforce called home; to this man I now called husband, but there was mystery as well and, of course, a splendid opportunity to make the life of Aunt Augusta as miserable under my own roof as she had made mine under hers. Not, perhaps, the most noble of aims or best of comforts to my own unhappiness, but in fairness to myself, I was then a young, bitter, and ignorant girl.

I thought back to the previous afternoon—to the look of unabashed dismay on her hard, white old face as she was handed down from Ambrose's fine, funereal coach by a footman. She surveyed the abbey with ill-concealed horror, and I wondered humorously to myself whether the sight of those grim, gray buildings—some actually merely grass-grown ruins—was bringing to mind long-forgotten and ghoulish scenes from *The Castle of Otranto*, *The Monk*, *Horrid Mysteries*, and other so-called "Gothic" novels of her youth. I hoped secretly and with malicious delight that she would come to find Thanatos Abbey as fearful as Otranto or Mrs. Radcliff's Udolpho.

"Welcome to my home, Aunt Augusta," I said, smiling complacently as I came forward to greet her. "May you be as comfortable here at Thanatos Abbey as you have always made me feel in Park Lane."

She ignored my greeting, if indeed she even deigned to hear it. "You are in good looks, Enid," she said abruptly, eyeing my lovely cornflower-blue silk dress and its lavish trimming of ecru-colored Brussels lace with jaundiced disapproval. By contrast, her own black weeds looked more stark and depressing than ever.

"Thank you, Aunt," I murmured politely, and curtsied with supposed deference. "How it grieves me not to be able to return the compliment, but perhaps it is only the long trip that makes you look so peaked. Rest should do wonders."

Ambrose came up beside us just then, kissed me on the cheek, and escorted us into the abbey while Jemmy Burkers, once more in the livery of a servant, supervised the unloading of her boxes from the coach. The charade was starting again, and I now must learn just what that charade was to be—and to what uses of my own I could conveniently put it.

That charade! The why of it! The many whys of my present life! This is the direction in which my mind now turned as I sat in that window and gazed unseeing out upon that moonlit scene. Why were we all here? Why indeed had Ambrose De'Ath come into our lives in the first place? Why had he had such an effect on Augusta Tregaron, the cold and self-possessed and ever-mistrustful Augusta Tregaron? Why was Jemmy acting the part of a servant when clearly he was on an equal if not superior footing with Ambrose in whatever this game was that they were playing at, and why—most personal of all the many whys—why had Ambrose chosen to marry me? What was I to him? I had no fortune (as yet) and no influence with my aunt. Why elope like a schoolboy with a stranger, and one, moreover, whom one has heard accused of perhaps the foulest crime in the whole catalog of human sins?

One thing was certain. Obviously his marriage to me was not part of the original plan. His conversation with Jemmy Burkers upon his arrival at the abbey after our wedding trip had made that clear enough. In fact, I would venture to say that Ambrose himself didn't seem to know why he had made me his wife.

I sat huddled on that windowsill and looked up once more at that cold and distant moon. Why? So many whys! And then, as dispassionately as that great cold moon looked down on me, I turned my gaze and looked down upon the man who lay stretched across my bed like a pale, dead Christ, crucified upon the shroudlike whiteness of the sheets.

His body was long and slender to the point of emaciation, the hair straight and black as the loam in a graveyard plot. He lay upon his back, his feet together and his arms stretched wide in an attitude of crucifixion as the pale rays of the full moon bleached his skin to cadaver whiteness and the black bars of the window frames crossed his body like so many lashings of a whip. I felt nothing—neither desire nor despair; attraction nor revulsion. The sight of him was as dead to my heart as I sensed the sight of me was to his own eyes. (His heart I simply could not read.) But we were married. Thanatos Abbey was my home; this was my husband.

The body stirred fitfully on the bed and I felt a wave of pity for it wash over me. It was so slender and pathetic and vulnerable. This, I thought sadly, was the first night of his return to the abbey—our first night together in many weeks—and it had meant nothing to me; to either of us, I had sensed, though we each had tried dutifully. The plain, sad truth of the matter was that neither of us really cared. Why? Why had he married me?

Ambrose moaned slightly and stretched his long body, waking abruptly as one does in a strange bed—a little lost, wondering where one has suddenly got to.

"Enid?"

"I am here, Ambrose, in the window."

"Oh, yes, I see," he mumbled, his body shifting on the bed so that the full moon outside cast the shadow of my figure like a dark blanket across the paleness of him. "Can't you sleep?"

"No."

"Bad dreams?" One could have cut the discomfort between us with a butter knife.

"No, not tonight. Last night."

"Oh."

"Ambrose?" I said no more, drawing in my breath rather, girding my loins for what I must say; the questions I must ask.

"Yes?" His tone was guarded.

"You don't really want to be here, do you? You don't really want to . . . sleep with me?"

A long pause in the quiet darkness. "No, I . . . I suppose I don't," at long last.

I stifled the tightness I felt clutching at my heart. "Why did you marry me, Ambrose?" I tried to keep the pleading out of my voice.

"I really . . . I . . . don't really know, Enid. I wanted you, I guess. I felt that you were right for me somehow."

"Right for you? Am I right for you, Ambrose?" His words amazed me. I could not fathom the man.

"Yes, Enid, you are. I think you are. I . . . I have a sense of well-being when I am near you. I am glad that I married you." He smiled tentatively at me.

"You just don't want to sleep with me, that's all," I remarked flatly, no irony meant by my words.

"I am sorry," he whispered at last.

"Don't be," I retorted proudly. "I don't really want you here either." Now it was he who drew in his breath in the darkened room. I had not meant to sound harsh or cold, but somewhere in my soul a door had closed and we both knew it. "You are my husband, Ambrose. I shall be faithful to my vows and shall carry on my duties as your wife with decorum and to the very best of my ability. That I promise you. In fact, I shall perform the first of those promised duties right now.

"You may take your nightgown and robe and retire to . . . to . . . You see, I release you—take you off the hook, as it were," I rattled on with a false brightness, my words pouring forth in a torrent that betokened the pain and the pride and the agony of feelings that welled up within me. "You don't have to come to me anymore, pretend to desire me, make excuses for not coming to me—none of it—not anymore.

"Thanatos Abbey. See, isn't it funny? This was once a monastery or maybe a convent and these rooms were all cells and the inmates were monks or nuns or some such thing and . . . and . . ." I stumbled over my words, choking on them even as I choked on the lump in my throat. "And they were all celibates and so are we, aren't we?" I looked across at him, half-laughing, half-crying.

He sat on the edge of the bed, emaciated, frail, and white, with his feet together as if they were held in place by a great iron spike; his bony knees were wide apart, his elbows resting on slender thighs, hands hanging limply before him. His head was down so that I could not see his face. He said not a word.

"Well"—I laughed shrilly—"if I am to live in a cell in an abbey, I might just as well be a nun, don't you think? I don't know much about popery, but don't they consider themselves to be married—brides of Christ or something like that?

"There, that's it. You can be Christ and I'll be the bride. It's perfect—perfect, isn't it? Now, go, do go on. Don't worry about me. I'll take my bed and sleep in it alone, and you can go . . . go to your casket with a clear conscience. See, I release you. What more can a dutiful and understanding wife do for her husband?" I broke down sobbing into my knees, which trembled as I clutched them to my chest in an agony of pain and confused emotions.

"You know, then, about . . . about how I . . . about . . . ?"

"About the coffin that you sleep in? Say it, why don't you? Yes, Jemmy showed it to me. I saw it, and let me tell you that it revolts me more than mere words can say," I retorted, my mind going back to the sight of that ebony box with its white satin lining, the smock-worked pillow and white satin quilted coverlet. Yes, he actually slept in it—and why not? Was not his home a veritable mausoleum, his carriage a hearse? Why should his bed not be a coffin? My voice had broken suddenly, becoming tearful and small, unable to hide any longer the bitterness and anger that I could not help but feel within me.

"Why," I whimpered, "why did you marry me?"

"I do not know, Enid. I do not know. I . . . I am going now. Is it all right?"

"Oh, yes," I cried in my pain and my pride, "it is quite all right. Go, by all means."

And he left, his long dressing gown slung over his shoulders to hide his pale nakedness from my last sight of it, his hand clutching the rumpled mass of the linen nightshirt that he had removed earlier. He slunk from my rooms like a defeated cur with not even so much as a tail between his legs, I reflected bitterly as he departed.

I was alone now, but was it not better to be alone than to pretend? I looked up once more at that pale, cold moon—so full and round and dispassionate—and sensed to the core of my being the plumbless depths of my aloneness as I had never sensed them before.

"Well, damn it, I am alone. What matter? So is every other soul in this whole bitter, ugly world—and most of them hide from it, run from it, fear it, and die from it—but not me! I know I am alone and I will not be afraid. I am not afraid! It is simply the way it is." Thus defiantly I railed aloud at that great silver disk, but the old moon made no answer. Yes, I *was* alone.

Despite the briefness of my slumbers, I awoke the next morning feeling rested and strong. A renewed sense of purpose surged through me like the burgeoning life in the belly of a pregnant woman. No, I was not pregnant with a child—probably never even would be, I reflected coldly, trying not to be pained by the thought of life as a barren woman—but I was pregnant with determination and with fire.

I would set about making my life here at the abbey as bearable as possible without a husband to lavish my starved affections upon and without a child to bring joy to my long days. I had already made a stab at making my rooms more attractive, and that was a start at least. Now I would set my mind to other, more profitable tasks: I would learn what plottings went on between my husband Ambrose and the subtle, crafty Jemmy Burkers, and then see to it that I put that knowledge to the very best use that I could. The old Madame, my mother-in-law, was a woman of great learning and even greater wisdom, and so for the sake of my intellect and in order to expand the narrow borders of my life, I would cultivate her and learn from her as much as possible. Most satisfying of all, I would, if I could, devil the very life out of Augusta Tregaron with as little mercy as she had shown me over the long years of torment in her brother's house.

And, I comforted myself still further, in a little less than three years' time I would, as a married woman, come into my fortune as set forth in the terms of my Uncle Llewellyn's will. Then I would, by wise use of it, set myself free from all of them, leaving them behind with as little sorrow as I might leave a crust upon my plate.

"I know I am alone and I am not afraid," I said aloud to myself as I gazed at my cold, hard face in my mirror. "It is simply the way it is," I enunciated precisely, watching my lips form the words: drilling their meaning into my mind like a sergeant major drills his men. With a last cold smile at my reflection, I left my rooms and walked down the narrow corridor toward the front of the abbey, passing, as I did, the door to Aunt Augusta's suite. Something strange—a small, nagging fearful thing—knocked momentarily at the doors of my memory as I passed. It was a vague feeling and inconsequential, as I thought then, but what is it they say about the origins of great oaks? . . .

Augusta Tregaron was already at breakfast, sitting like a small, spare black bird at the large refectory table that dominated the breakfast room. It might well have been a piece of the original abbey furnishings for all I could guess. I had never yet eaten there, usually preferring to have my coffee and toast in my own sitting room. In my aunt's honor, however, I had ordered the room to be opened and prepared for use.

The effect, as I came in, was quite enough to gladden my heart, for from her seat at the table (the which I had troubled to prearrange with the servants) she faced a massive, dark and irredeemably ugly painting representing damned souls in the torment of a fiery hell. It was gruesome and fascinating in its grim, Germanic way—dwelling on unspeakable tortures and the agonies of eternal damnation. Its fairy-tale fantasy had no effect on my own skeptical and unsusceptible nature, but I knew when I first saw it that it would work its way with Augusta Tregaron.

And work its way it did, for as I came into the room, so mesmerized was she by the painting on the wall before her that she did not even hear me enter. It was only the clinking of a serving spoon against one of the covered silver dishes on the sideboard that brought her out of her reverie.

"Good morning, Aunt. Did you sleep well?"

"That is a terrible painting, Enid."

"Painting, Aunt?"

"Don't be dull, girl. You know what I am talking about. This . . . this . . ." And here, at a loss for words, she performed the uncommon act of waving a forkful of scrambled eggs toward the object of her conversation.

"Oh, that. Actually, the technique is rather good, I think. *Menchen im Hades,* it's called; part of a series on Dante's works by a German artist whom Ambrose discovered in Munich. He committed suicide, I understand. Cut his throat with a cavalry saber." I leered gleefully. Augusta Tregaron shivered.

"Disgusting."

"Rather a neat trick, I should say. Couldn't have been easy." I smiled with relish and deliberately shoveled a forkful of kidneys into my mouth.

She looked away in obvious revulsion, but had soon to bring her eyes back to me, for nowhere in the room was there anything to see but tokens of death and damnation. The small chamber was paneled to a height of six feet in ancient black oak, above which a narrow band of hand-painted Gothic lettering—starkly black and gilt on a dead white ground—repeated over and over again the Latin admonition *Memento Mori*: "Remember you must die." Above that, a series of small mezzotints depicting various gruesome death scenes of some of the more infamous sinners of history and legend circled the room. Above them another band of *Memento Mori* met the joinings of wall and ceiling. The accent colors of window draperies, rug, and damask napery were the somber purple, lavender, and black of mourning.

Augusta Tregaron laid her eyes on me and reflected for a long while, her lips poised as if about to speak; and yet she spoke not. I pretended not to notice, but rather ate my eggs and kidneys and toast with a repulsive gusto meant to displease her the more.

"Do you wish to say something, Aunt?" I said at last, my mouth full of food.

"Must you eat in that revolting manner, Enid?" she asked with a twist of her cold, hard face.

"Is it revolting to you? Do forgive me, but this country air has done wonders for my appetite. I sleep like a baby and eat with the gusto of a bumpkin. Thanatos Abbey is like a tonic after years in the grayness of London's foul air. You'll see. It shall have its effect on you, too, Aunt Augusta." I smiled craftily at this happy thought.

"I wonder," she muttered to herself, her cold eyes straying to that terrible painting with another small, involuntary shudder. "Your husband Ambrose is very anxious that I should get on here, that we two should work together on his studies. He is convinced that Llewellyn is trying to reach me."

"Is he?"

"Is he?" she echoed me, puzzled as to my meaning.

"Is Uncle Llewellyn trying to reach you?"

"I . . . hope so. If he is, it is proof, is it not, that . . . that . . ." She trailed off again, her eyes fascinated by the painting before her, a fearful glimmering of her own torments yet to come lighting those hard, dark, birdlike eyes of hers. Though her face was turned to her left, toward me, yet those fearful eyes sought out that horrible picture. How I laughed within myself to watch her. Damnation to her, I thought triumphantly.

"Proof of what, Aunt?" I urged flatly.

"Proof that that thing," she said spiritedly, nodding to the painting on the paneled wall before her, "is a lie—that we remain aware and cognizant after death. That death isn't an end, but only a change. If Llewellyn is trying to reach me, can reach me, he will prove by doing so that there is no real death, but only of the body—not of the soul."

"Indeed! If Uncle Llewellyn can reach you, his reaching you will prove that death isn't a final end, Aunt, but it certainly won't make this painting a lie." I smiled serenely and took a long sip of coffee, letting the effect of my remark set in.

"It won't?" she asked abruptly, her eyes snapping away from the dark, grim canvas at last and riveting on mine.

"But of course not. All souls in hell are cognizant. That is the very idea of their agony and torment. If Uncle Llewellyn contacts you, he will prove, by doing so, that there is a form of life after what we call dying, but for all we know he is trying to reach you from the very gates of heaven or—less likely, considering his basic goodness—the very gaping jaws of hell itself. Who are we to know? We shan't know unless he tells us, shall we, Aunt?" I asked cunningly. I was enjoying myself immensely.

"You are little comfort, Enid, to the disquietudes of my soul." She sighed softly, and I could almost have believed her to be, at that moment, poised on the brink of some true, human feeling. It was too much! It was the last straw! I felt my heart tighten within my breast. My lips formed precisely the words I now spoke as a trembling passion of bitterness set every nerve of my body to quivering within me.

"And what, Aunt Augusta, have you ever done to ease the disquietudes of that maimed and battered little soul that I carried with me like a wounded bird when I entered your brother's house all those years ago that I, now, should entertain to comfort the self-created disquietudes of your miserable old soul?" If ever a woman could turn to stone as she spoke, then I turned to very granite with those words of mine.

A look of pain crossed that hard, crone's face of hers such as I had neither seen nor thought possible of her. "I am old, Enid, old and alone and afraid of dying . . . afraid of hell . . . afraid of nothingness."

"Nothingness," I scoffed. "You won't know the meaning of the word 'nothingness' until you've lived under my roof the kind of life you've forced me to live under yours all those endless, nightmare years."

She actually whimpered before the angry lashings of my tongue. I could not believe it, and yet, pressing my advantage, I went on. "You want comfort from me for the disquietudes of your poor old soul. All right. Comfort you shall have, then. There is *nothing* after death. We are animals, animated meat, and like meat we die—only we bury ourselves in this part of the world. In other parts, I understand, they eat dead men like so much steak-and-kidney pie.

"You're damned lucky, by the way, that there's nothing after death, because if there was, you'd really be *damned*. Hell, old woman, is right here on earth, and you've made it for yourself. If you had ever shown even a shred of pity, of mercy, of kindness to anyone in your whole blighted existence, then you might be able to look back on a good life and not fear death so very much at all. Of course you fear death! Why shouldn't you, when you've made life hell for everyone you've ever known." Nothing was going to stop me now. I let out all the grievances that I had harbored within me for all those endless, soul-numbing years.

"What did you ever serve up to my mother but hatred and mistrust? What seeds did you ever sow in Morgan Tregaron's heart but suspicion and lying tales of betrayal? And how you hated poor, pale, sad little Aunt Amelia. What did she ever do, poor soul, but marry your precious brother Llewellyn and try to make him happy? But you wanted them all, Llewellyn, Morgan, and Rhys, the one that died young. He probably gave up the ghost to escape you; that's what my mother always said. You wanted them all to yourself, to rule and control and own. There was no room in their lives for wives and children, was there? Not with Augusta Tregaron putting her nose in everywhere, spying, lying, and dividing whenever she could. How you must have hated it when Uncle Llewellyn took me in. No wonder you've made me the object of your hatred all these years."

She sat like a crumpled old hag such as one might see in the doorway of some low public house in the steaming bowels of London. Still I had no pity.

"Meditate on your life, Augusta Tregaron, and be damned glad that your dying, like all our dying, will end in merciful oblivion. You're getting away cheap, if you ask me, lady." I rose abruptly, and throwing down my purple linen napkin, stalked from the room in a passion of deep fury, nervous agitation, and utter disgust.

Ambrose was silhouetted in the partially opened front door of the abbey as I stalked from the breakfast room. Jemmy Burkers, standing arms akimbo before him on the broad outside step, was speaking:

". . . to talk soon. Go on in an' fetch the old lady on 'er tour of the abbey an' meet me in an hour or so. I'll be waitin' in your study." Without another word, he turned heel and walked off.

"Jemmy," Ambrose called after his "servant's" retreating form, "it shall go well. I've laid the groundwork splendidly. You'll see."

"But of course you 'ave, my lad. Was there ever any doubt? It's your job, arter all, what?" Jemmy called back over his shoulder in a patronizing tone that made me sick. Ambrose, my so-called husband, begging crumbs of praise and reassurance from the likes of Jemmy Burkers! I tried to slip down the corridor to my rooms without his seeing me, but I was too late.

"Enid," he called out to me, closing the great front door of the abbey behind him, thus robbing the immense dark entry hall of nearly all natural light.

"Yes, Ambrose?" I answered brightly.

"You look rather agitated."

"I have had words with my aunt, and am somewhat upset."

"You do not get on, do you, the two of you?"

I laughed harshly at the tameness of his description of our relationship. "No, we do not get on. You have heard her opinion of me; what she thinks me capable of. Should I get on with her under such circumstances?"

"That depends."

"Depends?"

"On the rightness of her accusations. If her opinion is correct . . ."

"The *rightness* of her accusations? If . . ." I could say no more. I was too stunned. What did he think of me? He had, before our marriage, seemed to defend me from Augusta Tregaron's accusations. Now there were ifs to his thinking. Ifs!

"My aunt is awaiting you in the breakfast room. She said something about you showing her the abbey. Your servant, too, seems to have asked you to show her about as well. Therefore, pray do so, sir, being careful only to keep from invading my private rooms while on your tour. Those are my own and I will not entertain visitors. No one! Do you understand?"

"Perfectly, Enid."

I turned away and started hastily down the corridor toward the back of the abbey, lest the tears that I felt welling in my eyes be seen by him and taken for a sign of weakness.

"Enid," he called out softly.

"Yes?" I kept my back to him.

"I am sorry for my ill-chosen words. *She* thinks she is correct. That, after all, is what counts."

"And you, Ambrose?"

"I . . . I do not know, Enid. And will not know or even speculate till you yourself have told me. Is that fair enough?"

I did not answer at first, but then at last: "Fair enough for now, Ambrose. It is precious little, I think, for a husband to offer his wife, but in fairness to you, it is more consideration than I have been given by anyone else in almost fourteen years. It is enough for now at any rate."

"We shall talk more of this one day."

"Perhaps. See to Aunt Augusta now, Ambrose. She is the heart of the matter for you now, isn't she, after all?" I retreated down the hall to my rooms without another word. There was nothing more to say.

It was in a rather defeated and weary mood that I sat by my casement window that morning after my confrontations with my aunt and Ambrose. Strong sunlight—the first strong sunlight that I had seen in that dreary place—streamed over my shoulder onto the canvas set before me in my work frame. I was calming down now, the steady rhythm of my needlework working its soothing effect on my agitated nerves. I was just beginning to embroider the emerald-green feathers of a fanciful and rather engaging cockatoo when there came a sharp tap at the window to my left.

I started and looked up to see a smiling Jemmy Burkers standing without in his full servant's livery. I remember thinking how ill it became him after seeing him so often in the evening dress of a gentleman. Despite his class, when dressed in evening kit he cut a fine figure indeed, being shorter, more solidly built, and infinitely more muscular than Ambrose. Jemmy had the catlike, athletic grace of a man who knows his own body and uses it well.

I rose, oddly not the least angered by his sudden and most unconventional intrusion upon my privacy, and opened the casement to him.

"Beggin' yer pardon, ma'am, but I was passin' across the green and saw you at yer 'broiderin'. You . . . you looked rather a sweet picture."

"D-did I?" I stammered, and then, to hide the fluster that I felt, I went on: "And so you thought you'd disturb that picture just to spoil it?" I felt ashamed of myself the very minute I spoke, but could not take back the words.

He gazed at me penetratingly for a long minute before he replied, and then, unexpectedly, his words were soft and kind. "No, Mrs. De'Ath. Not ta spoil it. Just maybe ta touch it for a minute; ta be a part of it fer a second or two. There ain't much 'ere that's pretty or sweet, arter all, is there? An' a man must 'ave something sweet before 'is eyes, upon occasion, mustn't 'e?"

I could not help the tears that filled my eyes at that moment. "Forgive me, Jemmy. I was rather rude, wasn't I? You see, despite what you may think about my class and my background and my opportunities in life as opposed to your own, I wouldn't know very much myself about pretty things or sweet ones either."

"I understand."

"Do you? Do you?" I cried. "I am not sure that I understand myself."

"You're fightin' a battle, my girl," he said gravely, "an' it's lonely an' 'ard and all up'ill, most o' the time, ain't it? An' sometimes it overwhelms ya, don't it? But you'll win through. My money's on ya, pet." He spoke so kindly, so touchingly, that I could not even take exception to the gross informality of his address. I doubt if he had even realized his breach himself.

"How . . . how do you know?" I whispered.

"I'm battlin' too, little girl. I'm battlin' too. Speak to 'er, will you? Open up to 'er. It's 'ard at first, but it'll 'elp. Now, get back ta that little green bird o' yours," he said, nodding past me to my embroidery stand. " 'E ain't got no wings yet. 'Ow's 'e gonna fly wi'out 'is wings, poor little blighter?" With that, he smiled crookedly, gave me a wink, and was gone off across the wintral, dun-colored grass of the "green," as he called it, and was soon lost from sight over a rise that led down to the cliffs beyond the back of the abbey.

That smile—that crooked, cocksure, smarmy smile—and that daring wink, so crude and typical of one of his low, cockney origins. What did he mean by them—pleasantry or insult? Familiarity or contempt?

Damn Jemmy Burkers, I thought as I jabbed my needle into the canvas breast of my fanciful little cockatoo. How dare he speak and act in such a manner to me? Who the devil did he think he was?

Well, one thing, at least, I would take him up on! I would speak to her. But not of myself, of course, as he had suggested. I would make her set him straight; make her exact from him proper respect for my person and privacy. So much—I smirked—for the cocky Mr. Burkers, sticking the needle viciously into my little green bird and adding a silken feather to his elegant emerald wing.

Ambrose was my next visitor, knocking at the outer chamber with a tentativeness that let me at once identify my caller.

"Come in, Ambrose," I called confidently. I had not really meant to banish him from my rooms entirely, and was glad of so quick an opportunity to make amends for my pique of the previous night and morning.

He entered with a curt nod, and noting the changes that I

had made during his protracted absence in London, stood for a while surveying the room.

"I did not notice, last night, how much you have done to alter the appearance of your apartment. It didn't suit as it was, I take it?"

"No, Ambrose, I found that it did not suit at all, for it was beastly gloomy and virtually smelled of death. I have had enough of gloom in my life, thank you." My tone was distant and vaguely reproachful.

"We are quite at odds, you and I, aren't we?" he said at last.

"I am your wife, Ambrose, and will act my part for the world to see, but within these little rooms, I am mistress. What life I can make for myself, I will . . . and . . ." I paused then, biting my tongue, wondering whether to dare say what I had to say.

"And?" he prompted.

"And I will not thwart you. I do not yet know your game, nor even all the players as yet, but do not be afraid, Ambrose. For now I see no reason to thwart you."

"I do not know what you say," he answered stiffly. "Games, players, thwarting . . ."

"Have a caution, Ambrose dear!" I warned with a smile. "Do not overplay your hand. Funny, but I have the feeling that your 'servant' Mr. Burkers would catch my meaning soon enough."

"My servant Mr. Burkers is a crafty, sly devil and not at all to be trusted," he snapped hotly, and with a powerful want of discretion for one so stolid and cautious as Ambrose.

"True," I concurred, "and I do not trust him. Nor," I added spitefully, "would I trust overmuch any dull-witted fool who was not man enough to be master of his own household."

"I begin, madame, to see that you are not at all what I bargained for."

"Oh, but you did not bargain for me, sir, as I must admit to my own shame, and if I am not what you expected in a wife, at least you can say that you got me cheap. It is *I* shall pay the price of my folly, sir, not you, for I sold myself for next to nothing, and that is exactly what I have got in return—next to nothing."

"Perhaps we deserve each other," he said, crumpling back under my cold and polite assault of words like a marionette whose strings have broken. I looked at him sadly. We were both victims, after all, and I could only pity him.

"Do let us make the best of it for now, Ambrose, until such time as we can rectify things. I'll try not to be so bitter. You try not to be so weak. The best of a bad bargain, shall we? After all, we're not bad people, Ambrose, only rather ... mismatched?"

"Yes, mismatched. You want to love life, no matter what it has done to you. I . . . I want only to steep myself in Death." He smiled ironically. "Yes, my ill-assorted consort, we'll do our best—starting tonight at dinner."

"At dinner?" I asked.

"That is what I came to tell you. My mother has invited guests for dinner to welcome you formally into the family and to honor your Aunt Augusta as well. Shall we present a united front before them all, or shall we air our private unhappinesses for all to see—like the common sort?"

"Whatever else you and I are, Ambrose, we are not of the common sort. A united front, by all means."

"We shall meet in the New Hall, then, at seven o'clock."

"At seven."

He turned to go.

"Enid, I am sorry."

"So, Ambrose, am I."

The door closed.

# 6

# THE COMPANY DINES

> I maintain that though you would
> often in the fifteenth century have heard
> the snobbish Roman say, in a would-be off-hand
> tone, "I am dining with the Borgias tonight,"
> no Roman ever was able to say, "I dined
> last night with the Borgias."
> —*Max Beerbohm*

> Serenely full, the epicure would say,
> Fate cannot harm me, I have dined to-day.
> —*Sydney Smith*

Although I had seen Jemmy Burkers several times since Ambrose's return to the abbey with my Aunt Augusta, and should therefore have by then become accustomed to his reversion to the manner and dress of a servant, yet it still came as a shock to see him that night in immaculate evening livery, striped vest and white gloves, standing at his post beside the double doors to the New Hall, where my mother-in-law awaited her guests.

So used had I become, however grudgingly, to seeing him in his place as master of Madame Henriette De'Ath's elegant and fantastic domain, that to see him ready to receive and announce her guests at the door while Ambrose now usurped, as it were, his rightful place at the old woman's side, actually rankled me. It was indeed a strange turn of events that I should find myself even thinking in such terms, and about Jemmy Burkers of all people. Perhaps it was because I knew in my heart that, lowly as was his birth and upbringing, he still stood taller as a man than did my husband Ambrose.

While Ambrose had, since my first acquaintance with him, steadily lowered himself in my respect and esteem, increasing intimacy with Jemmy Burkers had, albeit grudgingly, increased my regard—if not my actual respect—for his intelligence and even certain aspects of his character. Amazing!

"The young Madame De'Ath," Jemmy announced formally if not quite correctly as I swept between the open leaves of the painted and gilded French doors and on into that huge fairyland candlelit salon beyond.

"Thank you, Jemmy," I breathed softly. "It is odd this way, isn't it?" I could not help remarking to him *sotto voce* as I passed him and walked toward my aged hostess.

"Is it, madame?" he murmured.

It shouldn't be, I thought, but, oh yes, Jemmy, it is—very odd—and for the life of me I do not know why I should find it so. But that is quite enough, I chided myself severely. My thoughts must perforce turn to the two people before me. They were the important ones, and not that devious pretended servant behind us. What, after all, was he to me?

Old Madame De'Ath sat, small and erect and dignified as ever I had seen her, in a large, very old-fashioned bath chair which had been upholstered in fine French or Belgian petit point, its wooden frame and structure lavishly gilded. A small rubber-tired wheel protruded before it, its steering mechanism controlled by the long gold canelike stick that rose up from the front of the conveyance and which Madame De'Ath held in one gnarled, bejeweled old hand like a French queen might have held her mockery shepherdess's crook.

Her gown was of deep, dark old-rose silk brocade, stiff and gorgeous to behold; the neck cut square and low and edged in delicate gold lace, beribboned and bowed from low bosom to tiny waist, while the lush full skirt was parted from bodice to hem, revealing a delicate pale rose silk taffeta petticoat. Edging the front opening and hem of this wide skirt was a double border of gold lace in the gatherings of which sparkled amethysts, aquamarines, and a profusion of those bright pink gems that some call balas rubies.

Her wig was huge and high, and worn, like her gown itself, in the gracious and extravagant style of another age—the age of prerevolutionary France. The hair of it was rosy mauve in color and dressed with ropes of pearls and jewels of pink, blue, and amethyst. Long curls, or lovelocks as they were called in her day, hung down past her bejeweled ears to the thin, wrinkled neck, where they touched the gold necklace that she wore. This necklace was ornate, studded and festooned and literally dripping with bright jewels that shone like globules of liquid color.

As always, her face was white with arsenic and white lead, kohled about the eyes and spotted with black patches. The old lips were near to purple with rouge and the cheeks colored in similar fashion. The effect, while sounding utterly grotesque, somehow worked on that old woman, making her at once bizarre and magnificent; never diminishing her majesty however it made one question her mind. That arresting figure was so many things as one beheld her—dignified, powerful, young and old, ugly and beautiful, eccentric and noble, mad and sane all at once. And, as always, I loved the very sight of her.

She nodded her head gently as if commanding me to approach still closer, and it was then that I realized that I had stopped stock-still some ten feet from her and had been in a long and trancelike study of her person, to the utter disregard of personal propriety. Indeed, I had hardly noticed that Ambrose stood beside her, dutiful and funereal as ever, like the very personification of that corpse-spirit that lurked within the depths of his odd and melancholy soul, awaiting, as it were, its final, inevitable, eternity-long reign over his skeletal body and morbid mind. I looked at that skull-like face, the long, bony, cadaverous body, the dull, sunken eyes from which no spark of living fire seemed to flame forth, and wondered how long that corpse within him would be held in check by the simple, natural act of living. Not long, not long, yet every minute must be an eternity to him. Poor, poor Ambrose.

He came toward me, extending his long fingers to grasp my own small hand, and led me to his mother.

"*Ma mère,* may I present formally my wife Enid, whom, I am given to understand, you have met already during my absence in London."

"But of course. *Ma petite,* your presence in my salon is a pleasure, as always, but to see you by the side of my son is, naturally, the best pleasure of all."

"You are too kind, madame," I murmured, curtsying low, my eyes on hers and seeing in them a sadness and a knowingness that I knew reflected the expression in my own. We were playing a game this night, acting a charade, and we both knew the necessity and the sorrow of it. I grasped, moreover, that neither of us wished Ambrose to have an inkling of the frequency with which I had visited his mother in this room of hers, nor the part in our evenings which Jemmy Burkers had been wont to play.

The sound of voices came to our ears just then, and so with little further converse Ambrose led me to a place behind his mother's chair, where, my arm locked dutifully in his, I joined that formal family group to await the entrance of the evening's guests.

How strange it was to stand there statuelike and see that magnificent room from the viewpoint of the old Madame De'Ath; to await with her as she sat, like a resplendent, bejeweled spider, the coming of the evening's complement of flies for her delectation. The great doors opened at last and far down that long, glowing, candlelit room, Jemmy Burkers entered ceremoniously, his white shirtfront and gloves showing almost luminously above his dark livery in the warm yellow light of that fantastic salon.

"The Reverend Mr. Enoch Pond and Mrs. Peggy Pond. Their son, Master Lucas Pond." He announced those rather common names to us and then deferentially closed the double doors behind the trio who now approached. And what a trio they were! Even then, something about them nagged at me, but for the life of me I could not think what it was. Had I heard of them before? It seemed utterly unlikely.

The Reverend Enoch Pond was tall and florid, of great size and imposing bulk. He was a man of fifty-odd with a look about him of self-congratulatory, self-esteeming grandness. A large gold-plated watch chain, hung with a profusion of heavy, cheap ornaments, decorated his plain black waistcoat in the general vicinity of a corpulent midsection that was carried before him as if its very corpulence were a badge of success in life. There was certainly nothing meek or humble in the manner of the man; nor, must I add in fairness, nothing of ill humor either, for he had that unabashedly satisfied look of a man "crept in favor" with himself, as Shakespeare so aptly puts it.

If something made me mistrust him on sight, it was the worried, haunted expression of timidity in the eyes of his fat, round, dark little wife, stuffed—like too many feathers in a comforter—into the plain, high-necked flowered dress which she wore, ornamented only by a modest cameo brooch of brown shell and gold plate pinned at the throat and a small locket hanging from a chain of woven hair. The hair of this chain was silver-gray and matched the sparse locks on her husband's head, leading me to think sympathetic thoughts of the imprisoned Mrs. Pond with her husband literally around her throat even as (I sensed) he was figuratively on her back. In short, my sympathy went out in pity to the plain, timid little woman with the anxious eyes and terrible dress.

Master Lucas was a snively boy of seventeen or thereabouts, tall and awkward and too heavy about the hips and thighs to ever hope for manly grace. He had dull, watery eyes and an adenoidal look made all the more unattractive by a perpetual open mouth and the slightly bucked, rabbity teeth that resided therein. He seemed to be as mild as his mother and as completely the antithesis of his father (except in his height and promise of future girth) as ever true-born son could be. It took no more than a glance to suspect that in the Reverend Pond's eyes Lucas would probably be a great disappointment to his father if indeed he was not already.

The only mystery that this trio of guests presented to me as they made a galloping and almost herdlike approach to their hostess and her family was what on earth were persons such as these doing in the company of the eloquent, witty, and absolutely grand Madame Henriette De'Ath in the first place?

"Madame De'Ath"—or *Dee'*Ath, as he insisted on pronouncing it—the florid Mr. Pond gushed loudly as he actually dropped to one knee before the bath chair and clasped her tiny hand in his great red paws, "this surely is an honor, ma'am. I said ta the Mrs. here only this mornin', 'Peggy,' says I, 'if that don't beat all, bein' invited ta supper up ta the abbey.' Can't tell ya, Madame De'Ath, what a thrill ya give us all. Lucas'll remember this right on inter the next century, after we is all dust. Ain't that so, Lucas?" he called loudly over his shoulder.

"Surely is so, Pa," the boy concurred dully but dutifully. Perhaps, from his father's standpoint there was room to hope after all, I reflected.

"A comforting thought indeed, Mr. Pond." old Madame De'Ath smiled graciously, and I wondered how she kept the mockery out of her eyes and her tone as she spoke.

"*Reverend* Pond," he corrected patiently, as one accustomed to such a slip.

"But of course," she exclaimed effusively, and I had the distinct impression that this little exchange between them was not infrequent. "Pardon, *Reverend* Pond. We on this side of the Atlantic use 'reverend' as a title but never as a form of address. Pray forgive me. I shall—how do you say?—'get the hang of it' one of these days. Meanwhile, allow me to introduce my new daughter-in-law, the young Madame Ambrose De'Ath."

"Enid, Reverend Pond and his charming family are from a former colony across the waters, the United States of America," Ambrose put in gallantly.

"I am delighted, sir." I nodded and offered my hand, first to "Reverend" Enoch Pond and then to his timid, speechless little lady, who offered a plump, cold hand, wet with perspiration. Poor, nervous, fluttery little mouse, I could not help but think. Young Lucas I merely smiled at, not wishing to risk his clumsy grasp.

"Pray, ma'am," I asked Mrs. Pond politely and in an effort to set her more at her ease, "from what region of America do you come?"

"Why, little Madame De'Ath, from God's country, upper New York State; from Hydesville, a town that will one day be known to all the tormented souls of earth as the New Jerusalem," Enoch Pond interjected on behalf of his still-speechless little wife.

"Praise the Lord, yes," Mrs. Pond exclaimed shrilly and to my great surprise, for I had begun to think her a mute. Lucas followed with a crack-voiced, "Amen."

"Indeed," I murmured, trying to keep my increasing wonderment from showing on my face. Who *were* these people and, even better still, why ever were they here in the golden salon of Madame Henriette De'Ath? Moreover, as I pondered upon the Ponds (pun intended!), I became certain that they had been here before and perhaps even often at that, for despite their utter  gaucherie at the prospect of dining at Thanatos Abbey, they seemed completely at home in the salon itself and sat down unbidden in what appeared to be their usual seats once introductions had been made. Most curious indeed.

The doors reopened just then. Jemmy Burkers, playing his role to the hilt, announced still another guest: "Mr. Osric Ottermole."

We all turned our attention toward this new arrival, with whom, it seemed, I alone amongst the assemblage was unacquainted. At his approach, Mr. Osric Ottermole, he of the most appropriate name, sent through my person that mild chill of revulsion such as one experiences upon finding something fat and yellowish-white under an overturned rock. He was a small man, under five feet in height, completely bald, and even in that flattering candlelight of a repulsively sallow complexion. His deep brown eyes protruded like two large, shiny carbuncles from beneath small, puffy, lashless yellow lids. That characteristic, together with his firm, rotund little body and the sausagelike clumps of fingers at the ends of his plump, stubby arms, only served to confirm my first impression; that of some fat, juicy half-curled larva, all yellow body and brown dots of eyes, discovered under a stone or in the overturned earth of a hedgerow.

He approached with somewhat bustling, quick little steps, extended his plump hand to take Madame De'Ath's, and bowed to kiss it with pale, thick lips. His cheeks, I noted, were full, firm, and hairless, virtually shiny with scrubbing. In fact, upon closer scrutiny, his whole person had a scrubbed and immaculate appearance, and he smelled strongly of attar of roses as well, which fact I found both odd and somehow not unpleasant to discover. Perhaps it was because he looked as if he should smell of something else—earth, probably.

"Madame De'Ath, I am charmed, charmed as ever," he whispered in a small, rasping voice. I was surprised to find his mode of speech and accent that of a well-educated man of breeding, quite at odds with his uncommon looks and almost tradesmanlike brusqueness of walk and dress.

We were introduced and I accepted his good wishes on my recent marriage, finding myself rather liking the strange little man for his courteous, easy, and well-mannered ways. He was not only well-spoken but seemed both intelligent and good-humored as well.

"Mr. Ottermole is our local undertaker and has a very fine funeral-furnishing establishment in Wadebridge, my dear," Ambrose said by way of enlightenment.

"Indeed! How . . . how . . ." I stuttered, at a loss for the proper words. Does one say "charming," "delightful," "interesting"? I had never met a mortician socially before. What *did* one say?

" 'Enterprising' might be the word you want, Madame Ambrose," Mr. Ottermole interjected helpfully and with unexpected good humor at my impolite loss for words. "I come from good old English squire stock, you see, but along about my father's time our money began to run out at an alarming rate. The two of us, man and boy (as I was then), decided that there were three things everyone needed at least once in their lives—a doctor, a parson, and an undertaker. Father was too old to become a doctor and too dissolute . . . Pardon, Reverend, Ma'am." He smiled affably to the Ponds. "Too dissolute to be a parson, and that left only one thing.

"And so"—he laughed raspily—"we're the very best damned funeral outfitters in all of Cornwall—and the richest," he added merrily. "Rather set the gentry on their heels when we descended to trade, don't you know, but our success unsettled them even more." He chuckled good-naturedly. "It used to do the old man's heart good to bury the very people who had turned their noses up at him for going into trade. 'Now who's turning up his nose, lad?' he'd say while we were embalming some sour old party who snubbed us at church or neglected to invite my mother to tea. We had our fun, though, my, didn't we!" he added reflectively.

"Well, more power to you, sir." I nodded deferentially.

It was then that Jemmy Burkers reentered the salon, escorting my aunt, Augusta Tregaron, who marched forward, head high, arm resting on Jemmy's with a clawed, bemitted old hand extended on his forearm as did the ladies of Olde England on the arms of their knights in armor. She was head to toe in black as usual and looked, with her withered white face, almost as much a corpse as did Ambrose himself. Had her sharp old eyes not flitted, like those of a ferret, from face to face over the company already assembled, and over the grandness of the room as well, I expect Mr. Ottermole should have wished to measure her right then and there for one of his finest caskets.

Her confused reaction to the company before her was most humorous to me. Impressed as she always was by the gentlemanly Ambrose De'Ath and his funereal austerity, and now by the fantastic value and antique splendors of the New Hall itself, which she was viewing for the first time, yet nothing could have been more impressive to her sight than old Madame Henriette De'Ath, for there sat a woman even farther along in years than herself and yet one who was as absolutely gaudy with the resplendence of jewels and gold and lace and silk as she was bedraped with the dark trappings of mourning and death. Here was a woman bewigged and painted and dressed in a manner that my Aunt Augusta could only have considered whorish and vulgar, and yet this was no whore who sat with the majesty of a queen amidst all this luxury and beauty!

Augusta Tregaron's eyes riveted on her near-contemporary, taking in every nuance of Madame De'Ath's bizarre toilet. Her mouth remained shut tight as a trap until introduction forced her to recover herself and make reply, which was as well, for had she not made that effort to seal her lips, I suspect that she should rather have gaped like a bumpkin.

As further introductions were made all around, her obvious amazement at her hostess's appearance was transcended by her utter shock at the unsuitability of the common-as-dirt

Pond family and the physical and professional unattractiveness of the otherwise kindly and proper Mr. Osric Ottermole.

I smirked to myself at her ever-more-aghast expression and finally drew in my breath. The cast had now assembled, and the curtain, so to speak, was about to ascend. This, I remember thinking, was going to be *quite* a dinner party.

I have said that the cast was assembled, the curtain about to ascend, but that was not strictly true. Say, rather that at a clapping of Madame De'Ath's bejeweled old hands, the curtain—in the form of hinged panels fully ten feet in height—was drawn back by that most perfect of butlers, Mr. Jemmy Burkers, to reveal a room the existence of which was not only hitherto unsuspected by myself, but evidently by the greater part of the company as well.

As the entire paneled wall behind us slid noiselessly open, there was revealed a sight every bit as overwhelming to me as had been Madame De'Ath's salon upon my first viewing it. Before us, lit by three huge, lavish crystal chandeliers, was a long high room that appeared at first to be paneled from floor to ceiling in squares of polished onyx. The twenty-foot ceiling, arching over our heads in tentlike fashion, was mirrored over its entirety and thus reflected every point of light in those absolutely blazing chandeliers as if they were diamonds. The effect was one of almost more-than-daylight brightness and it contrasted sharply with the onyx blackness of the walls, which, on second glance, proved to be merely squares of common window glass, but given their exotic look by the utter blackness of the night sky without.

Surely, I thought, any ship bound for Ireland across St. George's Channel must see these very lights and marvel at their brightness. Perhaps even some poor peasants on the far coast were remarking, at this very moment, on the brilliant light from across the sea as they sat to their own rude meal of boiled potatoes.

But there was yet more to see: beneath that mirrored ceiling and its breathtaking load of blazing crystal stretched a long narrow table of ornately wrought gilt-bronze with a marvelous top set with mirrored glass. Upon its reflective surface were arranged eight widely spaced place settings in the very finest of Sevres porcelain—an old chinoiserie pattern in green and yellow, and long gone, I would imagine, from the Sevres catalogs—complemented by heavy gold cutlery and the finest yellow linen napery, by tall stemmed cut crystal goblets and exquisite silver-gilt salts, all of which sat upon that mirrored surface like so many lovely jewels upon a tray.

Down the center of this long, gleaming table ran a low, water-filled gallery of ornate *bronze-d'oré* filled with pale yellow water lilies, floating with their bright green pads as if on the surface of a golden lake. These flowers had no scent of their own, but from the masses of living plants which were set out in large yellow and green pots arranged in the corners and along the glass walls of the room, came the mingled scents of orange blossoms and roses, lilacs and lily of the valley and gardenias in such profusion as to almost stifle the breath.

In short, it was a fantasy room which appeared before our wondering eyes, and it was only the deep, uncultured cockney voice of Jemmy Burkers that broke our thrall, plunging us back into the reality of our own individual existences with his curt, "Madame De'Ath, ladies and gentlemen, dinner is served."

With that, Jemmy wheeled the old lady to her place at the foot of the table, and Ambrose, after escorting me to a place at her right hand, took his own at the head. Mr. Ottermole had the dubious honor of escorting Aunt Augusta to Ambrose's right hand before taking his own seat across from me (and therefore to Madame De'Ath's left). Beside him was placed poor Mrs. Pond, while her son Lucas sat on my right and his father just beyond, on Ambrose's left and therefore across from my Aunt Augusta. I had the distinct feeling that the seating arrangement was well planned. To what purpose my aunt had been seated opposite such a man as Enoch Pond I did not know, though by careful observation I hoped to find out.

A battery of waiters and footmen under the watchful and very professional eye of Jemmy Burkers served our sumptuous and almost overly lavish meal, poured our wines and generally saw to our needs as if we were dining in the bygone grandeur of Versailles rather than the home of a British gentleman on the rock-bound coast of Cornwall. Once more, I reflected, Madame De'Ath was proving her penchant for fantasy and mystery and romance, her remarkable ability to suspend reality and weave some semblance of a world that no longer *was*—a world, in fact, that *when* it was, was known intimately to such a few, and of those few, virtually all gone long since to Madame la Guillotine. Who was Henriette

De'Ath? Who was she really, I wondered to myself as I had so often since our first meeting, and as I would so often in future.

"Did you ever see her, Madame De'Ath? Did you really see Marie Antoinette herself?" Mrs. Peggy Pond was gushing. What was it about that little woman? Where had I heard of her before?

"Oh, but yes, Mrs. Pond," my mother-in-law replied, "and more beautiful and gracious she was than any praise of mine or any painting by a master could make her out to be. She had such *élan*," and then, in reply to the look of confusion on the good woman's face, she clarified most gracefully so as to cause no embarrassment, "such style, such dash, such nobility and confidence. She believed with her whole heart that France was hers. She had no dream, no inkling of the end that was in store. It was sad, rather, her great beauty and her great lack of insight." There was an expression in the old woman's eyes that indicated to me that she had slipped back, far back into the past, to the days of which this magnificent room was but a shredded, tattered remnant; to a day when a queen of France ruled the table and guided the conversation rather than . . . ? Than whom? Again, who was this old woman really?

"Were you there for the end, madame? Did you see her at the last?" I ventured to ask.

"But no," she replied, making a little moue as if to indicate the simplemindedness of my question, "else I should not be among this charming company tonight, should I?" she went on quickly, flashing a smile at Mr. Ottermole, as if to invite him to join the conversation (or change it?).

"I am glad that Mrs. Pond has brought up the subject, madame, of your original homeland. You have told many stories of others, but surely your own adventures must have been great. Your escape from the Terror, for instance?" Mr. Ottermole was not about to change the conversation.

Mrs. Pond, as well, urged her on. I thought it politic to remain discreetly noncommittal, for though I hoped she would speak of her personal experiences, I doubted that she would be any less reticent over the dinner table than she had been over the card table in her salon on the frequent evenings I had spent in her company with Jemmy. I turned my attention for the moment to my right, where Master Lucas sat stolidly stuffing his gaping mouth with all the solemnity of a police surgeon at an autopsy. (Morbid analogy, that, and I remember wondering at the time what on earth had possessed me to think in such terms.)

"I suppose, Master Pond, that you must find all this very boring. Madame De'Ath must seem out of another age to you, and rather cra . . . rather eccentric into the bargain."

He looked at me with those dull eyes of his as his masticating jaws ground to a slow and evidently thoughtful halt. He swallowed painfully and answered me in a most surprising vein: "Quite the contrary, Mrs. De'Ath" (he pronounced this as did his father—*dee*'Ath), "I find the old lady interestin', and as to my findin' her *crazy*, I think she's crazy like a fox. I just haven't tumbled yet to her game."

It was my turn now to swallow hard and, indeed, I very nearly choked on the wine that I happened to be sipping at that moment. "I have often heard it said, Master Pond," I replied, trying to recover from my initial reaction, "that the Americans are a canny people with a crude but effective way with words. You do nothing to dispel that impression, sir." I smiled weakly and lifted my glass to him in a sort of tribute I suppose.

"Always put it in a nutshell, ma'am."

"Indeed." And as Master Pond went back to filling his own shell with as much as he could stuff into it, I was left to ponder on the old admonition about telling books by their covers.

". . . often enjoyed perusing the memoirs of the few nobles who survived those terrible days in France, madame. Perhaps you yourself should put pen to paper," Mr. Ottermole was suggesting, as Mrs. Pond concurred with an urgent squeal. I thought I heard a snort of derision from her son just then, but it may only have been an excess of piggish snuffling into his Sevres asparagus "trough" that caused the disturbance. At any rate, Madame De'Ath demurred with a slight wave of her hand and a small moue of supposed embarrassment which I did not believe for a minute. I did not think then, nor do I now, that true embarrassment was native to her emotional range, nor even necessary to her for that matter.

"I don't read much, I'm afeared, folks," Mrs. Pond exclaimed in a fruity voice that betokened that she was nearing her capacity for wine-bibbing, "but I've heard tell of some great French lady what wrote her *mem*-wars a few years back, and she's made pots o' money at it."

"How fortunate for her," Madame De'Ath said in a voice that dripped icy sweetness. Earning "pots o' money" on her "*mem*-wars" was surely not only far beneath her dignity but also unnecessary as well, or so at least she seemed to be implying.

"I think, Madame De'Ath, that Mrs. Pond refers to the memoirs of the late Duchesse Eugénie-Marie de la Cressonière, which were published some fifteen or twenty years since. I remember reading them with relish at the time," Mr. Ottermole put in helpfully.

There was a momentary flashing in the eyes of Madame De'Ath that betokened both anger and some other discomfiture, both more subtle and more acute. I glanced at young Master Pond, noticing that he kept one gimlet eye upon her face as he raised his glass, and I guessed that he, even as I, was reading much into her expression. However, before she could recover herself and make reply, there came a sound of clattering plate which caused us all to take our attention from Madame De'Ath and look to Jemmy Burkers, who stood at a portable butler's tray against the wall just behind us. He was feigning a look of chagrin as he stooped to pick up the heavy silver-gilt cover of a serving dish.

"Beg pardon, Madame De'Ath," he mumbled obsequiously.

"Quite forgiven, Jemmy," she replied serenely, and looking down the long table toward her son, spoke his name with a bright gaiety that I did not trust. "Ambrose, darling, pray of what have you and the good Reverend Pond been speaking to entertain our honored guest, Miss Tregaron?"

"Why, *ma mère*, as ever we have been on my hobbyhorse, flogging away and trying to prevail upon my charming aunt-in-law . . ." (don't overplay your hand, Ambrose, I thought; the old woman's not stupid) ". . . to join our little circle."

"I've been endeavorin' ta explain the little spirit band that we've formed here at the abbey, ma'am," Enoch Pond interrupted, calling down the length of the table loudly, as if we were all deaf.

"Tell her, dear," Mrs. Pond urged with surprising animation and the bright-eyed flushed look of a temperate woman who has momentarily lost her temperance, "all about our callin', about the sisters and the New Jerusalem."

"Now, now, Mrs. Peggy, calm yourself. All in good time. My wife, Miss Tregaron," he exclaimed, addressing himself across the table to my aunt in a voice loud enough for us all to hear, "my wife refers to the little Fox sisters—Kate and Margaretta—whom God in his infinite wisdom has seen fit to cloak with the Mantle of Divine Revelation—"

"Amen," Mrs. Peggy put in shrilly, as my aunt, who throughout the entire evening had remained taciturn even for her, looked on in unabashed shock at the gaucheries of this irrepressible American couple and their stolid son, Lucas.

Again Jemmy Burkers intruded at what was evidently considered to be a pregnant moment, this time asking if the ventilating windows should be opened. After making an overly complex answer, Ambrose brought the conversation to more general topics, thus increasing the tensions at the table, at once frustrating the Reverend Pond's desire to sermonize on the subject of his odd beliefs and allowing for the piquing of my aunt's curiosity without in the least satisfying it. That this was his aim was evident to me by the satisfied smile he exchanged with his mother; that he had succeeded was shown by my Aunt Augusta's pensive face as we rose from the table a few moments later and made our way back into the great candlelit salon once more.

During the rest of the evening there seemed to be a pattern emerging: one in which the Reverend Pond and his family were allowed to expound just so far on the world of "spiritualism," as they called it, animal magnetism and the like, only then to be interrupted at some key point in their haranguing by the brazen interference of Jemmy Burkers or the more subtle manipulations of either my husband or his mother.

Master Lucas, as well as Mr. Ottermole and myself, took no great part in the general conversation, but each of us in our own way seemed aware of the tensions inherent in that evening. Aunt Augusta, clearly in my mind at least, was the chief subject of the game. That she was titillated by the Reverend Pond's dynamic and bizarre views on what he called "spiritualism" and the "departed souls beyond the veil," there could be no doubt. She was, moreover, spellbound by his delivery, which was dramatic, and inspired by what was—or seemed to be—his complete conviction on the subject. A fish she was, with a shiny baited hook dangling before her mouth, yet every time she came near to biting, that hook was jerked away. Obviously, when finally she was permitted to bite, the hook would strike deep and true—or so Jemmy and Ambrose seemed, between them, to hope. I say Jemmy and Ambrose quite deliberately, for I was not then sure of what part Reverend Pond played in the game—whether active participant, or passive co-conspirator himself with the others, or merely being manipulated as is a puppet on its strings.

As for my Aunt Augusta, I had lived long in the vicinity

of that wily old fish, and it would not have surprised me at all if she still managed to get exactly whatever it was that she was after—the bait they offered—and then be gone in a trice, leaving their fine big hook naked and unblooded. It would be interesting to watch, and since I cared not a fig for any of them, I thought that I would look on at their games with a fine sense of detached and high-minded curiosity; the clinical amusement, as it were, of an observer of the human condition. Surely, I thought then, there is no need for my own involvement in this charade. Little did I realize how that game would turn, and how quickly I would be pulled into the center of that little band of spirits to which Reverend Pond made such frequent and as yet still rather obscure reference.

At last the evening came to a close. While Aunt Augusta remained behind momentarily with her hostess, Ambrose and I accompanied the other guests to their waiting carriages. I happened to fall behind with Mr. Ottermole, talking on the subject of books and history, two interests we held in common. It was then that I seized the opportunity to make of him a request that I wished no other person to overhear.

"Mr. Ottermole, do you perchance still retain in your library a copy of that book of which you made mention earlier over dinner? *The Memoirs of the Duchesse de la Cressonière*, I believe?"

"I most certainly do, Madame Ambrose. I think that I must still have a copy of every book I have ever laid hands upon. Being a widower and of a naturally solitary disposition as well, reading has been for many years a consolation to my lonely hours," the little man answered quite kindly and with an openness of character that I found pleasant and refreshing.

"A consolation perhaps, sir, but a sauce to your wit and conversation as well, for I do not mind telling you that I find you a most pleasant dinner partner," I said smoothly, but meaning every word most sincerely. He was, in truth, as ugly in his person as a man might be, but what little of his company that I had had to myself had been decidedly enjoyable. "I am almost loath to ask, Mr. Ottermole, for at such short acquaintance, it is indeed a presumption on my part to . . ." I trailed off tentatively.

"Pray ask, young Madame De'Ath, whatever it is that you will of me. I am yours to command," he murmured with a gallant little bow.

"If I chanced to be in Wadebridge on the morrow, might I impose upon you by stopping by to borrow—"

"Say no more, my dear young lady." He smiled with a wave of his fat little hand, lowering his tone as if he, too, wished our converse to be private. "You shall come at four for tea and I shall show you over my library if you like. *The Memoirs of the Duchesse de la Cressonière* shall be at your disposal as well as any other books that you may wish to borrow."

"You are most kind," I said with sparkling eyes, as much because of his friendly affability and the prospect of an acquaintance to visit as because I had achieved my ends and had a promise of this particular book which I so much desired to read—and to read both quickly and secretly as well. With a sudden twinge I realized that I had not been out of the abbey once since my arrival over a month and a half earlier. "I shall do some shopping in the town and come to you for tea," I agreed in all eagerness.

Like two conspirators we made our pact, and lest we be noticed by the others, we hurried on down the corridor to rejoin Ambrose and the Ponds for their effusive and prolonged farewells on the front steps. It never occurred to me at the time to wonder why Osric Ottermole felt constrained to act the conspirator as I did. What, after all, did he have to hide? I was the plotter, not he.

At last the great abbey doors closed on one and all. Ambrose breathed a sigh and said with obvious relief, "Well, my dear, it all went off rather well, don't you think?"

"Indeed it did, Ambrose. A most interesting evening and really rather enjoyable, too!" We walked back through the hall together and along the left-hand corridor, which led to our respective bedroom suites. There were so many questions that I had in my mind to ask, and yet I lacked the courage to ask a single one. Never guessing the devious nature of my thoughts, Ambrose must have misinterpreted my silence and thought that I dwelt upon our own unhappy marital relationship, for he seemed embarrassed and abstracted, as if he was wondering how to say a discreet good night. As luck would have it, he was saved any discomfiture on that account by the sudden emergence of my aunt from the door to her own rooms, which were on the same passage as ours.

A sudden unaccountable chill, not the first such to do so, ran through my person as I saw her standing there with the door to my rooms beyond her on the left-hand side and Ambrose's door farther down on the right, lost in the looming darkness of the hall. Someone walking across my grave, the old Cornish country folk would say!

"Good night to you once more, Ambrose," she said abruptly with an unmistakable air of dismissal, and then, eyeing me harshly, "Enid, a word with you."

"Of course, Aunt," I answered with alacrity, seizing this opportunity to make the first night's parting after our agreement to live apart less awkward for us both. "Excuse me, Ambrose." He nodded with obvious relief and went on past us down that dark hall.

I followed my aunt into her set of grim little cells, eerie and medieval in the light of two single candles in small brass candlesticks. Somber reminders of death and the hereafter lurked in every corner and cupboard, leered from every grim painting and mezzotint on the black oak walls. I smiled serenely at the effect and turned my attention to the withered and hateful crone before me.

"Whatever do you make of those ghastly people, Enid?"

"Why, that they are indeed ghastly, Aunt, but then I hear that most Americans are. A crude race, but quite driving, ambitious, and clever in their own naive way. I have the feeling, somehow, that I have heard of—"

She cut me off. "It seems strange that a fine gentleman such as Ambrose is, a lady such as Madame De'Ath, should consort with such common—"

"Thanatology, spiritism, or whatever it is, Aunt Augusta, is a bizarre subject, I should think, and one that admits of an odd assortment of adherents. Mr. Ottermole, however, seems, despite his unfortunate bad looks, an intelligent and decent, gentlemanly sort." I added this last in an effort to see if she had noticed my liking for the little man. That, and any kindness she might have sensed in him that was directed toward me, would have made him virtually an enemy to her.

"Yes, yes," she said, dismissing him with a wave of her hand that indicated she had not noted our rapport. "I spoke to him but little. He seemed acceptable. The boy, of course, is a blockhead. I wonder, Enid, you could find a subject for converse with him." Aha, I thought, she saw me speak with Lucas and is curious.

"A few banalities merely to be polite," I said, waving my hand lightly in a gesture of dismissal similar to her own. "What do you make of my mother-in-law?" I countered.

"She is an eccentric. The way she dresses and the vulgar ostentation of her toilet and suite are scandalous, of course, but what can one expect? She is French after all, and you know what they are!" Did I? "She is a relic, as one can readily see, of that old France, which, happily, has had its day. She is probably senile and half mad into the bargain," Aunt Augusta snapped with finality, thus dismissing the grandeur, wisdom, and mystery of old Madame De'Ath as one dismisses a crazy cousin kept in the attic during her mad spells. Master Lucas, for all his seeming a "blockhead," had a far better idea of my mother-in-law than did Augusta Tregaron.

It was best not to take exception to her opinion, so I changed the subject, to my nearly instant regret: "How do you like your rooms, Aunt?"

"They are dreadful, Enid, as well you know. This whole wretched place is as grim as . . . as . . ."

"Death?"

"As death," she acknowledged, saying the word firmly. "I know, dear niece, that you did not want me here at first, and I can guess, as well, why you changed your mind so suddenly upon your arrival at the abbey. I know what you have had in mind, welcoming me to your 'home,' as you have called it." She stared long and hard at me. "I am no fool, young woman. No fool at all."

"I never thought you were, Aunt."

"You know me well enough to know my fear—my one fear—and you thought that this place would be a torment to me, didn't you? Do not dare to deny it, girl. I saw it in your face the very moment you greeted me. I felt the chill of this place the instant I laid eyes on it, as you knew I would. Yes, I will even admit that to you. This death-shrouded atmosphere in which Ambrose De'Ath wallows like a dissolute in an opium dream is as repellent to me as it is sacred to him. But he and I have, it seems, been drawn together for a purpose beyond our own petty desires and fears and discomforts. We are meant to be of some use to each other for a larger purpose, for God's will perhaps, as Reverend Pond has intimated. Therefore, Enid, I can endure this atmosphere for a time. I *can* and I *will*, do you hear me?" she insisted, staring with blazing eyes into my own, her whole body atremble with some passion—contained fury, perhaps.

"I hear, and I have no doubt, Aunt, of what you say. You have an iron will. *All* the Tregarons have a will of iron." I kept my gaze locked on hers, unblinking, my mouth an expressionless line.

"Do they?" she muttered with a curl of her lip.

"Now"—she smiled coldly—"as to your own doubts."

"My doubts?"

"Or fears, perhaps," she amended slyly.

"Fears?"

"Yes, Enid, your fears. Why do you insist so fervently that there is nothing beyond the grave?"

"It is my conviction, Aunt. I do not believe the fairy tale of resurrection and life after death. I am sure that this comes as no surprise to you. I have stated my beliefs—"

"Or lack thereof," she broke in dryly.

"Or lack thereof," I conceded seriously, "without shyness or modesty from my earliest childhood, as I was encouraged to do." I spoke matter-of-factly, but was indeed puzzled and unsettled by the strange turn of her questions. I could not catch her "drift," as it were.

"Why does the idea that my brother Llewellyn might truly be out there—'out beyond the veil,' as Reverend Pond has rather aptly put it—trying to reach me, bother you so, Enid?" She was cool and sharp now. I felt that I must be on my guard, but against what? What new hurt could she give me? What new trick had she yet up her black sleeve that I did not know and that I could not answer?

"The idea does not *bother* me, Aunt. It merely seems ridiculous."

"But suppose it *were* possible? What then, Enid?"

"It is *not* possible, Aunt," I said peevishly. Her game, whatever it was, was tedious and boring now.

"Allow for an instant that it might be. Say that one night this 'spirit band' of Ambrose's works and that we reach beyond the veil—*really* beyond it, to make true and actual contact with my brother. What then?" she pursued, her old voice cracking with the force of her insistence on her point.

"Why, we would contact him and he would indeed be speaking to us from beyond the grave, for as God is my witness, Llewellyn Tregaron is dead and I myself have seen him in his coffin." I stopped short for a moment as I fought off the vision of his embalmed body, blue with death. "And, of course," I went on, recovering my composure—such composure as I had under her questions, the import of which I had not yet come to understand—"you, Aunt, would be reassured, as you so desperately need to be reassured, and would, I suppose, stop fearing death."

"Never mind me, Enid," she urged like a lawyer before the bar. "Would you not then be *afraid*, learning—or rather, having it proved to you—that there is more than mere nothingness after death?"

"Be afraid? Why, no! Of what then should I be afraid? If I am not afraid of *nothingness*, why should I be afraid of a . . . a *somethingness*?" I stammered, struggling not only to express myself but also to understand the direction of her questions and guard myself accordingly. Somehow, I knew even as I spoke that I had failed and fallen into some trap she had laid.

"Because, my dear, if out of that 'somethingness,' as you so inarticulately put it, Llewellyn Tregaron can reach us and speak, would you not then be afraid that *others* too might break their silence?"

"Others? What others?"

"My brother Morgan Tregaron, perhaps. My murdered brother Morgan and his butchered wife as well," she snapped sharply. "Might they too not welcome a chance to reach out; to call to us from beyond the grave and avenge their poor murdered souls on . . . whomever . . . it . . . was . . . who . . . did . . . the . . . deed?" Her last several words dropped from her mouth singly, one by one, like bodies dropping through the door, thudding to the rope's end with that sickening snap of the neck. The trap had been well set, it had sprung beneath me, and I had dropped again and again with each word she uttered.

I stood before her like a statue—unmoving; sick at my stomach; too stunned to answer; too frozen with this new and devious torment of hers to even make a pretense of fighting back. Would she always win? Always? Even under what was now my own roof?

"Do not be afraid, Enid," she said with smooth malevolence, guiding me toward the door as one guides a blind man, "you say that there is nothing beyond the grave; that Llewellyn cannot reach us. I do not agree, of course. I know that he has already tried. But if, for argument's sake, you are right, why, there is nothing to fear. Nothing to fear at all."

I was in the hall now, my feet carrying my body, my poor benumbed body, toward my own door. Her quiet, crackling old voice sounded after me down the chilly stone corridor like that of a witch in some dark, Germanic fairy tale.

"If, on the other hand, Ambrose is right and Reverend Pond is right and *I* am right, why, then, Llewellyn Tregaron, Morgan Tregaron, Caroline Tre . . ." Her voice trailed off softly, mesmerizingly, as finally her door closed behind her with a small metallic snap.

How long I stood in that chill corridor, my hand poised on the skull-headed doorknob of my apartments, I do not know. How I ever slept that night is an even greater mystery.

God help me, I thought. God help poor Enid Tregaron.

# 7

# FEAR AND AN
# ANSWER TO FEAR

No passion so effectually robs
the mind of all its powers of acting
and reasoning as fear.
—Edmund Burke

Infirm of purpose!
. . . The sleeping and the dead
Are but as pictures; 'tis the eye of childhood
That fears a painted devil.
—Shakespeare

Sleep was long in coming, and when at last it came, it was a
fitful slumber filled with nameless horrors; ghosts from my
dreaded past rose up to haunt me, and every doubt that I had
ever had of myself and my worth as a human being and as a
daughter stabbed through me as a knife to my very heart's
core. Accusations and fears and horrors that had assaulted
my sight to the point where once my very mind was
threatened, returned in the wake of my wicked aunt's subtle
suggestion of new terrors to come.

Oh, dear God, no! I had loved my parents, loved them
dearly, and had it been possible, no greater bliss could have
been afforded me than to once more be enfolded in their loving and secure embrace as I had been so often in that wonderful time before the night of terrors had come upon us. But
not now, not some shrinking gray ghosts, pale and ludicrous
shades of what they had been in life, come from out of their
graves, from "beyond that veil" of which Reverend Pond
talked so surely, to accuse or chide or reveal truths that my

mind would not bear. No, it could not be. I would not allow it!

But how to stop it?

I slept at last, the kind of restorative sleep that comes when the mind and body have borne all that they can with justice bear. Then, from somewhere beyond us, mercy and pity send that kind of deathlike sleep that makes me, when I contemplate the actuality of my own eventual demise, realize that when it comes I shall probably welcome it as I welcome my deep slumber after the unendurable day that has passed.

From that deep sleep of escape and nervous exhaustion I awoke in the wee hours of the morning somehow surprisingly alert and more clearheaded than I could have wished, given the utter turmoil of my poor brain but a few hours earlier. I lay long in my bed, reflecting with something akin to equanimity on the events of the previous evening. As I did, I watched the cold early-spring sun rise and fill my small bedroom with its wan light.

There was really nothing to what she had said; nothing to those ridiculous hypotheses of hers that Uncle Llewellyn was "beyond the veil," as she put it, awaiting a chance to reach her and prove that life (or consciousness, at least) exists on the other side of the grave. And what was this "proof" that she had? Why, nothing more than some scraps of automatic writing done, or so it claimed, by old Madame De'Ath, and which I could dismiss as a hoax without the least qualm—especially now, having seen the old lady and realizing that in her mad moments she could probably be duped by Ambrose and Jemmy as well as anyone. Without knowing the details and having no real idea of the motive as yet, still I felt sure that Augusta Tregaron was the victim and butt of this game that I sensed was being played so slowly and carefully. That it was a game was a great comfort to me.

I turned my thoughts back to Aunt Augusta's belief in her brother's spirit reaching out. *If* such things could happen! *If!* What nonsense! Didn't she use her common sense and logic?

Why, if such things *could* happen, then the spirits of men far smarter and stronger of mind than my poor good uncle and far more needing of vengeance and justice than my dear murdered parents would long ago have recrossed that invisible barrier that divides us inexorably from the "undiscovered country from whose bourn/ No traveler returns"! How many proofs we would have had by now, of life after death, had the great and willful men of history, the pitiful, tortured victims of our hideous wars and shameful inquisitions had it within their power to cross over that barrier and exact their vengeances on us or even simply to reassure us of the life to come! But none ever have—and none ever will—especially not if they are asked to perform parlor tricks for addled, fearful old ladies. Would not that be too far beneath the dignity of one who had endured the agony of death itself and learned the answer to life's greatest mystery—the mystery of the grave?

*But if they could?*

That is what my aunt had thrown up to me! *If* they could, would I fear? Would I be afraid? The answer to that, I did not know; could not know—no matter what fearful images her tormenting question had conjured up in my poor mind and heart. Moreover, not only could I not know, I did not *want* to know.

I lay in my bed, and the sun came up; with it my strength and my spirits. No, I thought, I could not know, and since no logical possibility of Uncle Llewellyn—or anyone else, for that matter—returning from the grave existed, I would dismiss my wicked, spiteful, hated Aunt Augusta out of hand.

The real question was why Ambrose and Jemmy had brought her here; why was Ambrose trying to convince her that there was something to this thanatology business? I believed he did have a genuine interest in the subject. Everything about this house of his and the contents of his library as well as his own demeanor and mode of dress indicated as much. But what was he expecting to get from her? She was an old, old lady, strong-willed and selfish; afraid of only one thing, as she herself had had the strength and self-knowledge to admit (even to me), and that thing, death itself, of which few, if any, are truly unafraid. What could they make of this? What game play with a fearful, strong-willed old lady? And then I realized!

A fearful, strong-willed, *rich* old lady!

The light began to dawn.

When at last I left my rooms that morning, it was with a lively step and a bright-eyed glow. My blood pulsed in my veins and my quick brain throbbed with ideas. I was sure now that I knew what it was Ambrose and Jemmy Burkers were about, and I could only applaud their evil machinations deep within my bitter heart. These two rogues would exact for me that revenge that I had so long sought to wreak upon Augusta Tregaron. Well, so be it!

I swept into that small breakfast room with such alacrity that Ambrose looked up in surprise and smiled agreeably. Jemmy, who was serving my aunt sausages, grinned in undisguised pleasure and my Aunt Augusta gasped in utter dismay like the evil witch who discovers that the princess yet lives.

I knew at once that she hated my sudden and cheerful entrance; that she had expected if I made any appearance at all, I should be dull and tired and cowed by the fears she had tried to instill in me. Well, I had answered those fears and I was strong again!

"You are in health this morning, Enid," she said in a tone of near-dismay. "I should not have thought you would sleep well last night, given the troublousness of mind under which you labored when last we spoke." Her remark was pointedly aimed at reviving those fears she had sought to conjure. It would not work. Her dry, cracked old voice, sounding brittle as the rashers of bacon that Ambrose broke under his fork, would work no spell on me in the cold light of a sunny March day.

"You do look splendid, my dear. But pray, what troubles had you to wrestle with?" Ambrose asked with as much curiosity as concern. "You were fine when I bade you good night."

"Why, none at all, Ambrose." I smiled, ignoring my aunt entirely. "I cannot think what Aunt Augusta means. I slept that very 'azure-lidded sleep' of which Keats writes so eloquently," I went on animatedly as Jemmy poured my tea.

" 'In blanched linen, smooth and lavender'd,' ma'am?" Jemmy asked softly over my shoulder.

"Why, Jemmy Burkers, however do you know to quote *The Eve of St. Agnes*?" I looked up at him in surprise.

"Even servants may read, ma'am," he said with dignity, his dark face darkening the more, whether with anger or embarrassment I could not say.

"Why, yes, of course. Forgive me, Jemmy," I answered, feeling suddenly contrite as I remembered our many quiet evenings with old Madame De'Ath, she with her strange figured cards and he with his books.

"That will be all, Jemmy," Ambrose interrupted abruptly and with all the imperiousness of a master in his voice. "If we require anything else, I shall ring."

"Very good, sir," Jemmy muttered with seeming obsequiousness, and left the room at once. I did not like the hard look that had come into his eyes just then, but the sulky look on Ambrose's face aroused my curiosity even more. Had I not known better, I should have thought that he reacted with some jealousy to my little exchange with his "servant."

"Enid, in this house one does not engage in colloquies with the servants, however well informed they may appear to be, and one *never* apologizes to one of them, for *any* reason whatsoever. Do you hear?" Ambrose spoke in the tones of a parent to a child. I did not answer.

"It seems to me," Aunt Augusta remarked dryly and with evident satisfaction at Ambrose's attempt to humiliate me, "that that man does not know his place. He is altogether too obtrusive for a servant and seems to have an uncommon lot of knowledge for a person of his class."

"It is my mother's fault, Miss Tregaron. She has spoiled the creature with her unnecessary indulgences. It causes him upon occasion to overstep himself. I shall speak to him about it shortly."

"Pray do so, Ambrose. Servants, like children, should be kept well in line." This last was meant for me.

"And so he shall," Ambrose remarked darkly.

These two, I thought to myself as I observed them together, are far better matched to each other than either of them is matched to me. How sad that Ambrose could not have married the elder Miss Tregaron instead of having to settle for the younger one. And for more reasons than one.

Soon after noon, the carriage that I had ordered rolled around to the front entrance of the abbey and I was off to Wadebridge with all the enthusiasm of a prisoner let loose from his dungeon.

I had passed through the town but once, and that on my way to Thanatos Abbey, at which time I had scarce taken time to make any notice of it save that it appeared to be both small and unremarkable. Now, upon entering it once more and being handed from the carriage by a footman, I found that my closer inspection only confirmed that first impression.

Wadebridge consisted of an inevitable High Street along which ranged the usual establishments: local inn, greengrocer's, dry-goods merchant, bookseller's, and a variety of small half-timbered houses and bow-windowed shops. Finally, at the end of the street, a small, medieval-looking church and rectory stood in isolated dignity adjacent to the graveyard.

Beyond that, on a pleasant rise above the town, surrounded by a pleasingly old-fashioned garden which was just coming into its spring greenery, and backed by a copse of gnarled, wind-lashed ancient trees, was a Jacobean manse, the largest home in the area and that which my driver had pointed out as belonging to Mr. Osric Ottermole himself. He had said his ancestors were the local squires, and everything about the old house, the surrounding gardens and park and the extensive farm and grazing lands beyond, verified as much. This park, however, and much of the land behind, had been converted to other uses now—the uses of Mr. Ottermole's present occupation in life.

His trade establishment lay discreetly on the nearest end of the park to the graveyard, church, and town, and therefore as far away from the site of his ancestral manse as the acreage would allow. With equal discretion, his business, lodged in an old and well kept Georgian house, was whispered rather than proclaimed on a small polished bronze plaque beside the door, which read modestly:

OTTERMOLE AND SON
UNDERTAKERS & COMPLETE
FUNERAL FURNISHERS
ESTABLISHED 1815

The Georgian bow windows were draped in black crepe and displayed a tasteful line of mourning garb—hats, gloves, ribands, and armbands—as well as several exquisitely rendered miniature models of hearses, funeral carriages, and coffins, perfect in every detail right down to the little feather plumes on the carved and hide-covered wooden hearse horses. Here, in this funeral-furnishing shop, Ambrose must obtain his mourning habit, ordering from Ottermole and Son the way others order from a haberdasher and a tailor, a glovemaker and a bootmaker. His carriages and livery, too, must come from this place; even the very harness for his horses. How odd and how damnably sad and how funny, if one had a penchant, as I occasionally did, for macabre humor.

To the left, beyond the furnishings shop, was a drive leading back to a large group of work buildings—mortuary, stables, carriage houses, and the like, which stretched out into what had once been farmed land and where, in fact, several jet-black hearse horses grazed idly in spacious rock-bound paddocks. The whole arrangement bespoke the wisdom, discretion, taste, and canny pragmatism of both Mr. Ottermole and his immediate forebear.

By the time I arrived at the manse for tea, I had amassed a small but satisfying array of parcels on the seat of the carriage beside me. It gave me such pleasure to have got out of the abbey and away from its oppressive atmosphere. The irony of having left that dark place in order to take tea with a mortician did not then strike me, for despite his melancholy profession and truly unfortunate looks, the little man whose guest I was to be seemed a wholly engaging and pleasant person. To my eventual delight, nothing that was to occur would serve to change that assessment.

A maid, quiet and neat and well starched, opened the door to me and bade me enter. From out of the shadows of the central hall came just then a small, squat little soul of the female sex but of uncertain years, shy and diffident, looking up at me with huge wet brown eyes that I instantly recognized as a family characteristic of the Ottermoles.

"Madame Ambrose De'Ath? Pray, do forgive Mr. Ottermole," she said in a small sweet voice. "He shall be detained yet awhile and has asked me to beg his forgiveness and keep you company until his arrival." The voice was countryish in accent, but the words and manner were that of an educated young lady. She had an odd mixture of shyness and confidence, polish and gaucheness which, I suspected, resulted from the conflict of unfortunate looks and fortunate education.

"Miss Ottermole?" I ventured tentatively.

"But yes. Do forgive my manners, madame. I am so unused to visitors that I have quite forgot myself. I am Arabella Ottermole." She smiled demurely, showing a set of pretty, pearly little teeth rather like those of a doll.

And very much your father's daughter, I could not help but think as I surveyed the plump little girl—she was surely not much above eighteen, I judged—with her sallow, round face, pale straw-colored hair drawn back so severely as to render her, at first sight, almost as hairless as her sire, and of course those huge, liquid brown eyes. She was very young, as I have said, plain as a pikestaff, and while as well spoken as her father, unlike him, she seemed to be painfully shy, self-conscious, and uncertain of herself. These latter attributes, I felt sure, were due to her own realistic knowledge of her physical shortcomings and plainness. I felt a common sympathy with her, for while I had not the plainness of this girl, I certainly, thanks to Aunt Augusta, had had for many years the shyness, self-consciousness, and retiring qualities which she had. Sweetness, however, saved her nature, just as bitterness had all but destroyed my own.

She escorted me into a sunny parlor, made all the more cheerful with bright chintzes, large cages of twittering songbirds, potted indoor plants, and a rather informal, lived-in air more to be expected in a cottage than a manse.

"Do forgive the mess, madame, but I am always leaving things about," she fretted as she bumped a kitten off the settee and gathered up the scattered contents of a sewing basket, "and I fear Father is no better," she went on, picking books and papers off the good solid, comfortable old furniture and setting them in neat piles in a corner.

I could not help but laugh in delight at the cluttered and bustling scene before me. What a vast difference between it and the cold formality of Thanatos Abbey, where nothing was alive and singing, where no kitten tumbled, and no clutter existed except the jumble of skulls that peered in mockery of life from every gaping shelf and chest. Miss Ottermole, hearing my laughter, looked up in surprise, and I could tell that she thought me rude.

"Pray, do forgive my laughter and kindly do not be disturbed by my presence, Miss Ottermole. You cannot imagine how completely delightful and pleasant I find this sunny room with all its clutter and the menagerie scattering amongst the table legs." I smiled and pointed to a trio of kittens that played hide-and-seek with each other in the general confusion that reigned across the Turkey carpet, where balls of cotton had rolled and become tangled about the furniture and the tiny, furry bodies of the kittens themselves.

Her face relaxed just then, and she laughed easily herself, displaying those good, even little teeth, and suddenly I saw that when she reacted unselfconsciously there was almost a prettiness about her. "There is nothing like a litter of kittens to liven things up, is there?" she asked agreeably.

"Indeed not," I concurred, remembering that in my own early years kittens and puppies had played a happy part. In my uncle's house I had been allowed no pets, and those that I had had were sold off or put to sleep by Aunt Augusta. I scowled at the memory and put it from my mind. Brightening, I urged my companion to stop her fussing. "Now, do please stop this bustling about and invite me to sit down. I think that we shall be great friends, but only if you leave the room as it is," I chided earnestly, feeling quite comfortably at home with this girl and her happy, unpretentious parlor. "Please do obey me in this," I urged in almost elder-sister tone as she hesitated, looking about her at the room. At last she smiled again and nodded happily.

"Pray be seated, Madame De'Ath." She bowed in mock

formality. Once seated and with tea ordered, I asked my hostess whether she had ever been to Thanatos Abbey.

"Indeed I have," she said emphatically, "and so I think that I can guess why you like this room so very much." She smiled with the easy humor of a mischievous child and I realized to my own delight that once I had put her at her ease with me by my unexpected informality—who, after all, expects informality from someone called Madame De'Ath? —her initial shyness vanished completely. She gave promise of being as pleasant company as was her father, who just then popped his bald, yellow little head in at the parlor door.

"Getting acquainted, you two? Good! Shan't be a moment," and with that he disappeared. Turning toward Miss Ottermole, I saw that she followed his retreating figure with much warmth of expression.

"I think that you love your father very much, Miss Ottermole," I ventured.

"He is a very good, dear man, madame, and we have great fun together. I should not like ever to leave him," she added pensively.

"Really? Most young ladies look forward to leaving their parents, to find a husband of their own, to raise a family," I remarked by way of sounding her out.

"Not I, madame. My little world is here," she said quite definitely, "here with Father."

"You are a child yet, I think. There is a lifetime ahead of you," I suggested softly.

"I am eighteen," she answered proudly, "and have run my father's house for him since I was ten—when my mother died." She hesitated, looking up at a painting over the mantelpiece, a rather crude effort at portraiture by some country artist. Yet even the painter's obvious lack of talent could not hide the beauty of the subject, a small, pert young woman with a long, slender, graceful neck, wide gray eyes, curly blond hair, and an enchanting smile.

"You have your mother's smile, Miss Ottermole," I said, "and a very pretty one it is."

"Have I? Do you think so? Father says so, but then he is rather prejudiced, I fear. He thinks that I am very like her in my manner as well, but of course, I am most like him in looks, I think," she murmured.

"Is your hair curly by nature, Miss Ottermole?" I asked casually.

"Rather. I keep it back with oil and pins."

"Do you? My hair is straight as a die. If I were lucky

enough to have hair that curled, I think I should dress it to enhance the curls as your mother did, and not to hide them."

"You would?"

"Oh, yes. I think it would be most becoming."

She did not say more, but I hoped in my heart that I had given this dear, plain girl some food for thought. Properly coiffed and dressed, this child might have some of the prettiness of the young woman in the portrait. She was too dissatisfied and conscious of her looks to have made the attempt as yet. I found myself longing to give her a guiding hand, such a hand as none had given to me.

Mr. Ottermole returned just then, well scrubbed, neat, and robust. "Well, well, have you two young ladies got on well together? Good! I rather thought that you would. Didn't know, did you, Madame De'Ath, that I had a treasure here?" he asked, giving his daughter a little hug of pride and affection which seemed to both please and embarrass her.

"Indeed, I did not, Mr. Ottermole, but I am delighted to have made her cheery acquaintance." I smiled.

Over tea the three of us chatted of books and the latest news from London, speculated on the activities of the Royal Commission and its plans for the coming Great Exhibition of 1851, laughed at the antics of Miss Ottermole's kittens as they bedeviled some of the caged birds in the window, and generally had together a most agreeable afternoon.

As it drew to its close, my host sent his daughter out of the room and up to his study in order to fetch the book he had promised to lend me and which had, or so I thought, precipitated this visit in the first place. When she had gone, he looked at me urgently and with a father's concern. "What do you make of my daughter, Madame De'Ath?"

"She is charming, Mr. Ottermole," I said wholeheartedly and with the utmost sincerity.

"Honestly, madame, and without regard to my feelings," he urged.

"Mr. Ottermole, she truly is charming, well educated—"

"She went to Miss Mitchell's Academy in Portsmouth—one of the best," he broke in proudly.

"And it shows, sir. She is excellent company, as you yourself must know, since it is you who are the chief beneficiary of that company. Moreover, she comes by her social graces quite naturally, too. I think it is a family trait," I complimented him.

"I shall be honest, madame," he countered. "Her looks, as well, are a family trait."

"She has her mother's lovely smile and excellent teeth," I returned, refusing to take his meaning.

"And her mother's good nature, as well, but she has my stature and features, poor child. She is plain and lonely and clings to me like a limpet."

"She loves you, sir."

"Yes, and I am fortunate in that, but she is young and should have a suitor. She is shy and plain and won't venture to a dance or a supper or any party. I know she thinks she's too ugly for a fellow to look at her, or thinks that if one does, it's for my money and not her heart."

"Oh, surely you exaggerate, Mr. Ottermole. And she is not ugly at all," I insisted. "If she thinks that *you* believe that she is ugly, then you have done her a great deal of harm. It is what *you* think of her that shall determine what she thinks of herself." I was almost angry with the poor, well-meaning man by now. If one is thought to be ugly, then one will be ugly. If one is thought to be guilty, then . . .

"Well, *I* am, no question about it, and look at the beauty I had, madame. Adeline loved me, you know," he said, looking up at his wife's portrait with pride and an aching heart. "She had the pick of the county, but she chose me. And I was still poorish then, as well. She just loved me," he reiterated simply.

"I have not a doubt in the world that she did. And with her sweet nature, your daughter, too, will be loved," I reassured him, terribly embarrassed by his openness with me, and yet pleased by it as well. He was confiding in me with trust and as a friend and as a lady, whereas for most of my life I had been treated either as a child or as a guilty, criminous girl. It seemed that Mr. Ottermole saw better things in me, and what he then said only confirmed that thought.

"You are a lady, madame, young and smartly turned-out, if you don't mind my saying it. I . . . I don't know quite how to ask this, but I must for Arabella's sake. Can you do something with her? Help her looks, her style of dress? I know nothing of such matters. Money for stylish clothes, jewels, is no object. I . . . I . . ." He trailed off inarticulately with a wave of his hands in what might almost have been defeat. My heart went out to him, a worried father with a homely daughter and no woman about to guide him. He might well have been reading my mind by his next remark.

"If her mother had lived, she'd have known what to do. Things should never have come to this pass, if Arabella had a mother. It is hard for a man alone."

"Say no more lest she overhear us, sir. Be assured that I shall delight to make Arabella my friend and see if I cannot ... cannot bring her out a bit."

"Will you?" he asked with a grateful sigh of relief.

"Calm yourself, Mr. Ottermole." I laughed. "It is not so difficult a task as you may think. There is a great deal of excellent material in her with which to work."

We raised our teacups and toasted our conspiracy with a twinkle in our eyes. Arabella Ottermole, upon her return to the parlor with the books, found us deep in a discussion of the merits of medieval church architecture.

My nose was buried in the first few pages of Volume I of the three-volume *Memoirs of the Duchesse de la Cressonière* as my carriage rolled back through Wadebridge on its return to Thanatos Abbey, and so it was that I was unaware of the approach of Reverend Enoch Pond and his son Lucas as they crossed from the general direction of the inn and hailed my driver to a halt. Most unmannerly, I remember thinking, but then what can one expect from foreigners.

"Good evening, Madame De'Ath," Enoch Pond called out in his boisterous American drawl. Lucas muttered a more somber "Evenin', ma'am," and stood just behind his father, who had leaned his arms against the edge of the carriage with one foot braced against a spoke of the back wheel. Did he think he was in California or Kentucky or some such godforsaken region as red Indians and cowboys range about in?

"One of them as has always got eye ta book, I see," he remarked, nodding at the books in my hand and upon my lap. I smiled and hastily slipped them out of sight in the folds of my voluminous skirt. "Well," he continued, ignoring my sudden movement, "idle hands be the devil's workshop, as they say, an' books of virtuous subject matter lift the spirits," he harangued, angling his head in order to try to make out the titles of the books.

"How nice to see you, Mr. Pond, Lucas. Pray, how is Mrs. Pond?" I smiled, recovering my composure and ignoring his obvious attempt to learn what I was reading.

"Fine thanks, madame, and she will be the better for your askin'. We'll be seein' ya up ta the abbey Friday, won't we?"

"At the abbey?" I echoed dumbly. "Another dinner?" I wondered aloud.

"Naw, ma'am. No such honor as that," he scoffed with some genuine regret. Our reg'lar Friday-night circle. The first one in months. We come special from Manchester for this series of settin's. I suppose you'll be joinin' the band?"

"I have no idea, Mr. Pond . . ."

"Reverend Pond, ma'am," he emended patiently. A look of sulky annoyance crossed the boy Lucas' face.

"Yes, of course, Reverend Pond. As I was saying, I have no idea as yet whether my husband wishes me to join your circle, but I am sure that I shall see you on Friday, nonetheless. And now, do forgive me, gentlemen, but I must return to the abbey. My greetings to your lady-wife." And with that I indicated to the driver that he should be off.

The carriage lurched and we sped away, leaving the florid and puffing Reverend Enoch Pond and his enigmatic son Lucas in the middle of the High Street, the former waving self-importantly for all to see and the latter stolid as a milk stool beside him.

"Reg'lar Friday-night circle," he had said, and then I remembered! I remembered the packet of papers that Ambrose had given to Aunt Augusta at the house in London and which I had tried to burn up to spite her. The witnesses to that "automatic writing" of Madame De'Ath's had included Enoch and Peggy Pond, which was why their names had sounded so familiar to me and why I had had such a nagging feeling about them all during the previous evening. They, together with Jemmy, Ambrose, and Madame De'Ath herself, had formed a group of what Reverend Pond called "spiritualists" and what I chose to call "fakers" instead. The question that remained was whether the Ponds were innocent and sincere dupes or partakers in the plotting.

Well, that conversation had resolved me! I must talk to Ambrose—and soon. With that I turned once more to *The Memoirs of the Duchesse de la Cressonière*, perhaps not exactly the "virtuous subject matter" suggested by the Reverend Pond, but sure to be a damned fine read for a chilly spring evening. Perhaps even an enlightening one as well, I thought, remembering the look of annoyance and even of anger that had crossed my mother-in-law's expressive old countenance at the mere mention of this book.

I would take supper in my rooms this evening and keep my nose where it was—in the memoirs of Madame la Duchesse!

Upon my arrival back at the abbey, I bustled up the corridor with a footman at my heels, carrying the books and parcels from my afternoon shopping expedition. The hall was completely dark now save for two or three candles in sconces along the walls. The yellow light flickered eerily, and as I reached out to open my door, the gaping skull face of the knob seemed to shift and grin at me most menacingly. I recoiled with a small scream as if I had been bitten.

"Are you well, madame?" the footman asked.

"Quite well, thank you," I replied with a nervous laugh. It was, after all, just an optical effect of the flickering light on that grotesque doorknob, and I should have known better.

The manservant deposited my bundles in the sitting room and departed, yet I, all oblivious, still stood in that narrow corridor lost in thought. What was it about this hallway? Had I been of a foolish and gullible temperament, I might almost have believed in hauntings. Hardly a day had gone by since my Aunt Augusta's arrival when passing her door, going to or from my own rooms, had not given me a chill of trepidation. Something in that long dark corridor with my rooms to the left, hers on the right across the hall, and Ambrose' doors farther up the passage, lost in darkness and shadow, filled me with a sick and fearful feeling in the pit of my stomach; a chill that went to my very bones; that eerie and terrible sensation of something crawling over one's body in the dead of night or of a footfall on one's own grave.

Enough! I was letting Aunt Augusta's attempts to frighten me get the better of my stalwart spirit. I was too strong to be afraid of ghosts and childish things. I must not, like Richard at Bosworth Field, be afraid of shadows when there was battling yet to do. I stared hard at the several doors along the corridor, at the flickering candles in their sconces, at the grim, depressing old paintings in their wide gilded frames, and lastly, I stared at the skull-headed knob of my door. It winked again in the flickering light.

This time, dammit, I winked back!

# 8

# THE SPIRIT BAND

Yet meet we shall, and part, and meet again,
Where dead men meet in lips of living men.
—*Samuel Butler*

And whether we shall meet again, I know not.
Therefore our everlasting farewell take.
—*Shakespeare*

Once again that inevitable question: who was Madame Henriette De'Ath? So often since my first meeting with her, I had marveled at her and pondered the mystery (or so I sensed it to be) of her real identity, for whoever she was now, I was sure that she had not started out her life as a modest French commoner of merely aristocratic origins.

Plain Madame De'Ath, wife and eventual widow of an elderly Englishman of French Huguenot extraction, she might have been, mother to Ambrose De'Ath she was, but her maiden name and identity were still a puzzle and destined to remain so, it seemed, for I had been forward enough on several occasions to question her as to her own antecedents, only to be put off with evasive answers or, more frequently, no answers at all. When taxed persistently, she lapsed into that well-timed, convenient deafness and near-senility which her great age permitted her to affect and which her subtle talents as an actress enabled her to play at so convincingly.

And speaking of her age, I was able to put it, although she never admitted to a specific number of years, at somewhere in the early eighties. Eighty-three is what I judged her to be, which would have put her birth in the year 1767 or thereabouts. Ambrose was forty, having been born in June of the year 1810, and so he was the product of his mother's later years. I did know that she had been a wife but a year or two when Ambrose was born, so again, she had had time to have lived a rather full life prior to meeting and marrying the late Mr. Hugo De'Ath and bearing to him her only child while already in her early forties.

And so it came down to this: I wanted to know who Madame Henriette De'Ath might have been in France before the Terror; before the old order was brought to its knees before the reeking and vengeful rabble of Paris, murdered or scattered across the face of Europe as the wind scatters chaff. I wanted to know what she had done between her birth in about 1767 and her marriage in about 1808. She had been a young woman in her twenties when the French Louis XVI and his Austrian queen, Marie Antoinette, went to the guillotine. What had been her life then? Who had she been? Who had been her friends, her family? How had she, who was obviously, from everything she did admit or hint at, close enough to that doomed court to know it intimately, ever managed to escape the fate of so many French nobles and courtiers?

I looked at those little leather-bound volumes of the Duchesse de la Cressonière's memoirs and wondered. Picking them up one by one, I skimmed the pages, trying to let my eyes range over the names that were mentioned. Perhaps the name Henriette would leap out at me, coupled with a family name and description that would strike a chord of familiarity. If not, I would have to begin at the beginning and read the three volumes in order, which would be interesting, no doubt, but time-consuming as well. I doubted I had the patience for such a task.

And names there were aplenty: De Polignac, Princesse de Guéménée, the governess of the children of France, who communicated with her many dogs through the intercession of "mediating spirits," Mme de Lamballe, the Comte d'Artois, Axel Fersen, the child bride "Guichette," the notorious Comte Alessandro di Cagliostro and his wife, Lorenza, who ruled all Paris with their fantastic rituals and mysteries, the evil and predatory Jeanne de la Motte, whose treachery in the scandalous "affair of the necklace" brought down the Cagliostros and ultimately the queen of France herself. Mesmer, out of favor at court, but practicing his "animal magnetism" for the nobles of France, the young and infamous Mme Clothilde du Roc, the foolish Cardinal de Rohan, all were mentioned time and again in the pages of the duchesse's memoirs, but no name rang a bell; not one "Henriette" was mentioned.

Perhaps I was wasting my time—yet I could not but think otherwise when I remembered how the mere passing mention of this book and the name of de la Cressonière had made Madame De'Ath react so strongly. Why? Had she herself read them and found them irritating in some way? Inaccurate? Was she mentioned in them (as I rather guessed)—and to her detriment perhaps—or had she actually . . . ? But enough of speculation! I must read if I was to know.

Idly turning to the last pages of the last volume, I saw that they ended on a tragic note, with the young duchesse-to-be of the first volume, widowed now, her husband condemned and beheaded by the tribunal, her children dead, setting down her words in lonely exile in a country house in England, whence had fled some of the pitiful handful of survivors of the Reign of Terror. The last entry was dated 1806 and read as follows:

And so, dear reader, I have put down for posterity the romantic story of the halcyon days of old France. You have learned from one who lived it the tale of tragedy and madness that swept the unseeing, unknowing foolish court of Marie Antoinette and her poor husband Louis from that golden perch at the top of the world. You have learned for yourself of the luxury and idleness and indifference to human suffering that made way for the storming of the Bastille, the Revolution, the abolition of the monarchy and the Reign of Terror, from which, of my ancient and noble house, none have escaped save my single self.

That life that I have known is gone—perhaps even justly gone—and now, rather than approaching my middle years in the love of a good husband and surrounded by my children and grandchildren, I look forward to the long stretch of years as a homeless, friendless exile in a foreign land.

Adieu! The France of my youth is dead, and with it dies Eugénie-Marie, Duchesse de la Cressonière.

Finis

An interesting conclusion, sad and touching and Gallicly dramatic. Yet I wondered! The mood of the first volume, what little I had already perused at least, smacked of high spirits and the imperiousness of true nobility. It read like a narrative which the duchesse had adapted from diaries that she must have kept, for the details were most explicit. By reading between the lines, so to speak, one was left with the impression that she must have been, in her youth, a high-strung and strong-willed girl, opinionated and very proper, for she was narrow of mind and highly disapproving of much that she saw of French court life and certainly not above making her opinions known. Many of her appraisals of the celebrated people of her day were at least critical if not downright damning. Whether those opinions had been expressed in her heyday other than to the secret pages of her diary, I had no way of knowing, but I rather thought that they must have been private opinions and confided to no one, else she would have been much disliked and eventually barred from those circles she traveled in and described so well. There was no indication of such a barring, although her contact with the court ended more or less permanently when, in her early twenties, she retired to her husband's country home to await the birth of her first child. Not long after, the events leading up to the Terror began and the duchesse never saw the court or her queen again.

From what I could gather, the sad, defeated woman of 1806 was not the true Eugénie-Marie de la Cressonière, and I could not help but wonder whether, in the years following this memoir, she did not eventually recover some, if not all, of her former spirit and begin her life anew, as so many victims of the Terror had done; as Madame De'Ath herself had evidently done.

It was an interesting speculation and one that I kept in the back of my mind as I returned to Volume I and continued reading the memoir in its proper sequence.

There was no more exciting evening to be experienced in all of Paris than to take to one's carriage in the dead of night, masked and robed as if going to a *bal masque*, and ride swiftly down the Boulevard Beaumarchais to the corner of Rue Saint-Claude, in which isolated district stood the great dark house known to all Paris as No. 1 Rue Saint-Claude.

In that house, awaiting their nightly coterie of illustrious guests, were the mystical sorcerer Comte Alessandro di Cagliostro and his notorious and utterly romantic comtesse, whose beauty had captivated every heart in Paris.

Madame my mother had returned to the country,

leaving me in the charge of my eldest sister, Camile, Comtesse de Lambeth, who, like most of the bored young nobles of Paris in that dissipated and licentious age, had become a partisan of this so-called comte and his wife, Lorenza di Cagliostro.

And so it was, to my everlasting shame, that I, with the ill-contained enthusiasm for adventure that so often characterizes our innocent and impetuous youth, accompanied my sister one midnight in the spring of 1784 to that mysterious mansion of which all Paris talked unceasingly. What romance surrounded that place! What could one not imagine occurring behind those gray stone walls?

The line of carriages in the Rue Saint-Claude was long and it seemed an age before our turn came to draw into the deep, cobbled courtyard which rang with the clatter of hooves, the rumble of carriage wheels, and the bustle of grooms, footmen, and the lackeys of virtually all the fashionable people of the city in their finest liveries. Yet another age passed before we were at last handed down from our coach by the comte's extravagantly liveried footman and conducted up the broad stone steps, across wide terraces which were flanked by great alchemical braziers filled with licking, wind-whipped flames of golden fire. We were accompanied by yet more lackeys, those bearing high over their heads heavy bronze flambeaux that danced dramatically in that windy night.

The air smelled of the rain that was soon to come. Occasionally a large single drop would splatter down upon the gray stone of the steps, the gray slate of the flagged terrace as we hastened along toward the gleaming glass-paned doors that were even then being opened to admit us by a pair of tall, slender doormen in Turkish dress. I heard the hiss of droplets strike the leaping flames of the torches, and it seemed to my agitated sensibilities that it must be all the jinns of Arabia whispering to me in their devilish tongue, which, it was rumored, only Cagliostro himself could interpret aright.

The wind blew those tall old trees that encompassed that isolated house, waving the great branches as if they were the fronds of the merest willow on a riverbank. A terrifying peal of thunder exploded over our heads and caused both Camile and me to shriek out in alarm.

Lightning flashed just then, and I saw for an instant her masked face frozen in the blinding blue-whiteness of the light. I saw that she was as afraid as I, and the knowledge somehow comforted me. Reaching for each other's hands, we two sisters entered at last the sanctum of the mysterious Comte di Cagliostro.

The air within was heavy, laden with exotic incense and the atmosphere of the coming storm; all lit with soft golden candlelight that had the awe-inspiring feeling of a cathedral chapel about it. Everywhere were mirrors and rare furniture crafted from the most unusual woods imaginable. The window draperies and *portières* that divided room from room were the most diaphanous of silk gauze. Everywhere was cloth of gold, bronze, and damascened metalwork, bejeweled daggers and strange Arabian and Oriental curiosities.

As we entered the *foyer,* the floor of which was inlaid with colored stones and metals in the form of a large round zodiac, a gust of wind swept through the doors at our backs, sending the silken gauzes of the *portières* billowing like the sails of a ship, and for the next few moments I was able to see into the room ahead of us, huge and round, with a great circular table in its center and around which were seated at their ease some of the most influential noblemen and ministers of France, including the Cardinal de Rohan himself.

Between each of these great men was set an empty chair, and at each place, whether occupied or not, was a table setting of Sevres china, gold cutlery, and a veritable forest of tall-stemmed crystal goblets. In a throne of honor at this gorgeous table, his seat set higher than any of the others, including the illustrious cardinal himself, was the man I knew at once must be the fabled and mysterious Alessandro di Cagliostro.

He was small of stature, corpulent, and gross of face and figure, his skin a sallow hue even in that flattering golden light; his manner of dress was bizarre and gaudy with cloth of gold, brilliantly colored gems set in his buttons and studs and with a diamond watch and chain hanging across his gold brocade vest. He wore upon his head a Turkish fez wound around with colored silks and bound with ropes of pearl in the manner of a sultan of the East.

Taken all in all, he seemed even to my youthful scrutiny a gross and sensual man upwards of forty years in age, fantastically but unbecomingly arrayed and distinguished mostly by the compelling fire in his large dark eyes. It was in those eyes that all the considerable passion, wisdom, and drama of the man actually resided, and in them I could begin to see the secret of this man's great success in the world and influence on the men (and women!) of his time. But what indeed was his time? Some said that Alessandro di Cagliostro was five hundred years of age. It was even rumored abroad that he had walked the Via Dolorosa at the side of the Savior himself and had knelt at the foot of the cross. That such an outrageous and monstrous blasphemy could even be considered in connection with the man was some sort of tribute to his powers of persuasion, and so it was that I could not help but be fascinated by the very sight of him.

But alas, it was not to meet the illustrious comte that Camile and I had come to No. 1 Rue Saint-Claude that night. Rather our assignation was with Lorenza, Comtesse di Cagliostro, called the most notorious and bewitching woman in all Europe.

We had not long been in the foyer when we were greeted by mute sign by a young and very beautiful girl who then signaled us to follow her in silence. This girl, surely no more than sixteen years of age (and therefore even younger than myself), was dressed in a manner completely scandalous and remarkably dramatic. As she was so close to myself in years, my fascination for her person was even deeper than that of my sister, and so I found myself studying her at every opportunity on that mysterious night, and on others that followed.

She was a tall and slender girl, dressed in one single garment, and that a long, clinging shift of palest ivory gauze, caught at the waist by a rosy mauve girdle. Through this gauze every line of her shapely body was revealed in all the utter perfection of its youthful ripeness. Her breasts were full and round, the nipples hard and as deeply pink as coral through the thin cloth of her robe. The cleft of her buttocks, the dark shadow of her *mons de Venus,* the supple grace of her long thighs as she swung easily down the candlelit corridor with us, were all accentuated shockingly with her every step. As I followed her, I wondered whether I, so attired, would look even as she, and thinking that I would not, I ached with jealous envy of her person.

Her hair was darkly golden, and although bound in the manner of ancient Greece by rosy mauve ribbons, I could tell that it curled naturally. I found her face cool and imperious, and thinking it precociously haughty for one so young as she, I envied her the more. Her profile was classically elegant and her large, lustrous eyes promised passion and fire, although those passions and fires were banked and her gaze impersonally steady whilst conducting us to the apartments of her mistress, which we reached at last after climbing the narrowest of stairs, winding between the inner walls of the very house itself, and entering through the mirrored panels of a secret antechamber.

Awaiting us, surrounded by ladies masked even as were we ourselves, was the lovely Lorenza, Comtesse . . .

It was then that the book fell from my hand and I was asleep.

The following morning during breakfast I spoke to Ambrose, wondering, once I had begun, why I had found the prospect of doing so so difficult.

"I met the Reverend Mr. Pond and Master Lucas in Wadebridge yesterday afternoon."

"Yes?"

"Ambrose, they asked if I am to be in the 'circle' on Friday next. I assumed that it was the spirit band of which they spoke. I could not make them answer, since you had not seen fit to inform me of your plans. Do you intend that I join it?" I was deliberately passive in my attitude in order that Ambrose might answer honestly and off his guard, rather than to have him say what he thought I wished to hear.

"I think not, Enid. It does not seem appropriate."

"Appropriate?" I echoed. "Who then shall be a part of it, pray?"

"Mother, of course," he answered, still not grasping my displeasure. "The Ponds, myself, Jemmy, and your Aunt Augusta."

"What of Mr. Ottermole?"

"He sits occasionally, but has had to decline this sitting. He has a funeral to see to."

"But my aunt will be in the circle!" I stated flatly.

"Of course. It is, after all, your Uncle Llewellyn whom we wish to reach."

"Oh, yes"—I smiled—"Uncle Llewellyn. Tell me, Ambrose, suppose I wished to have a chat with the dear old fellow? Mightn't I join you all just to say hello for *auld lang syne*, as the poet says?"

"For heaven's sake, Enid, enough of levity. You are entirely too flippant in your manner to suit."

I clucked my tongue in sympathy with his annoyance at me. My, how naughty I was being. Poor Ambrose! Just then Jemmy entered the room and saved my husband the hearing of another "flippant" remark.

"Is my Aunt Augusta on her way, Jemmy?"

"No, madame. She has sent for her breakfast in her room this morning," he answered deferentially.

"Splendid," I snapped with satisfaction. "Then as we three are now alone and unlikely to be disturbed by the old witch, I think that I had better make things quite clear. Ambrose has just informed me, Jemmy, that my participation in the spirit band is not appropriate. That was the word you used, my dear, was it not?"

"I fail to see, madame . . ." Jemmy interrupted, still playing at servant.

"I have every intention, in spite of your objections, Ambrose; in spite of your 'failure to see,' Jemmy, of joining your little band of spirits on Friday evening and—"

"I don't think it would be wise, Enid," Ambrose broke in.

"Don't you, Ambrose, and why not?"

"Your aunt would not like it." He glared at me pointedly. I knew what he meant but refused to respond. "You are a skeptic," he went on, "a nonbeliever."

"And is Jemmy here a believer?"

At that Jemmy smirked and bowed in mockery toward me. "There are more things in heaven and earth, Madame De'Arth, than are—"

"Than are dreamt of in your philosophy," I finished up acidly. "Yes, Jemmy, I've read *Hamlet*, too. Now, just whom do you two think you're fooling with this trumpery spirit band of yours? I am no frightened old lady with both feet in the grave up to her petticoats, that you can fool me with your ridiculous games."

"Enid, that is enough," Ambrose snapped, his voice frigid.

"No, Ambrose, let 'er talk. She's got somethin' up 'er sleeve, I think," Jemmy countered, that crafty slyness that I so detested and yet respected coming into his voice.

"Thank you, Jemmy. Yes, my dear pair of rogues, I am quite on to you, I think. You heard—read in the *Times*, no doubt—of my Uncle Llewellyn's death, and seizing the opportunity, attached yourself to my bereaved Aunt Augusta at the time of her sorrow, with the intention of preying upon her obvious fears and grief in order to detach her from her fortune, or a goodly part of it at any rate. You intend to dazzle her with false hopes of a life to come, trick her with 'messages' from her dead brother, and swindle her—bilk her of her money."

"Swindle her? Bilk?" Ambrose protested with a look of indignation that did not fool me for a second.

"Cheat, swindle, bilk, fleece! Oh, there are probably many more words for it than that, but then, I am not overly conversant with the criminal language of the gutters. Jemmy would have a more colorful vocabulary than I with which to describe your little games."

"Shhh, lower your voice, madame," Jemmy whispered with something of a twinkle in his eye, and throwing aside all pretense of being a servant, locked the breakfast-room doors and slid into a seat at the table with us.

"Ambrose spoiled things, didn't he, Jemmy, by marrying me? That hadn't been part of the plan, and it rather delayed things, didn't it? Set you all off your pace, so to speak?" He nodded. "Well, I *am* married to you, Ambrose," I said emphatically, turning to my husband, "and I have it in my power to ruin your little scheme."

"Indeed you have," he breathed softly, realizing at last the full implications of my position. He knew he could no longer forbid me entry into the spirit band.

"Or . . ." I said slowly, pausing pregnantly.

"Or?" Jemmy urged slyly.

"Or I might just be willing to aid you and abet you."

"Abet us? You'd do that, Enid?" Ambrose blurted out in surprise. Clearly he had been afraid that his plan was doomed to fail now because of my presence, because of his impetuous marriage. Now I offered hope, and he snapped at it.

"Why not? She's got no love for the old lady. I've seen that from the very first," Jemmy exclaimed, his eyes dancing as he began to see the possibilities of my being an ally rather than a hindrance whose inconvenient presence has to be got around.

"Indeed, I have no love at all for the old lady, as Jemmy says. *You* know some of the reasons why, Ambrose, and if you, as my husband, keep those promises of silence and loyalty that you have made to me, then I, for my part, shall dutifully aid my husband in his endeavors—whatsoever they may be—and with a vigorous will to boot."

"Agreed." Ambrose nodded significantly. Our little pact made those few days earlier still held. Our front would remain united in the face of all.

"Well, that's between you two, arter all," Jemmy said sullenly. "You are 'usband and wife. But answer me this: why should you be so willin' ta see 'er fleeced?" His eyes were full of suspicion. "When she dies, the money'd be yours, wouldn't it?"

"I doubt that, Jemmy. I doubt it strongly, for reasons that are my own."

He cast a questioning and suspicious eye at Ambrose, but true to our bargain, Ambrose's expression remained impassive. I was gambling that my husband knew me well enough to know that, should he reveal any secret of my past to anyone else, I would be true to my word and ruin his plans for my Aunt Augusta's fortune.

I pressed my finger into the lace of the tablecloth, and looking slowly from one to the other of my companions, point by point laid down my law.

"I want the pleasure of watching at close hand, as one of the spirit band, everything that you do to set her up for the final denouement. I want the satisfaction of helping you to do it. Meanwhile, unless you think otherwise, I think that I can best serve by continuing to vex her and cross her at every opportunity. Any sudden change in my behavior would only arouse her suspicions. My pleasure will come when I see her brought to her knees and suffering.

"As you must know, I do not believe in the hereafter; in some rewarding heaven for saints and a hell of just retribution for sinners. Therefore it behooves me, for my own selfish satisfaction, to help her to find her just hell right here on earth—*now*—whilst I am alive and able to watch her suffer; whilst I can enjoy every second of it. Raise her hopes, Ambrose, as high as you can. To heaven itself. Make her believe with her whole heart that Llewellyn Tregaron really is waiting beyond that veil of Reverend Pond's with a message for her; make her pay dearly in whatever way you have in mind—and she'd pay anything you ask if you can prove he's out there—and then . . ." I paused in my long harangue for want of breath almost.

"Then?" Jemmy urged.

"Then give *me* the pleasure of telling her that it was all a game; that she's been gulled; that death and nothingness still mire her around like a morass; that like a worm in the beak of a bird, she *will* be swallowed up." I slammed my hand on the table for emphasis, and the cold light in my eyes was as the glare of a Medusa from which even two such rogues as Jemmy Burkers and Ambrose De'Ath must turn away their gaze.

"You are very hard, Enid," Ambrose murmured.

"You must 'ate 'er very much, Madame De'Ath," Jemmy whispered softly, a thoughtful, faraway look stealing into his dark eyes.

"Very much, Jemmy. Very much indeed."

"I find that sad," Jemmy murmured.

Ignoring him, I went on, "Oh, gentlemen, there is one more thing." They both looked at me, suspicious once again.

"Money." I enunciated the word carefully. "One-third of whatever she contributes to the 'cause'!"

"One-third!" Ambrose exclaimed.

"Pardon me, madame," Jemmy broke in, speaking softly and with reasonableness in his tone, "but to be fair all around—and I am, ma'am, by such upbringin' as I've 'ad, very adamant on the subject of 'onor amongst thieves—to be fair, your 'take' should be one-quarter and not a cent more."

"One-quarter?" I cried, politically ignoring his remark about thieves and its insulting implication.

"You are forgettin', ma'am, the elder Madame De'Ath," he answered mildly.

"The elder . . . My God, she's in this too?"

"Of course. The guiding spirit, one might say."

"Of course," I concurred. "I knew that you must be *using* her in some way, but . . . Oh, that crafty old witch! She's actually in on it! How very stupid of me not to have realized! How very naive!"

"Yes, rather, now I think about it," Jemmy agreed affably, "but as I said before, honor amongst thieves. One-quarter and not a cent more."

I looked at him thoughtfully for one long minute. It was true. It was he and not Ambrose with whom I had to deal; he and the old Madame De'Ath, who trusted him more than she did her own son. "Done," I exclaimed at last. "One-quarter and a full membership in the spirit band. In fact, that percentage answers another question that I might have had."

"Oh?"

"The Ponds! They have no share, therefore they are . . ."

"Dupes, merely dupes that I stumbled across in London during some of my researches," Ambrose began to explain.

"They come from New York State, as they told you, and they were family friends of these children, the Fox sisters, who claim to be able to communicate with the dead. It has caused quite a sensation over the water, and the Ponds—Enoch, actually—saw an opportunity to spread the word to England before anyone else did. He preaches 'spiritualism' in some of those poor-as-dirt but very earnest Nonconformist chapels that are springing up like mushrooms all over the landscape. London and Manchester and Liverpool are filled with them, and the Ponds go from parish to parish spreading their word. They are quite eager and gullible and have suited our purposes admirably these last few months, haven't they, Jemmy?" he asked smugly.

"Indeed they 'ave, my lad," Jemmy agreed in a congratulatory tone. "One of your better discoveries," he added expansively, as if petting a dog, "although I 'ave my doubts about that son of theirs, Lucas."

"A sullen, dull-witted block," Ambrose summed the boy up.

"Per'aps," Jemmy answered reluctantly. "Well, no matter! To the spirit band!" He smirked, pouring a cup of tea for himself and raising it in a toast. Ambrose rose abruptly.

"I had better inform my mother," he muttered, and turned to leave us.

Jemmy got up as well and locked the door again behind Ambrose's retreating form.

"What are you doing, sir?" I asked indignantly.

" 'Avin' breakfast with my new co-conspirator, if you don't mind, madame," he answered firmly.

"And suppose I do mind, Jemmy?" I challenged. Did he think that this pact changed our relative positions in some subtle way? If so, he would soon find out how very wrong he was.

"Then rise, Madame De'Ath, unlock the door, and leave. I shan't stop you. The door's locked to keep out stray servants wi' pryin' eyes and waggin' tongues, not ta keep *you* in."

"All very well and good, then," I conceded with a sniff of disdain. Perhaps I had more to gain by being civil, but one thing at least I could not let pass. "You know, Jemmy, I did not miss your snide remark before, and I am sure you also know that I did not like it at all."

"My remark, ma'am? My snide remark?" He was all feigned innocence.

"Your allusion, sir, to honor amongst thieves. The implication was not lost on me. I am not a thief!"

"Not yet, per'aps, but you're on your way to it, joinin' us dyed-in-the-wool thieves in our little game as you are." He smiled engagingly and I could not tell how seriously he meant his remark to be taken. *I* chose to answer it seriously, however.

"I hate my Aunt Augusta, Jemmy. Hate her with a passion. That is my motive."

"I know that, Enid," he said, "and I don't like it."

"Don't like it? Why should you even care, so long as it means I shan't inform on you?"

"I don't like what it does to ya, girl. I've said that I thought you were very lovely. I've thought so from the first—a fine, good-lookin' woman. . . ."

"So?" I said, looking away quickly to hide the blush that I could feel reddening my face.

"So this mornin', sittin' 'ere, smashing your finger into the table, sayin' what you said, you was ugly. 'Ate does that to a face—even a pretty one like yours. You turn ugly with your 'atred of that old bitch, and . . . and it 'urt me to see it, Enid. It 'urt me ta see it."

"Hurt you?" I cried scornfully. "Why on God's green earth should my hatred of my aunt, that 'old bitch,' as you so accurately call her, hurt you?"

"I guess, ma'am, I guess because I 'ad come to expect better of you, and I was disappointed," he said slowly and with what seemed to be genuine sadness in his aspect.

"You? What right have you, Jemmy Burkers, to expect anything of me—anything at all—or even to be disappointed in me, for that matter?" I cried out, my indignant voice near to a shriek. "Who are *you* to expect better of *me*?"

"Forgive me, Madame De'Ath. Once more I 'ave overstepped the bounds of our relationship," he said stiffly, rising from his untasted breakfast with a small bow. "I 'ad forgot our respective positions in life and 'ad come to think of us merely as two 'uman bein's." He moved toward the door, reached out, and unlocked it. "It was my mistake, and I 'umbly beg madame's pardon." He bowed curtly and left me alone.

The eggs stared at me like three cold, jellied eyes from off the plate before me. What an odd, odd man was this Burkers person. Well, no matter! Let the devil take him!

Friday night came on apace, and with it such a storm as might indeed have waked the dead from their eternal slumbers and summoned them forth to join our little band of "spiritualists," as Reverend Pond was wont to call us. The air was damp and cold. The night roared with wind, rumbled with thunder, and opened with endless torrents of driving rain.

Until the last of the wooden paneled shutters in the old Madame De'Ath's salon were closed over the casements, we could watch transfixed as, out across St. George's Channel, the sky split and gaped like the very mouth of the Pit itself. Long jagged flames of lightning licked across the heavens like the forked tongues of so many flaming hounds let loose from hell. Nothing daunted, our little band of stalwarts gathered, the unfortunate Ponds somewhat dampened and disheveled by their long and soggy coach ride overland from Wadebridge, but enthusiastic nonetheless for the endeavors of the evening to come.

Within that golden, candlelit salon, richly scented with the aromas of wax and leather-bound books and polished woods, shielded from the threatenings of the outer world by shuttered windows and the thick stone walls of the old abbey, we huddled about a marble fireplace, sitting on chairs of gilt wood and brocade that might once have graced the mirrored halls of Versailles itself. To stave off that penetrating chill from which neither walls nor roof nor shutters could protect us, we sipped cup after cup of steaming chocolate from elegant little porcelain cups.

Jemmy had been sent to fetch my aunt, and whilst we awaited her arrival, Madame De'Ath presided over our little group with charm and grace, relaxing us with pleasant inconsequentials of her long and interesting life. Lucas Pond skulked about in the corners, eyeing the books of astrology and occult subjects with well-disguised but nevertheless detectable curiosity. Mrs. Pond, wearing the same terrible print dress, hair chain and locket, and cameo, rewrapped a knitted shawl close about her overstuffed little person and smiled timidly, clearly out of her element but enjoying her adventure into the realms of the wealthy in spite of that fact.

Reverend Pond sat back serenely, his broad corpulence exposed to general view, accentuated by his large gold-plated watch and multitude of dangling charms. He had, as always, the self-satisfied air of a self-loving, self-praising man about him. He felt as if he had arrived, so to speak, and that all this grandeur was simply his due. He, unlike his poor, simple little wife, did not feel at all out of his element; indeed would have scoffed at such an idea had anyone dared to suggest it. Just looking at him, I sensed that he was feeling his own mightiness, and I longed, out of a certain sympathy I suppose, to warn him of how the mighty are apt to fall.

Ambrose played his part as host, but there was a nervousness about him that seemed uncharacteristic in one usually so phlegmatic. I realized that he was not yet reconciled to me as a co-conspirator, but put most of his behavior down to the effects of the storm upon his system and thought no more about it.

Now we merely awaited the imminent return of Jemmy with my Aunt Augusta. I had hardly seen her at all in the past few days. She had closeted herself with Ambrose for hours at a time, studying with him his extensive notebooks of supposedly documented accounts of contact between departed spirits and living persons. She had been much moved by these "proofs" of the life to come and had taken most of her meals alone in order to facilitate her reading and study. She had been so moved by all this material of Ambrose's that during the course of one of our rare meetings, she confessed herself much impressed and happily reassured that Llewellyn sooner or later would speak to her from the "Great Beyond," as she now called it. Of her cruel and taunting conversation with me on the night of the dinner she made no mention at all. It was as if she had forgotten it or dismissed it from her mind as being of no importance. Well, I had not! I still felt I owed her payment for it—and as ever, I bided my time.

The credit for her enthusiasm, I knew, belonged entirely to Ambrose, whose own obsession with death was leading me to believe that he more than half-believed in such nonsense as spiritualism himself. He was totally plausible to her and played his part in the game with deep conviction and authority. He was truly a "thanatologist" by his own definition of that odd word and no doubt without his special efforts and long years of quite genuine study, there would be no gulling now, of Augusta Tregaron or any other old ladies. Without his keen interest in such phenomena and a deep and abiding love of occultism, even the keener brains of the clever old Madame De'Ath and their wily partner, Jemmy Burkers, would not alone have been enough to convince so cold-hearted and suspicious a person as my aunt of the possibility of life existing after death. Jemmy had not the education and the polish of a gentleman, and Madame De'Ath was too old and eccentric to act alone in convincing her. Yes, Ambrose during these last few days had played his part flawlessly and set the stage for this night's charade to perfection. Had I loved him as a woman longs to love her husband, I might well have been proud of him.

I watched him and wondered. Did he feel any guilt or remorse for putting his hard-earned and quite genuine knowledge of "thanatology" to use in such a manner? What else was it but a form of prostitution to use his serious study in the fleecing of fearful old ladies out of their money? But no more of that.

The doors to the hall opened at long last and Augusta Tregaron entered on the arm of Jemmy Burkers, looking inevitably like some black-clad hag from out of *Macbeth*. Her frail, stiff body, indeed her whole manner, was as brittle and hard as the black mourning beads that edged her high neck and the cuffs of her long sleeves in a small, conservative condescension to fashion. As always, her ringless white claws curved like talons from the black, fingerless mittens that she seemed never to be without. Between her and her hostess there was the most dramatic of contrasts, for my mother-in-law wore yet another of her magnificent old French toilets, perfect down to the last strand of pearls and curl of her wig. How strange, the utter difference between these two strong, independent, and eccentric old women—one full of life, the other wallowing in death.

I surveyed my aunt with a certain smugness. Will you walk into my parlor . . . ? I thought, smiling to myself. Ignoring me, she paid her respects to the rest of the company and took her seat, stiff as a waxwork model, on the edge of a gilt-and-petit-point settee before the fire.

"Well, the band is now complete, but before we form the circle for the sitting, my friends—" Madame De'Ath started to speak.

"I beg your pardon, madame," my aunt interrupted unceremoniously, "but before another word is spoken, I must ask whether you intend that my niece Enid be a part of the circle?"

"But of course, Miss Tregaron. My daughter-in-law is most welcome in our little circle," she answered with ineffable grace and charm. My heart instantly went out to her in a feeling of gratitude that as suddenly turned to trepidation. Why had Aunt Augusta asked such a question? Surely my very presence in the room with the others must have implied my membership in the band.

"It will not do," she stated flatly.

Ambrose and Jemmy exchanged urgent glances, and a look of guilt passed across my husband's skeletal face. That expression was not lost on Jemmy, and he was clearly curious by now.

"Will not do, Miss Tregaron?" Madame De'Ath questioned.

"My niece is a skeptic. Her resistance to the very idea of spiritualism rules against her continued presence in this room." Her bitter old voice sounded as harsh as the cawing of a marsh bird in that serene and lovely old salon.

"My servant Mr. Burkers is a skeptic also, Miss Tregaron. Do you object to his presence as well?"

"No."

"And I have never yet heard young Master Lucas Pond express a personal belief in spiritualism—or, as they called it in my day, animal magnetism—yet both of these men have been in the circle from time to time and have not spoiled our sittings. Your niece is a skeptic, it is true, but she is intelligent enough, I think, and open enough to new things, to admit of the possibilities, if not the probabilities, of a spirit world beyond this life. Her presence should be no deterrent to our success."

Everyone breathed a sigh of relief at the reasonableness of her remarks, shifting or nodding in agreement and assuming the matter at an end, which it was not.

"I will not sit with her, Madame De'Ath."

"You *will* not, Miss Tregaron? Surely who sits in my circle is for me to decide?" my mother-in-law asked with deceptive softness in her voice. Her old eyes were hard and angry at this challenge to her authority.

Ignoring her, my aunt turned to me, "I put it to you then, Enid. Will you not voluntarily absent yourself from this room at my request?"

"I see no reason, Aunt, to absent myself from this room, nor indeed from any other in the abbey. You forget that this is *my* home."

"And you forget yourself. Once more," she snapped, "will you leave this room?"

"I will not."

Ambrose, demurring on my behalf, broke in just then. "Enid, my dear, perhaps, since your aunt feels so strongly . . ." Why was he not backing me up as he had promised?

"I, as well, feel strongly, sir, and as my husband you should support me in this matter," I retorted hotly.

"Indeed, I . . . I do," he said with no conviction in his tone, his whole body sagging limply. The man had no spine at all, and for an instant I found myself almost loathing him.

"Pray forgive me, Madame De'Ath." Jeremy spoke up with the tentative obsequiousness of a servant. How well he played his part!

"Speak freely, Jemmy. In the spirit band you are an equal member with us all," my mother-in-law said firmly.

"Thank you, madame. Well, it seems to me, observin' this colloquy as I 'ave been, that there is somethin' more to Miss Tregaron's objections to 'er niece's presence than merely 'er skepticism as to the fact o' an arterlife."

Oh, Jemmy be still, I thought urgently.

"That is very perceptive of you, young man," my aunt crackled condescendingly. No—she could not, she would not . . . "I have," she said significantly, letting her eyes wander over the assembled company dramatically, "as you all can see, urged my niece to leave of her own accord, but since she has refused, the consequences must be on her own head."

"Oh, no," I groaned, that sinking feeling in the pit of my stomach. Not here! Surely not here and now and amongst these people. Weak as he was, I had been able to count on Ambrose's loyalty and silence, but now, it seemed, they were not enough. Why was he not doing something? Make him stop her. Ambrose, you alone know what it is that she is about to say. Stop her for God's sake, for *my* sake. I should have known, I should have . . .

". . . only fair that you all should know," she was saying smugly and with such satisfaction, "that amongst this company tonight sits one who has more to fear from the spirit world than any of us; one who will resist the spirits and do all in her power to keep them from coming to us." Ambrose stood mute.

"And why should this person resist the spirits so?" Madame De'Ath asked calmly over the gasps of Mrs. Pond, who, together with her florid husband, sat agog at the hostile turn the evening was taking.

"Because she is a *murderess*, madame, and has every reason to fear that the poor victims of her brutal attack may come back to accuse their own daughter of her vile and most unnatural crime."

Amidst the shrills of Mrs. Pond and the general gaspings of the others, my own voice arose in an agonized wail of pain and dismay. I stumbled to my feet and ran blindly, my eyes stinging and blurred with tears, toward the doors at the far end of the room. In the wake of my hasty flight small tables went tumbling, a cacophony of tinklings and little crashes accompanying my departure.

Just as I reached the door, my arm was caught in a strong, almost painful grip. Ambrose?

"Let me go," I wailed hysterically, for I had lost all control.

"No, you'll not run away, girl. Not now; not anymore." It was Jemmy's deep voice and coarse accent that sounded in my ear. Jemmy! He whirled me around toward him and, taking me by both shoulders, proceeded to shake me till I thought my neck would snap. Still I went on resisting him, beating at his chest with my fists, sobbing and crying all the while. Finally he freed one hand and took to slapping me across the face. Still I could not regain my control.

"Jemmy, stop, for God's sake. Let her go," Ambrose called out down the length of the salon. Through all this he had not yet moved from his stance by the fireplace; had made no move toward me at all.

"Stay out of this, Ambrose," Jemmy shouted back over his shoulder menacingly.

"Let her go, Jemmy," Ambrose insisted. "It's true. She *is* a murderess. She killed her parents."

The words roared down the room like a rain of hailstones, stinging me far more sharply than all of Jemmy's cruel slapping. The effect on me was instantaneous. I stopped stock-still, my cheeks hot with blows, my tear-blurred eyes burning, and my shoulders bruised and sore with the force of Jemmy's grip.

There was utter silence in that room now. It was as if Jemmy and I stood in a time of our own, out of all contact with the rest of the world. My eyes were locked on his face, wide and coarse with its crooked, broken nose, thick brows, broad, square chin, and blazing animal eyes. The expression in them was at once of pain and fury, of question and accusation—and of sadness. Most of all such sadness and disappointment. It hurt me to see those eyes of his. It hurts even now to remember them.

Then suddenly he recovered himself, and it was as if all the stopped clocks in the world had begun to tick again. His eyes were blazing yet, but the old familiar craftiness had crept into his face again, making me think for an instant of the sly and wily Ulysses. This somehow comforted me. He took my hand and led me, docile and spent as a repentant child, back down the length of that golden salon past several overturned tables and broken *objects d'art* to where that little group of dismayed and uncertain souls awaited my return.

Each face, to this day, stands out in my mind's eye in

cameolike relief as I look back upon that horrible night: Mrs. Pond, white with embarrassment, her cheeks sagging, her eyes like two black raisins in the pale muffin that was her face; Enoch Pond with his great, florid countenance even more red than usual, his blue eyes large with shock and his mouth opening and closing mechanically as he puffed in and out like a blowfish on the beach at Brighton. Lucas alone of all the company chose to regard me with a frank and thoughtful stare, and I actually almost welcomed it as a relief from the unabashed shock of his parents' expressions, the hurt of Jemmy's.

Aunt Augusta looked triumphant as a Caesar at his coronation, and Ambrose, shamefaced, had turned away. Only Madame De'Ath, of all the group, seemed totally unmoved. She sat passively in her bath chair as she awaited my return. Did nothing ever surprise her or upset that remarkable equanimity of hers?

"Now, my dear"—she spoke to me softly after Jemmy had led me back to my seat—"have you quite recovered yourself?"

I opened my mouth to speak, but only a dry sob came forth.

"Some wine, perhaps," she suggested kindly, and before I knew it, Jemmy had offered me a glass of chilled champagne, which I gulped as if it were water. From somewhere over my shoulder a rather rumpled but otherwise clean linen handkerchief was proffered.

"May I be so bold, Madame Ambrose," Master Lucas mumbled with somewhat clumsy gallantry as he made the offer.

"Thank you, sir. You are most kind," I whispered, and made much use of his offering.

"Now," Jemmy Burkers announced abruptly, "when the young Madame De'Ath 'as quite recovered 'erself, we'll go on as if nothin' 'ad 'appened. Is that clear?"

"Jemmy," Madame De'Ath called softly to him. He whirled on her like an attacker.

"Can anyone 'ere—_anyone_, mind—honestly say 'e is without something in 'is past which precludes 'is castin' a stone?" There was an uncomfortable silence broken only by the rustling of Augusta Tregaron's skirts as she shifted upon the settee. All eyes turned to her. She began to speak, and then evidently thought better of it, snapping her mouth shut like a trap instead.

"No need to speak further, Miss Tregaron," Jemmy purred

nastily. "We all know *you* must be without sin. You've cast the first stone, arter all, 'aven't you?"

"Jemmy, you forget yourself," Madame De'Ath chided patiently in a way that made me think she applauded his remark despite its imprudence. "Come sit by me and calm yourself," she urged, patting the upholstered footstool beside her bath chair.

"Forgive me, madame, but I should prefer ta sit 'ere, beside Madame Enid and calm '*er*," he countered hotly as he knelt before me to refill my empty glass.

"It does you credit, Jemmy, that you wish to see to your master's wife, but that rightly is Mr. De'Ath's duty, and one which I am sure he is on the point of taking up," my mother-in-law remarked precisely, and suddenly each of them, having forgotten their roles as servant and husband respectively, returned to their proper duties; Ambrose coming to sit with seeming solicitude at my side and Jemmy to serve wine to the company as a balm to their agitated nerves.

Some minutes of silence were allowed to pass before Madame De'Ath, her misplaced rank as leader of the band resumed once more, began to address herself to me again.

"Are you sufficiently recovered, my dear?"

"Yes, madame."

"Excellent! Now, I do not wish to cause you any more pain or alarm than I can help, but it cannot be avoided now, you understand?"

I nodded solemnly.

"An accusation has been made against you tonight and before these witnesses which cannot be altogether ignored. Now, this is not a court of law and I cannot force you to speak if you will not—you understand that, my dear?"

"Yes, madame."

"Good." She nodded soothingly like a wise old fairy queen talking to the frightened child who has strayed into her kingdom. "I think it would be best if you were to answer your Aunt Augusta's accusation right here and now, whilst we are all assembled to listen. Then, you see, you will have had a fair hearing and a chance to explain—if, of course, you wish to explain—and clear up the doubts which, understandably, have been raised in our minds."

"There's no doubts, madame," Jemmy snarled. "The old bitch is lyin'."

Aunt Augusta groaned and clutched her hand to her cold old heart.

"That will be *quite* enough, Jemmy," Madame De'Ath

broke in sharply, and Jemmy Burkers, looking as dark as murder himself, leaned back against the paneled wall by which he stood, to await, as did the others, my explanation.

"Yes, Madame De'Ath, under the circumstances, I think perhaps it is best if I . . . I attempt to answer my Aunt Augusta's accusation. She has made it many times over the years, and in the presence of many people, including, once, your own son, Ambrose, who led me to believe that he gave her remarks no credence. I see now that he evidently believes her, and I wonder why, that being the case, he ever asked me to become his wife. That, however, is neither here nor there, and I do wrong to bring it up at such a time. Forgive me."

I paused, my hands trembling violently, Lucas Pond's handkerchief a knot of soggy, twisted linen between my wet palms. It was hard to see even so far as my hands, so blurred was my vision, so swollen my tear-filled eyes.

I was sick at heart and stammered much at first before I finally began to speak sensibly.

"Yes, I . . . I must explain at last. I never have, you know, not really. I . . . you see, Madame De'Ath, it is quite true that . . ."

# 9

# THE TRIBUNAL

What judgment shall I dread, doing no wrong?

Forbear to judge, for we are sinners all.
.—*Shakespeare*

"Jemmy . . ." My small voice was lost on the howling wind even as I spoke his name. The driving rain beat against my bedroom windows and lashed at my night shift as I opened the casement to him. "You'll catch your death out there."

"That I will," he shouted over the storm, "unless you let me in," and with that Jemmy Burkers leaped up onto the wide outer ledge of the window, and pushing the casement as far as it would swing, slid his agile body sideways through the narrow opening. He hopped to the floor and I shut the glass behind him hastily lest the rain drive in upon us any more than it had already.

"You are soaked," I scolded in a whisper, now that the storm was locked outside once more.

"So are you," he returned, eyeing the clinging wetness of my white linen shift in such a manner as to make me blush. I said nothing at all, but instead wrapped a shawl about me and huddled modestly in an armchair by the fireplace.

Throwing his sodden greatcoat across my bed, Jemmy bent to stir the ashes in the grate, where he soon had a fire going once more. As he went about his task, I watched the planes of his wide, rawboned face, fascinated by the playing of the flames upon his features.

He stood at last, one forearm braced along the mantel, his broad shoulders hunched, and his eyes blazing as he stared absently into the leaping tongues of fire. Standing thus, he made me think of Hephaestus, smith of the gods, in the light of his forge.

I did not know what to say. I did not know why he had come; still less why I had admitted him to my room, but oh, how glad I had been to see that crooked smile of his at the window. Behind me, the rainwater which had driven in at the open casement was collecting on the edge of the sill, and in the silence of that room I could hear it begin to drip, forming a puddle on the floor beneath.

"Look at that mess," I exclaimed for want of anything better to say. Actually the place could have been flooded for all that I cared for the rooms of Thanatos Abbey. "I should never have opened the window to you. You should not even be here, you know! Why on earth did you risk it? Suppose Ambrose had been with me?"

He snorted in derision.

"You forget, Mrs. De'Ath, that I *know* where Ambrose sleeps."

I did not answer. His words hurt too much.

"I'm sorry, Enid." He relented softly, seeing the look of pain on my face. "I . . . it's no' your fault 'e is the way 'e is. An' you know why I came. I 'ad ta see 'ow you were. You looked terrible when we finally broke up that—what shall I call it?—that tribunal."

"Jemmy, I do not want to talk about it anymore. I just . . . I just cannot. I've already said more this night than I have said to anyone in the past fourteen years, and tomorrow night . . ."

"You don't 'ave to say another word, girl. I didn't come 'ere for that. I . . ." He stopped, at a loss, it seemed, for words.

"Why did you come?"

"I just thought you might need someone near." He kept his eyes on the fire.

Neither of us spoke for a very long time after that. Then somewhere out in the labyrinthine halls of the abbey, a clock struck one and its sonorous note, something akin to a death knell, signaled the breaking of that mood which had grown up between us like a wall.

"Ambrose betrayed me tonight, Jemmy," I whispered brokenly, my voice catching on the aching lump in my throat.

He grunted.

"I did need someone near. That someone should have been Ambrose."

Another snort of derision from the figure by the fireplace.

"It should have been," I went on, "but it wasn't—and it won't ever be. I know that quite well now. But . . . but why is it you, Jemmy? Why are you so kind to me? Why, after the way that I've treated you, the way that we started out loathing each other, why have you changed?"

He said nothing.

"I admit it, Jemmy, I've treated you badly and with terrible contempt, yet tonight it was *you* who defended me, you who forced me to face those people when I tried to run away, you who protected me," and here I smiled a small smile as I touched my fingers to the still-red and swollen marks of his blows upon my cheeks. "You were not gentle," I chided good-naturedly, "but you were effective. Without the—"

"Don't say no . . . any more," he muttered.

"Oh, Jemmy, I must! Do you not see that I could not have borne up tonight—no, not for a minute—without you? You were mad, you know, leaping to my defense like that. It might have spoiled everything."

"I didn't care."

"I know you didn't. That's what is so wonderful. You threw all caution to the winds for my sake, while Ambrose— my husband Ambrose . . .

"I . . . I have always been alone, you see, since that night when I was a girl. Nobody has ever defended me or helped me. I have, since that night, met with either silence—which can mean anything—or else dreadful accusation. Comfort never. I . . . I . . . I thought Ambrose would be different. He seemed, when first we met, to want to defend me and protect me from my aunt, but it was all a sham, and I do not understand it or . . . or . . . I don't understand him and I . . ."

There was no longer any coherence to my words or to my thoughts—only a jumble of painful and inarticulate feelings of such a nature that I had never allowed myself to show to anyone before. With that sudden letting go of all my pent-up emotions came such a floodtide of tears as I had not shed since my childhood—since long ago, since perhaps even longer ago than that terrible last night of what had been my childhood. I had not cried then; I had not dared to cry then.

All at once I was enveloped, warm and safe as a child, in Jemmy's strong and comforting arms. Lifting me from the chair, he ensconced himself in my place and sat back, holding me whilst I sobbed.

He did not speak, did not try to quiet me; he simply let me run my course until I fell into a spent and exhausted sleep with my arm draped across his chest and my tearstained, burning face buried in the warm curve of his neck. It was exactly what I had needed, and by some miracle this strange, crude man had known it, had sensed my need as if it were his own; perhaps in a way it was.

When I awoke, it was already morning. The ashes were cold in the grate and the puddle beneath the sill had dried up. I lay in my bed with the covers drawn up about me and tucked in tightly, as if I were a child. Jemmy and his greatcoat were gone, evidently back through my window, which, though closed, was not locked. Beyond the panes of glass, it was still gray with dense masses of cloud scudding swiftly across the skies.

Another day—and tonight another meeting of the "tribunal," as Jemmy had so aptly termed it. I had hardly been able to tell my story—though I had truly tried to—and nothing had been resolved. Madame De'Ath had suggested that we meet again when I might have regained my composure, suggesting, moreover, that Mr. Ottermole be present, since he was so often one of the spirit band.

Realizing that I must at last end the silence that I had kept for so many years and face the consequences, whatever they might be, I consented to her proposal, insisting only that Mr. Ottermole's daughter, Arabella, be present as well. Why? As an ally? Perhaps that was part of it, but really it was more, because I truly liked this poor, plain little girl and her father and wanted them to judge me upon a hearing of my own words and not some time after, on hearsay or the ignorant gossip of the Ponds.

And so the spirit band—the tribunal, if you will—was to meet that night to hear my story in its entirety and to hear my refutation of my Aunt Augusta's ugly accusations against me. Then, doing what no judge and no jury had been called upon to do by the queen's law, they would presume to judge me; to decide once and for all my fitness to join their precious spirit band, and therefore, by inference, my very guilt or innocence of the horrendous crime of parricide which had hovered over me these past fourteen years.

My fitness! My guilt, my innocence! By God, I wondered, how had I got myself into this? How had I allowed these people—these bizarre strangers—to have a part in my poor life? Would it never end? Would I always be ripe for judgment, ready for condemnation? Would Augusta Tregaron always win?

Would it never end?

Yes! It must!

Jemmy had said that it would. He had said that it all would be well, would come right in the end, and so I had trusted him—and had trusted Madame De'Ath as well, for it was she after all who urged me to put myself in their hands this night. Was I mad to do it? I did not know!

But one thing, at least, I did know—one thing *was* sure: Jemmy had come to me in the night because he had sensed my need. He had come to comfort me, and I had been comforted! For that single act alone, I would be grateful to my dying day.

Ambrose stood alone in the grass-grown ruins of the ancient chapel of the abbey, the black of his mourning garb stark against the broken ruins of the gray granite walls and rain-washed greens of the fresh spring turf.

His head was down, and it seemed almost as if he were speaking to himself. He looked up just then, and catching sight of me on the lawn before the abbey, the expression on his face changed; registered something near to panic, I thought, or at the very least some acute embarrassment.

I turned away, back toward the doors of the main building, regretting deeply that I had ventured forth, and hoping to avoid having to speak to him; it was too late. He called out after me, and so I was forced to halt and wait till he caught up to me.

"Good morning, Enid."

"It is morning, Ambrose," I acknowledged stiffly. "As to whether it is a good morning or not . . ."

"I was just out inspecting some of the damage."

"Damage?"

"This storm has played havoc with the grounds. There has been some flooding and—"

"Flooding? There are no cellars here, are there?"

"No, no cellars," he agreed a trifle hastily. "Mother's glasshouses. Several panes have blown out and shattered. I've had to send for a glazier. She fears for her gardenias."

"Does she? How terrible! I feel for her," I remarked flatly, something in his evasive manner troubling me.

"Enid, about last night . . ." he murmured tentatively.

"What about last night?"

"You do understand, don't you? I had to go along with your Aunt Augusta."

"Did you?"

"We've got precious little money left in the kitty. *You* haven't a sou, and our only hope is getting some money out of her. If I had backed you up, she should have been furious. And . . . and . . . after all, it is true that you . . ." He broke off lamely.

" 'It is true,' you were about to say, that I *did* kill them, right, Ambrose?" I finished his sentence for him.

"I did not say that, Enid."

"You did not have to; it is what you were thinking, nonetheless; what you have thought all along. The thing that sickens me, Ambrose, is that I realize now that you always believed me to be a murderess. You *married* me thinking— nay, actually believing—that I, as a child of not yet fourteen, had been capable of killing my own parents. You believed it and still you married me! Even risked my aunt's wrath to do it! Why? I cannot think why, and frankly, it frightens me."

"Frightens you? Why should it frighten you?" he asked, genuinely curious, as if he could not understand my thinking. I was not sure that I understood it myself.

"Does it not frighten *you*, Ambrose?" I said at last. "What kind of man marries such a woman as I am—am presumed to be? I wonder, husband mine, and so, I think, should you. What sane man marries a murderess?" That was a very good question, and I looked long at his cold, skeletal mask of a face. What man hid behind that face?

He was looking at me in surprise. Had he never asked himself that question before? Did he, at least, not know his own motives in marrying me? No, I rather thought not. Moreover, my direct questions seemed to take him aback. I do not think that he wished to hear them, let alone probe at his own motives and learn the answers. He chose to attack instead, offense ever being a good defense.

"It is time you realized that you are in this game now quite as deeply as am I. You're too clever by half, you are, young woman, and have outsmarted yourself, I fear. Your trouble is you want to eat your cake and have it, too."

He stammered on hotly, "I . . . I want . . . I *need* your aunt's money. You want some twisted form of revenge. Well, I don't care two pins about your revenge—have it if you can—but I *do* want that money. It is the only way to continue my studies in thanatology and to keep up this home of mine."

"Home," I snorted.

"It is not my fault that you two hate each other, nor my fault that you did what you did—if you did it," he added intensely, with a finger upraised to silence my protests, "but if I have to get what I want out of her by going along with her hatred and mistrust of you, then, by damn, I will. I'll play it to the hilt; call you a murderess to your face before her if it will wring a pound out of those grasping old claws of hers.

"Hell, woman, we're down to pennies and ha'pennies. There's no bloody time for honor or gentlemanly niceties." I watched him intently, marveling to see such impassioned emotion in his aspect.

"Why, Ambrose, you do have a passion after all—other than your ridiculous mania for thanatology and death, of course. Money! You love money!"

"No, you are wrong. I *need* money. I do not love money. I do not love anything," he remarked precisely.

"I stand corrected. You don't love money. You don't love anything," I demurred, bowing sarcastically. "Well, it is true that I did not like being betrayed last night, Ambrose, but at least now I understand it better. You stood to lose your two great 'needs'—I'll not use the word 'love' to you again *ever*—this mausoleum of a house and my Aunt Augusta's money. Of course you had no alternative but to join forces with her in her hounding and tormenting of me. And you don't feel the least bit guilty about it, do you? What, after all, is a little torment between husband and wife?"

I turned heel and stalked off, not wanting to look any longer on his contemptible face lest I be sickened by it.

"See that you don't forget that, Enid," he called after me in a warning tone that I did not like at all.

"Forget what?" I asked hotly, reeling about to face him again in my anger.

"Husband and wife. We are still husband and wife, you know, and I will not tolerate behavior on your part that is any less than beyond reproach." His tone was cold, haughty, and utterly nasty.

"You dare say that to me? You, who betrayed me to my aunt before that company?"

"I have not betrayed your bed, Enid, nor do I intend to."

"Betrayed my bed," I exclaimed in disgust. "No, you have not betrayed my bed, Ambrose, any more than you have ever given me one single moment of pleasure in it. Do not worry; my behavior will be above reproach, but not for your sake, sir! Say, rather, for my own!

"Now the devil take you, sir. The devil take you and Augusta Tregaron both, for by God, if ever I have seen two creatures who deserve each other more, I cannot think when it was."

The doors of the abbey slammed shut at my back and I tore down the corridor toward my rooms in a passion of fury and hurt and indignation.

The tribunal was to meet at nine o'clock that evening. Strangely, as the time drew near, I found that *I* was not frightened or even particularly nervous. Rather, I felt a deadly calm steal over me, as if I had at last girded myself for the ordeal and would see it through. Perhaps I needed to see it through.

The tribunal would hear me, would hear my Aunt Augusta . . .

And the tribunal would tell me the answer.

The tribunal would decide.

I dressed in red in honor of the occasion, a dark wine red suggestive of the blood that I was accused of spilling. This was a calculated act on my part, and one of pure bravura. The gown itself was of deep velvet, tight and well-fitting in the bodice, with bared shoulders and a low, wide corsage of the untrimmed red velvet. The skirt was full and worn with the wide crinolines that were just coming into fashion at that time.

With my pale skin and simply coiffed dark chestnut hair, the bloodred velvet made a startling contrast indeed. As I stood before my glass, I could not help be pleased with the dramatic quality of my appearance, and yet it was too austere by far. It wanted a certain air of reckless panache such as I sensed in my mood that night and which I wished to express somehow in the style of my toilet.

Jewelry must be added to create the proper effect, and so I chose from amongst my jewels a parure of pavé turquoise set in gold and accented with pearls and diamonds. It had been a gift of Ambrose upon the occasion of our arrival in Paris, and I had not yet worn it. The necklace was in the form of a pavé turquoise serpent which circled the throat. From its mouth issued forth a forked tongue of sinuous gold links set with tiny pearls.

The bracelet, also of a serpentine design, circled my wrist, forming a knot of writhing coils from which the snake's tail seemed to slither down the back of my hand, whilst the head appeared to be wriggling some inches up my forearm.

Along the left side of my red velvet corsage I scattered a cluster of small matching brooches, each in the form of a tiny coiled serpent. Several others I attached to the broad velvet skirt, as if the cunning little snakes were tumbling toward the hem.

I wore no rings, choosing to keep my hands bare of all ornament—bare even of my wedding band, which I removed and buried amongst the trinkets at the bottom of my jewel case. So much for Ambrose!

I stood back and surveyed my appearance in the glass. The dramatic effect of those bright and brazen turquoise-and-gold serpents, with just the merest accent of darting, pearl-encrusted tongues and evil little diamond eyes, made the bloody color and deep texture of the rich velvet all the more apparent. I was genuinely pleased with the contrast of my severe coif, stark gown, and colorful accent of such lavish and grotesque jewels. The resultant effect was one of daring—just as I wished it to be.

After all, was not my very mood one of daring?

Was it not a daring thing I did that night?

One last long look at my figure in the glass; one long last sardonic smile at the enigmatic woman whose face was my own face; whose form was my own form.

> I have set my life upon a cast,
> And I will stand the hazard of the die.

It was some minutes after five. They had gathered themselves, this little tribunal, in the great, dark, brooding front hall of Thanatos Abbey, and now sat, quiet and rigid, in a small circle before one of the cavernous stone fireplaces, the light of a crackling fire playing on their pale, solemn faces as it might once have played upon the Inquisitors of old Spain. Indeed, the very iron candlestands and suits of armor, the dark tapestries and stone walls of that long, low hall effectively suggested some reenacted scene from the Spanish Inquisition.

A scene! Yes, that was it! As I entered that dark and solemn hall with the howling wind of a rising storm whistling about the low eaves, I was reminded of the parting of the curtains upon a play. A peculiar sense of detachment, which had already had its beginnings in the carefully calculated preparation of my toilet, swept over me now in a wave; the stage was set, the cast assembled, and now I, their leading player, was making my entrance, and making it as befits a suspect heroine—to a hushed and expectant house.

I took my own good time, walking slowly and gracefully down the center of the long room toward the gathered group, eyeing them carefully, gauging the effect of my appearance and dress upon each of them in turn.

The first to see me was Jemmy Burkers, in his servant's livery, standing broad and strong near the fire. His eyes lit up in admiration at the sight of me. He knew! He sensed the intentional daring and defiance of my dress and aspect, and he nodded, ever so slightly, to signal his approval of me. How fine he looked at that moment, his dark face ruddied by the flames, his dark eyes alight with admiration, a small smile playing across his crude and interesting face. That was Jemmy!

Aunt Augusta sat like the small black bird of prey that she was, within the wide confines of a high-backed wing chair, the shadow of the tall fire screen that shielded her face from the heat casting her pale white face into a darkness out of which only her piercing, malicious little eyes could be seen, regarding me with hatred and ill-concealed contempt. Brazen, blood-drenched scarlet girl, the expression on her accusing features seemed to cry out almost audibly. So much for Augusta Tregaron.

Ambrose stood beside her chair on the far side of the fireplace, his arm resting across its wide upholstered back almost protectively. Pale as a corpse in his dead black mourning, his eyes registered shock and annoyance as he watched me approach. He recognized my jewels. Did he remember, as well, the happy moment in which he had presented them? I rather thought not! Most likely he remembered their price and regretted the purchase. Why had this man married me? There must be an answer somewhere! Why does one marry a parricide? He nodded coldly at me, and I lowered my eyes in return. Ambrose De'Ath! My husband Ambrose!

Mr. Ottermole, sitting somewhat away from the others on a straight-backed chair, saw me then, and smiling quite genuinely, rose, approached me swiftly on short, plump little legs to offer me his arm.

"Madame Ambrose, you are breathtaking," he exclaimed, taking my fingers in his round little hands and holding me away to his arm's length in order to survey me. At his first approach, I had been somewhat annoyed. He was spoiling, after all, the drama of my stately and elegant entrance, but no, I was wrong! His genuine delight at my arrival and appearance, his charming and gentlemanly courtesy, were perfect, setting me at my ease, as perhaps an actress is set at ease by the first speech of her fellow player.

I smiled serenely at the dear little man, a sense of tremendous release washing away the tenseness I had felt. He liked me! Despite what he must have been told of my aunt's accusations, despite the fact of my evil past, his bulging brown eyes were warm with unmistakable friendliness, his plump, smooth yellow face was all reassuring smiles.

He patted my hand as if to comfort me, and escorted me in bustling fashion the rest of the way down that long room to where the others waited.

Great, florid Reverend Enoch Pond, embarrassed and unsure of how he should behave toward one such as I, half-rose from his seat on the settee, half-bowed, barely touched my hand in greeting, and muttered a halfhearted, "Evenin', ma'am." I could hardly have expected more.

Mrs. Pond, seated beside her mate, pursed her lips and lowered her eyes with a slight nod of her head. It was as much as she could muster, being what she was, a timid, simple soul, prejudiced by her spare, harsh life and the spare, unyielding religion that was so much a part of it. They were, husband and wife, small of mind, rigid in their narrow values, and rather uncharitable and intolerant of human frailty and pain. They tended, I suspected, to condemn what they could not understand. They would condemn me, and so I expected nothing from them. So much, I thought, for the Ponds.

Lucas stood apart, at the side of the fireplace, but came forward to bow and kiss my hand with a sort of clumsy gallantry that I had noted in him on the previous evening as well.

"Ma'am," he murmured, "if you be needin' a lend o' my kerchief, it's right here waitin'," and with that he patted his breast pocket and risked a small, tentative smile.

"You are most kind, Master Pond. If I have need, I shall not hesitate." The boy nodded and returned to the fireside, ignoring the pointed rumble of disapproval that issued from his father's throat. Master Pond was a surprising young man!

Mr. Ottermole led me then to a settee opposite that of the Ponds, where his daughter Arabella awaited me, wide-eyed. She patted the empty seat beside her by way of invitation.

"Thank you," I whispered as I sat next to her, settled in, and adjusted my skirts.

"You look so beautiful tonight, Madame Ambrose," she returned in awe, her large brown eyes gliding over my toilet in something near to disbelief.

Her own gown of sprigged muslin was girlish and pretty, but too lacking in color and style to enhance her plump figure, her pale face, and light yellow hair. Her coif, I noted, was softer, however, and made her look prettier than she had when first we met.

"I am glad you asked that I be here tonight," she whispered urgently. "You have a friend in me, madame. You have a friend."

"Thank you, dear." I smiled, trying not to let unsuitable tears of sentiment well up in my eyes. "It is most kind, but I asked for you, not as an ally, but rather so that you might hear my story from my own lips and not some garbled tale from others. Do you understand?"

"Yes, madame," she replied sedately, having sensed the seriousness of my mood and of this moment. I drew in my breath then, and turning my gaze, I looked upon the last member of this assembled tribunal, Madame Henriette De'Ath.

She sat in her gilt-and-brocade bath chair, which was drawn up close by the fire near Jemmy. It was, I realized with surprise, the first time that I had ever seen her outside the confines of her own apartment, and it seemed a strange, almost unnatural thing. She was, after all, a creature from another age, and belonged in the golden salon and mirrored dining room of her private quarters; not here in the grim Great Hall of Thanatos Abbey.

She, too, had dressed to suit the occasion, and contrary to her usual flamboyant toilet, was attired in a severely simple high-necked gown of dark garnet taffeta, trimmed in a shade of deep wintry blue velvet. Her wig was simple—small and curly, of a dappled gray color—and dressed with small pins set with garnets, pearls, diamonds, and pavé turquoise stones. In short, her usually garish style was toned down, the effect smart and somber and utterly tasteful. Moreover, her chosen scheme of colors and textures echoed my own manner of dress remarkably, and seemed to betoken visibly an empathy that I sensed had existed, unacknowledged, between us, from the beginning.

I studied her unabashedly for a long moment, drinking in the striking beauty of her wise old face, the nobility of her entire aspect. There was nothing of eccentricity and madness in her on this night. Rather, she might have been some allegorical figure representing Truth and Justice and Wisdom. Everything about her bespoke temperance and the balanced scales of a wise life well-lived, hard lessons well-learned, just kindness well-meted. I looked at her and loved her. Did I live to be old, such a face would I wish, by my living, to have earned as this old, old woman, by her living, had earned for herself. Noble, gracious lady, Madame Henriette De'Ath!

"Madame, my mother-in-law," I spoke at last, "I thank you for your kindness and patience before my unnerved and uncontrolled behavior last evening. I thank you for your kindness in sending for Mr. and Miss Ottermole, as well.

"They and the rest of this company form the only society in which I now, as Ambrose's wife, am able to revolve. It is only fitting, therefore," I added, addressing myself now to the entire group, "that all of you be gathered and that you hear once and for all my answer to the accusation of my Aunt Augusta that I have, in my youth, committed a dreadful and violently unnatural act of murder. I began to explain last evening, but was unable to go on for very long. Tonight I am composed. Tonight I shall tell you the story of my past—that past which I have ever tried to keep hidden from the world at large, even as my aunt has bruited it to every willing ear."

"Insolent girl," my aunt muttered.

"Pray be silent, Miss Tregaron," Madame De'Ath commanded gently but with force. "Last evening you put forth your niece's unsuitability to join our spirit band on the grounds of her wishing to prevent the spirits of her murdered parents from returning from beyond the veil to accuse her of their deaths. You have reiterated those accusations most eloquently as we awaited her arrival this evening.

"It is time now for Enid to speak, and I wish her to do so at length and without any interruption whatsoever. This is no more courtesy than you yourself have already received."

Augusta Tregaron glared but said no more.

"Are you ready to begin, my child?" Madame De'Ath asked.

"I am, madame."

I drew in my breath and spoke, at last saying aloud to this gathering all the things that I had held within me these past fourteen years; telling at last the tale of that dreadful night as I knew it:

"My memories, the earliest of them, are of a small, happy, close-knit dear family circle; my mother Caroline, my father Morgan, and myself together with the small household staff of kindly servants. We lived in a small and well-appointed house in Wales—near Cardigan, where my father had business.

"It was sometime around my eighth year that things began to change. There were many business dealings and an expansion of trade that caused my father to move us out of the peace and quiet of a Georgian row house in Wales to the grimmer prosperity of a Georgian row house in London, close by the home of my Uncle Llewellyn Tregaron, who lived in Park Lane with his wife Amelia and his unmarried sister, my Aunt Augusta.

"I had never known my father's family very well until that time. They had come originally from Wales, had prospered in the family business there, and had eventually resettled in London in 1810 at the request of their father. There were three brothers: Llewellyn, who was the oldest; Morgan, some few years younger; and the very youngest, Rhys. The overseer of this family of three brothers was their elder sister—or half-sister, rather—my Aunt Augusta. She was ten years Llewellyn's senior, fully seventeen years older than Rhys, and she had cared for them almost as a mother due to the constant sickliness of her stepmother, whom her widowed father had married when Augusta was nine."

"All of this is nothing," my aunt broke in suddenly. "None of this has anything to do with the events of the night of June 14, 1836. Get to June 14, Enid, get to June 14 if you dare," she shrilled, her eyes blazing, her old lips trembling with agitation.

"Silence, you old witch," I snapped. "This is my night. I shall tell the tales on this night!"

Turning my eyes to each of the tribunal in succession, I went on with my story, Augusta Tregaron's interruption having the effect of making me angry and therefore increasing the tempo of my words.

"She was a demon possessed when it came to her half brothers. Rhys was young and in love; he wanted to marry the girl and bring her with him to London, but Augusta would have none of it. Before they left Cardigan she contrived to have the engagement broken by his fiancée's family—something to do with a congenital weakness of mind which she claimed Uncle Rhys had inherited from his dead mother. Rhys never recovered from the shock of the broken engagement. He took to drink and finally hanged himself in the attic of the house in Park Lane. That was in 1813.

"Augusta had lost him, yes, but at least it was not to another woman. She had been able to see to that."

"Lies! Lies!" the old woman muttered to herself. No one seemed to hear her.

"Morgan, my father, did not marry until 1820, when he was already thirty-five years old. Augusta was so against the marriage that he actually returned with his bride to the family home in Wales in order to escape her destructive presence. God only knows how much I wish that he had never returned to London again. They might yet be alive."

I almost began to weep. Lucas Pond made a step nearer to offer his handkerchief, but I waved him back. I would not break down now. I could not. The tale was not yet told.

"Augusta lived with Uncle Llewellyn in the big house in Park Lane. In July 1822 I was born, and my uncle came to Wales upon the occasion of my christening. While there, he met a friend of my mother's, Amelia Langley, and fell in love. They corresponded secretly—*actually secretly*—because of Augusta's tyrannical jealousy and possessiveness, and saw each other on my uncle's ever-more-frequent 'business' trips to Cardigan. At last, in 1825, when Uncle Llewellyn was already forty-two, they married, and after a wedding tour of the continent, returned to live in Park Lane.

"Seemingly there was nothing that Augusta Tregaron could do. The marriage was an accomplished fact. She seemed to accept it with grace, but she stayed on, running the house as she had always run it, and undermined the marriage in every way that she could."

Before my aunt could raise her voice in protest, I silenced her with a look. "I have in my possession, to this day, letters from my Aunt Amelia to my mother cataloging the endless small torments and miseries to which she was subjected by the subtle machinations of Augusta Tregaron—much the same sort of miseries that I myself have endured at her hands over the years, I suppose.

"Yet, to be fair, it is true that Amelia Langley Tregaron was a weak and spiritless young woman to begin with, good-natured and docile, disposed to general ill health which was soon compounded by several miscarriages. In 1830, she gave up the ghost at last and passed out of our lives almost as if she had never been there at all.

"My mother was next. Aunt Augusta wanted more and more of my father's time, wanted him to move us all into the big house in Park Lane, wanted to rule our lives as she ruled Llewellyn's. Gradually my father weakened. He began to suggest that we actually do give up our own house and move in with his brother and sister. Mother resisted; Augusta Tregaron planted suspicions in my father's mind.

"Mother, she said, was too lavish a housekeeper, spent too much of my father's hard-earned money, entertained too often. She resented my mother's good nature, her lovely clothing and jewels, her happy, carefree home. She resented my mother's many friends and knew that they laughed behind her back at the crazy old spinster sister who had to run everyone's lives for them. Finally she hit upon it—the ultimate weapon—my father's jealousy of his beautiful and very much younger wife.

"Aunt Augusta told my father that his wife was unfaithful, that she was resisting a move to Park Lane because it would force her to give up the freedom and privacy that enabled her to have a lover behind his back. My father, so wrapped up in the business, had long given my mother her head in many ways. He had never questioned her dinner parties at which he was a silent but willing host; never questioned her attending the theater and the opera on nights when business affairs kept him away from home; but now, with Augusta Tregaron sowing the seeds of distrust and suspicion in his mind, he began to change.

"Suddenly my parents were arguing constantly. There was an air of bitterness; there were tears and accusations and protests and denials and recriminations. My mother was distraught, innocent, maligned, and helpless against the force of my father's implacable suspicions, suspicions fed constantly by the evil tongue of Augusta Tregaron.

"That was the family Tregaron; that, then, was the setting for the night of June 14, 1836—a sultry, hot, miserable night—the kind of night on which tempers flare almost preternaturally. My father had made the announcement that we were indeed making the move to Park Lane; that packing of valuables would begin at once; that our furniture was to be sold at auction; and that we would move within the month.

"My mother burst into tears and fled the room. I shouted at my father, raging at his cruelty and selfishness and his false suspicions. I was but one month from my fourteenth birthday, and although still quite young, I was no mere child. The atmosphere of that house had changed me much, and I had grown up quickly. I felt I had an adult's right to protest. I railed at my father and he struck me across the face for my 'insolence.' I threw down my napkin and ran from the dining room, up the stairs to my own room, and locking the door behind me, I cried myself to sleep."

I stopped just then, realizing suddenly that I was gasping for breath and that my words were beginning to tumble from my mouth in an incoherent jumble of sounds.

"Jemmy, a glass of sherry, I think," I heard Madame De'Ath suggest.

"No, madame, I am recovered now. There is not much more to tell," I protested, raising my hand to stop Jemmy from filling a glass from the decanter that stood on a table beside my mother-in-law's chair.

"I was awakened at six-thirty the next morning by a series of horrendous shrieks and cries that seemed to fill the halls of the house. There was the sound of footfalls, doors slamming, the high-pitched screeching of a policeman's whistle outside in the mews at the back of the garden. I trembled in my bed, sleepy and confused and afraid. Some time elapsed—minutes perhaps, a quarter of an hour, an eternity anyway. There came a banging on my door. I . . . I rose and crept to it in my night shift. It was Bridie, the Irish serving girl. She was sobbing and calling to me to open the door. I remember turning the key in the lock and starting to pull it open when suddenly someone pulled it shut again from the other side. A voice said, 'No, don't let the child see this, for God's sake. She'll go mad.'

"It was my Uncle Llewellyn. He . . . he opened the door slowly, just enough to slide in without letting me see into the hall.

"'Are you all right, child?' he asked.

"'Yes, Uncle. But I am frightened. Someone screamed. They woke me up. I heard a Peeler's whistle.' I began to cry, and he put his hand on my bowed head very gently. It was the only time I remember him touching me, I think. 'Where is Mama?' I cried. 'I want Mama.'

"'Your mama is dead, child,' he said.

"'No! Papa? Where is Papa?' And suddenly I felt so afraid as I asked that question. There was a feeling . . . a . . . a . . .'"

I sobbed a dry, racking sob, caught my breath, unable for the moment to continue. The room was so tense, the listening tribunal so silent—even the flames in the great, cavernous fireplace seemed to have ceased their crackling.

I went on at last, my voice sounding small and frail and childlike in that huge and gloomy hall.

"'Your papa is dead, too, child.'

"'No!'

"'And Janet.'

"'Janet, too?' I said. 'Janet, too? Poor old Janet?' I remember I cried then a little, shedding tears for our old cook because she was dead, but I did not cry for Mama and Papa. No one could understand that afterward. They saw that I shed no tears for my parents, and they said . . ."

"That you killed them," Augusta Tregaron croaked out of the silence.

"That I killed them," I echoed her solemnly. "The police came then—the Peelers as they were called—and they asked me questions. I couldn't answer; I had been asleep. I didn't understand.

"Then . . . then they made me wrap up in a dressing gown . . . I . . . I didn't have my slippers on. My feet were bare . . . I . . . I was so afraid, but they made me walk out into the h-h-hall."

I closed my eyes against the horror; the sights that I now relived—seeing them again and describing them aloud for these people, these strangers.

"There were great smears on the flowered wallpaper. Dark red streaks. Someone has got jam on their hands and wiped it on Mama's walls. Mama will be angry. It wasn't me. I hope she doesn't think it was me.

"I felt something wet on my bare feet. 'I've got jam on my toes,' I said to the police constable. 'I've stepped in jam, sir.'

" 'Never you mind, miss,' he said. They led me down the h-h-hall to Mama's room. There were people all around. Bridie sobbing, and Maggie too, her little sister Maggie; Aunt Augusta standing rigid as a statue. She looks frozen, I remember thinking. Uncle Llewellyn had his head bowed and his back to me. He was sobbing. There were others—men in tweed suits, Peelers in their blue jackets and copper buttons. One was a police surgeon with a little leather valise.

"They all stood back, like waves parting before me as I approached, and then I saw what had made them all come there.

"I . . . I didn't see it as they saw it. By some miracle, by some trick of my mind, I saw it then even as I see it now whilst I describe it to you. . . .

"I saw a . . . a scene just as I might have seen it on a stage. It was my mama's canopied bed, the curtains drawn back and in some disarray. It looked very small and far away, as if I were seeing it upon a stage from very high up in the gallery, or as if I were looking at a tiny bed in a room in a doll's house. It . . . it just wasn't real. Thank God, it wasn't real.

"There was a figure, a big doll in the bed, and she . . . she looked just like Mama, but her eyes were wide open and made of glass. She had her mouth open wide too, as if she were trying to scream and couldn't. There was jam, thick dark red jam, thick with strawberries, all over her face; all over the nightdress, all over the counterpane.

"I saw a knife, a hunting knife that was my papa's. Someone had stuck it into the big doll that looked like Mama, and it had stayed there. I . . . I didn't like it. Why didn't someone pull it out?

"The counterpane was half pulled off the bed and heaped along the floor beside it. And then I saw the other doll, dressed in a dressing gown like Papa's. That doll seemed broken, all of a heap on the floor. The back of its head was gone—all . . . all . . . all . . ."

Jemmy made a move toward me, but I waved him away.

"The head was all smashed in and covered with red jam . . . that and something grayish-yellow. I remember making a face in disgust—jam and horseradish, I thought to myself. Someone's been throwing jam and horseradish about.

" 'I don't like this place,' I cried out. 'Take me away, take me away.'

" 'Did you do this, child?' someone asked.

" 'Of course she did! The house was locked. No one broke in. She's the only one left alive.'

"I remember those words distinctly. The voice was Aunt Augusta's, the accusation, which I did not understand then, was hers. Uncle Llewellyn muttered, 'Oh, God, no. Don't let it be so.'

" 'I don't fling jam pots,' I shouted. 'I take care of my dolls. I don't stick knives into their stuffing. I don't break their heads. I'm a good girl. Ask Mama. I behave.'

"They all looked at me as if I were mad. They took me away; I washed the jam off my feet and they took me to Uncle Llewellyn's house in Park Lane.

"And that, Madame De'Ath, is all I know, all I remember of the night of June 14, 1836, and the morning of June 15. Nor do I have any real memory of the weeks following. After that, one day simply flowed into the next, and one year into the next. No accusation was ever made by the police, no action was ever taken against me, no word was ever said except by Augusta Tregaron. And that is all I know of my own knowledge and out of my own memory. The *facts* are another matter. . . ."

I sat back in my seat and closed my eyes briefly. No one

had spoken, for which I was grateful. "I'll have that sherry now, Jemmy, if you will be so kind."

"I've been 'arsh wi' you, Enid." He spoke *sotto voce* as he offered me the glass. "To 'arsh by 'alf. I'm sorry for it, girl."

I made a sign for him to be silent. Arabella Ottermole sat just to my right, and I feared the girl would hear his unsuitably personal remark. She, poor child, was lost in thought, however, and had not heard his indiscreet remark. No one had.

"The *facts*," I said at last, "were these. After my outburst against my father's decision to move to Park Lane, I went to my room, locked the door, and after some time fell into a deep sleep from which I was not awakened until the screams of the maids and the entry of the first Peeler. I heard nothing of the murderous attacks that took place that night. I saw nothing.

"On that night, the two housemaids, Bridie and her younger sister Maggie, were away. Mama had given them permission to visit their mother after dinner was served, provided they were back to light the fires and heat the water as usual in the morning. The only people in the house that night, therefore, were Mama, Papa, the cook Janet, and myself.

"Sometime during the night after I fell asleep, my mother was stabbed to death with a hunting knife that belonged to my father and which he had used to repair the wire of the bell pull beside my mother's bed only a day or two before. Its usual place was on the desk in my father's study at the back of the ground floor. He used it as a letter opener, I believe.

"My father, whose body lay on the floor beside my mother's bed, bore superficial bruises and several minor cuts and punctures of the hands and face, which were evidently inflicted with a small sewing scissors that came from a work basket that my mother kept near her bedside. This scissors was found underneath my father's body when it was moved.

"The actual cause of my father's death, however, was a series of blows to the head; one to the front side of his temple, many more to the side and back of his skull.

"The blood, the smeared handprints on the walls of the hall, the trail of blood down the corridor, all led to Janet, the cook, who was old and had been with us as long as I could remember.

"It was theorized that she had heard the attack on my parents and come down the attic stairs to their aid. She was wearing a robe which had been drawn on hastily over her night shift. She must have received the first blow of the knife just inside my mother's bedroom door, for she had one stab wound in the chest, and an isolated spurt of blood on the bedroom wall by that door seemed to correspond. She evidently fled down the hall toward the back stairs again to escape her attacker. She was caught at the top of the stairs and stabbed several more times in the back, leaving a pool of blood. She must have either fallen or crawled down the steps to the ground floor, for she was found near the back door. A police whistle which was always kept by that door to summon the Peelers was in a pool of blood by her side. She had died bravely, trying to summon help.

"When Bridie and her sister returned to the house in the morning, they found the back door locked but unbolted as it should have been to permit them to gain entry without rousing the household so early—it was before six-thirty—and it was then that they discovered Janet's body. It was their screams that awakened me.

"There is no more to say. You all know now exactly what I know."

Augusta Tregaron sat still as a waxen figure. Out of a mouth that hardly moved, she muttered the final period to my long tale: "You murdered them. You killed my brother Morgan."

"That is the one thing you have not said, Madame Ambrose. You have not actually answered your aunt's charge," Mr. Ottermole suggested quietly, almost apologetically.

"Did you do it, Enid? Tell us once and for all, for God's sake, and end all this accusation and argument." This from Ambrose.

"The truth is, ladies and gentlemen, the truth is that I slept through the entire night and did not hear a sound until the housemaids came home and discovered Janet's body in the lower back hall."

"Liar," Augusta Tregaron cried out. "Liar. You waited until you had your chance, you waited until Caroline was sleeping, and you stabbed her. Your father—my poor, poor brother Morgan—came to her aid and you struck him down—blow upon blow over his poor skull.

"You beat his handsome face and bashed and bashed till his brains were gone. You devil," she shrieked, rising from her chair and literally hurling her frail, thin, brittle old body upon me where I sat. "You devil, it wasn't jam, it wasn't horseradish. It was his blood, it was his brains—my dear dead brother's brains."

Ambrose and Mr. Ottermole had to pull her off me. She

had never done such a thing in all the years that I had known her. In all these years Augusta Tregaron had never lost control, and now, as I watched, she shrank back into the huge wing chair, her thin body shriveled and racked with sobs.

"My brother's blood, my brother's brains. She killed him," she cried, pleading with them all to believe her.

I was stunned, sickened at my stomach by what I saw. I could hardly bear to look upon such raw emotion in her after suffering all those years of cruelty and torment at her hands. I did not know what to say, how to react.

"I . . . I swear I have never seen her like this," I said to no one in particular. "I do not understand."

"You have never told her before how that night seemed to you; what you thought happened on that night. Now you have, my dear, and she is reacting to your words. She is in great pain, reliving that morning, the discovery of her brother and his death in such a violent and ugly manner. One must pity her." Madame De'Ath spoke softly.

"Pity her? Pity Augusta Tregaron? She has made the last thirteen years of my life a hell on earth, and you say that I should pity her?" I cried out indignantly.

"Have pity, young woman," Enoch Pond intoned piously. "Say with Christ, 'Blessed are the merciful.' "

"To hell with Christ, Reverend Pond. Christ didn't have to live with Augusta Tregaron for over thirteen years. I did!"

Mrs. Pond literally squeaked at my impious retort. Murder can be nothing, she must have thought, for a creature who could dare to speak thus. My fate with the Ponds must be sealed already.

"Yes, Enid," my aunt hissed suddenly over the general tumult of voices in that dark, grim hall, "I did make those years a hell for you. I made up my mind to punish you in every way that I could, since no one else would.

"Llewellyn refused to believe that a child—especially you, his dear niece—was capable of such a crime. The police were fools as well. Bumbling and incompetent. They admitted that you were the only likely suspect, but they too said that you were a child and no child would be able to do such a thing. They theorized a burglar hidden in the house, a lover of your mother's, the maids bent on robbing the house with the aid of some criminal accomplice; everything but the truth.

"The truth was a locked house, three corpses, and one lone living being left. You, Enid. You killed my brother." She spat those words at me in a fury of passion far more human than the flat, icy statements with which she usually abused me. I could almost understand her anger; almost feel something akin to sympathy. She had feelings after all, this cold and brittle old hag.

"I . . . I slept through that night. I heard nothing." How could I make her believe me?

"The truth is—" she went on.

"The truth is," I interrupted in anguish, "the truth is I do not know if I did it or not. I have *never* known. I just do not remember. May God forgive me, I may well have done it, after all. I just simply do *not* know!"

The verdict of the tribunal was as follows:

*Madame De'Ath* (with that judiciousness I would have expected of her): Guilt not proven.

*Ambrose De'Ath* (out of his own conviction—*hope* even—as well as to please my aunt): Guilty.

*Augusta Tregaron* (out of her deep conviction and utter hatred of me): Guilty.

*Jemmy Burkers* (injudicious and surprising to me): Not guilty.

*Reverend Enoch Pond* (with typical self-righteousness): Guilty.

*Mrs. Peggy Pond* (surprisingly, and after much soul-searching and in great fear of her husband's wrath): Guilt not proven.

*Lucas Pond* (out of youthful gallantry and rebellious contempt for his father): Not guilty.

*Osric Ottermole* (with a wisdom and judiciousness not unlike that of Madame De'Ath): Guilt not proven.

*Arabella Ottermole* (with the awed, romantic naiveté of "heroine worship"): Not guilty.

The result—three condemned me out of hand, three felt the charges unproven, and three exonerated me of all guilt.

"Well, Enid," Madame De'Ath remarked after she read the verdict from the little slips upon which each had written his opinion, "you have told what you know of that night and have heard the verdict of us all. If we constituted a jury and a court of law, you should go quite free."

"It is a mockery," my aunt muttered.

"That is quite enough, Miss Tregaron. It was you who raised this issue, forced this confrontation. You and your niece both agreed to this tribunal, as my servant Jemmy Burkers has so aptly termed it. You *both* agreed to abide by its decision. Now it *has* been decided that Enid Tregaron De'Ath is acquitted of the charges you have raised against her. You must abide by that verdict, as must we all.

"And now, Enid, let me welcome you once and for all to the spirit circle. Unlike any of the rest of us, you have earned your membership in something like an ancient 'trial by ordeal,' and I think it is very much to your credit that you submitted to it at all. In my opinion, you certainly did not have to."

"No, Madame De'Ath, I suppose I did not have to, but you see, in reality, I did a cowardly thing; not a brave one at all."

"How so, my dear?"

"I left it to you all to answer for me, to decide for me, the truth of my Aunt Augusta's accusations, and whilst I accept your acquittal happily, indeed gratefully, you see . . ."

"Go on."

"I . . . I am not sure I know quite how to put it, madame. You see, I came into this hall tonight and submitted myself to your verdict with a will, but if it were up to me . . . if *I* had had a vote in this tribunal, I should have agreed with your personal verdict, madame; the verdict of you and Mrs. Pond and Mr. Ottermole. I should have entered a verdict of 'not proven,' for you see, I still do not *know*."

# 10

# THE PASSING
# OF A STORM

Casca:   Cassius, what night is this!
Cassius: A very pleasing night to honest men.

Casca:   Who ever knew the heavens menace so?
Cassius: Those that have known the earth so full of
         faults.

                           —*Shakespeare*

"Arabella, you are a dear girl, but you must not, you know, make of me something that I am not." We were walking slowly along the cliffs away from the abbey. Below us, the wet sand of the beach showed evidence of the fearful storm that had raged these past two days and which now seemed to have truly passed. Great gouts of seaweed, dead creatures— fish of the waters and fowl of the air—lay scattered along the line of highest tide or trapped in amongst the eternal rocks that jutted into the sea like great bony black fingers. The gulls, like the scavengers they are, came out to swarm amongst the corpses. It was a scene of great sweep and passion—the endless sea and rocks and birds, the gray skies and the smells and sights of death laid out below in one vast panorama.

"I love nature," I said aloud, although more to the air than to my lone companion. "It stirs my soul—all of it—the storms, the life and death of it all. At moments like this, I feel at one with it, alone with it, and unafraid of it."

"It frightens me rather," Arabella whispered timidly.

"Does it? Perhaps that is because you don't quite understand it. We are—or at least we should be—at one with all this. It is not nature that frightens me, Arabella. It is people."

"People?"

"Yes, people. You see those gulls down there amongst the rocks?"

"Yes."

"They are picking for their dinner, their very survival. They scavenge and kill to eat."

The little girl beside me shuddered involuntarily.

"Look," I went on, pointing to a great black crow that sat motionless and gleaming against the brilliant, rain-drenched green of a meadow farther along the path on our right, away from the sea. "Do you see that bird? He, or one of his fellows, will pick at the egg of some smaller bird and carry off the unborn young, sitting in the grass and making a meal of the little sluglike thing in the broken shell."

"Ugh!" She shivered.

"And when that bird is done with his meal, out of the ground will come a host of beetles and ants to finish off the little that is left. In the span of a single day nothing will remain of that unborn creature in the stolen egg. What, Arabella, would you call that scene, which, mind you, is enacted in nature day after day even unto the end of time? What would you call it?"

"I should call it death and cruelty. It is too terrible."

"No, child. You are wrong. It is life. Life going on in the only way it knows. Blind nature providing for the survival of its own. Cruel—yes, there is cruelty—but it is a blind and innocent cruelty. It is not deliberately malevolent." I paused.

"Only man is deliberately malevolent, Arabella. Only man kills for reasons other than survival. Only man tortures for the sake of torture.

"Those gulls, that great black crow, the sea down there that spews up carnage with every wave, the storm that strikes terror and unleashes death with every shattering fork of lightning—all those forces are natural, innocent and cruel and eternal.

"Augusta Tregaron is not a force of nature. Augusta Tregaron is a force unto herself." I lapsed into a brooding silence, never slowing my solemn pace along the narrow track at the top of the cliffs, my eyes never leaving the carnage of the just-passed storm.

"What did you mean, Enid, that I must not make of you something that you are not?"

"Only that—that I am not some heroine out of a romantic novel like *Jane Eyre* or *Wuthering Heights*. I am . . . am . . ." I faltered, at a loss for words. I was not quite sure what it was that I was trying to convey to this plump and lonely young girl by my side.

"Oh," I said at last, waving my hand impatiently, "I guess that I am trying to say that the Brontë sisters are not writing my life for me. Do not look upon me as a maligned and innocent heroine with a happy ending right around the corner. I . . . I may well be all that she says I am." I looked up, out toward the water.

Out across the channel, too far for the eye to see, lay the south coast of Wales. A long time ago I had been happy in that place. Would I ever be happy again—anywhere?

"You are my *friend,* Enid," Arabella was saying comfortingly and almost fiercely. "I may be young. I think that you are trying to say that I am a child still and must grow up; not believe you to be innocent merely because I *like* you.

"Believe me, Enid, dear sister, I am not so young as you think. I, too, have had hurts; I, too, lost a mother young. One grows up rather quickly under such circumstances. Oh, I know I have not suffered as you have suffered; yet still I can feel for you. Feel for you and admire you for your strength and your abiding fortitude in enduring what you have."

I blinked away the tears that welled in my eyes. "Arabella, you are a very kind young woman. I am not used to kindness."

"I know that, Enid, and it makes me sad. I hate that old woman, your aunt," she said fiercely, impetuously, sounding suddenly like a child again, protective of me, but injudicious and overwrought nonetheless.

"That is not right. You have no cause to hate her."

"She has hurt you, my dear friend. That is cause enough, is it not?" she asked, laying a hand on mine, looking up with those great warm brown eyes, so like her father's.

"No, it is wrong to hate."

"She hates you."

"She thinks she has cause. Maybe she has."

"No," Arabella returned adamantly.

"Child, child, do not defend me so. I may well be guilty, as she says."

"No! I believe in you, Enid, even if you do not."

We came to a fork in the path just then, and so turned our steps inland, away from the sea. My mood passed suddenly and I turned my thoughts away from the previous night, from the tribunal, and from Augusta Tregaron.

"You looked quite pretty in that muslin dress, my dear."

"It is the only really good dress I have," she murmured. "If only I could look like you. Last night you looked so beautiful, so elegant, that I could have wept. No girl in a novel—"

"Aha, you see." I laughed sharply. "I have caught you at it. You do think of me in that silly, romantic way."

"No, no," she protested, "it was your looks, the high color of your toilet—"

"I dressed in that manner quite deliberately, and for an effect," I admitted simply.

"*Did* you? It was a brave thing to do—so defiant," she breathed.

"Yes, I daresay it was. It helped me, you see. Whistling in the dark, rather," I explained.

"I should do that," she said at last.

"How so?"

"In my own little way, I mean," she amended hastily and with some self-consciousness. "I am plain and homely and I dress so that I feel the want of looks and spirit in me. I yield to it, so to speak . . ."

"Yes?" I urged, liking the direction of her thought.

". . . but if I fought it, fought my homeliness . . ."

"You are *not* homely."

"And you are not *guilty*. See"—she laughed merrily—"we believe in each other."

And I laughed too; actually laughed about the greatest pain of my life. It was a first sign of health—small and tentative—but I saw it for what it was and actually dared a tiny moment of rejoicing. Perhaps more storms than one were beginning to pass.

"I shall be as brave and defiant as I can about my looks, dear friend. Will you help me?"

"With all my heart," I agreed, giving her an exuberant little hug.

"And we shall have to test, too," she said with conviction.

"A test?"

"Yes," she answered with rather more nonchalance than she had been wont to show even just moments earlier. "That tall young fellow—Master Pond, isn't it?—hardly looked my way all last evening. If I set about to turn his head and actually did turn it a bit, would not that be a good test?"

"Oh, quite," I said seriously. "A very good idea," and I turned my head away quickly, biting my cheek to keep an impolitic smile from forming on my lips.

"Enid, are you angry at Father?" she asked suddenly.

"Angry at Mr. Ottermole? Certainly not! Why ever should I be?" I asked in surprise.

"Well, last night, he did call for a verdict of 'not proven.' "

"Which was very just. Did you not hear me say that that is precisely how I should have voted myself had I been able?"

"Yes, and that is why you think that I am young and worshipful of you, I suppose—because I lacked the discretion of forbearance or whatever to say 'not proven.' "

"There is something to that, Arabella. I should have thought you more grown, perhaps, and less biased in your friendship."

"What of Master Pond? He, too, thinks you are innocent."

"Master Pond is young and gallant and"—here I could not help a smile—"perhaps a bit defiant of his father."

"Oh, his father!" she scoffed. "Pray what do you think of Reverend Pond?"

"Very little. I am not overmuch impressed with clergymen to begin with, which is a shameful thing to say to a young and impressionable girl, I suppose."

She smiled delightedly, showing those pretty little teeth of hers. "I am not so impressionable as you think," she retorted, knowing that I only half meant what I had said. "I think Reverend Pond is dreadfully pompous and full of himself. In fact, he is fuller of himself than he is of God. Or perhaps that is a good thing?" At that we both laughed very heartily. How nice it was to have a friend! To laugh!

"Why do you think Jemmy Burkers voted you innocent?" she asked abruptly and rather sharply. "He does not strike me as either impressionable or overly gallant."

"I do not know, Arabella. I truly cannot think why," I answered in all seriousness. A vote of 'not proven' would have been far more prudent and sensible on his part and would not have hurt the outcome in any way. Why *had* he plumped for total exoneration? It really piqued my curiosity.

"Do you think he loves you?" she asked.

"Loves me?" I exclaimed, aghast. "He is a servant, Arabella, and moreover, I am a married woman."

"So, he is a servant. What of that? A cat may look at a king! And as for being married, your shoulders are just as white, your hair just as glossy, your lips just as ripe as ever they were before you became a wife." She shrugged.

I stopped dead in my tracks and looked at her in amazement. "Arabella," I cried, "what *have* you been reading?"

"Well, he *is* rather good-looking in a brutal sort of way and . . . and . . ."

"And *what?*" I cried indignantly.

"And . . . Oh, Enid," she replied, a pained expression of

sympathy passing across her face, "Ambrose is really such a pill. Really he is."

I wanted to laugh; I wanted to hug her girlishly and giggle and agree—oh, yes, Arabella, Ambrose is *such* a pill—but of course I could not. Instead I drew myself up to my fullest height and said with dignity, "Arabella, you forget yourself. Ambrose De'Ath is my husband."

She looked up at me askance but made no reply. "You know," she said at length, "Father must think a good deal of you to have let me stay the week. He may have voted as he did out of prudence, but if his instincts leaned toward your guilt, I should not be here, should I?"

"No, I suppose you should not," I agreed.

"Have faith in yourself, dearest sister, please?"

"I'll try, little one, I'll try."

The path began to wind back toward the abbey, its low piles of gray stones and slate roofs still dark and wet from the rain. We walked back toward it arm in arm like loving sisters, and as we did, I prayed that this young girl's faith in her new friend would not—as I feared—prove unjustified. I wished for her sake to be truly worthy of the faith that she placed in me so innocently.

I needed, I think, to be believed in and trusted at last after all those years of suspicion and accusation.

"Oh, look," she cried just then, and following her eyes, I saw a wondrous sight.

The sun, brilliant and clear, had just come out from behind a passing cloud and now shone down upon the abbey. In that sudden brightness the lawns sparkled like emeralds, the old stone walls glowed like polished agate, and every pane of glass in Madame De'Ath's dining room and adjacent glasshouses caught the sunlight and reflected it like a facet on a diamond. It was a brilliant and breathtaking sight which left us gasping in awe and delight.

"Oh, Enid, may our futures one day glow for us with such beauty and such brilliance." She sighed feelingly.

"May they indeed, my child. Oh, Arabella, it only wants a rainbow to complete the picture," I whispered.

And miraculously, there it was—spanning the sky like the long graceful arch of a bow, one end lost in the misty clouds over Wadebridge, the other far to the southwest, out across the huge sea itself. A rainbow!

"Enid, you are magic. You wished for it and it happened," she said in awe.

The wind blew, the clouds moved, the sun hid, and all was as it had been, gray and dull and muted.

"Don't be silly, child. There is no magic."

Later that afternoon, after luncheon was served, I retired to my rooms to rest, feeling truly calm and unperturbed for the first time in days. I stretched upon a lovely old French *méridienne* couch which Madame De'Ath had been kind enough to send to my apartments for my comfort after a complaint I had made against the stiffness and discomfort of the medieval furniture in my suite.

Now, in a taffeta dressing gown, I reclined gracefully, feeling for all the world like the renowned Madame Récamier (who had died only a few months previous, in 1849) or even a fully clothed (but not unglamorous) version of Canova's statue of Princess Pauline Borghese. Thus settled, I resumed the memoirs of the Duchesse de la Cressonière where I had left them off:

Awaiting us, surrounded by ladies masked even as were we ourselves, was the lovely Lorenza, Comtesse di Cagliostro. She was swathed from head to toe in a robe of vibrant, iridescent blue cloth embroidered all over in gold thread in the form of strange characters—pictographs—of ancient Egyptian style and representing the lost language of the ancient civilization of the Nile. Her hair, the golden hair of her northern Italian race, hung about her shoulders undressed and unadorned save for a golden fillet circling her high, pale brow. Her lips were deep red and set in an austere and medieval smile, the lustrous dark eyes like the banked embers of a smoldering fire. Hers was a beauty of which a Dante might sing; for which a Dante might suffer.

Upon reflection, it seems to me now that that very austerity of expression was framed with calculation for the intent purpose of making men suffer; to agonize over and be tempted by a beauty they might never obtain—although it was rumored that for the right sum of gold and jewels placed in her husband's outstretched palm, a night in the arms of Lorenza di Cagliostro might indeed be bought, and often was. But no matter!

She greeted us, the last of her expected guests, with a strange sign of her graceful white hands. We approached, the mirrored panel clicked shut behind us, and there we stood, a dozen timid, nervous young ladies *en masque*, crowded into a tiny, dimly lit antechamber with the magnificent Lorenza and the slender, diaphanously clad and nameless young girl who had conducted us hence.

Still under an admonition of silence, we were conducted into a great circular room, which, I imagined, must correspond with the circular room that I had glimpsed below and in which the illustrious comte himself was entertaining his noble guests to a midnight supper. This hall was lined in tall, gilt-framed mirrors which reflected our moving forms in a veritable infinity of splintered fragments only dimly seen in the light of a scant dozen black candles burning in gilt-bronze sconces spaced around the room just below the vast and vaulted ceiling.

In the center of the floor was what seemed to be a small round stage, carpeted with silken rugs figured in the manner of Egyptian hieroglyphs and strewn with pillows of butter-soft gilded leather. Circling this central stage was a series of curved, backless couches or divans, covered in cushions of black silk fringed with gold. Across each of the twelve divans was draped a long cord of gold satin, the significance of which none of us yet grasped. There was a thirteenth couch, set high above the others on a dais. It was bare of such a silken cord. Beside each of these divans was a low fruitwood table. No other furnishings disturbed the symmetry of the room at which we gaggle of shy, somewhat intimidated ladies marveled, nudging each other silently, since none dared speak aloud.

Suddenly the complete silence was broken by the faint sound of oddly discordant music, of lutes and pipes and tinkling cymbals. Faint as it was, the sound filled that large room almost magically, seeming to come from nowhere and yet everywhere at once. It was a marvel and sent a delicious chill through my very bones, a chill as of ancient mysteries revealed.

All at once the mirrored walls began to open as if moved by an unseen hand, and there appeared, behind twelve hinged panels, twelve tiny mirror-lined cubicles. With that unexpected movement, the whole dim room was filled with reeling fragments of light, and our reflections appeared before our eyes from every angle in a myriad of endless forms.

Conducting us one by one, the slim girl in the sheer ivory gown brought us each to our own little chamber.

To each of us in turn she whispered the same injunction:

"Cast off the garments of this world and seek the raiment of the next."

Thus she spoke to me, and I found myself alone, locked into a tiny compartment of my own, cut off from Camile and the others as surely as if I had been set adrift in a casket. Each of the walls was mirrored, and for the life of me I could not tell which it was that hid the door. Until such time as it reopened, I was little more than a prisoner.

The "raiment of the next world" which I had been instructed to seek out hung upon a gilded bronze hook, several of which projected from the gilt frames of the mirrored panels. It was a single shift of sheerest ivory gauze. Beside it hung a girdle of light blue silk. That was all. I found myself trembling with excitement, and I laughed nervously as I prepared to don the fragile little garment.

Only moments before, I had surveyed the near-nakedness of our slender young guide and wondered if I, robed thus, would look as lovely as she. Now, if I dared, I would find out! If I dared? Of course I must! Had I any choice? Dared I be the only one of the twelve to refuse? And that girl! She was no more than sixteen. I was nearly nineteen. If she could dress herself without shame in such a manner before all eyes, why then so could I!

Reasoning thus, and throwing all modesty to the winds, I donned the gauzy shift, girdled my waist in the manner of our guide, and barefoot even as she, I awaited the eventual opening of the cubicle door. After some few minutes, it swung back soundlessly, and I stepped forward into the big circular hall.

A wave of nervous titters went through us all as one by one we emerged from those tiny dressing chambers, still masked as before but suddenly near-naked in our new raiment. Again, one by one, we were conducted to our separate divans. The music played on, mysterious and still unknown of origin, floating on the air almost mystically.

There was an abrupt clapping of the hands, and we saw that Lorenza di Cagliostro, whose continued presence in the hall had heretofore gone unnoticed, now stood before us upon the high dais that held the thirteenth divan. She raised her arms and from her shoulders the oddly figured iridescent blue robe slid into a heap on the floor at her naked feet, revealing herself in just such a simple shift as our own, save that it was of purest, sheerest white gauze, girdled about the waist with a rope of solid gold in the shape of a serpent. This garment clung to her like a wet skin, accentuating each line of her ripe and comely body.

"Ladies of Paris, gracious ladies of noble blood, initiates into the Rites of Isis of the Order of Egyptian Freemasonry, you have fulfilled your initial obligations, taken the first of your vows; have sworn to safeguard for all time the secrecy of our Holy Rites, and now, with the completion of your initiation on his night of nights, you shall enter into the Realms of the Life beyond our Life—that life revealed only to the Ancients of Egypt and Greece—and now imparted to you initiates through the grace and favor of him who is the last of the Ancients upon Earth; He who is the Grand Copt of the Rites of Osiris of the Order of Egyptian Freemasonry; He who calls himself mortal before the skeptics of this world—the Comte Alesandro di Cagliostro.

"I, called Lorenza, Comtesse di Cagliostro, am your guide, Grand Mistress of the Rites of Isis, and hand-maiden of the Grand Copt. Follow my commands as you would those of Him who is our Master, and the secrets of the Underworld are yours."

Her words had a soft and almost mesmerizing quality about them. Her voice was low and fluid, the slightly accented French indescribably majestic and lofty in its every intonation. We were indeed hers to command.

"Do you join in this Mystery of your own free wills?" she asked.

A pause as we all looked nervously about, unsure of how we should reply. And then: "We do," we initiates blurted out more or less all at once, and one by one we reaffirmed our memorized oath of allegiance to the Grand Copt and the Grand Mistress as well.

"You are, all of you, privileged of your sex, privileged of your race and nation, privileged of the age in which you live. You will see much this night, you will dare all, and you will not falter. Woe to you who falter in the service of the mysteries of Isis; in the Rites of Osiris."

"We will not falter." The young guide spoke up in a clear, bell-like, and mellifluous voice, motioning as if to prompt us, and so, taking her cue, we all vowed after her that we would not falter. Even as we spoke, the air around us became suffused with the heady, spicy aroma of rare incense burned in unseen braziers. The music swelled as well, and our wandering attention was drawn to a portion of that circular mirrored room which was swinging back like a wide double door. Out of the impenetrable blackness beyond the threshold romped twelve lively young women who proceeded to perform an antic dance about the room, circling us around and around with an almost frenzied abandon as the music increased its pace and intensity.

These young girls were all perfect in their face and form, their bodies dyed that dark red color so characteristic of the ancient Egyptian race, their lovely forms utterly naked save for tiny girdles of gold cloth which circled their slim hips. Their hair was black and plaited in the ancient manner, held back from their brows by thin golden fillets.

They reeled and cavorted shamelessly before our wondering eyes. None of us upon the divans moved or spoke a word. I for one was shocked but dared not show it lest I be thought a child. Especially did I not want to lose face before that young and lovely girl whom I had singled out from the first as an object of my interest, for I was ever cognizant of the fact that she was even younger than I and yet so immersed in the Rites of Isis that she sat with remarkable poise upon the right hand of the Grand Mistress herself. I wondered at length who this girl might be.

There was, however, little time for speculation before these twelve naked creatures were each circling an individual couch. The dancer nearest to me swept the silken cord from beside me on the cushion, and binding my wrists together in a trice, drew the cord along the floor, where she bound its other end to the ankles of Camille, who sat upon the next divan to my right. Just then, I saw that another of these dancing girls was binding the cord of my neighbor on the left about my own feet.

At first, quite naturally, we all squealed and struggled, but then, over our own shrill cries and protests, rose the hypnotic voice of the Grand Mistress herself.

"Even thus are you bound, O Women, by the silken cords of your masters, by the soft bondage of your fathers and husbands, your sons and your lovers. Struggle in those bonds, O Women, lest you be unworthy of your sister-Goddess, the Great Isis herself.

"Struggle" she called out over the music. "Struggle," she called out in the heady, incense-laden air, and as we obeyed, struggling with our silken bonds, all at once we were beset by a host of laughing naked men, some young, some old, and some merely boys, but all only dimly seen in the darkness of those few guttering black candles. They pawed at us and snarled and sought to work their wills upon us, cajoling us to yield ourselves.

The air was filled with shrieks and cries as we women and girls, bound and terrified, sought to ward off these would-be violators of our persons. Some, such as I myself, fought as virgins, to ward off the first violation of our innocent bodies; others, like Camile, to protect the honor of their husbands; but whatever the reason, we *did* fight, we *did* struggle, and began to find that when we worked in pairs and threesomes, ensnaring those lecherous attackers in the very cords that bound us one to the other, we could overpower them and win.

"Struggle," Lorenza di Cagliostro urged. "Struggle," the girl at her side cried out joyously, and suddenly, with great dramatic moans and cries, the men lay down at our feet, tangled in the silken webs, defeated and beseeching in their demeanor.

There came the distant, jubilant chiming of merry bells, and over that the delighted laughter of the dancing girls. Then, to each of us, they gave a dagger, dancing away with an air of tittering mischief after placing the weapons in our hands.

"Cut away your shackles, turn your shameful bonds into weapons, and drive your persecutors from our midst," Lorenza commanded.

I drew the sharp little blade across the cords that bound me to my neighbors, freeing my wrist and ankles easily. Taking up the ropes as all the other women in the circle took up theirs, I brandished them triumphantly as a whip and lashed them over the bare buttocks of a pale old man who groveled at my feet. Each of us, breathless and fearful though we had been during the attack, began to feel a strange sense of renewal. We laughed now as we drove the cringing, crawling men and boys before us, herding them till they struggled and climbed, one over the other, up a pair of steps and over the threshold, back through the double doors from whence they had come.

The mirrored panels swung closed on the last of them, and we all, breathless and mirthful, laid down our silken whips and daggers and flung ourselves upon the divans, flushed with the success of our symbolic victory, at which point the dancing girls joined us on the divans, greeting us with hugs and kisses and praise of our task well done. The Grand Mistress let us laugh and chatter amongst ourselves and with the girls for just a while, watching us with hooded eyes, the barest smile upon her carmine lips. Then, at another clapping of her long pale hands, a second pair of doors flung back, revealing a large, dim room, bare save for gauzy hangings and a long, narrow *bronze-d'oré* table set with mirrors upon its surface and laden with huge trays of silver and gold which were heaped to overflowing with rare fruits and piles of strange sweetmeats. There were crystal bowls of odd, brightly colored sherbets and cut-crystal ewers of unusually tinted wines, and delicate long-stemmed goblets from which to drink them.

"Your victory over your masters deserves a reward. Lie back, initiates of Isis, and let your handmaidens serve you," our Grand Mistress called out over our chatter and exclamations of awe. The dancing girls arose at once and ran to lift the great trays carrying them gracefully around the circular room, setting them down upon the small tables beside our divans. For each of us, upon our own table, was set a tray of rare delicacies, a ewer of wine, and a glass; at our feet, a maiden to serve us.

The excitement of our binding, the onslaught of our attackers, driving them from our midst—it had all been strange and frightening and exhilarating. The joy of our victory, our affectionate treatment at the hands of these red-painted "Egyptian" serving maids, had all served to make my head reel. The incense was stifling, the reek of the men's naked, aroused bodies, and the musky perfume of the girls themselves assailed my nostrils all at once, making me giddy and light of head.

"Some wine," I commanded of the naked wench at my feet, and she poured the strange liquid, the color of pale amber and flecked with tiny, floating speckles of fire like an opal, which I drank greedily. It was as if I drank pure honey that had dropped from the sun itself, so warming was its thick amber sweetness.

I ate greedily as well, oblivious to all around me, bent totally upon the fascination of my own senses. It seemed that every part of me was awake to touch and scent and sound and sight and taste as it had never been before. I looked about me. I wanted to touch everything—the sharp-edged cutting of the pattern on the crystal ewer, the cold wetness of the lime-green sherbet in the bowl nearby, the warm liquid of the opalescent amber wine, feel the round, firm red breasts of my serving girl. Across the room, one initiate was doing just that to her wench.

I drank in the smell of musk on the bodies of the maidens in the room, enjoyed the heady bouquet of my wine and the aroma of the incense that made my head throb so.

Around me floated a thousand sounds—soft moans of quiet ecstasy, as of someone caught in a dream; low, suggestive laughter; the tinkling of glass on glass; the rustle of bodies on silken cushions. Over all floated the ever-present sound of that strangely discordant music. At my feet, the serving maid sighed languorously and arched her body like a cat.

"All around me—even in the dimness—I saw so much of color, wondrous color; the green wine in a ewer across the room, the cool ivory of a gauzy shift as it lay in a soft cloud upon the floor at the gold-clawed foot of a divan, the dark red and pure white of two bodies as they entwined upon the deep black silk of a cushion, the darkly golden hair—bound in ribbons of rosy mauve—upon the head of the slender beauty who sat, still as an idol, on the right hand of Lorenza di Cagliostro.

Most of all, I was awake to taste—the sense of the opal-amber wine on my tongue, the oddly bitter fruit upon my lips. I desired to taste the rose-pink sherbet on a tray across the room, run the tip of my tongue against the cold glass of the mirrored walls that reflected us all to infinity. What, I wondered, would be the taste of the long droplet of sweat that ran between the perfect breasts of the wench at my feet? It dropped into her lap, and still I longed to taste it.

I cannot say what happened then. It was the most sacred part of the rites for us, and though I have dared reveal this much, no more of that first night of our initiation dare I describe, for though I have long ago forsworn the Order of Egyptian Freemasonry, yet am I bound by certain oaths that I must hold inviolate to my dying day—and even beyond.

A chime somewhere in the hall struck four of the clock. I laid down the book, somewhat shaken by the sensuality of those old French days before the Revolution, and prepared to join Ambrose and our guest, Arabella Ottermole, in Madame De'Ath's salon for tea.

Quite enough of reading for one afternoon!

"I 'ave not 'ad a chance yet to say one word to you. Why did you ask that girl to stay? 'Er room is adjacent to yours. If . . ." Jemmy spoke in a hurried, impatient whisper, placing his hand on my arm as if to restrain me.

"I did not ask her to say. She asked if I would mind, and I said that I would not if her father had no objection and could spare her. He had none, and so here she is," I whispered back. We stood in one of the corridors leading to my mother-in-law's salon, both of us apprehensive lest we be seen in such intimate converse by some servant or—worse yet—my aunt or Ambrose.

"Jemmy, do let me go. I am expected for tea and am late already," I insisted, pulling away from him.

"No, I must speak. I think they are all in there by now anyway, and shan't see us. Your aunt, of course, is still sulkin' in 'er tents like Achilles."

"Homer now! You do surprise me, Jemmy."

"Don't patronize me, Enid. Now, when is that girl goin' 'ome?" he asked, his hand still holding me back. It made me angry, and I was not civil to him.

"She is not going home. She is staying the week out as my guest. Since her father is joining us for the séance next Friday, she plans to leave with him that night. Now, dammit, sir, let me go," I snarled angrily.

"Rot," he exclaimed, ignoring my anger, "the 'ole week! We 'ave to talk, Enid. I cannot wait out the week." There was a look of urgency and concern in his aspect that I could not ignore. He was being damnably possessive and presumptuous in his manner, but it was, it seemed, only for my own good, and I could not really, therefore, say him nay.

"Where can we meet?" I relented at last.

"Your rooms will not suit, with the girl right next door. And she's with you nearly all day, isn't she? Can you climb out the casement of your sitting room—the window that's the farthest from 'er room—an' slip around the back wall of the abbey to the ruins of the chapel?"

"When?" I breathed softly, finding the prospect of an assignation in the ruins of a chapel somewhat exhilarating.

"Midnight. The 'ole place is as quiet as a grave by then."

"Lovely analogy, Jemmy Burkers, lovely."

"I won't risk comin' ta the window to fetch you," he went on seriously. "Miss Ottermole might 'ear. Just meet me as near to midnight as you can. I'll be waiting." He resumed the impersonal dignity of a servant and bowed his great black-maned head to me. He began to withdraw back down the corridor, but suddenly checked his progress and called out in a *sotto voce* whisper, "Oh, an' don't forget ta dress warm. It's chilly out there o' nights." He turned away again.

A midnight assignation in the ruins of an ancient chapel! And with the likes of a lowborn cockney servant, my social inferior in every way, my husband's supposed man, and yet, in truth, almost Ambrose's master, partner with us in crime—a villain sly and clever! And yet, a villain who had shown to me such tenderness and concern as even my own husband could not muster. And, as Arabella Ottermole had remarked earlier in the day, he was rather good-looking in a brutal sort of way.

I regarded him thoughtfully as he retreated down the hall. There was something in the set of his shoulders . . . Yes, Jemmy Burkers *was* good-looking—in a brutal sort of way. Midnight . . .

I slipped along the rough-hewn blocks of granite, feeling the tug of stone and mortar on the woolen fibers of my heavy, dark shawl. The night was clear, the sea calm, the heavens black and strewn with stars. There was a clean chill in the air that refreshed my senses and left them keen to sight and sound. It was a natural acuity of sense and not such a drugged and debased arousal as had been described by the Duchesse de la Cressonière in her shocking and unwholesome tale of the "Rites of Isis." With a shiver of disapproval, I put that debauchery from my mind once more and drank in the beauty of the night—and the excitement of my adventure.

At the end of the farthest wing of the old abbey I turned, and there, in the light of a waning half of moon, stood the grotesque and skeletal ruins of the ancient chapel—all bare granite bones reaching to the sky like the bony ribs of some long-dead monster. I moved silently across the freshly green spring lawns, stepping carefully lest I lose my footing on the tumbled stones, half-embedded in the turf along the crumbling foundations of the ruined building.

Once I had stepped within that rectangle of broken walls and skeletal arches, I found myself on a soft, deep carpet, more mossy than grassy, that gave beneath my feet in a disconcerting manner—as if I trod on living flesh. That thought made me shudder, and I drew my shawl around me closer, as if against some sudden change in temperature. Jemmy was nowhere to be seen. Had he forgotten our appointment? Had something held him up? I dared not wait too long.

"Enid."

There was a figure, a deeper black against the blackness of a massive stone altar that stood at the far wall of the chapel, well away from where I waited.

Had he been there all the while? I wondered.

"Jemmy?"

" 'O else? Come. 'Urry," he whispered, his low voice carrying to me clearly on the chill, crystalline night air.

I crossed the spongy turf with gingerly steps, hating the feel of it beneath my slippered feet. Jemmy stood by the ancient, rudely carved Romanesque stone, a dark lantern, shuttered yet still showing tiny points of the light imprisoned within, set on the altar beside him.

"Oh, Jemmy, this is not a good idea. The moon is too bright, these walls too low. If someone chanced to see us . . ."

"Stop worryin'! Enid, d'you trust me?"

"Trust you? I . . . I suppose I must. I am here with you, after all." Why was I asking such a question? He was beginning to frighten me, or perhaps it was just the mood of the place.

"Good! No' every girl in Christendom is brave enough or trustin' enough ta foller a feller down inta the very bowels o' the earth." He smiled in a totally winning manner, his face looking especially handsome and youthful in the pale and flattering light of that half-moon.

"Into the bowels of the earth? Oh, Jemmy, whatever are you going on about?" I asked, more exasperated by what I took to be his levity than frightened by my precarious position alone with him amidst those sinister ruins.

"I'm takin' you down 'ere. We'll be safe as death." He stomped with a booted foot upon a paving stone at the base of the altar.

"Do stop! I think you really are trying to frighten me, Jemmy."

" 'Course I am, girl. Then you'll cling like a limpet an' I'll have to 'old you tight an' protect you." He smiled devilishly.

"I thought you were serious, that you had important things to talk over. I can see that you do not. Therefore . . ." And I turned to walk away.

" 'Ere, girl, I *am* serious. I do 'ave things to say, and down 'ere is the safest place ta say 'em." He spoke in earnest now, and with the dark lantern in one hand, he stooped and pulled aside a long narrow slab of stone at the foot of the altar.

"Jemmy, a secret passage!" I exclaimed. It was rather like something out of *Horrid Mysteries* or *The Monk*. "If Arabella could see me now, why, she'd be sure that I was a heroine out of a novel."

He chose to ignore my silly remark. "There are steps, but they're narrow and very rough-hewn. Are ya game ta try 'em, girl?" he asked.

"Rather," I answered delightedly, "but do light my way for me, please."

"U-uh, can't. The light'd be too risky, and I've got ta follow you ta close the stone over us," he answered. "Go slowly and feel your way. It's only about eight feet down."

I set my foot on the narrow step, barely able to see more than a foot or two into the pit that seemed to yawn below me. "Oh, Jemmy," I breathed, "this is scary."

"Go on, you're doin' fine, girl. I'm proud o' yer pluck."

"So am I, thank you." I groaned as I turned and backed into the hole, literally feeling my way down the steep flight of narrow, worn little steps, which were scarcely deep enough to rest my feet upon with any security. Below me all was pitchy blackness, the air stuffy and suffused with a damp, musty odor that made me think of graves.

Once I stopped to rest my aching fingers. I had gripped the edges of the steps so hard as I backed down into that void that they locked on me momentarily, arching like claws upon the stone of the steps. Looking up, I could see Jemmy's form just above me, astride the opening like a colossus, his black livery outlined against the night sky by a mass of twinkling stars. It was a ghostly and terrible figure that he presented standing thus, and I wondered for a moment, was I mad to place myself in his hands like this?

"Go on," he whispered, "you're nearly at the bottom. Don't go no . . . any . . . farther. Just stand and wait till I'm beside you."

"Don't worry. I shan't stray a foot farther than I have to," I answered dryly. "Whatever is down here, anyway?"

"Bones o' bishops and monks and such," he answered lightly as he handed the shuttered lantern down through the opening to me. " 'Ere. Mind you grasp it by the 'andle, 'cause it's 'ot, and don't open it till I've got the stone back in place."

"No, seriously, Jemmy," I insisted as he swung himself, agile as a cat, down through the opening after me and turned to slide the flag into place above our heads.

The darkness was impenetrable now, not even the stars and moon visible anymore.

"Bones o' bishops," he reiterated patiently, and I laughed nervously at the thought.

"How silly!"

"Slip the shutter, girl, and I'll show ya," he spoke up, the first time since our meeting above using a normal tone of voice. It sounded extraordinarily loud and echoed oddly in the damp, musty dark. I groped at the lantern in my hand.

"Ouch! It *is* hot," I exclaimed. The shutter opened just then, and I looked about me in surprise and dismay. "You were right. Bones and bones and bones," I repeated in awe as I swung around and around in the tiny low room in which I found myself standing once the lantern was opened and I had light enough to see.

"The abbey crypt, my dear, full o' bones o' bishops and monks and probably a deal o' 'apless rats and other creatures what strayed in and couldn't get out—forced ta spend eternity in the company o' this pious brother'ood," he went on grandly, taking me from wall to wall and introducing me, as it were, to the ranks of rudely crafted oaken shelves that lined the walls from floor to ceiling. Most of them were open and simply heaped with a jumble of rotting, splintered long bones, and large ones, those of arms, legs, and pelvises predominating, the smaller bones having long since vanished into dust.

"There aren't many skulls," I remarked as I looked upon the moldering relics of those ancient monks. There were skulls aplenty, God knew, in Thanatos Abbey itself.

"Naw, Ambrose plundered the best and the soundest o' them long ago. They've formed the basis of 'is collection, I think."

"Charming! I should have known, I suppose," I commented dryly. "What are on these other shelves? The ones sealed with stones and mortar?" I asked, for amongst the many open racks were several that had been sealed off and their coverings carved with crude, nearly illegible Latin inscriptions.

"Those are the 'igh muckety-mucks o' the abbey—bishops

or what-'ave-you. Thy didn't deign to 'ave their bones mixed up wi' the common lot."

"Why didn't they just bury everyone?"

"There's only topsoil ta speak of 'ereabouts; only bedrock with the barest coverin' o' dirt. They dumped 'em in this," he said, patting a big Roman sarcophagus that sat in the center of the small, low crypt. "It was kept full of quicklime. They'd put the corpse in, the lime would reduce it ta bones in short order, and they'd fish 'em out and shelve 'em."

"Disgusting." I grimaced.

"Good as any other way, I reckon." He shrugged. "Didn't leave much for grave robbers to pick over, though," he added thoughtfully and almost wistfully.

"Grave robbers," I exclaimed, "now there's a hateful breed of monster—Burke and Hare and all of their ilk. Digging up maggoty corpses for their gold teeth and wedding rings, selling bodies for dissection. Ugh!"

"I suppose," he mumbled, "that it's a livin' like any other."

"Yes, the perfect living for a gentleman of sensibility and breeding," I sniffed dryly, feeling suddenly waspish. "Pray do let us get off this morbid subject or I swear I shall go mad. You have lured me down here into the bowels of the earth for a purpose. We are safe, we are alone, more or less anyway," I remarked, eyeing our surroundings askance. "Do please speak." I felt edgy, something in his manner having changed in the last few seconds. There was now a sort of sulkiness about him, and although I was not precisely afraid to be there with him, I felt I did not want to stay very long.

" 'Ow do you feel after last night?" he asked gently. "You seem to 'ave come through all right."

"Surprisingly, I am quite calm, rather as if it is all over now and I can begin to forget it, get on with other things—the séance next Friday night, Arabella, things like that."

"Forget it?" he mused. "I realize, Enid, that last night's vote was quite a victory. I knew that it would be. I knew that you'd come out of it all right from the moment you walked into the 'all. You looked splendid—defiant, brave, and utterly commanding . . . beautiful. My 'eart went out to you, really it did, but . . ."

"Is that why you voted for my innocence, Jemmy, because I looked beautiful?" I asked, feeling terribly hurt. Didn't he believe in me after all? Well, what if he didn't! Who was he that I needed his kind regard or trust? I glowered angrily, more at myself than at him.

"No, of course not. I 'ad rather intended to vote 'not

proven' like 'er, but then I 'eard you out and that made up me . . . my . . . mind. I voted as I did because I know you—and because I know what 'appened that night. That's all."

"You know?" I asked, incredulous.

"I believe I do," he said serenely, and then sharply: *"Enid, are you a murderess?"*

"Jemmy," I cried, frightened and hurt all over again. The word "murderess" echoed and reached in the confines of the chamber.

"Answer me, woman," he shouted harshly. "Answer me! *Are you a murderess?"*

"I . . . I don't know. Jemmy, why are you doing this to me? Stop it!" I wailed.

He did not stop, but repeated the question a full half dozen times at least, till, between the sound of his voice and the constant reechoing of it off the stone walls of the crypt, I began to think that I should soon become hysterical. I clapped my hands over my ears in agony.

"Yes . . . no . . . yes . . . yes . . . perhaps I am. I don't know, Jemmy, I truly do not know. Why do you ask again and again?" My voice was a shriek of anguish now, sharp as a knife edge in that terrible place.

"Enid," he said, this time very softly. "Enid, are you a murderess? Is it in your nature to kill?"

"My . . . my nature?" I asked, stopped completely by the abrupt change in the tone and volume of his voice.

"Yes, Enid, think," he urged. "Is it in your nature to kill?"

"No . . . no, it isn't," I replied thoughtfully and with a strong sense of wonder. I had never, in all these years, asked myself that simple question.

"Isn't that the answer, then?" he asked simply.

"Is it? Is it . . . could it be as simple as that?" I asked in a sort of rapt, hopeful wonderment.

"Not quite, my dear, but nearly," he whispered, coming around to grip me in his arms, "nearly."

I backed away, not in alarm, but rather in excitement. I was too nervy to submit to being held, even by a comforting friend. "You know something, Jemmy. You know something. Tell me," I fairly shouted at him.

"No." He shook his head slowly. "I can't do that. It is quite true that I think I know, but I'm not dead sure, and even if I were, I don't think I should tell you, girl."

"It's true, then," I cried, backing away, around the stone sarcophagus. "You know that I did do it."

"Shhhh," he whispered softly, trying to calm me with a gesture of his strong, wide hands.

"Answer me! I did it, didn't I? You know somehow that I did it, don't you?" I shrieked. "Oh, Jemmy, you have me so confused."

"Enid, Enid, calm down. I voted you innocent. Based on all that I 'eard last night, I voted you not guilty."

I whimpered softly, crying fretfully to myself.

"Stop that! Listen to me. It is true that I think I know what 'appened that night—when was it?—June 14, 1836. Right?"

"Yes, yes. Please tell me."

"I can't, girl. *You* must tell *me*," he countered.

"How can I?" I pleaded in despair at making him understand. "I don't remember."

"You *must* remember. You'll never 'ave a moment's peace until you do."

"I . . . I'm afraid, Jemmy," I cried, overwhelmed by panic, knowing that he was right and fearing all the more.

"I know you are, Enid, but trust me. Don't be afraid to know the truth. Until you do know it, you'll 'ave no peace on earth. That old woman, your aunt, will 'ave power over you till the end o' your days, if you don't. She'll 'aunt you from the very grave, she will, if you don't remember what 'appened on that night."

"I'm afraid," I said again.

He took me in his arms then. I made no protest.

"I'm with you, Enid," he whispered, hugging me to his breast, enveloping me in his strong, muscular, protecting arms. "It won't be so bad, will it, if I'm wi' you?"

"No, Jemmy, perhaps it won't," I murmured brokenly, shutting my eyes tightly against the sight of those bones of long-dead monks. If only I could shut my eyes as easily to the undead past; but that, alas, could no longer be.

Jemmy held me for a long, long time, and for a long, long time I clung to him. I really was *afraid*.

Jemmy Burkers may have been right! Perhaps I did have to remember that night so long buried in my mind; the murder night of my parents—but not yet! I did not want to remember it yet—not now! Therefore, for the next few days I refused to admit of any thought but that it was a happy thought, saw no face but that it smiled in return at my own smile, and set about no task but that it was a pleasant task. It was the first peace I had known in some time, and I relished it. The past would have to wait.

And wait it did!

Much of each morning was spent in walking along the cliffs with Arabella, laughing and talking of books and gossip and in such idle chatter as girls of her age are wont to pass the time, but which I, thanks to the enforced solitude and isolation of my own girlhood, had never known. In her charming, sisterly company I enjoyed a taste of that youth which I had never had, gratefully entering into her girlish nonsense as if I myself were eighteen.

Yet never did I forget that my ultimate task—to which I had been set by her father—was to help and polish and guide, as best I could, with an older woman's understanding of the uncertainties of youth. Somehow, despite no little fear on my part that (given my terrible history) I was unworthy and unequal to the task, I began to succeed quite well with her.

Partly, I suppose, due to her unquestioned and unshakable view of me as some rather dashing and romantic figure from a ladies' novel, and partly due to my own firmness in attempting to guide her, she actually bloomed a good deal in those few days between the Saturday night of the tribunal and the Friday evening of the first full-fledged séance of the spirit band.

Our afternoons were spent in cutting patterns and sewing. With fabrics of mine that had only recently arrived from Paris in the final aftermath of my wedding trip to the continent, several of her own dresses which were sent for from home, and with the further aid of a dressmaker from Wadebridge who came each afternoon, Tuesday through Thursday, we set about creating a stylish wardrobe for Miss Arabella Ottermole. Trimming hats, making lists of accessories to be purchased in town or—more excitingly—sent for from Plymouth, engaged still more of our time. Endless hours of each evening were devoted to experimentation with hair style, the practice of facial expressions before a mirror, and all sorts of other little things to enhance the charms of and minimize the liabilities of my lively and ever-more-poised and confident young companion. It was all lighthearted yet purposeful fun and acted as a tonic upon my soul, making me feel somehow more worthwhile, less bitter and closed off from the world around me.

Or perhaps for the first time in years I began to see that the world around me might not be so terrible after all.

On several afternoons we were invited to take tea with Madame De'Ath in her candlelit salon. Once we actually dined there with her alone—but only once—for she generally dined with Jemmy each evening, treating him as an equal in those private moments, as she could not before most others.

On those occasions when we joined her, the old woman was at her most magical and spellbinding best. Arabella was fascinated, as indeed was I, and I could see that the old woman was herself trying to give the girl some encouragement, praising each new little touch of style or manner in a nonchalant and subtle way, gently discouraging little gaucheries, letting the child talk on of her books and few experiences of life, listening with complete attention and interest. It was a charming and a gracious thing for the old woman who—one might think—must find a rather plain and naive eighteen-year-old girl somewhat tedious. If such was the case, she did not show it by even so much as the drooping of an eye.

Those afternoon teas, combined with our morning chats as we walked, and the general improvement of her looks and wardrobe, worked something akin to a small miracle on Arabella. She really blossomed and took on stature, and as she did, I found myself taking a proprietary pride in her.

And then, a rather lovely thing happened, something that increased my own personal happiness. We had bid adieu to my mother-in-law and were leaving the salon when she called me back. Arabella went on to her own room, and I returned to face Madame De'Ath.

"Do not think, my dear, that I am unaware of what you are doing for that girl," the old woman said softly.

"Doing, madame?" I asked in some embarrassment and confusion.

"Yes, doing, my dear." She smiled, looking up at me over the silver tea things with those wide, lustrous dark eyes of hers, so youthful and alive despite her great age. "She is an awkward, motherless girl, and you are guiding her into bloom. It is a kind, generous, and lovely thing to do, and I merely wished you to realize that someone was observing, approving, and being pleased by your most excellent efforts."

"Madame," I stammered, "I can assure you that I do it . . . I . . . It gives me pleasure, madame. My motives are entirely selfish."

"In some senses, yes," she acknowledged. "There is selfishness in growing a rose, in raising a child, in giving love and guidance where it is needed, but it is a small sin compared to the beauty of the flower, the joy of the child, the sense of security and contentment that the guidance and the love bestow."

I stood blushing like a fool before her.

"I am not very good at receiving praise, madame," I mumbled at last.

"And yet it is praise that you have earned, child. You must learn to accept it with a gracious nod of thanks. Will you not try?"

"I will, madame." I nodded solemnly, feeling truly like a child before her, thanked her for her remarks, and turned to leave.

"You have the promise of being a fine woman one day, Enid. Only be patient," she called after me down the candle-lit room.

"You are kind, madame, and give me hope. I shall try to be worthy of all your good thoughts."

The doors closed behind me and I stood for a moment in the hall outside the salon. My eyes welled with tears of my mixed emotions. I felt terrible—guilty and sneaking like a thief. She had praised me so kindly, and what was I doing in return but trying to riddle out the well-kept secrets of her very life.

And those well-kept secrets, I felt sure, were to be prized from the Duchesse de la Cressonière's ever-more-fascinating memoirs. Each night before I slept I tried to find time to read just a bit at least, finding them quite shocking really, smacking as they did of the bizarre decadence of pre-Revolutionary Paris and the debaucheries of a bored and jaded aristocracy. As I read on, I found I had not lost sight of my original interest. I was still endeavoring to learn if I could the real identity of Madame Henriette De'Ath.

I had from the first believed she was far more than she claimed to be, but as I read more deeply into those volumes (the mere mention of which had caused such a reaction in my normally placid mother-in-law), I began to find that I did not wish to identify her at all with such a life and such times as those of the duchesse. And *now*, with the old lady praising me, trusting me as she did, I felt so much the worse.

Yet, the more I read, the more I realized that I was indeed entering into the world of Madame De'Ath's remote youth. A certain distasteful conviction grew within me, a seedling of suspicion from the first, that now came to full flower: Madame De'Ath was herself the author of these words.

Madame De'Ath was herself the Duchesse Eugénie-Marie

de la Cressonière. I hated the very idea, resisted the thought with all my might, and yet the more I read, the more I became convinced. If only I could become so engrossed in the content of the memoirs that I lost sight of the author as a person and could make of her just such a heroine as I sensed Arabella was making of me.

Such a trick of the mind would be a godsend, would enable me to forget Madame De'Ath as I read the book, separating once more the identity of the young and ever-more-debauched duchesse-to-be from that of the grand, gracious old lady whom I knew as Henriette De'Ath. It would have been more satisfactory that way.

Which is not to say that it would be the more accurate. Indeed not! The mystery remained. Who was Madame De'Ath? Her kindness to me did not make my task easier. I felt ever more guilty in attempting to probe that past she so obviously wished to hide with romantic evasions.

Yet probe I did!

And to be honest, the memoirs of the duchesse were one devil of a good read, regardless of the ultimate answer to the mystery of Henriette De'Ath!

And so, though plagued throughout that day with many reservations and feelings of guilt, yet that night I read on regardless. Was this the way Pandora felt when she decided to open the box? I wondered to myself as I rolled over in my bed, made myself comfortable, and opened the book into the yellow light of my bedside candle. Perhaps, but enough of thinking! I would escape, instead, into the romantic world of the adventurous duchesse:

The licentiousness and peculiar devotions of the Rites of Isis and the attendaant, even more outré Rites of Osiris troubled me from time to time over the spring and summer of 1784, and occasionally I even dared to wonder what the nuns who had schooled us in the convent would have thought of so many of their aristocratic former pupils being immersed in such uninhibited rituals. Yet, I plunged myself into them even as grossly as did any of the other fashionable young and old noble-women of Paris, even including my own sister. It was, after all, the thing to do, and I, like all the others caught up in that heady and dissolute time before the Revolution, kept up with the heights of fashion whatever they might be, wherever they might lead. Were we not, after all, wealthy and reckless and free from all the petty conventions that bound the masses? Other than an occasional thought given to the nuns who had schooled me, I never dwelt at all upon my Catholic religion at the time, for it could hardly compare in excitement and daring with the mysteries of Egyptian Freemasonry and the tangled webs of glamour spun by the magnetic Comte Alessandro and his beauteous wife Lorenza and their lovely young assistant and disciple. And so, I must perforce admit that for many long and exciting months, thoughtlessly, I allowed myself to be caught willingly and willfully in their toils.

But then, one night in the autumn of the year, there came a time of reckoning for me; a single moment in which I came face to face with the mirror-clear reality of the utterly debased and sinful mire in which I had wallowed, virtually unthinking, for the previous few months. That realization, frightening and dramatic as it was, changed the course of my very life and redeemed me from the teetering edge of the Pit itself. And it came about in the following manner:

It was the habit of the Grand Copt, as Cagliostro was called, to enter upon us at some point in our mysteries, and his manner of entry was grandiose in the extreme. There would be a loud and arresting chiming of distant bells and then the "heavens" would literally open up, the arched vault of the ceiling over our heads, splitting like the halves of a shell, and from the center, his feet set upon a golden orb of great size, would descend our Master, the Grand Copt of the Rites of Osiris of the Order of Egyptian Freemasonry, naked as a newborn babe save for a diamond star upon his forehead and a living serpent coiling and writhing in his hand.

Thus unattired in the guise of the Ancient Wisdom, the Truth of the World, he would come to us and command us, those of us yet clothed, to disrobe, dispensing with our raiment, to bare ourselves "body and soul" to "Truth"; the which, of course, we did without hesitation. Was he not the Grand Copt, the demigod of our profane worship?

Then, stepping from the great golden ball upon which he had made his dramatic descent, the comte would alight upon the small carpeted stage in the center of the room and recline thereon, exhorting us to be diligent in our application to our studies, instructing us in the wisdom of the ancient and occult forces of the universe, teaching us to relieve ourselves of the binding control of men who had heretofore been our masters, and who must now be cast out and made no more than slaves to our own licentious passions and pleasures, even as we had once been slaves to theirs. It was tempting and daring thinking to us who had been raised to believe we must count our beads and submit to husbands and fathers and bear sons for the aristocracy and the Church.

At the end of his instruction we, one by one, would approach him and do our personal obeisance (the nature of which must ever remain a secret from the common run of mankind) before his sacred and godlike person. This farewell having been enacted, the Grand Copt would remount the golden ball and rise again until he had disappeared from our sight and the vaulted ceiling reclosed behind him to the accompanying clangor of those distant bells.

Following this ritual, the music would rise to a new pitch, strange wines and exotic foods would be passed around to us, and we would take our pleasure amongst ourselves or in the pleasant company of the agreeable dancing girls who were at once our handmaidens, our sisters, and our slaves.

On this particular night of which I speak, I had been singled out by the Grand Copt for an especially fine performance of my sacred duties in the Rites of Isis and for my "beauty of body and soul," as he put it. I had drunk deeply of the heady wine and breathed deep of the rich incense-laden air, which seemed at once to both arouse and yet drug the senses. His praise on top of this excess emboldened me to do a thing that I had longed to do; dare a thing that I had long desired to do.

The handmaiden and companion of the magnificent Lorenza di Cagliostro, the slim young guide of my first night in the house at No. 1 Rue Saint-Claude, had ever been an object of my curiosity and, later, my desire. I wished to know her, to share some intimacy of regard with her, to share her friendship and her affections. In short, she had become an object of awe and mystery to me, and I wished to know and be known by her.

Throughout each of the rites, she had sat with stiff and regal dignity at the side of the Grand Mistress, and like the illustrious Lorenza herself, neither partook of the Mysteries nor appeared to wish to do so. They both sat above us all, watching with hooded eyes, instructing and guiding us, but never one with us, never joining in our rituals, our revelries, or our—how else to say it—our debauches. Somehow this very aloofness fired my desires and whetted my interest the more.

I knew by now who she was, this slim young girl, diaphanously robed, regal and aloof with a sophistication beyond her years, sitting at the side of the Grand Mistress. She was called Clotilde du Roc, and while her antecedents were unknown, it was a fact that she had been the mistress of Mesmer at the age of thirteen, had left him shortly before his fall from favor at court, and had joined the ménage of the Comte and Comtesse di Cagliostro. Under their tutelage she had become, at sixteen, the second-most-desired and sought-after woman in Paris, ranking only just behind the magnificent Lorenza herself, as an object of passion.

Every nobleman and courtier of Versailles desired her and hoped to have her, although few had actually attained to her favors, whatever their aspirations, for her career as a courtesan was guided by the expert hand of Comte Alessandro himself and she was obedient to his training in all things. At present she was rumored to be the mistress of no less a personage than the great and powerful Cardinal de Rohan, who, although he would soon fall into disgrace over the notorious "affair of the necklace," was at that time at the height of his influence at court. It was a current scandal in Paris that Clotilde du Roc carried with her a gift from her lover, de Rohan, which was as inappropriate as it was shocking—a large and priceless crucifix of bloodred rubies hung on a rosary of huge and perfectly matched pearls; part payment, it was suggested, for delights unsurpassed by any of the libertine cardinal's many previous mistresses. He was, they said, her utter slave, and through her, Cagliostro's slave as well.

This, then, was the imperious young girl who sat beside the Grand Mistress of the Rites of Isis; this, then, was the object of my every waking thought. I was entranced by her and jealous of — I disapproved of her, yet envied her, wanted to be her, yet hated her. Most of all, I was curious, and that curiosity, fired by the drugged wine and perfumed air, filled me with strange desires. All around me in the dim light of the great mirrored hall with its black silk divans, the sounds of pleasure reached my ears, riotous and suggestive. I brooded, my eyes searching through the moving darkness past the writhing bodies of antic dancers to the regal beauty who sat on the dais beside Lorenza di Cagliostro. My red-painted handmaiden was bored by my inattention and reached out beseechingly from her languorous pose upon the floor at my feet. I brushed her aside with an oath. Arising from the divan, I approached the dais slowly, walking carefully and purposefully amidst the bodies and cushions and the spilled wine upon the floor. In the perfumed air, the sound of that strange atonal and abandoned music jangled, thrilling down my nerves like fire as I steeled myself for what I wished to do. I was resolved. Tonight I would bestow the kiss of Isis upon the lips of Clotilde du Roc.

I bowed low before the grand mistress, made the sacred signs of the order, and then approached the lovely girl at her side. She looked down at me with those wondrous, wide dark eyes of hers, and in them I saw so much—a wisdom borne of age, though she herself was young, understanding and pity, power and madness, majesty and sensuality, fire and ice—all embodied in one great pair of luminous woman's eyes.

I opened my mouth to speak but the words stuck in my throat.

She was shaking her lovely, darkly golden head slowly from side to side. And then she spoke, the first words that she ever addressed to me personally, and the very last as well. "Sister in Isis, the way of Lesbos is not my way; the kiss of Isis is not my kiss."

No matter how gentle the tone, the rebuke was staggering, striking me to my heart's core even as would the sting of a lash. I reeled back as if I had been struck, looking horror-stricken with utter humiliation, into the depths of those fathomless eyes of hers; saw her shake her head in sorrow and pity as if she looked upon a lost soul. *I, a lost soul!*

I left that house—the house called No. 1 Rue Saint-Claude—in the chill of that cold autumn night in November of 1784 and never returned again. Even now, I often wonder if the terrors and trials of my subsequent life have not been the price I have had to pay for my sins, and indeed, my shriven soul trembles even now at the nightmare of debasement and debauchery from which I was saved on that night by the reproachful, pitying eyes of the beautiful and majestically lovely and aloof young woman known to all Paris as the shocking and notorious courtesan Clotilde du Roc.

Whatever she may have been, she saved me from a debasement far worse than her own, and I for one shall remember her gratefully till I yield up this life of sorrows.

I laid the book down with a sickening feeling in my stomach. No! I would not, could not believe that Madame De'Ath, *my* Madame De'Ath, had written those words! And yet, God help me, I knew it must be so! The very turns of phrase reminded me of her. Every word that I read reminded me somehow of her.

So long ago! In 1784! That was so long ago—sixty-six years! A lifetime. Had that wonderful old woman *ever*—even a lifetime ago—committed the sins that the duchesse described and attributed to herself so shamelessly?

The very thought made me sick at my stomach. It could not be—and yet it *was*. I knew it was! It must be! I put the book aside and resolved to read no more. I no longer wanted to know. Let the Duchesse de la Cressonière rest in the peace and obscurity that she had chosen for herself.

And so I shut down the lid on Pandora's box. I could not know then that it would not work; that the lock was already broken past all hope of repair . . . .

# 11

# THE SÉANCE

While yet a boy I sought for ghosts, and sped
Through many a listening chamber, cave and ruin,
And starlit wood, with fearful steps pursuing
Hopes of high talk with the departed dead.
                    —*Shelley*

I am thy father's spirit,
Doom'd for a certain term to walk the night,
. . . But that I am forbid
To tell the secrets of my prison-house,
I could a tale unfold whose lightest word
Would harrow up thy soul, freeze thy young blood.
                    —*Shakespeare*

We gathered in the salon at nine, Arabella and I both in deep-hued, high-necked somber silks, Lucas and Mr. Pond in their usual plain, ill-fitting black long coats and waistcoats, Mrs. Pond in a simple dark gray worsted pinned at the throat with her shell cameo. Mr. Ottermole arrived in mourning garb, having just returned in some haste from funeral obsequies conducted some miles away in another parish. He looked at his daughter, pretty and demure in her rather stylish and severe dark dress which fit well and made her seem slimmer, and glowed with a wonderful fatherly pride. It was all the reward I could have asked for my efforts, and more.

Madame De'Ath wore a plain steel-gray wig, deep purple gown, and a simple demi-parure of gray baroque pearls and huge dark purple amethysts set in heavy old-fashioned silver settings.

Jemmy, in his evening livery, saw to our comforts like the good servant that he pretended to be. We only waited upon

Ambrose and my Aunt Augusta. When they arrived, the séance would begin.

I sat stiffly, feeling all at once a nervousness that rather surprised. What, after all, had I to fear? My aunt had done her very worst only the week before, and I had come away from her challenge as an accepted member of the company—accepted at least by most. Augusta Tregaron and Enoch Pond were forced by the votes of the others to tolerate my presence. Ambrose, of course, had voted as he did more for the sake of my aunt and the need to remain in her good graces than because he actually believed me guilty. Or so I tried to tell myself. I still could not bear to think he could have married me believing me to be a murderess—and yet, that is really just what I knew he had done; married me truly thinking I had murdered three people. Why does a man marry such a woman? Why, for that matter, is a man so obsessed with death and its mysteries as was Ambrose? I wondered.

The nervousness grew in me and I could not yet understand why. Through this sitting, or séance as they called it, we would be attempting to contact my Uncle Llewellyn's spirit—nonsense, of course, as well I knew, but necessary to whet the appetite of Augusta Tregaron, reassure her of the possibility of contacting the dead, and wring some money out of her for the "Thanatological Foundation" which Ambrose claimed that he wished to found with her aid. Nothing in that for me to be nervous about!

Yet I *was* nervous.

And I should not have been, for only that morning they had explained it all to me, Ambrose and Jemmy; that we were going to skip the automatic writing and other small tricks and preliminaries with which they had at first intended to ensnare my aunt. Ambrose had decided that she was ripe already for the first full-scale séance and so that night "contact" would be established between ourselves and "my uncle." It would all be trickery and sham, of course, but only we four—Jemmy, Ambrose, Madame De'Ath, and myself—would know that. To the others, it would all seem genuine.

What, I had asked, would be the illusions that they used? They refused to answer, feeling that the less I knew, the more natural would be my own reactions to what I saw. I, after all, was supposed to be the utter skeptic and play the part of one who was only reluctantly convinced by the startling "proof" that the séance would produce before my very doubting eyes. My reactions, even more than those of the others in the spirit band, would be important to my aunt. I must, they urged, play my part well.

Maybe that was it—*stage fright!*

The séance, after all, was little more than a performance, or "gaff," as Jemmy termed it in his own cockney way.

Yet I could tell that Ambrose did not think so. He pretended that he thought of it only as a sham, but his pretense was not quite enough to fool me. I had come to realize that one reason that he kept himself closeted with my aunt was that with her he could be himself—expose to her his true feelings and his own absolute belief in the possibility of life after death. Or his *need* to believe. Before his mother and Jemmy and me, all of whom believed in nothing supernatural and who looked upon séances as a clever charade, he must pretend that he felt as we did (fooling none of us, by the way), but in the company of my Aunt Augusta—why, with her he could confess the truth of his own insane convictions and meet with nothing but approval and respectful attention. Yes, Ambrose De'Ath actually believed in the existence of departed spirits on the other side of the veil as surely as he believed—or wanted to believe?—that I was a murderess.

Suppose he was right? And on both counts?

No, it was not stage fright that had me so nervous that night. It was the fear that despite Jemmy's assurances, despite all the belief that had been expressed in me, and despite the fact that I knew this séance was set up to gull a fear-ridden, rich old lady out of her pounds and pence, yet I was still afraid that Ambrose and my aunt might be the wiser ones.

They believed me guilty—or *wanted* me guilty—and perhaps they were right. They believed that Uncle Llewellyn would contact us tonight. Perhaps he would! Suppose whatever illusions and trickery had been planned by Jemmy and Ambrose failed or was set aside by the *real* Llewellyn Tregaron? *What then?*

And how would I know? I was not a party to whatever tricks they had set up to fool her. I was supposed to sit there safe in the knowledge that whatever I saw was utter tomfoolery and sham.

Yet, suppose it wasn't all sham? Just suppose . . .

I had not time to finish my thought. The doors to the salon swung open just then and Aunt Augusta entered, leaning lightly on the arm of her favorite "nephew," Ambrose. Black-clad skeleton and black-clad crone, they made their way in a slow and stately dead march to the little cluster of gilded chairs and settees where we all awaited them.

Ambrose nodded, avoiding my eyes as he generally did of late, but Augusta Tregaron glared at me with a sort of hot, triumphant gleam in her hard old eyes. You shall reap your just reward, she seemed to say. You shall learn the truth, my girl. Although she said not one word of this aloud, yet I could almost hear the words assault my ears as she stared at me in that fashion. She had come full circle in her thinking. I realized that now she actually wanted me there that night; that she was actually looking forward to my participation in the séance.

My nervousness increased a thousandfold.

"Ladies and gentlemen, members of our spirit band both new and old, I bid you welcome," Madame De'Ath greeted us at last. "As you know, it was originally intended that on Friday last we spend the evening in acquainting the new-comers amongst us—Miss Tregaron and my daughter-in-law, Enid—with the ways of automatic writing, chiromancy, the tarot, and various other methods of attempting to penetrate the veil and reach out to those souls who have gone before. The Reverend Mr. Pond is particularly adept in the recent American phenomenon of 'spirit rapping' as discovered by his fellow townspeople in Hydesville, New York State, the Fox sisters. 'Spirit rapping' is a somewhat crude term to my way of thinking, but nevertheless an apt one." She smiled, nodding with charming deference to Enoch Pond. He responded with the puffing pride of a pouter pigeon.

"Our plans were interrupted by events upon which there need be no further elaboration on my part. We were all a party to them and they are quite behind us now." This last she said very firmly, as if to warn the company that she would brook no further remarks on the subject. "However," she went on smoothly, "because of the delay and because of a certain natural exuberance which I think we all share, to get on in earnest with our experiments, my son Ambrose has suggested we dispense with further preliminaries and attempt a full-scale séance at once."

There was a general murmuring of approval amongst us at this suggestion.

"Excellent." She smiled, clapping her long, slender, and be-jeweled old hands together in delight. "We are agreed that we shall get on with it. But, dear friends, before we enter the spirit room and begin our journey into the realms of darkness, I have asked the Reverend Pond to say over us a prayer of blessing for this, our most serious and pious undertaking." This last my mother-in-law said simply and unaffectedly, yet with the slightest, tiniest curling of her lip, so subtle that I doubted it was noticed by any but me. She was my true soulmate in that at least—she could laugh and enjoy her own hypocrisy.

The Reverend Pond rose, harumphing, from the settee and stood before the fireplace with a suddenly put-on expression of piety and that look of manly, fervent, two-fisted religious zeal that seems to characterize certain poorly educated, self-deceiving preachers on both sides of the great Atlantic.

"Let us pray," he said, raising his hands heavenward in a big, sweeping gesture that I judged to be rather dangerous in a room full of delicate furniture and *objets d'art*. (Having already caused some small chaos of that nature myself during my attempted flight from the room the previous Friday night, perhaps I was overly sensitive.) At his gesture we all bowed our heads—all save I, that is, who chose rather to nod slightly in order to get a good view of his performance "in the pulpit," so to speak.

"Oh, God," he roared out abruptly, "we are sinners" (I could have guessed *that* was coming!) "ripe with all our manifold sins and wickednesses naked before thine eyes. Yet, O God, do we seek the ways of truth and delve amongst the paths of righteousness for thy name's sake. Sorely tried," he shouted, as if he thought the Lord to be rather hard of hearing (heaven, after all, *was* a long way off), "sorely tried though we be with our iniquities, yet hear us and grant to us success in our humble and heartfelt endeavour of this night to come. Direct, O great director of all, our steps on the path. Lead us through the veil and grant that we may call upon the spirits of your loving children gone before and carry back with us their message of hope and of the life to come.

"Trusting in thee, O God, we enter into the dangers and adversities of this night with humbled hearts and unconquerable souls, soldiers in thy army, servants of thy right hand." Presumptuous prater, would he never stop?

Mercifully he paused for a great gulp of breath just then, and Madame De'Ath broke in serenely, "Oh, thank you, Reverend Pond. That was truly inspiring."

"What, what? I . . ." he began, goggle-eyed and open-mouthed, like a great netted salmon. He was about to say that he had not finished, but thought the better of it, conceding to the inevitable with a mighty "Amen" deeply intoned.

"Amen," we all responded, several with audible sighs of relief. Arabella made a little face at me and then caught herself, looking across the room at Lucas, fearful of his having seen her reaction to his father's benediction. He had seen, and he replied by raising his eyes to heaven and shrugging his shoulders quite eloquently. Arabella giggled behind her hand. I made a mental note to remind her never to laugh behind her hand—it was too gauche and moreover had the disadvantage of hiding that pretty smile which was one of her best assets.

"And now, ladies and gentlemen, we shall enter the séance room, which has been set aside for the purpose of spirit communication. None of you save Ambrose and my personal servant, Mr. Burkers, are yet acquainted with it, and there will be some admonition necessary once we have entered, due to peculiarities in the history of the room itself, but more of that later. Jemmy, the panel, please," Madame De'Ath instructed.

"This way, please," Jemmy Burkers said, directing our attention to a narrow panel of painted wood beside the small fireplace before which we were gathered. At a touch of his fingers to a certain portion of the gilded molding, the entire panel swung inward, revealing a corridor, like a tunnel, at the end of which we could see the dim light of flickering candles.

With a few gasps of surprise and several nervous titters and humorous remarks about secret passages, we stepped one by one over the threshold and into the stone-lined corridor. Mrs. Pond was just ahead of me, timid as a titmouse. Suddenly she stopped and grasped my hand impulsively in hers.

"Oh, Madame Ambrose, do stay close. This is ever so eerie."

"Indeed it is, but I am sure we are all quite safe."

"Will you forgive me, dear?" she whispered in my ear.

"Forgive you?"

"Yes. I dared not say I thought you were innocent outright, although I knew you must be. It was hard enough to vote 'not proven.' Enoch was furious with me and said I was disloyal and foolish."

"You believe me to be innocent?" I reiterated in surprise.

"Of course. You are a terribly brave and defiant young woman—rather too outspoken, I think—but I do admire you so in a way, and I cannot think that a child, as you were then, could kill her own parents, her own mother. It is too unthinkable."

She shivered slightly and went on, "It was as much as I dared, to vote 'not proven.' I have never defied Enoch so . . ."

"And it was much appreciated, Mrs. Pond. I think you, too, are brave."

"Do you?" she asked in surprise.

"It is not an easy thing, I think, to disagree with such a strong-willed man as is Mr. Pond," I murmured tactfully, "and I thank you for your faith in me as well." How odd, I reflected briefly, that others seemed to have more belief in me than I did myself. We squeezed hands, Mrs. Peggy and I, as if to reassure each other, and entered the room at the end of that long dark corridor.

It was a stone chamber, very large and very nearly square, very chill and dank and strangely drafty, although there were no windows and no doors save the one by which we entered. The floors were of flagstone pavings joined with mortar.

In its exact center was set a huge round table with ornately gilded legs. Its surface was covered entirely in black baize. Ranged around it were ten wooden chairs, straight of back and hard of seat, armless all, save one, and that was a large thronelike armchair of gilt wood upholstered in black horsehair. It was set some few inches above the others, as if on a small dais. The whole arrangement made my head swim with a sudden and overwhelming sense of having lived through all this before, which was nonsense of course, but frightening nonetheless.

The only illumination came from clusters of black tapers burning in two tall iron candlestands which were centered against opposite walls, and from one small blue flame that leaped from hot coals in the pierced brass covered pan of a tall seventeenth-century *parfum* set against the center of the nearest wall.

As we filed into that austere and chilling room, we stepped back against the cold walls nearest the door and waited. The last to come in was Madame De'Ath herself, leaning for support upon the arm of Jemmy Burkers with one hand while her other grasped a tall, elegant walking stick with a huge knob of dark, satiny silver set with jewels and pearls.

"Pray forgive me, dear companions, if I avail myself of a somewhat more comfortable seat than those afforded to you, but I must have a chair with arms and some cushioning to support my old bones. Pray forgive the impertinence."

And of course, without a murmur, we all did. Aunt Augusta may have sniffed slightly. She, after all, was nearly as old, but if she felt slighted, she had the grace to make no issue of it. I, for one, was rather amused, seeing how the clever old woman used her supposed infirmity to make sure that she obtained the seat she wished and probably needed in order to control the effects she would be using in the séance. Thus, one small and seemingly humanitarian concession to her age would lead to the rigging of the rest of the events to follow.

Jemmy conducted Madame De'Ath to her chair, set on its slightly raised platform, and with its back to the corner formed by the left-hand and farthest walls, and saw her safely into it.

"Remove this, please," she requested, handing him her walking stick, which he then placed in the corridor outside the room. Pulling closed a heavy wooden door, ancient and worn and set with wide iron bands, he sealed off the passage behind us. He slid the big iron bolt, and we became virtual prisoners in that great square cell. "Now, as to the seating, I shall decide that at once. Hmmmm," she mused, "as much by whim as by logic, I expect. Yes, Miss Tregaron, you shall take the seat directly before you. It is easier that way," and Ambrose, ever the good and attentive nephew, helped the old woman to her seat at once. Placed thus, she faced the farthest wall, with the nearest wall at her back. The wooden door to the corridor was behind her to the left and the *parfum* directly so.

"Ambrose, dear, pray sit beside Miss Tregaron to attend upon her during the séance." That placed him directly opposite his mother, with the nearest wall to his left and the right-hand wall to his right and the angle formed by them directly behind him.

"Lucas Pond next," she directed, and he took his seat beside Ambrose with his back to the right-hand wall, one of the two candlestands behind him. "Enid beside Master Pond, and dear Mrs. Peggy, do take the chair to the right of her."

This set Mrs. Pond and me with our backs to the angle formed by the right-hand and far walls in one of the darkest parts of that dim room. I sat with Lucas to the left and his mother on the other side.

"Now, let me see. Mr. Ottermole, I shall have you sit beside Miss Tregaron on her left, with your daughter beside you." That placed the Ottermoles across the table from Mrs. Pond and myself, with their backs to the angle formed by the nearer and left-hand walls. The door to the corridor was just to Mr. Ottermole's right.

"Reverend Pond, you shall sit by me," she said with devastating charm as the big red-faced preacher took his chair, deeming it to be a seat of honor. He faced his son across the table; the left-hand wall was at his back and the candlestand behind his chair, Miss Ottermole to his right and Madame De'Ath to his left.

Now only one chair remained vacant, and that one Jemmy Burkers quickly filled. Thus situated, he had the far wall at his back, Mrs. Pond to his left, and Madame De'Ath to his right. He faced my Aunt Augusta across the table.

"Now," she said lightly, "have we all settled in? Excellent!" She surveyed us all through the dim light of the room with the expression of a kindly disposed schoolmistress.

"Are we ready to begin, madame?" Jemmy asked.

"I think not quite yet, Jemmy. Ambrose must speak to us first about the character of this room," she said. "Do you not agree it is best, my dear?" This last was directed across the table to Ambrose.

"I do, *ma mère*," Ambrose replied solemnly. "Ladies and gentlemen of the spirit band, this room, as you can see, has but one entrance, and that barred by a heavy iron-bound door. It is windowless as well, and therefore would seem to be perfectly suited to use as a séance room. So indeed it is—from the purely physical standpoint—but this room has an unfortunate history, which has prevented us from using it for a large gathering such as this up until this evening.

"It seems to have been used, in former times, as a place of confinement and—dare I say it without a shudder passing through us, each and every one?—a place of torture."

"Oh, dear," Mrs. Pond cried out in alarm.

"But this was a holy place, an abbey," Miss Ottermole put in. "Monks did not do such horrid things."

"I can see that I have neglected my daughter's education sadly," Mr. Ottermole remarked, adding dryly, "An accurate history of the more lurid aspects of popery, my dear, is unfit for childish ears, but you are a young woman now. Remind me later to fill you in."

We all laughed at that small bit of wit, but were quickly, brought back to the main issue as Ambrose cleared his throat pointedly.

"In the course of our few private sittings in this room, my mother and I have found that great personal force and resistance is needed to drive away those aimless and hostile spirits whose bodies were maimed and tortured in this room and whose anguished souls were released into this atmosphere. They are vague, aimless, mindless spirits, trapped here at the scene of their terrible final dissolution, unable to rise heavenward; too martyred by their deaths to warrant hell.

"I do not mean to frighten or alarm any of you. These

beings, while occasionally aggressive in their outward manifestations, are quite harmless to our flesh-and-blood selves, and should be ignored—indeed, *must* be ignored, for it is only our minds that may prove vulnerable to their wild ravings. Should these tortured creatures seek to penetrate your thoughts, put from your minds all else but the goal of this night. Do not let these beings gain entry through the portals of your minds. Do you all hear and understand?"

We all nodded in solemn but timid assurance. The seeds of fear had been effectively planted, however, and we would all be easy prey for whatever tricks they had up their sleeves to fool the company. Artful!

"Our sole aim here tonight is to attempt to reach beyond the veil of this life to the departed soul known in life as Llewellyn Tregaron, brother to Miss Augusta Tregaron here present and uncle to my wife Enid, also here present. This attempt to reach his soul has been prompted by a remarkable incident which took place on the night of December 9 last between the hours of ten and twelve midnight. The Reverend Mr. Pond and his wife, Jemmy Burkers, and myself were witnesses to the incident.

"We had been having chocolate in the salon and were discussing the phenomenon of automatism, there being many forms at which my mother is quite adept, owing to her receptive and clairvoyant nature. In an attempt to demonstrate the correct method of performing 'automatic writing,' my mother took pencil to paper, using the simple expediency of repeating her signature over and over upon the page. This she continued to do for some time, hoping that a straying spirit might enter the vessel of her body and use her hand to express itself.

"The rest, I believe, is generally known to you all. Gradually, over a period of time, a signature began to emerge, the signature not of my mother, Henriette De'Ath, but rather that of one Llewellyn Tregaron. At the very time that this was occurring here in Cornwall, the soul of Llewellyn Tregaron was in the act of departing this life and passing out of his body some two-hundred-odd miles away in London.

"Moreover, that name had a somewhat familiar ring, and I sensed that I partly knew the man, whosoever he was. When the next batch of London papers arrived by post, there in the obituaries I found the name of Llewellyn Tregaron. I then realized that I had met the man many years before and that I had known his late brother Morgan as well. By some chance, some miracle, we in this house had opened ourselves to the spirit world at the very moment of Llewellyn Tregaron's passing, and he, aware that a friendly soul—if not an intimate one—was reaching out into the unknown, was able to make contact with us, however briefly, through the medium of my beloved mother.

"Realizing the implications of this occurrence to the success of my researches into thanatology, I flew with all possible speed along the high road to London in order to see if the Tregaron family would be willing to aid me in my endeavors. The rest you know. I have come back to Thanatos Abbey the richer for having a lovely wife and a new aunt who has proved a deep companion to my researches into the realms of life after death.

"And now, enough," he exclaimed, the tone of his voice changing abruptly from the cold, droning monotone of his long introductory remarks to one of lightness and some charm. "I return you to the care and guidance of my dear mother, who is an adept in these areas of animal magnetism and spirit communication which we shall now attempt. *Ma mère.*" He nodded his skull face deferentially in the direction of Madame De'Ath.

"Excellent, Ambrose. Now, dear friends, I shall instruct you in your several duties. First, we shall all join hands around this table, do you understand? *Bien.*" She smiled as we all nodded and took our partners' hands in our own. Mrs. Pond's, as I held it, was plump and warm and unpleasantly clammy to the touch; her son's was a rather dry and large hand, all knuckles, the grip a bit overtight. I looked about me to see that all of us seemed a trifle embarrassed or overly eager or cool, depending on our several dispositions. Having gripped our partners' hands as we were instructed, we found that in doing so we were forced to sit up quite straight in our seats with our arms widely extended, for the table, being very large, was really intended to seat more than ten.

"All right, you may relax for the nonce," she said, and we all let go and leaned back in our chairs "but once I have finished instructing you, and the circle is reformed, *it may not be broken for any reason whatsoever.* Is that clear? To make sure that you understand, if the circle is broken whilst I am in a trance—as may well happen—or if one of us is being used by a spirit or a spirit guide for communicative purposes of any sort, the breaking of the circle may endanger my life or the life of any of you. It is only the combined strength of our joined forces, linked both physically and psychically by our clasped hands, that protects us from the depredations of the world beyond the veil. If we break the spirit circle formed by our linked hands, we risk a rending of the veil and an invasion by those restless, undisciplined souls that have not yet found their eternal peace and which wander aimlessly in search of they know not what.

"Do I make myself understood?"

We all reiterated our solemn understanding of our duties. All very clever. With our hands linked, and forced into the upright position that the size of the table made necessary, we would be uncomfortable, intent on the seriousness of our endeavor, and easily distracted from whatever manipulations they would have to perform to create the effects that I knew we would shortly be entertained with. The key to much of it would be the link between Madame De'Ath and Jemmy Burkers, and I made a small wager with myself that whatever secret breaks occurred in the spirit circle, they would be between the hands of those two collaborators.

"Now," she went on, "I shall ask Master Lucas and his father, the Reverend Mr. Pond, to extinguish the candles in the stands behind their chairs. When they have done this, we shall be in virtual blackness. They shall have to grope back to their seats, but once I hear that they are reseated, then we shall all join hands and begin.

"Jemmy Burkers shall be my earthly guide should I fall into a trance, since he sits beside me and knows what it is that my trance state entails. Should I lose consciousness, it is from him that you shall take your instruction. Now, with your aid, I shall attempt to enter a trance that renders my own soul unconscious and opens my body to animation by some friendly spirit—in this case, hopefully, that of Llewellyn Tregaron himself, or if not him, then one who has been in communication with his deceased soul and will act as a spirit guide for us.

"I must enjoin you all to be absolutely silent unless you are instructed otherwise. Your only duties, other than to keep this circle closed at all times, are to listen and watch and—above all—to concentrate with every fiber of your being upon the name of Llewellyn Tregaron. Do you all understand?"

"Yes," we all replied as one.

"Is there anyone among you who feels unable or unwilling to participate? If so, please speak now."

None spoke up.

"Splendid. Master Lucas, Reverend, will you each perform your duties, please?"

The two men rose and one by one extinguished the

candles, the Reverend Pond with a bronze snuffer and Lucas, in the devil-may-care fashion of youth, with much moistening and consequent singeing of fingers, a feat of derring-do which Arabella watched in admiration. They felt their way back to their seats in the virtually impenetrable blackness of the chilly stone room. Now only the tiniest blue flame in the covered *parfum* behind my aunt gave any light at all, and that so feeble that no face was visible in the gloom save the nearest ones perhaps, and then only as an oval of gray in the looming dark.

"Join hands, please."

The séance had begun at last!

Out of that blackness, the soft, strong old voice of Madame Henriette De'Ath:

"Llewellyn, Llewellyn Tregaron, we call upon you now. Reach out to us, call across the veil of death itself and reach out to us, we who are kindly disposed, we who wish no harm to you.

"Augusta is here, your loving and much-bereaved sister Augusta, who loved you in life and grieves for you in death. Come to her, reach out to her, Llewellyn."

Her voice was becoming a droning, toneless parody of itself, the inflection flat and monotonous.

"Call out to Enid. Enid, your beloved niece is here, willing to pierce the veil and reach out to you, Llewellyn. Come to her, reach out to her, Llewellyn."

Was I wrong, or did there come just then a hollow, distant whooshing sound, as of wind coming from far away? It grew suddenly even chillier in that stone-bound cell. Mrs. Pond shuddered, the little thrill of her nerves passing through her fingers and into my own. Lucas, on my left, tensed suddenly. There *was* something! The atmosphere of the room had changed drastically. There was a terrible oppression that seemed to engulf all of us at once.

"Listen," Madame De'Ath whispered urgently.

There it was again. A faraway rushing as of air, coming from nowhere and yet everywhere at once. There was a rustling of clothing and a shifting and creaking of wood as we all sat up tensely, blind in the blackness, intent only to listen and to hear.

And then it came.

The damnedest, most hideous gobbling sound, mindless and inane, like the burblings of a loose-mouthed, drooling idiot child. It was everywhere around us, coming from the very air itself, waxing and waning in its intensity and volume, so that while one moment we were straining as if we were deaf, to hear the slightest sound, yet the next we ached to clap our imprisoned hands over our ears to protect them from the terrible onslaught to our senses.

We were not totally silent, but cried out and gasped in fright and wonder. I, skeptic that I was, remained cool, attempting to pinpoint the origin of the sound and fix its source. I could not.

"Away, poor spirits," my mother-in-law cried out suddenly in a voice of majestic command. "Away and trouble us not. We have dealings with Llewellyn Tregaron and will brook no interference with our goal.

"Llewellyn, Llewellyn Tregaron, come forth if you can and reach out across the chasm that divides your soul from ours," she commanded, her voice rising over the wild babbling of the mad voices that had invaded our séance. (I say "voices," for I did not believe for a second that it was "spirits," tortured or otherwise.)

The sounds rose to a howl of bizarre and mindless gibberish, and suddenly, even more powerful than it had been before, came the commanding voice of my mother-in-law, Henriette De'Ath. "Begone, poor wild spirits of the night. Away with you," and one by one we all joined in, led first by Ambrose and eventually by Jemmy. "Away with you," we enjoined, and gradually the mindless wailings and babblings receded and were heard no more.

I found myself trembling, Mrs. Pond's hand now cold and damp in mine and Lucas's grip on my fingers tighter than ever. It had been quite an experience!

"Thank you, friends. I think we have passed through that ordeal and shall be quite free, now, of uninvited guests," Madame De'Ath whispered. "You have all done quite well. . . ."

Her next remark was never uttered, for out of the darkness came an alien voice, sounding far away, yet very clear and bell-like in tone:

"Pegeen?" it called in a lilting Irish brogue. "Pegeen, my wee one," the voice whined in a long-drawn-out and plaintive manner.

"Mama?" I felt Mrs. Peggy Pond's hand go rigid in mine. She pulled, as if to raise her hand, but I did not let go my grip. The circle remained closed.

" 'Old onto 'er," Jemmy muttered in the dark.

"I am," I replied tensely.

"Mama?" she called again in a tiny child's voice. "Is it you, Mama?"

"Pegeen," the voice went on, whining and bell-like, speaking now in Gaelic, which none of us at the table understood save Mrs. Pond herself, who listened, and then, in a flood of tears replied in the same tongue, her voice returning to that of childhood in a most bizarre and chilling manner for those of us who sat as mute witnesses to the strange incident.

The bell-like voice floated in the air for a few more seconds, and then there came that strange rushing sound and it was gone.

Mrs. Peggy let out a shriek and almost leaped from her seat. Only Jemmy and I, holding on to her hands for dear life, prevented a breaking of the circle.

"Mama, stay, Mama," she called out plaintively to the now-empty air.

"Mrs. Pond!" My mother-in-law spoke up sharply, trying to bring the woman back to attention.

"Mrs. Peggy," her husband called out in the darkness, his usually sure voice sounding oddly thin and trembling. "Mrs. Peggy, are you recovered, are you quite yourself now?"

"Ma, it's me, Lucas." The boy spoke up abruptly on my left, his hand still gripping mine like a vise. "Come to your senses, Ma."

"Lucas?" she asked dazedly. "Oh, Lucas, it was my mother. Nobody ever called me Pegeen but her. She died when I was still a girl, when Papa took us over the water to America. She died on the boat. Oh, Mr. Pond, Enoch, she *was* here. She brushed my cheek like a cold breeze and promised that someday we'd be together—a long, long time from now, she said, but we'd all be together again.

"Lucas, it's true. It was your very own grandmama." Mrs. Pond began to cry tears of relief and joy, utterly convinced that she had truly rent the veil and heard the voice of her long-dead mother. It was as chilling and as dreadful an experience as I had ever witnessed, and I somehow felt sullied, knowing that I had been a part—however small—of the deception practiced upon this poor, naive little woman indiscernible in the darkness at my side.

"Mrs. Pond"—my mother-in-law spoke up then—"pray calm yourself. Are you quite sure that it was your mother who spoke to you? None of us here understand Gaelic—am I right in this?" and we all muttered our agreement, disembodied trembling voices in the blackness of that chilly room—"and so we have no way of knowing what was said. Are you sure it was your mother with whom you spoke?"

"Oh, yes, madame, I am that sure! She said that Papa had joined her and the wee brothers and sisters that had died as well—all save the one that wasn't baptized in time—and that we'd all be together again, but not for a long time yet. Oh, madame, it was wonderful," she exclaimed, and I could feel through her very fingertips that a new calmness had taken hold of her body and soul. Her voice became firmer and stronger, and she was no longer afraid as she had been earlier.

Perhaps, I thought to myself, the sham was not so bad after all, if it would help the poor timid little soul in some way or other; but that was only rationalization on my part. It was still a mean trick that had been played on her, and there was only one person at that table who was so bad—as far as I knew—as to deserve to be the object of such trickery, and that was my own dear aunt, Augusta Tregaron.

There was a sudden gasp and intake of breath in the darkness. "Look," the voice of my aunt urged upon us all at once. "Look." And turning our attention from Mrs. Peggy we saw what it was that she enjoined us to see.

A dense mass of smoke or some such substance resembling smoke was hovering over the center of the room several feet above our heads. It glowed visibly in the blackness; turned and coiled with a sinuous grace, changing color from pale blue to yellow to green and back again. We were utterly transfixed by the sight, and save for an initial exclamation or two, there was not a sound in the room.

"Llewellyn?" my aunt called out. "Llewellyn, is that you? Are you trying to reach me?" her old voice cracked out in the blind darkness of that strange room. "Llewellyn?" As she spoke, the dense mass above us seemed to move and swirl the more, as if in actual response to her call.

Except for her own words, there was utter silence still. The colors seemed to grow deeper in hue for a second, and then they faded away completely, leaving the strange eddying gaseous matter hovering in the air above the center of the table like a glowing and luminescent cloud.

"Llewellyn," she pleaded with the darkness, with that swirling mass of smoke, her voice sharp and shrill, the very sound of it fulfilling my every hope for revenge against her. And yet, it was so pathetic, so heartfelt! What right had I to tamper with her so? A hollow sense of guilt crept over me. Oh God, I was far worse than any of these other charlatans around this table—Jemmy or Ambrose or Madame De'Ath. They only wished to rob her of money, and would with their trickery give her hope of a life to come. I wanted to wait until they had fooled her into believing in that life to come: into believing that she would one day be with Uncle Llewellyn and the others again in another world; I wanted to wait until the moment when she truly believed, and than I wanted to dash her every newly built hope and dream and belief and shatter them beyond repair. I wanted to laugh and gloat at her and torture her with her greatest fear. Was I really so cruel? Perhaps she was right! Perhaps I was a murderess! Was the cruelty I planned for her any less evil than murder?

But I had no further time to reflect on the morality of my machinations. Things began to happen too fast.

*"It is him,"* she whispered, her sharp voice suddenly muted with awe. "I see his face!" And it was true! There in the whirling, sinuous smoke was the face of my Uncle Llewellyn Tregaron. It seemed to appear from nowhere, a vague, nebulous, but nonetheless recognizable image, swaying and writhing in the strangely glowing, curling eddies of gray matter that hovered in the air above us like a cloud. But then, as quickly as it had appeared, it had disappeared, and with it the glowing mass of smoke itself. The room was plunged again into that impenetrable blackness.

"Llewellyn . . ." she called out, lamentingly and forlorn, in a voice that nearly broke the heart.

"No, Aunt, do not despair." I cried out impulsively, the sound of my own voice actually shocking me as I heard myself speak. "He is still here; I sense him! He is still here!"

*My God, what had possessed me to cry out like that?*

*And then I knew!*

The very air around us was suffused with scent, the strong and unmistakable scent of a certain blend of tobacco, aromatic and rich with spices, so familiar that I had recognized it before I was even conscious of having done so. It was the aroma of my Uncle Llewellyn's favorite—nay, *only*—pipe tobacco; the very tobacco that I had delighted to smell whenever I entered his library; the tobacco that I had given to him on every birthday of his since I was a child, and that was so much a part of his person that I would ever identify it with him until the very day I breathed my last.

"Enid, yes! He *is* still here. I can feel it, too. Llewellyn, it is I, Augusta! Speak to me. Reach out and speak to me." Her voice was shrill and pleading and desperate, utterly heartrending and pathetic—even to the likes of me. I felt another surge of horribly mixed feelings. What was I doing to her, to this poor old woman? Had I a right to tamper so with her very heart and soul?

"Pray calm yourself, Miss Tregaron," Madame De'Ath urged.

The scent filled the air now, overpowering in its intensity. I found myself gasping for breath.

"Uncle Llewellyn," I called out. "Dear, dear uncle, I did love you. Did you never know? Did you never know how much I cared?" The tears were streaming down my face now, hot and wet. I could hardly breathe, my words coming in gasps.

Out of that impenetrable darkness came the deep, cold voice of Ambrose De'Ath: "Enough! Light the candles, gentlemen. I think that Miss Tregaron has fainted."

The spirit circle was broken.

"Miss Tregaron. . ." I heard the voice of Mr. Ottermole calling, followed by the sound of her cheek being gently slapped. There came the urgent scraping of chair legs on stone, lucifers being struck in the dark, points of yellow light leaping to life, exclamations and small, inarticulate cries of concern.

As the Messrs. Pond, father and son, relit those black tapers one by one, a scene emerged of ghastly pale faces frozen like masks, each of us shaken and frightened by what had happened and each of us fearing the worst had befallen my aunt.

She was slumped in her chair, Mr. Ottermole and Ambrose attempting to revive her with much chaffing of the hands and patting of her cheeks.

"Her reticule," I called out. "She has a vial of salts with her at all times," and pushing my way without ceremony past both Lucas and Ambrose, I slid to my knees before the unconscious old woman who was my aunt and fumbled in the little black-jet-beaded bag pinned at her waist. From its depths I drew the familiar little cut-glass-and-gold vinaigrette without which I had never known my aunt to be in all the years that I had lived in that house in Park Lane with her.

I uncapped the little vial and held it under her nose, the sharp smell serving to begin her recovery almost at once; but it was not the unpleasantness of the smelling salts that sent another thrill of terror up and down my spine. It was the rich and pungent aroma of that rare, almost exclusive blend of special tobaccos that still hovered in the air around us as palpable as a curtain.

"No, Aunt," I had cried out, "do not despair, he is still here, I sense him; he is still here."

My God in heaven! Was he? Was he still here? Had he indeed reached out to us across the veil?

*Was Llewellyn Tregaron amongst us even now?*

It was long past midnight. Lucas Pond, looking shrewd and narrow around the eyes had herded his parents, both rather overcome by the events of the evening (though each in a different way, to be sure—she somewhat exhausted and he rather toned down, as if the fear of God were in him), into their hired coach and sped them off into the night.

The Ottermoles had lingered, partly to see that my aunt was recovered sufficiently from her faint so as to be out of any danger, and partly to thank Madame De'Ath and myself for our hospitality to Arabella. She had, by the way, managed to turn Master Lucas' head a bit, as she had intended, and I had seen them exchange words and glances more than once during the course of our eventful night.

It was just before they were about to take their leave that another strange thing occurred which rather troubled me. I had just that previous night finished with the first volume of *The Memoirs of the Duchess de la Cressonière* which Mr. Ottermole had been so kind as to lend me and had all but made up my mind to read no further into the second. Therefore, upon leaving my Aunt Augusta's room after seeing her safely to sleep, I decided to take the book and return it to its owner while it was on my mind and before he left the abbey.

Fighting the sick feeling in my stomach that now attended my every step in the hallway between my Aunt Augusta's rooms and my own, I entered my sitting room and went to find the volume in question. It was not there! The second and third volumes were where I had left them, but the first had vanished entirely.

Returning to the salon where Madame De'Ath, Ambrose, and the Ottermoles awaited me, I entered with an expression of perplexity which they all immediately misconstrued.

"Is Miss Tregaron ill?" Arabella asked with concern as I approached the little gathering.

"What? Oh, no, no. She is sleeping peacefully now. I . . . I must confess to you, Mr. Ottermole that I am in some embarrassment," I replied, really quite without thinking.

"How so?" he asked.

"Mr. Ottermole, I have intended all evening to return the first volume of the book you were so kind as to lend me, but I find that it is mislaid." And then I realized! I had not wanted my mother-in-law to know of the book at all. Too late now! "I . . . I cannot . . ." I trailed off lamely.

"Oh?" Arabella exclaimed, and then, blushing in a way that immediately aroused my suspicions, she went on to explain. "I forgot to tell you. I knew that you had finished the book and so I took it to pack amongst my things this afternoon. Do not be alarmed that you have lost it. It is quite safe." She smiled winningly and I had naught to do but smile in return, although I knew that she was not telling the truth. I would not contradict her right then and there.

"Ah, good, I am so relieved," I exclaimed. She had *not* known that I was finished with the book, for I had not even mentioned the fact to her. She was hiding something. What? And more interesting—why?

"What book is that, my dear?" Madame De'Ath asked harmlessly, as if it were the idlest question imaginable.

"Just a history book, madame, Gibbon," I answered swiftly, before Arabella made a more elaborate and therefore more indiscreet reply. Despite my error in admitting that I had borrowed a book at all, I still did not wish to admit what book it was, although it was only too likely that she had guessed already. Mr. Ottermole, I noted, made no reply at all to any of this exchange. Bless his perceptive soul, I thought gratefully.

They left not long after this, and the three of us—Ambrose, Jemmy, and I—returned to Madame De'Ath's salon to discuss the success of the first séance. As we entered, the old woman called down the room with a glass of sherry raised in salutation, "Here is to a splendid evening. It could not have gone better, my dears, even down to the fainting spell, since it has not proven serious and the lady in question is not in danger," she added with no great show of genuine sympathy. She was alive and jovial, her wise old eyes sparkling with excitement. "Do not worry too much, Enid, about the old woman's fate, or bother to feel much guilt. People have a way in this life of reaping the reward that they have sown. She does not deserve much sympathy from you, after all. She has treated you ill and you are entitled to the revenge you seek."

Perhaps I was, but would I enjoy it as I had thought I

would? "Revenge is sweet," they say, but was it? What was the price in harm to my own conscience and character?

"You did the 'Pegeen, Pegeen' call superbly, madame," Jemmy was saying, laughing and mimicking in an exaggerated manner the very inflection of the "spirit" of Mrs. Pond's "mother." He poured himself a sherry and sprawled on a settee, one of us now, and no longer in his character as a servant. I rather liked it that way. He was no longer a servant in my eyes, but a man.

"I have not lost my touch over the years, have I, my boys?" she remarked with a smile and such an expression as showed me she was not innocent of the vice of vanity.

Ambrose had scowled at her use of the words "my boys," and now countered Jemmy with some praise of his own. "You were perfect as ever, ma mère," he remarked, adding, "and I must say that the aroma of the tobacco was the final touch needed to convince her. Even more effective than the smoke and lantern slide; better than them by far, in fact. She was totally convinced. And you were very helpful, too, Enid," he added expansively and with a touch of pomposity that irritated me no end. "You said just the right things, and your reactions tend to carry more weight with her than any of ours, saving mine, of course, could possibly do. I've reversed my opinion entirely, as a matter of fact, and am truly glad now that you are one of us, my dear." He raised his glass high in tribute. Jemmy smirked.

"Why, thank you, Ambrose," I replied. "I must confess that my reactions were all quite genuine. Not knowing what to expect, I behaved more naturally than ever I could have had you explained it all to me step by step beforehand as I had wished you to do. You know best, you, and Jemmy."

" 'Ow'd you manage the tobacco trick, by the way, Ambrose? Was it burnin' in the parfum be'ind the old lady's chair? That one even took me by surprise," Jemmy said with interest.

"Yes, how did you do it, Ambrose? It worked splendidly," Madame De'Ath asked.

"It actually frightened me," I admitted.

Ambrose looked dumbfounded. His already cadaver-pale face went dead white. His hand trembled as with the ague, the dregs of his sherry sloshing in the glass. "I say, don't joke like that." He smiled nervously, his lips quivering visibly. "I didn't have a thing to do with it. How the devil do I know what tobacco the old man smoked?"

I felt my stomach turn over. My tongue stuck to the roof

of my mouth and my throat went dry. Jemmy laughed. "Ambrose, you always were a good actor. I . . ." And then, seeing the look on Ambrose's face, he stopped abruptly, swallowing the words he had intended to utter, a look of blank stupefaction crossing his coarse handsome dark face.

He looked at me, a hopeful gleam in his eyes. "You . . ." he started to say, but I shook my head slowly, my eyes stark with the terror I felt mounting within me, the same terror that I had felt in the blackness of that stone-bound séance chamber; the same terror I had felt when I sensed that Uncle Llewellyn was indeed amongst us.

"Well," Madame De'Ath remarked calmly in the ghastly silence that ensued when each of us realized that something inexplicable had happened. "Your English Bard has always said that there are more things in heaven and earth . . . etc., etc. Wherever it came from, Ambrose's clever trickery or some subtle trick of the minds of all of us working in concert, the effect was quite remarkable. The old lady will be showering us with coin o' the realm in no time at all. Perhaps she shall make a small gift to you this week, Ambrose, my son. What do you think?"

His eyes lit up at the thought of money. "I shall suggest it, Madame my mother," he said with a restraint that hardly matched the gleam in his eye.

"Excellent! And next week she shall see even more—come away convinced, in fact—and pay a good deal, I think for the privilege." Her tone was so pleasantly cool and business-like and cheerful that gradually we returned to our senses, forgetting, as I am sure she intended us to do, the mystery of the pungent tobacco aroma that had come from nowhere—been amongst none of the tricks that they had planned—and spoke instead of other things.

"By the way, Enid," Jemmy asked, "is the old crone's 'eart all right?"

"Oh, yes, sound as a bell. She's just given to occasional fainting spells, not so much a frailty as a device for avoiding disagreeable situations—but I do think that this spell was genuine, however. The excitement rather overwhelmed her, and it nearly did the same to me, I might add."

"Well, good for it! I'd 'ate ta 'ave the old bitch's death on our 'ands."

"She'll survive the séances, Jemmy," I assured him dryly. "It will take more than a few airy spooks to kill Augusta Tregaron." And how right I was, although I could not know it then.

We soon adjourned our evening, and Jemmy, accompanying me down the hall toward the great front hall of the abbey, asked me how I liked the gibbering of his mindless, tortured souls.

"That was you?" I asked in surprise. "Indeed I did like them," I exclaimed laughingly. "However do you do it?" And with some amusement I watched as he threw his voice in the echoing hallway, making ghoulish noises that somewhat resembled those of the "mindless spirits" of the séance.

"The full effect depends on speaking tubes. I'll show you 'ow it all works one day, my girl," he explained. "Now, get some rest. It's been quite a night, arter all." He bowed and with a smile turned off toward his own rooms in the servants' quarters in the farthest wing of the sprawling house.

"Jemmy," I called after him, "what of the tobacco?"

"Ambrose," he replied softly, his voice carrying down the corridor. " 'E's 'aving' us on, Enid. It must've been 'im."

I stood for a while in the Great Hall before I braved the eerie and frightening hallway that led to my own rooms. Ambrose was as fearful of that tobacco scent as we all had been. Jemmy was wrong. He was wrong, and it scared me to death to realize it.

That tobacco! Its aroma still clung to my hair and clothing. It was real! It had been there in that room that night, and with it, I would swear, had been my dead Uncle Llewellyn Tregaron! A chill went through me, running down my spine like ice water. Suddenly I was very unsure of myself. Too many things were happening that I could not explain; too many feelings that I could not understand were crowding in upon my besieged soul.

*What next?*

# 12

# EXPLORATIONS

A brief reflection solves the mystery.
—Bishop William Stubbs

Only those who brave its dangers
Comprehend its mystery!
—Longfellow

Dammit! There had to be an explanation! With logic and common sense, I could begin to guess at the various tricks that had been used to create the effects of the séance, even including the aroma of that rare and distinctive tobacco.

My reactions to the sudden manifestation of the scent during the séance itself had been natural and emotional. It had been so sudden and unexpected in its coming, so evocative of the living presence of my uncle that I had reacted on a purely emotional level. That, together with my aunt's fainting spell, for which I admit I felt no little guilt, made me as vulnerable to suggestion as the others, despite my own private knowledge that the whole evening was an elaborately staged charade.

But they had all denied knowledge of the ruse—if ruse it was—of the tobacco; all of them: Jemmy, Ambrose, and Madame De'Ath. And then, too, even if it were a ruse, where had some one of them got possession of that rare tobacco in the first place? None of them seemed to know aught of it, and why play silly games if they did? Ambrose had looked positively ill at the realization that Jemmy was not responsible for the effect. Jemmy had reacted as if he believed Ambrose to be acting—which I myself doubted; his reaction was altogether too genuine to be mere dramatics. Madame De'Ath had seemed a bit nervous—uncharacteristic—and had changed the subject at once. Indeed, we had all been grateful to get off the subject.

No, I was not the only one who seemed frightened by the aroma of Llewellyn Tregaron's pipe tobacco as it filled that room with its pungent perfume. Was someone lying? They had to be! There had to be an explanation, and I had to know! But how?

It was nearly two in the morning by then. I was in bed but totally unable to sleep, and almost dizzy from overmuch reflecting—to no point whatsoever—upon that séance and the tobacco that had seemed to be burning from some mysterious place beyond the veil of life and death! Enough! I was actually beginning to frighten myself all over again.

Perhaps I could read myself to sleep. I reached for the memoirs of the shameful duchesse and was immediately confronted with the other, smaller mystery of that eventful night: where was Volume I of the little leather-bound set that Mr. Ottermole had lent me?

Arabella said she had taken it, and surely I had no real reason to disbelieve her or to be annoyed with her either. And yet I did both! Why? She was, after all, only returning the book to its rightful owner, and perhaps she wanted to read it herself. Then why not simply say so! No, there was more to it than that, as I had been able to read in her face when I brought up the subject of the missing volume in the first place.

And that was another thing! Madame De'Ath knew now that I had borrowed books from the Ottermole library—an unnecessary thing entirely, considering the number of books in the libraries of Thanatos Abbey. She was anything but a stupid woman, and she must have seen through my lies even as I saw through those of Arabella Ottermole. There were at least two sets of Gibbon in Thanatos Abbey; I would hardly have needed to borrow one from someone else. Moreover, I would place a wager that my mother-in-law had remembered that the only book ever mentioned in company with the Ottermoles had been those damnable memoirs. She must know what book it was that I had borrowed. What must she be thinking of me? Did she realize why I was reading them? Yes, more than likely she did, I supposed with a sigh. Well, there was no help for it now!

I was thinking too much—and to no purpose! I arose from my bed, restless as a cat. The séance and its aftermath had unsettled me, and reading, in this case at least, would only have served to unnerve me the more. Outside the sky was clear, the moon high and bright. No storm approached, and so it was not the electric atmosphere of distant thunder that agitated me thus—nor even Aunt Augusta. She was well, after all, and sleeping peacefully.

It was still the séance of course; the pungent unmistakable aroma of Uncle Llewellyn's pipe tobacco which conjured up so vitally the impression of his living presence. That, and the fact that I wished to escape the pernicious effect upon my thoughts of those damned, insidious little books with their tale of licentiousness and debauchery that I could not bear to attribute to my lovely, mysterious and wise old mother-in-law. I did not want to believe of Madame De'Ath that she had done such things; worshiped, in degraded ways, the fat, ugly little charlatan Comte Alessandro di Cagliostro, or that she had ever debased herself by the unnatural desire for her own kind; sinned in such a debauched way as that!

I paced around the tiny room like a caged creature.

No wonder that she did not want those books mentioned. She had probably only published those memoirs—so long ago, nearly fifty years ago—in order to live. Perhaps their publication paid the price of her survival in England after the Revolution sent her into exile. Now, her anonymity assured by a new name, her security by the comfort of an honorable place in society as widow and mother, she did not want the secrets of her horrible past laid bare. And yet I *knew;* I *knew,* and I could not ever *unknow!*

I felt sick at heart.

Action was the only answer. I must move. I must do something—anything.

I must learn the secret of the séance room, find out from whence the scent of Uncle Llewellyn's tobacco had come, or else . . .

or else what?

or else bring back Uncle Llewellyn myself.

I know now, as I write of all this, that I was not myself on that long-ago night when I went like a thief through the silent corridors of Thanatos Abbey in search of my dead uncle's ghost. I was so strangely "other," my nerves throbbing in my body like taut strummed wire, my brain keen with a kind of unnatural exaltation, my ears sharp as the ears of a night creature, my eyes open like an owl's.

I had drawn a dressing gown on over my night shift, wore soft, comfortable slippers, and carried a candle in a small brass holder, although I did not light it at once, choosing rather to feel my way out of my rooms and down the long corridor that led to the front hall of the abbey and thence away to the other wings of the sprawling old place. The windows along my path were few and small, but there was enough light by which to move down those silent, deserted halls, picking out various objects along the way—small points of light upon a polished suit of armor, a gleam of velvety gilt on a picture frame or the yellowy warmth of the polished dome of one of Ambrose's many skulls.

It was a waking dream, that nightmare walk through the unlit corridors of Thanatos Abbey; the silence so great that one might have heard the old place breathe or sigh in its slumber, and one would have gone quietly mad at the sound. I walked slowly, as if I trod through corridors of molasses, thick and heavy, weighing me down at the ankles, holding me back yet drawing me onward with every forward step through the sticky, sucking stuff.

It seemed an endless journey ere I arrived at the double doors of the New Hall. If they were locked, why, then my tortuous walk had been for naught; if they were open, then my adventures would begin in earnest. The knob turned, the lock clicked, and the door swung inward. There was not a light to be seen at first, for all the windows were shuttered as usual and the tall doors leading to the glass-walled dining room were closed as well.

I stood on the threshold and tried to accustom myself to the deeper darkness of that long salon. Gradually I could make out light emanating from two places; far down the room on the right, many feet beyond the secret panel that led to the séance room, was a pale bar of light along the floor. It came from under the door of Madame De'Ath's boudoir, which I had never seen. Nearer me, on the same wall, just before the place where I judged the panel to be, the dull red glow of a dying fire winked like the eye of a demon from the fireplace. That was all.

But it was enough.

I stepped just within the door and eased it closed behind me, my forefinger finding the catch of the lock and snapping it into a locked position. I wanted no one coming in behind me. I stood tense and expectant in the dark. No sound came from my mother-in-law's bedroom. She might even be asleep, the light under her door merely the last glow from her own fireplace or even a candle carelessly left lit at her bedside. Never mind, I had to go on with my task.

I picked my way carefully down the room like a child playing at being blind, and came at last to the red embers of the fire. Just to the left was the panel which hid the passageway to the séance room. I inched my fingers along the gilded molding just as I had seen Jemmy do earlier in the evening. The wood felt smooth to the touch; the tips of my fingers glided along the gessoed curves and grooves, unable to find any obvious latch or button at first, but then I felt it, high up, at a level just over my head. It was a small section of the molding that, when depressed, tripped a latch in the panel of the wall and opened a narrow door.

As the panel clicked open, I felt a rush of cool, damp air. The faintest, barest suggestion of Uncle Llewellyn's pipe tobacco hovered in the atmosphere. Only that! There was absolutely no sense of his presence left at all. I pushed the panel shut at my back and groped down the chilly stone passage, still loath to light my candle.

The inner door, heavy and bound in iron, was closed. I prayed it was not locked, but had no need to fear. It bore no lock, but only a bolt which slid closed from the other side in the séance room itself. I pushed at the door, and it creaked inward with a slight grating of iron on iron.

Blackness as impenetrable and inexorable as a grave.

I groped in my pocket for a lucifer match and struck it, the sound and smell of the sulfuric acid as it ignited almost causing me to cry out, so high-strung were my nerves by this point. Not bothering to light my own candles, I walked, match in hand, to the nearest candelabrum and lit the stub of one of the black tapers instead. Then, one by one, I lit them all, going around the near side of the huge table to light those in the stand on the right-hand side of the room as well.

What now?

I stood and surveyed the room. Nothing had changed. It was exactly as I had seen it at my last glance upon leaving earlier that night, except now I was alone, the chairs were empty, and several of the black candles were burned so low in their sockets that they were in imminent danger of guttering out.

The table, so large and round, must once have been very grand indeed, as I could see by a closer inspection of the ornate design of the gilded ormolu legs. The top, I surmised, had probably been of inlaid woods, although all of its surface was now covered over in black baize. I touched the edge and found that the cloth had been tacked down all around the circumference of the table, and so I could not lift it and examine the real surface. Taking my own candle now and securing it in the little brass holder that I had taken with me, I lit it and leaned across the tabletop to see if there was any sign of a break in the baize-covered surface. There seemed at first to be none, and then something caught my eye. It was merely a subtle, slightly different texture in the black baize covering in the very center of the table; that and nothing more. Yet, because it was there at all, it warranted investigation.

I have said the table was large, and indeed it was. In fact, in order to investigate that odd little imperfection that I noticed in the cloth of the covering, I had actually to lean across the surface and pull myself onto the top so that I lay stretched to nearly my full length across it before I had my eyes directly over the center of it. I set the candle down beside me and, on my stomach, with my body propped by my elbows, I observed that strange patch of peculiarly rough texture in the smoothness of the broad baize tabletop.

It was a small round circle of the very finest wire mesh that I had ever seen painted black and set into the baize in place of a corresponding circle of the cloth that had been removed. I touched it gingerly, and it yielded slightly, indicating that the table beneath it had been cut away as well. I put my ear to the mesh and heard a strange, hollow rushing sound, much like the sound one hears from the interior of a large seashell.

I found nothing else suspicious during the course of an inch-by-inch examination of the rest of the surface, and so, wriggling back onto my feet, I took the candle and crouched down on the floor beside the ornate ormolu legs. There were many of them, ranked in pairs around the circumference of the table, for it was a gateleg style, and was (or had been at one time, anyway) capable of being closed up into a smaller and more convenient rectangular size for storage or transport. Placing the candle on the floor beside me, I pushed at the two nearest legs. They did not budge. I looked and saw that they had been attached to the flagstone floor by means of brass braces and screws. Interesting! The table had been made into a permanent, immovable fixture for some reason.

Sliding the candlestick along the floor ahead of me, I crawled underneath the table. In the exact center, below the spot where the wire mesh had been substituted for baize cloth, stood a length of narrow iron pipe attached to the underside of the table at its top end and descending into the stone floor at its other end. More interesting still were the two other pipes—or more accurately, speaking tubes—which rose out of the floor and curved upward along the underside of the table toward the two places at which Madame De'Ath and Jemmy had been seated. Each of these tubes was fitted with a wide funnel-shaped mouthpiece.

I crawled out from under the table, unmindful of the dust which now covered my clothing and hands, and sat in the wooden chair that had been Jemmy's during the séance. The mouth of one of the tubes was fixed to the underside of the table directly before me. With my right hand—the one which Madame De'Ath would have been "holding" and which he would, therefore, have been free to use—I drew the mouthpiece forward so that its open funnel was level with the tabletop. I bowed my head and lowered my face into it, finding that it fit over my mouth and jaw like a mask or a medical inhaler. I made the sound of a low laugh or chuckle and suddenly that same sound, distorted and magnified many times, broke the silence of the room from every corner, much as had Jemmy's gobbling, mindless "spirits" earlier in the evening.

I sat back smiling and pushed the mouthpiece back into its place. Trickery, simple trickery, using devices that were common aboard ship or between waiters and kitchen help in the pantries of gentlemen's clubs. If I hunted long enough I would find outlets in all the corners of the room, which was why the sounds, hollow and distorted, appeared to be in the air all around one as one listened.

What other marvels did this room hold secret?

I arose from Jemmy's chair, which, unlike all the others, save that of Madame De'Ath herself, was stationary, riveted to the floor as were the legs of the table. Again interesting. I investigated.

The legs of both chairs proved hollow, their tops, where they were attached to the undersides of the seats, having tiny vents or tubes or even taut strands of wire feeding down through them. I could even feel a slight flow of cool, moving air from two of the legs. Along the underside of the right edge of Jemmy's chair, within easy reach of the fingertips of the right hand, was a row of small keys and stops not unlike those of an organ. I depressed one of them, and a stream of air came forth from one of the hollow legs in a great rush. Pneumatic pressure of some sort.

"Just perfect," I found myself muttering aloud. "Just perfect for propelling a chill breeze or—"

"—or the pungent aroma of ghostly tobacco smoke, per'aps."

I screamed out loud and shot bolt upright as if I had been sprung on an unseen hinge, every nerve of my body aquiver with fright.

"Jemmy," I called out, "for God's sake, you nearly killed me. Where are you?" I asked, turning and seeing him nowhere in the room, although his voice, a mellow, teasing baritone laugh, seemed to be coming from directly behind me.

"Sorry, girl. Didn't mean ta scare you, but I couldn't resist the temptation. Stand up," he directed, "and turn around slowly."

I did as I was asked, and found myself facing the blank back wall of the room.

"Now, blow out yer candle."

"No," I protested. "Most of the others in the stands have gone out by now. It will be too dark."

"The darker the better," he replied. " 'Sides, I've got a light wi' me. Don't be afraid."

I was certainly not going to have him think that I was afraid of him! I blew out the candle obediently. The room was in almost total darkness again, the blank stone of the back wall looming like the sides of a crypt. All at once, in the dark, I saw a bizarre parody of Jemmy's wide, coarsely handsome face, his dark eyes glowering at me out of the blackness, his head suspended in midair like a disembodied thing, the eyes deep pits, the brow low and beetling like the brow of an ape, the high cheeks hollow and the mouth a pouting, sulking gash. There was a terribly strange, nebulous quality about it, as if it were not a face of this world but seen, rather, through that veil of which Ambrose and Reverend Pond spoke so freely and knowledgeably.

My every canny instinct told me it was a trick like all the other tricks that I had discovered, and yet the effect was so terrifying that I could not help but gasp at its sudden appearance and then its even more sudden disappearance.

"Oh, Jemmy," I pleaded, "you are frightening me. Where are you? How did you do that?"

"Walk straight ahead of you," he instructed, his disembodied voice every bit as uncanny and unnerving as his disembodied head had been the moment before.

"Slowly," he cautioned.

"I can't go any farther," I argued as I came to a halt before the blank back wall.

"Put your 'and out and touch the wall, gently, gently," he

said, his voice sounding almost as if he faced me, which, of course, was impossible.

No! It was not impossible after all!

The "stone" wall was not stone at all. When I raised my hand to touch its rough surface, I touched, instead of stone, an expanse of smoothly stretched, slightly yielding fabric. I let out a squeal of surprise and withdrew my hand as if the wall were hot!

He laughed, and there he was again, his face illuminated grotesquely in the near-darkness. He was no more than two feet away from me, with only a partition of tautly stretched and painted fabric between us like a translucent wall.

"Step back, Enid," he directed, and as I did, he pushed the cloth and the whole wooden frame on which it was stretched, out of place revealing that he stood in an alcove some three feet square which lay behind the "stone" partition.

He entered the séance room and opened the shutter of a dark lantern that he carried. Holding the light just under his chin, he recreated the grotesque shadows that had made his handsome face seem so strange and other-worldly.

"It's a theatrical trick. This rigid frame is stretched with scrim and painted—by yours truly—ta look like the stone of the other walls." He demonstrated by putting the partition back in place over the opening of the alcove; the wall once again appeared to the casual and unsuspicious eye to be a solid wall of blank stone.

"It's always kept quite dark in 'ere, of course, an' no one is ever near enough to the wall ta see it well, so it works out fine. The room is so nearly square anyway that no one would ever think there might be an alcove or irregularity anyway. Next week, yer 'uncle' is gonna appear right in there, all wavering and blurry be'ind the scrim, and the old lady's gonna be sure 'e's just waiting for 'er ta join 'im in paradise."

I made a face at his flip remark.

"Wot's the matter? I thought you 'ated 'er so? I thought you was . . . were . . . out for revenge?"

"So I am. I . . . it . . . it's not a very nice thing we're doing, is it, Jemmy?"

"Not very," he agreed simply, "but it's wot you wanted. You were the one that wanted revenge."

I frowned.

"And what is it you want, Jemmy? Why are you in this?"

"Me? I ain't got no malice like you, if that's what you're thinkin'. I only want out—out o' England where a man can't breathe. Out o' England, where a poor, mad, death-obsessed eccentric like Ambrose De'Ath is a respected gentleman wi' a place in society and wi' clubs ta belong to and debts 'e can run up sky-'igh wi'out a penny to 'is name, while the like o' me, because I've got no formal schoolin' and no name . . . Wot's the use o' explainin'? It don't matter," he broke off dejectedly.

"No, please, go on, Jemmy. You know my story, and it is very different, isn't it, from the spoiled and pampered upbringing that you thought it was. Knowing the truth of my past helped you to understand me better, and that understanding on your part has helped me very much. It is only fair that I try to understand you better now."

He nodded. "I tried, the other night, to begin. In the crypt " he added slowly.

"Yes," I went on. "It is time that I know something of you . . ." And then, in a flash of insight, I understood what he was trying so hard to say; I remembered something that I had heard him say that night in the crypt below the ruined abbey chapel. I suddenly began to understand. "Go on," I urged gently, and sat in Madame De'Ath's big upholstered chair to give him my full attention.

He leaned against the table and looked down at me with troubled, angry eyes. He looked very handsome. Something in the depths of me ached as I gazed up into that face of his. It was almost as if I saw it for the first time.

"I'm a better man than Ambrose is. Takin' all in all, I am," he reiterated defensively and with bitterness in his low voice. "I'm stronger and tougher and smarter . . . and . . . and kinder as well. But 'e's a gent, 'e's 'ad education, and 'e's been polished by continental travel. 'E 'as a name. 'E knows who 'is father was—an' 'is mother. So that all makes 'im better'n me, they say. Right? Don't it?"

I did not answer.

"Don't it? In't that wot you've thought all along? That 'e's better'n me?" As his anger grew, his carefully tended attempts to improve his speech went by the boards and he spoke even more in the low manner and rhythms of his cockney origins. I did not mind somehow, for the contrast between his more carefully governed speech and the original only served to make me see how hard he had worked to better himself, how far he had come already, and how much farther he would come in the future with loving patience and guidance. I saw how cruel it was that he should be thought low for things he could not help and against which he obviously struggled so valiantly and patiently. I felt ashamed to remember how I had derided him for imitating his "betters" when, without such an effort on his part, he would stand no chance at all in this world of ours which judges so by outward appearances and so little by heart and character and striving.

"Yes," I answered at last. "I did once think that Ambrose was a better man than you. But I did not know you then—either of you. And to England, the England we know, he is a better man still, and perhaps always will be. But, for what it is worth to you, England is wrong and so have I been wrong—in the past."

"I don't know who my father was. My mother din't either, I'll wager." He laughed ironically. "But that I'll never know, and I really don't care anymore." (And I knew that he always would care down in the unplumbed depths of his soul, but no matter now.) "I was six or thereabouts when she died—died o' gin, most like. I don't know that fer sure either, 'cause I wasn't there when it 'appened an' 'er dyin' din't make much difference in me life anyway. I 'adn't seen much o' 'er. She'd been loanin' me out fer a year or more already—"

"Loaning you out?"

"Aye, ta some cronies o' 'ers, gents whose perfession was . . ."

"Grave-robbing," I said as he hesitated. "Well, why not. You said the other night that it was as good a profession as any other. I expect you were right, and that it is."

"I was gonna tell you about it the other night. I 'ad it all resolved in me mind. That's why I brought you down there, in fact. Thought it might make it easier in a way. I wanted ta let you know what it was like fer me—growin' up, I mean, but you . . ."

"Jemmy, forgive me. When I was a little child, the great bugaboo was the body snatchers—Burke and Hare. Well, you know. Children of the 1820s and '30s trembled at the thought of grave robbery and the 'Burkers.' Oh . . .," I gasped. Suddenly that word stuck in my throat. His name. He had no name from his unknown father, and so they called him that because he robbed graves. Poor Jemmy. I closed it out of my mind and went on. "After my parents . . . died, I used sometimes to be afraid that their bodies would be stolen. I grew up and got over such morbid and childish thoughts, but the childhood memory is still there. Do you understand?"

"Sure, nothin' personal," he said, and fell silent.

"Your name . . ." I urged gently.

"They called me Jemmy from early on, 'cause 'Jemmy'

means 'smart' in street talk, but 'Burkers' stuck arter they loaned me off of 'er. Ya see, they used to use me ta squeeze inta mausoleums an' crypts through vents an' the little windows they 'ave in 'em. Lots o' us grave robbers got called Burkers arter Burke an' 'Are made a name for themselves. I was little an' I'd get inside an' open the coffins an' rob the corpses for 'em, passing the goods out to the chaps outside. I'd find rings an' lockets and pocket watches, Bibles an' whatever mementos. We'd even take the clothes off of 'em an' sell 'em."

I winced, thinking of a boy—*this man* as a boy—doing such horrible things. How could one blame him, wild, orphaned little animal, surviving in the only way anyone ever taught him?

"We didn't kill nobody like Burke an' 'Are, though," he was reassuring me. "Leastwise, *I* never did, an' I don't know fer sure if any o' the others I was in with did or not, but we did snatch bodies. Arter a few years, I was too big fer squeezing inta crypts, so I 'elped dig an' load bodies from new graves an' wheel 'em through the streets in a barrow to the anatomists and the medical schools. I'm strong, as you've noticed. I got that way 'aulin' bodies." He snickered.

I shivered.

"I'm sorry, Enid. I don't 'ave nothin' pretty to say about my life—my past life, that is—but I want you ta know. It's important that you know."

"Is it? Why?" I asked, afraid in a way to know the why.

"Never mind," he said with a disappointed look in his eyes. "Barin' my soul, ya can chalk it up to if ya like," he replied softly.

I could not answer.

"Anyway, a turnin' point came when I was eighteen or so. I couldn't read or write very well. I groveled fer a livin' in the graveyards o' London and environs, lived in rented beds an' such 'oles as that, but I knew that there was more ta the world. I saw rich mourners in the graveyards, dressed in fine clothes; people o' taste and refinement who treated each other wi' kindness and 'ad sensibilities. Young, pretty ladies such as yourself an' gents like Ambrose is supposed ta be, an' I thought they must be so much better'n me. I thought the 'ole world must be better'n me an' my kind.

"Amongst my own, though, I was quite somethin' else," he said with a quick, cocky smile. "They singled me out fer me brains from the first—that's where the 'Jemmy' come from, as I said—an' later on fer me strength and agility as well."

"I've frequently had occasion to notice all three, Jemmy." I smiled, remembering the several times that I had been somewhat mishandled by him or watched his lithe and catlike movements. His acuity I had often noted as well.

"I was somethin' fine wi' the ladies, too. The females, I mean. I've never made love to a *lady*." He added this last slowly and thoughtfully, his eyes on me in such a way that I had to turn my head away from his gaze.

I knew then that he wanted me. Dangerous ground we trod, Jimmy and I.

"I'm not sure 'ow old I am," he went on abruptly, changing tone and subject completely. "About thirty-five now, I judge. Anyways, as I was sayin', I was about eighteen or so then. It was late one spring night an' I was comin' through a street in St. Giles near what they call the ' 'Oly Land,' as bad a slum as any in the 'ole o' London, an' an old Judy that I knew comes runnin' up, a disgustin', toothless old 'ag what I'd buy a peg o' gin fer occasionally out o' pity. It was three in the mornin' an' she's all agitated, tellin' me she 'ad a fresh body on 'er 'ands, a young gent wot poisoned 'isself an' 'ad fine clothes an what would I give 'er fer 'im an' 'is rig?

"I calmed 'er down an' got 'er ta explain. It seems she met a toff in a gin shop. 'E said 'e 'ad a room in the district an' asked 'er ta go back wi' 'm, that 'e'd pay 'er well fer what 'e wanted."

"Which was?"

"Fer any ordinary toff what liked low women—an' many of 'em do, ya know—sex, of course," he answered matter-of-factly, "but this bloke 'ad somethin' else in mind. 'E took 'er to a room 'e rented off a courtyard in one o' the rookeries o' St. Giles. She expected there'd be a bed, o' course, but there wasn't no bed—only a coffin on the floor of an empty room." He paused.

"My God, Ambrose," I breathed.

"The chap—'e was about twenty-three or so—was dressed all in black. 'E 'ad the coffin open an' four candles at the corners. 'E poured some wine and insisted that they drink. Then, 'e said, all 'e wanted was fer 'er ta lie in the coffin an' let 'im sit an' watch 'er while she lay there as if 'e was mournin' like. Then 'e'd climb in an' lie on top o' her fer a while. That was all."

"All," I repeated. "Wasn't that quite enough?"

"No sex, I mean," he explained.

"Oh."

"She pretended ta drink though she knew by now 'e was

not sane an' feared 'e might actually be poisonin' 'er. She only 'ad a sip or two. 'E drank 'is down. She got in the coffin; 'e lit the candles an' sat beside 'er like a mourner. She fell asleep almost at once, scared as she was, poor soul. Probably all the gin she'd 'ad. She was scared of course, but 'e'd promised 'er a sovereign. Fer a sovereign those old 'ags'd do anythin' a chap asked, ya know."

"Horrible!"

"Aye, an' I didn't think you was much better when I 'eard you two 'ad married," Jemmy snarled nastily.

Suddenly I realized what it was he thought of me when he arrived at the abbey and reviled me and dragged me to Ambrose's bedroom, which I had never seen. "Oh, Jemmy, you thought that I *knew* and that I aided him in his sickness and his perversion? You thought that I lay in a coffin for him? That I . . . ?" I could not go on. It was too horrible to contemplate.

"Yes, that is wot I thought at first. That you needed to marry for money—as indeed you did—an' that you joined Ambrose in 'is little game o' death as a way o' pleasin' 'im. I didn't know 'e'd kept it all from you an' that 'e'd tried ta be a normal man fer you. 'E *did* try, Enid, ta be a normal man for you, din't 'e?" Jemmy asked pointedly and in a tone I must reply to, no matter how personal the question.

"Yes, Jemmy, he did try. But not for long and not well. I have not one truly happy hour to remember of our intimacy, which is sad, I think, but no matter now. We are finished, Ambrose and I, as husband and wife. We only live in the same house and bear the same name. That is all." It cost me greatly to say those words, and perhaps I did not have to say them to this man; should not have said them to him, in fact. Yet, somehow I wanted him to know. I could not have him believe for a second that I could submit to the perversity of Ambrose's madness or that I could share a bed with such a man as him whom I must perforce call husband.

"That's all right, then," he said with some kind of satisfaction in his tone. "Just so's ya keep away from 'im now. But back ta me poor old friend wot lay shiverin' in that coffin. Next thing she knew, she was wide-awake an' 'e was on top o' 'er an' as 'eavy as a deadweight. She couldn't rouse 'im an' in 'er ignorance figured 'e was dead. She robbed the body o' money and rings an' was running about lookin' for a burker ta sell the corpse. That, my dear, is when I came on the scene.

"She took me ta the room. True enough, there was a coffin

an' four candles. In the box was a young man in mourning clothes o' very good cut an' style. 'E wasn't dead as she thought; only drugged. I smelled the dregs o' the wine an' knew at once. 'E'd dosed it wi' laudanum so's she'd go out an' really appear 'dead' an' 'ed'd drugged 'imself so 'ed 'die' as well."

"And it was Ambrose, wasn't it?" I asked in disgust, numb with revulsion and yet having to hear it once and for all.

"It was."

"And what did you do?"

He laughed. "I could 'ave burked 'im fer good an' all; sold 'is body, clothes, the coffin, an' the 'ole lot, but I thought better of it. I *was* smart, you see, an' I'd never killed anyone an' wasn't likely ta start then. I figured I stood more in the long run 'elpin' this madman than 'inderin' 'im. I took 'is ring and wallet an' watch back off the old Judy and replaced 'em. I gave 'er almost all the money 'e 'ad an' sent 'er packin'.

"I found 'is identity an' 'is address from papers 'e 'ad on 'im, locked up be'ind us an' 'ailed a 'ackney coach just like 'e was simply a drunken toff an' I was 'is servant out ta 'aul 'im back ta the bosom o' 'is family.

"It was the best an' the smartest thing I ever did in me life, 'cause ya see, I took 'im ta the 'ouse in London that 'e was rentin' at the time an' delivered 'im into the 'ands o' Madame 'Enriette De'Ath, who is the noblest an' wisest lady in the 'ole world. When I delivered 'im into 'er 'ands I put myself into 'er 'ands as well an' I've never regretted it for one minute since." He stopped abruptly and said no more, though I could see such pain mirrored in his sad face.

I reached out to touch him on the arm. "Oh, Jemmy, I'm so sorry."

He drew away from me instantly. "Don't touch me now, Enid. I've got control o' myself right now, but I don't know 'ow long it will last if you touch me. And I don't want pity, you know. I only want you ta try and understand me. That's all." He smiled down at me with a funny face. "Enough o' that now, right? Ancient 'istory, arter all, right?" he said lightly, his mood changing all at once.

"Right." I smiled up at him in return.

"C'mon," he said, pulling me up by one hand, "I'll show you 'ow it all works, since you're 'ere. An' that reminds me, what were you doin' 'ere anyway, girl?" he asked scoldingly.

"I wanted to see how everything works," I answered simply, resigned that he would talk no more about his past, at least for now at any rate.

"Did you, now? Well, you do 'ave pluck, I'll grant you, but you should 'ave asked," he chided overbrightly, determined to change the subject and our mood as well. He would not tolerate my pity, and we had both come perilously close to deep feelings during the course of his remarks on his sad past. This was no time for either of us to express deep feelings, and he was wise enough to know it, I wise enough to be guided by his judgment.

"I was not sure that I would be answered," I replied dryly.

"You're a sneak, that's what you are, my lady." He smiled. "Find anything?"

"Of course! A patch of wire mesh in the center of the table, pipes, speaking tubes, hollow chair legs, and pneumatic-pressure keys."

"My, my, quite the jack, ain't ya?"

"Jack?"

"Detective, my girl, detective."

"Yes, I suppose I am, and I really have only one serious question."

"Which is?"

"How the devil did you get in here with me? I locked the door to the New Hall behind me . . ."

"And that was your big mistake. I wasn't comin' in 'ere at all. I walked by ta look in on Madame De'Ath one last time before turnin' in myself, just ta see if the maid 'ad tended ta 'er fire properly. When I found the doors locked, I got rather upset. I wasn't sure what might 'ave 'appened. She never 'as those doors locked in case she rings during the night, the servants an' me can get to 'er. I went outside an' down through the crypt."

"The crypt? Whatever . . ." I stopped short and dodged past Jemmy and into the alcove behind the scrim partition. To the left in that narrow recess was an opening hardly wide enough to slip through which contained a flight of steps that went down a few feet and turned sharply to the right and thence out of sight. "So this is how you got in!" I exclaimed in delight, feeling rather like the heroine in a novel who finds the secret chamber and solves the age-old mystery of who killed Grand Duke Osbert back in the seventeenth century or some such nonsense as that. "What's down here?" I asked as I made the first tentative step downward.

"Go on an' look for yourself."

I slipped sideways through the opening and edged my way down the precipitous and narrow steps, carefully and one at a time. Below, after the turning, the steps opened into another crypt, similar to the one under the altar in the ruined chapel, but far larger, corresponding in size to the séance room directly above it. This crypt, unlike the other, was almost completely bare of bones, however, and filled with other, far stranger baggage.

"Fascinating," I cried out, my eyes lighting up with delight. It was the inner workings of a magician's workshop, the sanctum of secrets that triggered the mainspring of the clockwork séances conducted in the room above our heads. Along the ceiling ran a network of pipes and speaking tubes, wires and ropes that disappeared into the walls and the ceiling at each corner of the room. A large organlike contraption—very old and much abused by time—sat near one wall, its pedals and keys and stops wired tautly into the ceiling at the point just above which the chairs of Madame De'Ath and Jemmy must rest on the floor of the séance room.

On wooden shelves and tables rested an array of candles, braziers of cold ashes, circular disks of colored gelatin, drawings of my uncle, copies of his photgraphic image transferred to glass, pots of paraffin wax and paint, all sorts of paraphernalia both mechanical and chemical to be used in the deceptions being practiced during the séance that had just been concluded and those which were yet to be conducted. It was a bizarre and rather theatrical conglomeration of devices for the manufacture of mystery and illusion, and I love the very sight of it all, wanting, like a child, to know how everything worked.

"There's the tunnel ta the crypt under the chapel. It was built in early times as a precaution against raiders from along the Welsh and Irish coast. The monks 'ad an escape 'atch, so ta speak, in times o' trouble," Jemmy said, pointing to a small opening in one corner of the room. "It also accounts for the mysterious 'other-worldly' draftiness of the room above. Nice spooky effect, that, what?"

"Indeed," I agreed, hardly hearing him in my excited exploration of the devices in the room. "Jemmy, this is all so very interesting. Whatever is this?" I asked, poking at a paint pot with a label bearing a skull and crossbones, sure sign that the contents was poisonous.

"Phosphorescent paint for illuminated effects."

"Like the smoke tonight?"

"Naw, for glow-in-the-dark things like floatin' 'ands an' flyin' objects. The smoke was trapped in this covered brazier 'ere," he said, indicating a covered pot on a table directly under the pipe that came down through the center of the room below the table in the séance room. "I just unlidded it by pushing the right button on me chair upstairs. The smoke rose up the pipe through the funnel opening at the end and came out above through the wire mesh in the center of the table and massed as a dense cloud over it. Then all I did was pull the next stop under my chair, and the lighted candle in the lantern on the table 'ere sent a ray o' light up through the pipe inta the darkness of the room above. The light struck on the smoke an' illuminated it. If you'll notice, this rig 'ere is a wire rim wi' flanged edges like one o' them German angel-chime candle things. It held a disk o' tricolored gelatin that spun in the 'eat generated by the candle an' made the smoke appear multicolored until it melted in the hot air. After the gelatin melted and the colors faded, I pushed another stop and a photograph on glass of your uncle slid into place between the candle and the end of the pipe—sort o' like a child's magic-lantern slide. The light cast the image up onto the smoke over the table, causing a blurry but very effective image o' dear Uncle Llewellyn ta seem ta 'over in midair."

"How did it move and turn so eerily? The image actually writhed on the smoke as if it could move on its own, like . . . like a living being."

He laughed. "So simple, girl, so simple. The old lady was looking directly at it, concentratin' on it an' speakin' at the same time. It was the force of 'er own breath that stirred the air an' made the smoke swirl."

"So simple," I agreed.

"The simpler the trick, the better. Less goes wrong. Madame is very good at throwing her voice, and the speaking tubes do the rest. She learned a few sentences of Gaelic and played Mrs. Peggy's mother to perfection. The dear lady wouldn't remember, but she's said enough over the past few months that we've known 'er for us to know what ta 'ave the mother say that'd sound convincing. An' she died so long ago, any Irish-sounding 'ghost' saying a few personal things would convince someone so gullible as Mrs. Peggy."

"It wasn't a very nice thing to do. She's only a kind, simple, and harmless soul, after all. It's my aunt we're trying to hurt, not Mrs. Pond."

" 'Ow did we 'urt Mrs. Peggy?" he asked softly, "Really, now, think, my dear! She was assured o' a life ta come and 'appiness wi' 'er nearest an' dearest at some time far in the future. She believes in a life ta come anyway, an' now she's been reassured straight from the 'orse's mouth, if you will, that she's gonna 'ave a long earthly span follered by an 'appy arterlife. No 'arm done that I can see, an' the gaff 'elped convince yer aunt an' set 'er up fer 'er own experiences o' the evenin'."

"Well, when you put it that way, I can hardly say you nay," I agreed reluctantly. "By the way, speaking of my Aunt Augusta's experiences of the evening, the tobacco smoke was such a sudden and unexpected thing that it absolutely frightened the life out of me. I truly believed that he was amongst us as a sentient being. Despite the little game you seem to be playing with Ambrose, I cannot, I *will* not believe that the aroma of his tobacco was unplanned and just happened. Which of you set it up, and why all the obfuscation about it?"

"Obfuscation!" he exclaimed with a laugh. "Blimey, lady, wot a word!"

"I'll define it if you like," I retorted tartly.

"No, no need ta define it. I'm such an expert on the gentle art o' obfuscation that you might think the word was invented for me."

I was not amused. "Answer me. That damned scent upset me so much I took my courage in my hands and crept through the corridors of this damned mausoleum just to solve the mystery if I could."

"Solve it 'ow?"

"Either by finding out the source of the trick or . . . or . . ."

"Or?" he urged when I faltered.

"Or by conjuring up my uncle's spirit myself if I could," I answered shamefacedly.

He laughed and laughed. "I 'ad you sold, did I? You thought 'e might really 'ave come back from the dead? And smoking 'is favorite tobacco inter the bargain? Oh, girl, you're as gullible as poor Mrs. Peggy, ain't ya?"

"I am not! It . . . it just spooked me, that's all. Now, how did you do it, and why wasn't Ambrose in on it, or Madame De'Ath, for that matter?"

"Doin' it was easy. I simply stole a 'andful o' tobacco out o' yer uncle's 'umidor when I paid me respects ta yer aunt in London. I 'ad no idea at the time that it was such a rare blend. That made it even more convincin', of course, and 'ence even more effective. That's why it 'ad such an effect on you. You bought it for 'im an' knew it was an exclusive blend, so it convinced ya all the more. By the by, that's 'ow I got the photographs as well. The old lady was so upset by you runnin' off ta marry Ambrose that she welcomed my occasional visit. I took every opportunity ta snoop an' pinch what I could." He laughed again, in delight at his own ingenuity and nerve. I sighed in relief. Uncle Llewellyn was dead after all, and not hovering about in some nebulous afterworld, smoking a ghostly pipe and leaving ghostly tobacco ash behind. How ludicrous it all seemed now I knew the truth, and how foolish I felt for having been so gulled by Jemmy's trickery.

"Jemmy, one more thing. Why did you want to fool Ambrose with the effect?"

" 'Cause Ambrose wants to believe in the afterlife just as much as your aunt. If 'e thinks that the séances are workin' in spite o' all our trickery and games, then 'e'll work all the 'arder ta convince the old lady. They'll be 'appy an' so will we."

"But surely he can see through such a sham as well as I can?" I protested.

"Aye, if 'e were entirely sane, an' if 'e weren't so obsessed wi' death an' dyin' that 'e'd do anything to prove there is life arter death. But 'e's not. An' neither is she. They're two o' a kind, Enid, Ambrose De'Ath and Augusta Tregaron."

"Yes, Jemmy, you are right. They have an obsession with death in common, all right."

"They 'ave one more thing than that in common, Enid," he said in an odd tone of voice.

"Oh, what is that?" I asked offhandedly.

"You."

"Me?" I exclaimed.

"Think about it, girl. That's all. Just think about it."

I did not want to. Something told me not to; not now, anyway. "Jemmy," I said as I wandered around the room, poking into all sorts of oddments that were part of the séance-conducting apparatus, "wherever did you learn all these tricks? Paint and transparencies and images on smoke and strange voices—all of it. From the people you knew in London? No, I think not," I answered my own question. "Not from Ambrose?"

"Lord, no. He's as dull as they come. I learned it all from the old madame."

"From Madame De'Ath? From *my* mother-in-law?" I asked, incredulous.

"I don't know why that should surprise you, Enid. Your mother-in-law, as you call 'er, is the sharpest *sharper*, the best *betty*, the finest *broadsman* that I've ever seen, an' I've seen my share. She's an expert at *dookin'*—which is palmistry to you—swindlin', screevin' and forgin'. Well, I could go on."

"What is a broadsman?"

"A card sharp."

I winced. "And a betty?"

"She can pick locks."

"Pick locks," I exclaimed. "My God, man, what are you saying about her?'

"That she's the cleverest crook goin'. I've never known a better or a classier crook in all me life; that she's our ringleader, our sharper. I'm 'er *nobbler*, or special assistant—the *jemmy* one, the smart one and Ambrose . . ."

"And Ambrose?" I urged.

"Ambrose is our buttoner. He's the toff, the gent, the front who entices our dupes—your aunt, for instance, or that prater, Reverend Pond, who ain't worth money to us, but who adds a sort o' low-class dignity and stability to the act, being o' the cloth an' all. He really believes all that spiritualist nonsense 'e spouts, the old fool."

"Never mind Reverend Pond. Get back to my mother-in-law. Madame De'Ath a crook and a sharper? That elegant and wonderful old lady?"

"She is elegant an' wonderful! I never said she wasn't, did I? She's so fine a lady that I'd lay down me very life for 'er if I 'ad to," he retorted. We were practically shouting at each other now, so agitated had we both become by our conversation.

"Jemmy, who is she?"

"Who is she? She's Madame 'Enriette De'Ath, widow of 'Ugo De'Ath, late o' this parish."

"No, Jemmy, not who is she *now*? Who *was* she? I think I know; I'm sure that I know, in fact, but you tell me."

"I can't."

"Why not? Don't you know?"

"I know, but it's not my place to betray 'er confidence. Ask 'er yourself, if you like. She might even answer you, for all I know."

"I'll ask Ambrose," I replied evasively.

"Don't."

"Why not?"

" 'Cause he don't know."

"He doesn't? *You* know and her own son doesn't?"

"Ask 'er yourself, I said."

I walked around the strange organlike device, pacing nervously, impatient and anxious. Jemmy stood in the center of the room, near the table of braziers and candles and gelatin disks from the previous evening's séance.

"How can I ask her?" I said, waving my arms above my head in agitation. "It's so rude. And now I'm more confused than ever. How can Madame De'Ath be all those things you say—a cheat, a sharper, a card sharp, and a swindler . . . and what else? Oh, yes, forger. She's a lady and an aristocrat."

"Is she? Yes, I expect she is aristocratic. But then 'ow, Enid, can a low-life like me read Shakespeare and Byron and Keats, and appreciate fine wines and good food? An' 'ow can a gent like Ambrose De'Ath, Esquire, be a madman who sleeps in a coffin, believes in spirits, an' who lives like a king wi' 'ardly two pence ta rub together? And 'ow can a lovely, innocent little girl sleep through a triple murder an' grow up an embittered, vengeful woman wi' no idea in 'er 'ead o' whether she committed mass murder or not? What does Macbeth say? 'And nothing is but what is not.' The secret o' survivin' in life, my girl, is never bein' surprised by nothin'; by being quick on yer feet an' fast in yer thinkin'—an' never bein' surprised.

"That's why Ambrose is such a fool. I sprang that tobacco trick an' 'e fell for it. It didn't take much to fool 'im, an' now 'e thinks it really is Llewellyn Tregaron smokin' out there in the great beyond. Ludicrous, ain't it? Now, you was scared by it too, but you recovered and set out to investigate for yourself. He'd never do that. 'E's too eager ta be convinced. 'E don't want the *truth*. 'E wants fantasy an' unreality."

"Perhaps you're right, Jemmy. I'm not so experienced in life as you, though. A great deal still surprises me. I've thought all along that Madame De'Ath was something wonderful and elegant and perfect." I felt strangely washed-out and sad as I spoke now.

"And so she *is*—all those things. But she's also more than that—and a great deal less as well, if the truth were known," he said, adding the last remark gently, as if to soften it.

"If the truth were known," I repeated, reflecting on all he had said, on all I had learned that night—of the séance, the mysteries of which were mysterious no longer; of Jemmy, whose history was cruel and ugly and terrible and yet who was rising above his past with a strength and determination that one must admire; and of Ambrose, whose sickness of mind was greater even than I had judged it to be.

But was the truth known? No, not enough of it—not

enough for me, at any rate—and somehow, for me, the key to it all was the mystery of Madame Henriette De'Ath. Once the pieces of her own history fell into place, so too would the mystery of her son, Ambrose, and his vile obsessions be solved. Then I would know why he had married me, believing me to be and actually *wanting* me to be a murderess. Then I would understand Jemmy and the attraction between them, the lady and the wild, low boy of the streets. I would understand the power she had over him, a power that changed his life and started him out of the gutters of London toward some better future.

What was she—lady or crook, mother and widow, or duchesse and forger?

As I left the secret crypt under the séance room that night and passed down the narrow corridor into the New Hall, I was totally obsessed with confronting Madame De'Ath once and for all; obsessed with solving the mystery of her bizarre and conflicting past. Only then, I thought like a thing possessed, would I be satisfied; only then would I have solved the last mystery of all.

Such was my state of mind as I entered the New Hall, leaving Jemmy to clear up a few things, that I actually believe that had the light still shone under the old woman's door, I would have knocked and sought to confront her then and there. *She was the last mystery.* I was so sure of this that it never occurred to me in my strange blindness and lack of perception that *I myself* was the last and greatest mystery of all.

Perhaps, at the time, it was just as well I did not know that while there was but *one* lone Pandora, she was a Pandora confronted by *two* boxes.

# 13

# A DREAM OF
# FAIR WOMEN

A queen, with swarthy cheeks and bold black eyes,
Brow-bound with burning gold.

She, flashing forth a haughty smile, began:
"I govern'd men by change, and so I sway'd
All moods. 'Tis long since I have seen a man."

"Alas! alas!" a low voice, full of care,
Murmur'd beside me: "Turn and look on me;
I am that Rosamond, whom men call fair,
If what I was I be."
—Tennyson

"Aunt Augusta," I whispered tentatively as I opened her door and entered. I was chilled to the bone, not with cold, although the halls of the abbey were in a state of perpetual chill, but rather with an absolute *fear* that was always present in the atmosphere of the hall between those two doors—hers and mine—whenever I chanced to be passing. At times it was virtually unbearable.

I stood there in the open doorway, that horrible fear hanging over me like a pall, and looked at the old woman in her bed, motionless, with the counterpane rumpled around her and the stale smell of a long night's sleep heavy in the air. All at once, I wanted to scream. I wanted to run.

In my mind I did both. In my mind I turned heel and ran back across that dreadful hallway to my own little room, to hide under my own little counterpane and sleep and sleep and sleep.

Nonsense! I was a big girl now!

"Aunt Augusta, Aunt Augusta, are you awake?"

The old woman stirred in her bed. "Enid, come in. Come talk to me," she croaked, her voice harsh and rasping.

I crossed the cold, ugly little room and drew back the draperies, letting in the light of a bright, early-spring morning. That was better, I thought.

"You frightened us last night. We were afraid you were seriously ill," I said. "Do you feel recovered this morning?"

"I do, thank you. I suppose you're disappointed," she said testily as I helped her to sit up and went about arranging the pillows at her back.

"Disappointed?"

"That I did not die right then and there," she snapped.

"Why, why, no, I . . ." I stammered, and then stopped, and getting a grip of myself, went on more firmly: "Aunt Augusta, you mistake me entirely. I do not wish you dead. When you fainted last night, I was, for a moment, in the greatest concern that you had indeed died of shock, and I felt utterly terrible. It was with no feelings but those of gratitude and relief that I saw you come around under the influence of the salts I found in your reticule.

"I am most sincerely glad you are well, even if I do wish you could have awakened less your usual nasty self."

She looked at me penetratingly, her sharp old eyes very thoughtful. "You mean that, do you? Yes, I see you do. You are glad I didn't die last night. Why? What has come over you? You are different, Enid," she stated almost accusingly.

"I have discovered that I do not hate you, Aunt. That is all."

"The tribunal has not changed my mind, Enid," she countered, as if to prove that however much I might have softened, *she* had not. "I know what I know. You did kill——"

"I will not discuss it, Aunt," I said firmly. "Shall I ring for your breakfast, or will you be rising?"

"Ring, then. I shall spend the morning in my bed," she answered.

I pulled on the cord by the fireplace and brought the old woman her shawl to wrap about her shoulders against the chill of the room.

"You felt him, too, Enid!" she stated, not as a question demanding confirmation but rather as a fact without dispute.

"I *thought* I felt his presence, Aunt," I corrected simply and without guile. "As to whether it was actually . . ." I must be careful now. I must not allow myself to appear too convinced as yet, for she knew me for a skeptic and would be suspicious of any sudden about-face on my part.

"Stop playing at words, Enid. I *heard* your voice in that room last night even though I could not *see* your face. It was a conviction with you that he was there. You felt it and you believed it! You said I should not despair when his image faded from my sight; that he was still amongst us. You sensed his presence even more quickly and more strongly than I did myself at first—a fact which surprises me no end but which I cannot deny, since I was witness to it myself.

"And he *was* there!" she hissed at me like some strange animal. "The aroma of his tobacco, surrounded us like an embrace. We felt him, you and I, felt him and felt the comfort of his presence. Llewellyn *was* amongst us last night, Enid, and you know it as well as I do," she insisted vehemently.

"Yes, Aunt," I concurred without argument. It was a difficult position to be in. The previous evening, my impressions had been genuine and natural reactions to the occurrences of the moment. She was remembering them and judging me accordingly. But now I knew that it was all a lie and sham. The scent of his tobacco which had made me react so believably before her had not come out of the ether from beyond the grave, after all, no matter how frightened I had been and no matter how nearly convinced I had been of my dead uncle's living presence. But that was then and this was now. Now I must behave the skeptic once more lest I arouse her suspicions. Now I must act!

"You cannot deny it," she protested.

"I do not deny it. I do not know."

"You do know, you willful girl, and are being perverse just to vex me. I know you too well, Enid. You will vex me and cross me at every turn," she fretted.

How strange! I was in such a position that I could virtually do no wrong no matter what I said to her. Ambrose would be very pleased with the outcome of my part in the séance; Jemmy and Madame De'Ath completely satisfied. All was going quite well.

Why, then, did I feel so very terrible? Why was I not happily anticipating the revenge that would soon be mine?

Perhaps the answer lay in what I had just said to her only moments earlier: "I have discovered that I do not hate you, Aunt."

And it was true; I did not hate her anymore, even in spite of the long years of hellish treatment that I had suffered at her hands. Hate destroyed, and I had come suddenly to realize that I wanted never to hate again.

"Now I know you are well, I shall leave you, Aunt. If I see Ambrose I shall tell him you are awake."

"Tell him I wish to speak to him, Enid."

I nodded and turned to leave. My hand was on the knob when her cracked old voice called out to stay me. "Oh, and Enid, Ambrose has asked me to help him to found a society, a thanatological society, to further the study of the 'occult phenomenon,' as he calls it, and to hire the finest brains to aid in the pursuit of tangible proof of his—our—theories of life beyond the veil."

"He has mentioned such plans to me, Aunt, from time to time," I replied guardedly, my mind racing to find the right replies to the questions that I expected might follow.

"Financial aid," she stressed, which did not surprise me, money ever being an important and powerful tool to her. Witness her using her influence over my Uncle Llewellyn to prevent me from gaining control over my own money before my thirtieth year at the very earliest. In that instance, she was using money as a weapon against me.

"I am aware that it is financial aid of which you speak, Aunt," I said in a voice dripping with venomous sarcasm. "It is one of the sorrows of my present circumstances that I am not free yet, by the terms of the various wills that govern my own inheritance, to help my husband in his most interesting and perhaps worthy ambitions. If my money were, as it should be, my own to spend as I deemed fit, I would not dream of having him borrow or seek endowment in any direction but my own. It is too demeaning for him—and therefore, for me."

"You would endow his society?" she asked in surprise.

"Of course," I snapped in an anger that I hoped was convincing. "Do you think that I like knowing that he has had to come to *you* of all people for money? Because he is my husband, and my duty lies with his best interests, I must endure his having to ask you for help, but if I had my inheritance in hand, I should not let you give him one bloody farthing."

"Enid, your language."

"My language be damned, Aunt! I want you out of my life—not dead, mind you—but out of my life for good and all. If Ambrose accepts financial aid and research assistance from you for his thanatological society, then, dammit, I am even yet bound to you," and I saw her crafty old eyes light up at this, just as I had gauged that they would, "though I detest the very idea. Of course I would heap my riches upon him if I could, if only to release him from any need of you," I raged dramatically.

"As it is," I added more gently, as if I were being forced to relent reluctantly, "after the events of last night, I happen to think that there really may be something to what he is doing. I will not admit it yet for a certainty, but perhaps you two are right about life beyond the veil, and since I cannot help him financially at this time, perhaps it is best, if you wish, that you do so; I hate the very idea, as you may imagine, but I will not stand in my husband's way, no matter what my feelings are toward you.

"It would be an unwifely thing to do," I added for effect, and then worried if I had not overplayed my hand. I was saved at that moment by the maid's entry upon the scene. "And now, here is your maid. Good day, Aunt. I shall send Ambrose to you shortly."

I left her room flushed with an excited sense of accomplishment. She would give him money now, I was sure. My fine piece of acting just now had almost guaranteed it!

Success was at hand, and yet, as I hastened down the corridor toward the breakfast room, the heady sense of my own cleverness began to wear off and I found that I did not really like what I was doing. Even if she was a miserable selfish old woman, cruel and responsible for my remaining impoverished with a fortune years away in my uncertain future, yet did I have the right to cheat her like this? No, I began to think that I was not a very nice young woman. I began not to like myself at all. Yet, the *die* was cast. How could I turn back now?

It was nine-thirty; I had finished my breakfast, told Ambrose of my conversation with Aunt Augusta, and sent him packing like a lover gone a-wooing to her bedside. No sooner had he left when a maid entered the room with a note which she delivered into my hands.

"The coachman is waiting, ma'am, for a reply," she informed me.

The note was from Mr. Ottermole and read as follows:

My dear Madame Ambrose,

There are some urgent matters I must discuss with you at once, and so I pray you will return by my carriage to take luncheon at the Hall with Arabella and . . .

Your obedient servant,
Osric Ottermole

It was a most abrupt and surprising missive and I sensed his concern in that very abruptness, for Mr. Ottermole was by nature a most courtly and ceremoniously courteous little man, hardly given to peremptoriness at all.

I folded the little square of paper hastily and slipped it into a pocket of my morning dress.

"You may send the driver and footman around to the kitchen for some tea, Bess, and say that I shall be ready to return to Wadebridge in half an hour's time."

What could it be? Had it something to do with *The Memoirs of the Duchesse de la Cressonière?* Or perhaps with the events of last evening? I hastened to my rooms and made my toilet at once.

My curiosity was piqued and I would answer Mr. Ottermole's summons posthaste.

Arabella Ottermole sat primly upon the big soft sofa in the Ottermole parlor, one of the kittens, noticeably bigger now, asleep in her lap. She looked at me rather sheepishly as I entered the room on her father's arm, and smiled in greeting. Something was indeed amiss.

And then I saw that there was another in the room. Lucas Pond, stiff and formal and uncomfortably seated on a straight-backed chair in a far corner of that pleasant, cluttered, sunny room. He leaped to his feet self-consciously upon seeing me already in the parlor. Clearly he had been lost in thought and had not noticed our entry at first.

"Madame Ambrose," he fairly exclaimed, coming across the room to grasp my hand. His eyes, I noticed at once, were red-rimmed and dull for lack of sleep, but otherwise he seemed well enough.

"Master Pond, I am surprised—and delighted, of course—to find you here," I said in greeting. But actually, I was quite abashed at his presence. What was the boy doing here? What could he have to do with the "urgent matters" to which Osric Ottermole had made mention in his note?

Nothing perhaps—or everything.

I sat beside Arabella, and taking a kitten of my own to fondle, waited patiently for some explanation of my hasty summons from my host and his daughter. After some slight hemming and hawing, Mr. Ottermole began.

"Madame Ambrose . . ."

"Please, enough of that rather starchy formality, if you please. My mother-in-law is the only 'madame' I know, and I do not care for any other name but my own. Therefore . . ." I trailed off with a gesture of dismissal.

"Very well, then, Enid," the dear little man conceded, putting his chubby thumbs into the front of his vest and leaning back somewhat more at ease in his gentleman's parlor chair. "I am rather embarrassed by my impolite young daughter here. She and Master Pond here have a confession to make."

"Please, sir, it was all my fault," Lucas Pond protested chivalrously. "I put her up to it. Don't blame Miss Arabella," and speaking thus, he turned to give her an urgent look of concern.

"Miss Arabella" blushed prettily.

"I think you had better explain," I urged, more curious now than alarmed. There was too great an air of youthful mischief to arouse my greater concern.

"Master Pond became aware somehow that you had borrowed a book from me. Last night, before the start of the séance, he accosted my daughter in the front hall of the abbey and learned from her the title of the book in question."

"I'd already guessed," the boy interrupted. "I was only lookin' to be sure."

"Whatever," the little man said with a wave of his fat little hand, turning his great brown carbuncle eyes at Master Pond with some slight but amused disdain. "He suggested that she—how shall I put it?—*filch* the volumes if she could, and lend them to him for a quick look."

"He was only going to steal a glance," Arabella put in defensively, and then blushed at her own unfortunate choice of words.

Master Lucas explained further. "I saw by the bookmark being in the first few pages of Volume II that you had finished with the first. I asked Miss Arabella's permission to take that one while she returned the others to your rooms."

"I wondered, Arabella, how you came to know that I'd finished that first volume," I remarked. "I had not mentioned the fact to you at all, regardless of what you said last evening."

"Pray forgive me, madame . . . Enid. I . . . I really meant no harm. And the volume is not lost, after all," she added brightly. "Lucas has returned it to Papa already."

"Has he indeed? What a quick study you are, Master Pond," I remarked sarcastically.

"I was up with it all night, ma'am," he explained with a stifled yawn, "and am sufferin' for that fact now, I might add."

"My sympathies. Now, why was the book such an object of curiosity that the two of you resorted to the petty theft of my private apartments?" I asked dryly and with some severity in my tone, lest the import of their bad behavior be lost upon them entirely. I was, as I have said, more curious than concerned at this point, but I had no wish to condone their actions by letting them off too lightly. The reward of my severity was the expressions of pained embarrassment on their young faces. It was enough.

"I wanted to read the memoirs for the same reason as you, ma'am," Lucas said simply. "The old lady didn't like the mere mention of this Duchesse de la C., and it set my mind ta thinkin' as it did yours. I was already suspicious of her, and any clue I could find would help, wouldn't it? When Pa an' me spotted you comin' from this house with books the next day, I put two an' two together and come up with 'memoirs.' I've been wantin' ta have a look-see ever since."

"And now you have, thanks to your pretty little accomplice in crime," I said only half-seriously.

"Well, she is pretty, ma'am, I'll grant you," he said solemnly as Arabella blushed crimson and Mr. Ottermole's eyes gleamed with feeling, "but as to bein' a partner in crime, the fault is entirely mine." He shook his big head slowly for emphasis.

I found that I really rather liked this seemingly stolid and oafish youth. He was smart and gentlemanly and gallant, if rather overly solemn in his demeanor, awkward yet in his painfully youthful looks and terribly "American" in his speech and lack of polish. I chanced a look at Arabella. She was regarding him even more thoughtfully than was I, as if judging for herself if he was the raw material of a good match. Interesting! Perhaps he was.

"Why do you think that she brooks no mention of that particular book, Lucas?" I asked, getting back to the main issue.

" 'Cause it reveals too much about her, ma'am. Because it tells who Henriette De'Ath really is—and what she's up to!'

"What she's up to!" I could not help but exclaim.

"Master Pond and I have talked at some length on this matter over breakfast this morning, Enid," Mr. Ottermole spoke up. "The boy was here before eight to return the book, explain his actions in taking it, and to voice some concern, for all of which things I must heartily commend him, however much I may disapprove his behavior of last evening.

"While waiting your arrival from the abbey, I have glanced

over those passages in the book which seemed to Lucas to be pertinent to his point and have generally refreshed my memory on the first volume as a whole. I have not read it, you see, in some twenty years or so. In fact, I remember at the time trying to interest Madame De'Ath in reading the book or talking of her own history vis à vis that of the duchesse whom I even wondered if she might not have known in Paris in the early days. She would have none of it and put me off with much firmness. I put her reactions down to the painfulness of her experiences and thought no more of it. Until, of course, it came up again recently. Now, I wish I had pursued it long ago."

"And I heartily wish I had not read it all. In fact, I have read quite enough myself, for I find the duchesse's debauchery very distasteful. Therefore I have brought along the remaining volumes of the book," I added, withdrawing the two remaining volumes from my bag and placing them on a nearby table. The kitten jumped from my lap in alarm as I extended my arm. "There," I stated with finality, "safe and sound. All three volumes home where they belong.

"Now, as to the mystery of Madame De'Ath, I confess that I am suddenly in some embarrassment. I did read these memoirs with an aim toward learning what she herself chose not to reveal. I, too, feel that I have now discovered her true identity through reading this book, but she is my mother-in-law, and I feel it would be both indiscreet and disloyal of me to indulge in such speculation with you all, especially since to do so would be so clearly a violation of her wishes in the matter."

"Excuse me, Enid, but do I understand you to feel that you know her identity now as a result of your reading?"

"But yes, Mr. Ottermole. Have I not just said so?"

"And knowing that identity, you *still* feel constrained by loyalty and discretion?" he pursued with an emphasis that puzzled me.

"Why, yes, of course! Shouldn't I?" I asked in astonishment.

He was even more astonished than I, and so, I noted in utter amazement, were Master Pond and Arabella.

"Why, no indeed," he exclaimed. "I certainly should not if I were you . . . unless, of course . . ." He broke off abruptly and looked to Master Pond, who nodded shrewdly as if reading the elder man's unspoken thought.

"Miss Enid, ma'am," the boy asked carefully, as if

broaching a delicate subject, "just who is it you think Madame De'Ath really is? Do speak up, please, for there is more in this than you seem to think."

I sat there rather stunned, looking from one serious, concerned face to another. "More in this than I seem to think!" I repeated. "You are rather frightening me." I looked with pleading eyes at Mr. Ottermole.

"You are not being disloyal, I can assure you, Enid." He smiled reassuringly. "Who is it you have concluded that she is?"

"Why, who else? La Duchesse Eugénie-Marie de la Cressonière, of course!" I cried. "She wrote those memoirs long ago, perhaps—nay, surely—as a necessity in order to eat, but now, quite understandably, given some of the book's shocking revelations, she wishes to put that shameful past behind her and live in a shriven and repentant obscurity. Who can blame her?" I exclaimed in her defense, stopping suddenly in my harangue when I realized that Lucas and Osric Ottermole had both leaned back in their seats and were nodding their heads at each other in what I took to be a relieved understanding. Even Arabella seemed to know what it was that they saw. I felt suddenly quite out of the picture.

"Stop this! Pray inform me if you see some error in my thinking. Who else could she be, and why should her identity at this point have any other than the most superficial significance? It is nothing more than a matter of historical curiosity after nearly seventy years, I should think!"

"Enid," Mr. Ottermole said gently, leaning forward in his chair toward me in a serious and confiding manner, "the true identity of Madame De'Ath has implications to the here and now that are of the very gravest import for us all, and it is only the implicit conviction of the three of us in this room with you that you are an innocent victim of the old woman's machinations that enables us to speak to you as we do now. My dear young lady, there is a plot afoot at the abbey, and the proof of its existence is to be found in the pages of that very memoir you have been reading, and in the real identity of the woman you call mother-in-law—Madame Henriette De'Ath."

I felt my face drain of color and my stomach wrench into a knot. What did they mean? What was it that they knew?

"But that was all so long ago! It is past history, that book!" I protested.

"The seeds of the present are ever rooted in the past, my

child," he answered placidly with the preaching tone of one who speaks in aphorisms as a habit.

"Who is this plot against, then?"

"Against all of us, since we are made dupes by it, but its principal aim is against your poor aunt, Augusta Tregaron."

"Aunt Augusta?" I was sick at heart now. What was going on? How could they know? "Mr. Ottermole, Lucas, pray do be clear. What is going on? To begin with, if I am wrong, then just who is Madame De'Ath if not the former Duchess de la Cressonière?"

"My dear," he began to address me, and then broke off, saying to Arabella, "Daughter, take your friend's hand, for I fear she is about to be shocked."

"Yes, Papa. Dear Enid, do not be upset by what Papa says. We shall decide amongst us what to do, and it will all come right in the end, won't it?" Arabella said comfortingly.

"Enough. Please get on with it," I insisted impatiently.

"My dear Enid, your mother-in-law is none other than one of the most adept and notorious charlatans of pre-Revolutionary France, mistress of the hynotist Mesmer, apt pupil of the greatest fraud of all time, Comte Alessandro di Cagliostro and his licentious wife Lorenza. Your mother-in-law was once known and celebrated in Europe, and later, briefly, in London itself as the greatest courtesan and poseur of her day—the remarkable and mysterious lady known as Clotilde du Roc."

"Clotilde du Roc!"

They all nodded solemnly.

"The child-mistress of Mesmer, the consort of Cardinal de Rohan and countless other great men of France and later of Italy and England. She dropped from sight around 1810 and has not been seen or heard of since—until now."

"It is unthinkable, Mr. Ottermole. The aristocratic duchess, Eugénie-Marie de la Cressonière, yes! But a notorious charlatan and trickster, a courtesan . . ." And even as I spoke, I knew that they were right. Jemmy had said that she was both a great lady and a "sharper" and a forger as well. In fact, months ago when Ambrose had first come to the house in Park Lane and presented the alleged signatures of Uncle Llewellyn that he claimed his mother had written automatically at the very hour of my uncle's death, I had told my aunt that Henriette De'Ath, whoever she might be, was most likely a consummate forger. And now I knew that that was precisely it—a mistress of the art of forgery. And why not? Was it not one of the many convenient tricks of a dishonest trade that such premier fakers as the Cagliostros would have been at pains to teach a clever and willing apprentice to their devious schemes? She had been their accomplice, and being both smart and ambitious, she had learned well; so well that over half a century later she not only still practiced her trickery, but passed her knowledge along to her son and her boon companion, Jemmy Burkers.

"A plot, you said." I broke off my reverie and urged Mr. Ottermole on in his explanation.

"Lucas here spotted it at once in his reading. He marked certain passages and pointed them out to me this morning. I have come to the same conclusions that he has drawn."

"Go on."

"Very well. The large round table at which the duchesse first sees Cagliostro seated with the Cardinal de Rohan and several other notables . . ."

"Yes?"

". . . is the table, the very table, baize-covered now, at which Madame De'Ath conducts her séances. Cagliostro used to conduct 'spirit dinners' at which the ghosts of great men of the ancient world 'dined' with his living guests. It was probably just such an occasion that the young duchesse glimpsed through the billowing curtains on her first evening at the mansion on Rue Saint-Claude. He also conducted sessions of 'animal magnetism' at that well-known round table. Madame De'Ath still uses the term—an old-fashioned one—in favor of the newly coined 'spiritism.' Now, just as did Count Cagliostro in the Paris of the 1780s, Madame De'Ath uses that table in the England of 1850."

"You are saying that we sat at the table of a man who has been dead since 1794 or thereabouts and that the séance was conducted in such a manner as he might have conducted it—and by a pupil of his arts as well?" I reiterated slowly, trying to give myself time to think. I knew, of course, that he was right, but nevertheless, this was a serious turn of events which I must deal with even while I wrestled with the revelation of Madame De'Ath's true identity.

"I am," he said firmly, with a grave nod of his bald yellow head. "Can you not see that in the very furnishings of her house; the manner in which she creates, in that salon of hers and in the dramatic effect of that dazzling dining room, a world of fantasy and illusion? It is the same technique that was used in the mansion of the Cagliostros over sixty years ago. The use of incense and mirrors—both distractions and distortions to take one's senses away from reality, the use of very dim lighting or no lighting at all, black candles, sounds coming from nowhere and yet everywhere at once, unnerving effects to break down one's natural resistance to unreality; to shake one's ordinary common sense and to open one to trickery and obfuscation. Or, in the ordinary run of evenings with her, the effective use of opulence and glamour to utterly charm and distract the senses. She makes anything seem possible when one is in her company."

"Well, she does do that, I will admit," I conceded with a rueful smile.

"The dining table, sir," Lucas urged with a no-nonsense practicality about him.

"Ah, yes. We dined, do you remember, at a long gilt-bronze table set on its surface with mirror? A most unique piece of furniture, would you not say, and of extremely high value, to say nothing of the setting itself—a room of glass and mirror and crystal chandeliers?"

"Indeed, most unique and certainly very valuable," I concurred as I absently stroked the kitten that had returned to my lap. I held Arabella's hand with my other, free one, hoping that she could not feel how I trembled in every fiber of my being. This was a terrible turn of events.

"Let me read from the memoir," Mr. Ottermole said, raising a finger to stay further comment as he ran his thumb over the edge of the first volume of that devilish little book. I heartily wished that I had never seen it. True, I now knew, for what it was worth to me, the identity of my mother-in-law, but what did it avail now that they all knew, and that by their knowing, the plot to relieve my aunt of some of her fortune would be exposed as well? Dammit! It was the very last thing that I had wished to happen. Damn Lucas Pond! That seemingly dull boy was too clever a man by half.

"Here it is," Mr. Ottermole exclaimed at last, "on page ninety-seven." He put a pair of fragile-looking wire-rimmed spectacles on the end of his nose, and peering down through them, read the following: " 'Then, at another clapping of her long, pale hands, a second pair of doors flung back, revealing a large, dim room, bare save for gauzy hangings and a long, narrow *bronze-d'oré* table set with mirrors upon its surface . . .' The table, Enid, at which we dined some few weeks ago, a unique table, and one which, I have no doubt, once belonged to Cagliostro himself, even as many of the other furnishings of her suite may have once been his. After he and Lorenza were banished from France in the late 1780's, he did reside in England for some time. Perhaps he left their valuables in the hands of confederates—or one confederate in particular, if you understand my meaning."

"Clotilde du Roc," I muttered, more to myself than in answer to his conjecture. They were right. She *was* Clotilde du Roc, the slim and elegant child-woman, so poised and beauteous and desirable that she had even fascinated one of her own sex with her celebrated charms. Yes, I could well believe that the Henriette De'Ath that I knew in 1850 was the same Clotilde du Roc who had been the talk of Paris in 1784.

And suddenly, with a strange feeling of relief, almost an overwhelming sense of relief, I realized I was glad that she was Clotilde, who had turned away the duchesse with all her unnatural yearnings, and not the aristocratic Eugénie-Marie, who could be a prey to such desires in the first place. I had come to hate the debauched and degraded sensuality to which the duchesse had become such an easy and willing slave, seduced into unnatural vices by fashion and idle living. I had hated the very idea that my magnificent Henriette De'Ath could ever have been so besotted as that, but now I knew! She was not Eugénie-Marie, but Clotilde, and being Clotilde, she had rejected the kiss of Isis, the way of Lesbos. Oh, she was still a villainess, to be sure, but crimes against nature, at least, were not numbered amongst those villainies. Far better the mistress of a cardinal than of a duchesse, I thought to myself, and as I did, I almost laughed out loud with sheer pleasure at that notion and the way I had put it in my own mind.

"Madame De'Ath is a great lady," I remarked to no particular purpose.

"She is Clotilde du Roc," Arabella put in, obviously rather scandalized by it all. The young, I realized, are often far more intolerant than their elders. But then, that held true of me as well, for was I not far less tolerant of all this than, say, Mr. Ottermole would be, or surely, Madame De'Ath herself, who was the kindest and most tolerant person I had ever known. Then, too, she would be, having seen so much more of life—and such a varied life, at that—than most people would in several lifetimes.

"But nevertheless," I insisted to Arabella, "a great lady."

"She is out to cheat your aunt," Osric Ottermole added as a reminder, "and she is doing it with Ambrose's help—your husband's help—and with the help of Jemmy Burkers, who, I have suspected, nay, *known,* for some time now, is no more a servant in that house than I am myself."

"Why should they do such a thing?" I asked by way of argument, knowing all the while quite well why.

"For money."

"Money? Why, Ambrose is wealthy, the abbey is worth a fortune . . ." I protested, lying of course.

"The abbey and most of its contents are entailed upon a cousin of his in the event of Ambrose De'Ath dying without male issue. He is, of course, married now, but nevertheless . . ." He said no more on that subject, seeing the look on my face. "You mistake, Enid, or have been misled rather, if you think your husband is wealthy. His expenses so far outstrip the income from his father's estate that he is in debt to everyone he knows, from his club in London to the greengrocers in Wadebridge, to every bookseller and curiosity shop between here and Paris—and to myself as well," he added deprecatingly.

"To you as well," I said in dismay. Even to a friend was he in debt, as well? Unthinkable!

"For funerary equipage, mourning clothes, and funerary haberdashery of every sort purchased in ever-increasing numbers over the past few years as his obsession with death has grown deeper. My dear, your husband owes me over three thousand pounds. The debt was even greater at one time, but he paid off some of it about a year ago, only shortly after having had a wealthy elderly couple as his guests in the abbey for a few weeks.

"They were there in order to try to contact their son who had been killed in India. They 'contacted' him, and as a result, rewarded Ambrose with a gift of several thousand pounds to aid his researches. At the time, I gave it little thought, putting it down to obsessed scholars with sincere—if peculiar—beliefs in the hereafter, and I dismissed the whole incident.

"I dabbled in animal magnetism with them after all, even if only as an intellectual amusement. There are so few amusing or cultivated people in Wadebridge, you see, and the De'Aths are a fascinating family. I might even have gone on, continued to dabble in the occult with them, with never a thought in my head of chicanery, were it not for the shrewdness and sharp observations of our astute young Master Pond here."

I looked at Lucas Pond with hooded eyes, trying not to show how annoyed I was with his cleverness. At first glance, this boy was young and awkward and stolid, yet withal, he was actually a shrewd, honest, and promising young man.

"Master Lucas," I said at last, "you are to be commended for your keen sense of observation and deductive reasoning. However, I hardly know what to say. We have no shred of proof. Madame De'Ath may deny her past and call us over-imaginative busybodies for our pains. Ambrose most sincerely does believe in a life after death, and as far as Jemmy Burkers is concerned, I will admit that my mother-in-law indulges him in ways that no servant should become accustomed to, but after all, she is old and eccentric and has a right to indulge her whims if she so chooses. If she spoils Mr. Burkers, why, it has done no harm to his education and general well-being, and he acts as her factotum with the utmost respect for her person and with an unshakable loyalty that I find quite admirable." I hoped that I sounded reasonable.

"You are being unwise, Enid," Osric Ottermole chided gently. "They are a charming and interesting crew, perhaps, but they are, or have recently become, at any rate, a hotbed of crooks as well, and they are out to cheat your aunt, using us all here, and Master Pond's innocent parents also, as dupes in their devious game." As he finished, his tone become quite severe.

"I have no love for my Aunt Augusta," I declared, changing tack quite suddenly and with very little thought, more's the pity. "Suppose what you say is true; suppose they convince her that Uncle Llewellyn is waiting beyond the veil for her, and as a result, she gives them money? What of it? She is rich. She can afford it, and whatever price she pays, she will be paying for the conviction that she will see her brother again and that she herself will not drop into an abyss of oblivion when she dies, but rather will pass over into some better world.

"She is terrified of dying," I went on vehemently, "and of a nothingness beyond the grave. Believe me, no price would be too great for her to pay, if by paying it she assuaged those terrible fears of hers. And if they can, with their trickery—if it is trickery—reassure her, why, then, let them. She has nothing better to do with her wealth.

"I'll surely never see it, she hates me so." I had spoken feelingly, hotly, and from the honest depths of my soul.

"What are you saying, Enid?" Mr. Ottermole asked directly.

"I am saying, all right, you may have uncovered a plot. What of it? Let the spirit band continue on its merry way. Let Ambrose collect his ill-gotten gains if he can. Perhaps he'll even pay you something on his debt, Mr. Ottermole," I added fliply, regretting that last remark even as the words flew from my mouth.

"I do not care about the debt. I would rather absorb it myself than regain it by helping Ambrose De'Ath to cheat old ladies," he growled at me with some anger in his tone.

"I am sorry. I should never have said such a thing," I replied contritely.

"But, Miss Enid, what is it you *are* saying? That we go along as if nothing had happened?" Lucas asked, observing me narrowly.

"Yes, exactly."

"But why?" Arabella protested, looking at me in wonderment.

"Because I ask it of you," I said simply. "Friends, I *promise* you that until I walked into this room an hour ago and you apprised me of it, I did not dream that Madame De'Ath might actually be such a notorious character as Clotilde du Roc. It does, however, explain much that I have puzzled over and prove to me that she is indeed a consummate charlatan and that, trained in her youth by the masters of her craft, so to speak, she comes by her talents logically and quite naturally." And here I could not help but think to myself of Jemmy's revelations about her devious talents. He had been telling me who she was with his every remark, and yet, still, I had been dense; had been convinced she was the other, more debauched of the two women. Better a rascal than a dissolute. "Now," I went on, "given all that, there is something else—a new development—which affects seriously how you handle this situation you have discovered. You see, I have reason to believe that, unfortunately, it is already beyond the point of turning back and undoing the damage that this séance has already done.

"I have seen my aunt this morning. I am relieved to say that she is well and has suffered no ill effects after her spell, *but* she is now virtually convinced of Ambrose's theories. One more session like the last—this coming Friday—and she will undoubtedly endow his 'thanatological society' with great willingness and even joy. The money will be no loss to her, I can assure you," I added dryly.

"Now, if after having been convinced—and as I say, she is virtually to that point already—that she has an afterlife awaiting her, she were suddenly to be disabused of that conviction, I think that it might serve to destroy her utterly. I would actually fear for her life, in fact." I stopped, letting the weight of my words sink in, for I meant them sincerely.

"I see." Mr. Ottermole nodded. "Go on." Lucas, for his part, was silent, but I saw him nodding quietly to himself.

"I warned you once, child," I said, turing to Arabella, "that I was no poor, put-upon heroine out of a novel. I have not always been good, and I confess to you now that once I did wish my aunt's destruction. I do not wish it anymore. I have learned that I have no need of revenge and I no longer have any desire to disabuse her of her pathetic and desperate belief in some supernatural life to come, if it comforts her, but—and I became sure of this only this very morning—if she *were* disabused of her near-conviction at this already-too-late date, it might well accomplish for me, against my will, what I had originally hoped for—her suffering and her end."

Arabella smiled at me ruefully.

"It is a dilemma," Mr. Ottermole exclaimed. "To expose the plot might cause trouble of an even more unpleasant sort than we have got already, yet morally we cannot let them go on with it. What about my telling Ambrose that I'm on to him and letting him take it from there?" he suggested.

"I fear it would be useless, sir. Ambrose more than half believes in thanatology himself. In spite of the fact that he must be a party to this deception, Ambrose is utterly convinced that my uncle actually was in that room with us last night. I thought so too, at first, but realize now that it was a trick. He *must* be aware that it was trickery—or *should* be—but insists that it was a true contact between our world and the next," I added so that they should have a true picture of the situation at the abbey—minus, of course, my own culpability, as much as possible. I was ashamed to admit my own deep part in this situation for which I was having more and more regret as time wore on.

"He is far gone," Mr. Ottermole lamented with a clicking of his tongue and a shaking of his bald head. "That poor boy. The seeds of his madness were sown in childhood and now they spring forth, flower, and branch. Enid, my dear, it is blunt and cruel to say, but I have known Ambrose De'Ath since he was born and I know that his mind will not much longer bear the weight of the madness that lurks within him. You must be prepared for the worst, which is a terrible thing to have to say to a young bride, but you are strong and must be told.

"When I heard that he had married, I almost had hope. I know that Madame De'Ath was pleased, but alas, I have seen no change for the better. And from what you say, it seems his madness grows upon him. Poor Enid! Poor Madame De'Ath!" he lamented.

"Poor Madame De'Ath!" Arabella repeated. "Why, Papa, just moments ago you were condemning her for a charlatan and a loose woman. She is a shocking person with a lurid past," the girl exclaimed primly.

"Wait, wait, my dear." He laughed at his daughter, holding up one plump little hand in protest. "You mistake me greatly. I do not like her present use of her 'talents' to cheat Enid's aunt—or anyone else, for that matter—and I surely do not like being used as a dupe in the process, but I do not condemn her past.

"Hers is a magnificent history, detailed far better in footnotes to the life of Alessandro di Cagliostro or Cardinal de Rohan, or any of several other powerful men of her heyday, than even in the few referencs to her in the pages of this memoir here. She was the greatest mistress in an age of great mistresses. She was a lady of legendary wisdom and charm and beauty, gaiety and power, remoteness and majesty. She was, nay, *is*, a truly romantic figure!

"If she employed the trickery of a Mesmer or a Cagliostro, she added to those dishonest skills her own vast talents as a woman of mystery and a mistress of charm; as a warm companion and a gentle teacher. Always, those lovers of hers who wrote of her, wrote with high praise and great admiration.

"She is still a woman of greatness and glory; I dearly love her as a friend and have loved her thus for over thirty years. It has been an honor to be the companion of such a lady, and if she has failed in any aspect of her life that I know of, it is only in trying to raise the demons that have plagued her poor stepson's twisted mind. And God knows that failure has not been for want of trying, for—"

"Her stepson?" I cried, breaking in on his romantic defense of Madame De'Ath.

"Oh, yes. What, did you not know? Ambrose De'Ath is not her own blood. Did she never tell you?"

"No, she did not," I said in complete amazement, "nor, I might add, did Ambrose himself," I said with mounting indignation at having been kept so in the dark. How could I have lived so long in that house and known none of this? I was suddenly too angry with Ambrose to be quite rational.

"Pray calm yourself. It is understandable that *he* should not tell you of his true relationship to her," the little man said with a wave of his hand and an effort to soothe my indignation. "Ambrose, in his delusion, no longer acknowledges his step-relationship to her. He is convinced that she is his very own mother and would deny as an aspersion on them both any implication to the contrary. That is why he resents her favoring of Burkers, the servant, too, I think. He looks upon it as a betrayal by his very own flesh and blood."

"But why? What would it matter that she is his stepmother? Why deny the relationship? It would not change their feeling for each other, surely?" I persisted in confusion.

"It does not change hers. She has tried to reach out to him and help him ever since she first came to Thanatos Abbey—or Abbey De'Ath, as it was called in former times, before Ambrose renamed it a few years ago. She came here over thirty-three years ago as the second wife of Ambrose's father, Hugo De'Ath. She has remained faithful to her responsibility for the twenty years since old Hugo's passing, and will do so, I have no doubt, until the end. But the delusion is not hers. It is Ambrose's own delusion that she is his real mother. You do not know that sad story, do you? No, I can see you do not." Osric Ottermole shook his dome of a head sadly at the memories that our conversation had awakened in him.

"The boy was under four years of age when his real mother died; childbed fever it was, just like that which took Princess Charlotte of Wales, who might be queen this very day had she lived. It was my father who laid her out up at the abbey—in the very room that is now Ambrose's bedroom, if I'm not mistaken. I helped him. I was a boy of nineteen then, just the age Lucas is now.

"She was a pretty woman, dark and pale, rather like you are in looks, Enid, and she was laid out in a black oak coffin in her white wedding dress. There were four candles at the four corners of the box, and a chair for Hugo De'Ath, who was in great grief, as you may imagine, and determined to sit a vigil over her body all night. Poor man, he knew as well that the infant girl in the nurse's care in a room down the hall would soon be following its mother. It must have been a very hard vigil to keep.

"Finally, however, sleep overcame his determination to remain awake and he nodded in his chair. Sometime during that awful night, unbeknownst to anyone, the boy Ambrose crept into the room after his father. When old Hugo woke in the early morning, it was to find the horrifying sight of his only son and heir, Ambrose De'Ath, asleep in the coffin of his mother, snuggled up against the corpse as if they were two babes asleep in the woods. It was such a heartrending sight that, unwise though it may have been to shock the boy thus, he cried out, poor man, in alarm and woke the child. Ambrose began to cry, fondling his mother's dead face and playing with her stiff hands, cajoling her to wake up and play with him.

"When Hugo tried to remove the child, the boy fought like a devil and, with maddened eyes, clung to her corpse. It was a nightmarish experience for them both, of course, and I know that the memory of it troubled Hugo De'Ath to the end of his days. The boy never recovered at all," Mr. Ottermole concluded sadly.

"Poor Ambrose; poor, poor deluded madman," I lamented, my heart filled with a kind of hollow pity for him. How could I hate him now or be revolted by his horrible obsession? He was mad and had been so from one terrible long-ago hour in his early childhood. Poor mad Ambrose.

But what of myself, chained by a golden band to that madness for the rest of my days? No, that was another matter. I would not think of it now.

Lucas spoke up then. "All this is very interestin' history, sir, but we are really forgettin' the main point. What are we to do about this plot? You have discounted, for very sound reasons I may say, discussin' it with Ambrose De'Ath himself, or the old lady Tregaron, but something should be done!" the boy urged politely.

"Indeed it must, Papa," Arabella agreed.

"Enid, when you return to the abbey, tell Madame De'Ath all that we suspect of her séances and plotting, seeing to it that, for his own sake, your husband is not a party to the conversation," Mr. Ottermole instructed. "Tell Madame De'Ath that I shall expect a message from her before Friday next, giving any suggestions or remarks that she may care to make in defense of her endeavors. And, by all means, send her my respectful greetings as well. Make it clear to her that I consider us to be far too old and too fast friends and neighbors for this affair to change my kind regard for her—unless, of course, the outcome be not to my liking."

"Father," Arabella cried out in dismay, "you speak so romantically of her."

"Ah, my dear little girl, you are a product of these middle-class times when our lively little Hanoverian queen is being tamed by her boring and priggish Coburg mate. The age of my youth and that of my dear father before me was an age of golden license and passion and sensual joy. It was the age of Marie Antoinette and tumbling heads, of impostors and rogues like Giuseppe Balsamo, who called himself Cagliostro the immortal, and Mesmer, who talked to ghosts. It was the age of Napoleon and Josephine and of Madame Récamier and the Princess Pauline Borghese; of Lady Caroline Lamb and mad Queen Caroline of Brunswick, who was our sovereign George's embarrassing and tragic wife.

"Ladies sent locks of their privy hairs to their potential lovers and risked pneumonia by wetting their muslin gowns in order to render them transparent before they made their entrance into a ballroom. Beau Brummell walked the streets of London with his 'fat friend,' the Prince Regent, and the old Duke of Wellington told a former mistress to 'publish and be damned' when she tried to blackmail him. It was a great age—and Clotilde du Roc was a queen of that age. We shall not see her like again."

"It is very strange," I murmured.

"What is strange, my dear?" Mr. Ottermole asked distractedly, his romantic soul lost in the glamour of the past that his words were conjuring up for us.

"She is an old, old lady. At least eighty-three, I should judge, and yet everything you say of her, everything she has ever been or done, even the beauty that she must once have had are still there—still to be seen, or sensed at least. There is such majesty in her aspect and such glamour as well. At times even a sort of inspired madness. Sometimes when I watch her, I can see a girl of sixteen or eighteen in her face, or the poise and grace of a mature and elegant lady in her thirties. It is true, I can see her as a mistress and a lover, and yet as a mother, too. She enthralls and captivates utterly with the power of her being. It is so strange." I ended lamely, drained of words, and all of them somehow seeming trite and inexpressive of what I wished to convey. Mr. Ottermole spoke just then:

> Stiller than chisell'd marble, standing there;
> A daughter of the gods, divinely tall,
>   And most divinely fair.
>
> Her loveliness with shame and with surprise
>   Froze my swift speech; she turning on my face
> The star-like sorrows of immortal eyes,
>   Spoke slowly in her place:
>
> "I had great beauty; ask thou not my name:
>   No one can be more wise than destiny.

Many drew swords and died. Where'er I came
    I brought calamity."


"That is Tennyson, children, and when I first read that poem many years ago, I wondered to myself if he had not known Henriette De'Ath."

"Jemmy Burkers quoted Byron," I said. I quoted Jemmy's reference:


    She walks in beauty, like the night
      Of cloudless climes and starry skies;
    And all that's best of dark and bright
      Meet in her aspect and her eyes.


"Well, my dear, Mr. Burkers has more sensibility than I would have thought. I commend him for it, but it only serves to prove my point." Mr. Ottermole smiled, nodding approval. "Byron knew her, too. And Shakespeare and Spencer did, and great poets yet unborn will know her one day."

"That doesn't make sense," Lucas Pond said stolidly, with a look of boredom on his countenance. Arabella looked fascinated if a bit puzzled withal, and I smiled my encouragement, for I loved the wide streak of romanticism in this homely little man. He went on speaking, his tone soft and wistful with just that touch of the poet that is in so many otherwise unprepossessing little men.

"In every age, my dears, there is a Clotilde du Roc, a Helen of Troy, an Elizabeth, a St. Joan of Arc, a Madame De'Ath, a—yes, I shall even venture to name her, though her greatness will be, I think, of a different nature than theirs—a Victoria. It is the Mystery of Woman of which I speak, and in every age there are those who transcend their more mundane sisters and come to personify in their single selves the whole of man's eternal 'Dream of Fair Women.'"

# 14

# AFTERNOON OF
# THE JEWELS

... heaps of pearl,
Inestimable stones, unvalu'd jewels ...
—*Shakespeare*

One pearl of great price.
—*St. Matthew*

The carriage had barely come to a halt at the abbey doors before I alighted, dashing past the footman like an impatient girl instead of a well-bred woman, but my spirits were too high, my eagerness too great to stand on ceremony.

I raced along the corridors of the abbey and did not check my pace until I was at the very doors of the New Hall itself. I knocked and heard from beyond the painted panels a command to enter. I flung the doors to their widest in my exuberance and made the first few steps of my entrance, stopping almost at once as my eyes met a blinding blaze of dazzling light that transfixed me where I stood.

The New Hall by daylight! The New Hall not seen as a golden and mysterious candlelit salon, but rather, exposed to the full glare of the harsh, bright afternoon light of a spring day. All the windows were open and unshuttered to the fresh spring air; the tall, wide doors of the dining hall were thrown back, and light streamed in at every pane of its three glass walls, turning the great crystal chandeliers overhead into gigantic glittering spiderwebs of spun sugar.

No shadow remained save the shadowed face of the room's only occupant. At the center of that blazing, daylit suite, near the threshold of the dining hall itself, stood Madame Henriette De'Ath, she who was also the notorious Clotilde du Roc.

She wore a simple pale blue satin shepherdess dress, or at least what had passed for such simple garb in the glamorous age of Marie Antoinette of France, a small gray wig upon her head, covered by a lace-edged scarf and yellow straw hat that was tied under the chin with a wide blue satin ribbon. Over her arm was a basket filled with early-spring flowers and in her gloved hands a pair of common garden shears.

"Come in, my dear. I was just about to trim the gardenia trees. Will you keep me company?"

"*Oui*, madame," I said, and came forward toward her, still seeing only the outline of her tall, graceful form against the bright light of the room beyond the threshold where she stood. Her face was in shadow even yet, and her features consequently dim to my eyes. How odd, I reflected: I had never seen her stand before to her full height. She had always been either seated or wheeled as if an invalid in that enormous bath chair of hers, or leaning on the arm of Jemmy Burkers with only her head and shoulders remaining erect and noble of carriage. Now, as she stood awaiting my slow and thoughtful approach, I saw that she was quite tall indeed, her entire manner and bearing as magnificent as that of a queen, despite her great age.

Her eyes flashed fires of challenge as I came up to her. She knew I knew.

"You have read enough, I think?" she said simply, her eyes still sharp as she gazed at me.

"*Oui*, madame. Enough and more than enough," I replied more stiffly than I had intended. It was my guilt that I sought to cover. I felt as if I had somehow betrayed her.

"I confess to having been annoyed at first, but it really does not matter." She shrugged and turned toward the banks of potted trees and plants at the nearest corner of the glass-enclosed dining hall. "Does it?" she asked, her back to me as she snipped at a topiary tree.

"No, madame, it does not. I . . . I am glad, rather, that you are who you are and not who I *thought* you were. . . ."

"And who was that, my dear?"

"I thought at first, foolishly I now admit, that it was the Duchesse de la Cressonière. . . ."

At this my mother-in-law half-turned and laughed, her old head thrown back, the network of wrinkles on her face and neck stretched to youthful smoothness by her action, her dark eyes merry with ironic light. "That simpering, priggish, easily led little fool? I be her? Never! Little Eugénie-Marie, who grew up to be a fat old duchesse and ended her life a suicide?

She was convent-bred and unimaginative and dutiful; if easily led by strong-willed, domineering nuns, imagine how much more easily she was led astray by the likes of such masterly charlatans as Cagliostro and Lorenza—and my humble self. I pitied her and her kind—and had contempt as well. She did what all the others did, followed where all the others were herded. They followed every whim of fashion, however debauched or silly or extravagant, and by their doing helped to bring down a throne and a kingdom. Ah, child, never could I have been one of them!" She smiled.

"*I* was one of the people," she said with pride. "A peasant girl and a Huguenot, one of an ancient Protestant family that had fallen on the hard times meted out by Catholic France to all the Protestants in her midst. We were poor and of no account, but my mother always instilled in me the pride of all our former distinctions, the strength of our sturdy stock and the desire to rise above the miserable lot that had befallen us solely as a result of our religion.

"Then, when I was nearly twelve, she died—my mother died—and I chose to leave my father's house not many months later, taking the road to Paris with all I owned tied up in a simple scarf. I was determined to make my fortune."

"A brave thing to do, madame," I murmured, bethinking myself of how I, with forty pounds a year of my own, had not been brave enough to leave my hateful prison in Park Lane and fend for myself in London.

"A foolish thing to do," she said simply, "but no matter now. It was what I chose to do at the time. They say that God protects children and fools; I being both, he guarded me well in his way. He put me on that very high road on the very day that a man of great power and perception was to pass."

She stopped to arrange some blossoms in her basket, setting it on the mirrored surface of the long *bronze-d'oré* dining table. I looked down upon her face reflected in the bright mirror. It was so old and yet so firm with inner strength and power and beauty. This lady was indeed a marvel, I thought in awe.

"The man was Franz Anton Mesmer. He was an Austrian physician and he had come to Paris first in 1778. He effected 'miraculous cures' amongst the nobles of France and within a few years had become the most celebrated man in Paris. He was a genius and a sorcerer. Like every other great charlatan, poseur, and fashionable man of religion, he understood the foibles of human nature and used them to his advantage. He cloaked all his doings in a shroud of mysticism and secrecy. He knew that people loved to be amazed and fooled, and so he amazed them well—and fooled them well—and they, in turn, paid him well.

"I was walking on the road as I have said, when a great wooden coach came rumbling up behind me from the direction of Strasbourg. They were huge, high, clumsy, uncomfortable things, those old traveling coaches of yore . . . and a man looked down at me from the window as it passed me by. Not five seconds later it rumbled to a halt some way down the road.

" 'Come on,' he called out the lowered window in a heavy German accent. 'Hurry! I have to be in Paris tomorrow.' His whole manner was impatient and peremptory and condescending, none of which I liked. Therefore, I took my time, walking with all the dignity and independence that I could muster.

" 'I am Clotilde du Roc, *monsieur*,' I said with a polite curtsy. 'With whom may I perhaps have the fortune to ride?' I asked with a poor attempt at sophistication.

" 'With Franz Mesmer, *mademoiselle*, physician to the great and wealthy men of France. Will you ride?'

" '*Oui, monsieur, Merci.*'

" 'Come up, then,' he ordered impatiently, flinging open the door.

" 'I await your footman, *monsieur*,' I said stubbornly.

" 'You await my . . .' he cried, but then relented with a laugh at my presumption. The lazy footman, resentful and sulky, was ordered down from the box and made to assist me into the coach as befits a lady. I sat opposite *monsieur* and regarded him carefully and with all the poise that I could muster.

"He was a man of nearly fifty at the time, still quite handsome in a wicked sort of way, and, I could see at once, not unsusceptible to the charms of the fair sex."

"He seduced you," I murmured, lost in the shocking thought of an innocent child in the toils of such a debauched and worldly man as Anton Mesmer.

"Say, rather, we seduced each other, my dear," Madame De'Ath corrected me dryly, her painted eyebrows arched as she looked askance at my fatuous remark. "I was a farmgirl, remember, and no farmgirl is still very green at twelve. Why do you think they call it 'country matters'?

"Oh, it is true that he was the first, but I was not totally unknowing and I was an eager and an apt pupil, whether the arts he taught we were of an animal nature or of an intellectual. In short, I was a pretty, willing, sensual, and bright little sponge of a girl, and, as he saw at once, a fine potential companion to his endeavors. We were fast friends long ere the coach rumbled through the eastern gate of Paris some three or four days later."

"Three or four days!" I exclaimed. "But, madame, he said . . ."

"Never mind what he said. We dallied three or four days along the road to Paris." She smiled knowingly.

"Country matters, madame?" I breathed in mock scolding.

"Mesmer was a genius, as I have said," she went on blithely, "but a temperamental one and quarrelsome into the bargain. I had not been with him more than two years, living with him at his mansion in the Place Vendôme, when he began to fall from favor with the court. He had made too many enemies, you see. Something which never pays.

"The king ordered two commissions to investigate his practices, the nature of which had become suspect. Amongst the members of the commissions was the merry old ambassador from the newly formed United States of America. He was Benjamin Franklin, and I had enjoyed some amorous dalliance with him from time to time. It was he who helped to discredit Mesmer's medical cures in a much-heralded experiment that failed utterly. Anyway, it was Franklin who advised me that my protector was about to be sent from court in disgrace and that it would be wise to seek other friends. And so, seeing the handwriting on the wall, and not being overly scrupulous about loyalty at that rather selfish and self-seeking time of my life, I left Mesmer and joined ranks with a far greater, wiser, and more successful charlatan and sorcerer—the illustrious Comte Alessandro di Cagliostro himself.

"He had been attempting to lure me away from Mesmer for some time already, wishing to enlist me in his 'Egyptian Mysteries' as an accomplice of his wife in her role as 'high priestess.' It was all trickery and nonsense, of course, those 'mysteries.' At any rate, it seemed quite natural that I should join his cause and that of his wife Lorenza. She was a lovely and enigmatic lady and I came to adore her as one adores an older, much-loved, and respected friend. I remained faithful not only throughout all their years of great power and popularity, but also during the years of exile in London and as wanderers in Europe. They ended their days in misery, he in an Italian prison and she in the confines of a convent, lonely and isolated." Her soft dark eyes filled then with unshed tears.

"And now, that is all; that is enough, I think," she said lightly. "Perhaps one day I shall tell you more, but for now I find life stories tedious, don't you?"

"No, madame, not yours," I replied simply and honestly to her rhetorical question, though I did not expect a reply.

There came a knocking on the outer door. "Ah," she cried. "Perfect! Here comes Jemmy to join us." She bade him enter, and I saw him start visibly as he saw that I was in the room.

"Madame De'Ath," he murmured, coming forward to hold her hand and kiss it as if she were his queen. "Enid." He nodded, his dark eyes searching my face, wondering what it was he saw in my bright eyes.

"Enid and I have been discussing Clotilde du Roc, Jemmy," Madame De'Ath remarked with pointed nonchalance.

"Oh?"

"She has been reading the memoirs of a late, talkative old acquaintance."

"Ah, yes, I see." He nodded. " 'Er that was mentioned at the dinner party last month. Well, no 'arm in that, is there?"

"No, none, as it happens." Madame De'Ath smiled at me quite warmly. "My daughter-in-law does not condemn her old mother-in-law for the sins of her 'shocking' past, do you, my dear?" There was an edge of irony in her voice. This woman clearly apologized to no one for her past. She kept it as private as possible, not out of any shame or fear of condemnation by others, but merely because it was hers, a personal thing to be shared only with intimates.

"It would be presumptuous, madame, for one who has been branded a murderess to condemn the past of another. Of the three of us here, I am the only murderer, am I not?"

"And are you so sure of that? So sure that you are a murderess? Are you sure that you deserve such a label?" she asked gently.

"I really do not know. I suppose that I shall never know."

"Enough talk of the sad past," she exclaimed all at once. "Jemmy, be a dear and ring for tea, please, and have the maid arrange these flowers," she said, handing him the basket and shears and taking me by the arm affectionately, distracting me from the unhappy thoughts that had threatened to overwhelm me just then. "Over tea we shall do nothing but laugh and tell amusing stories and get crumbs all over the carpet and butter in the marmalade jar. I insist upon it, do you hear?"

We did laugh over that tea, the three of us, and Madame De'Ath regaled us freely and easily with stories of her true past, sharing with me things that heretofore had only been told to Jemmy, who was her pet and her pupil and her "son" in spirit, if not in law, as was Ambrose. She had never had a child of her own body, something which I think may have been the deepest regret—perhaps even the only regret—of her long and adventure-filled life. It was during that gay and lively afternoon tea party that I came to understand at last what an important part it was that Jemmy Burkers filled in the last years of her long, eventful, and dramatic lifetime.

For nearly eighteen years now he had been with her, first merely as a watchdog over the grotesque doings of her stepson Ambrose, and then gradually, as her sympathy for and understanding of the nature and intelligence of Jemmy Burkers grew, she had begun to refine that nature and train that untutored intellect, broadening his knowledge and educating him far above his normal station in life. She had made him see the worth of his own self, his brain and his talents, but with that new self-knowledge had come a restlessness and a desire to make of himself more than could ever have been made of a man of his class in England.

The disparity between the class of poor, deranged, obsessed Ambrose, who would ever be a gentleman of breeding, no matter what the eccentricities of his warped mind, and his own class made Jemmy anxious to leave the dark shores of England behind him for the brighter prospects that he felt awaited him in America, where self-made men were carving empires out of the wilderness and where gold had just been discovered in a place called California. Only money—or the lack thereof—held him back. And if all went well, even that might change.

"I've put by every cent I've been able to these past five years, but it's 'ardly a proper stake yet."

Madame De'Ath looked at him with affection as he said this, love and pride in her eyes such as a mother might have for a child of whom she was proud; of a son whom she loved. Before, she had always guarded herself in front of me, but now she let her true feelings for this man shine through. "I have often said that I would give him some of my jewels to sell, but he will not hear of it," she said with a sigh.

"Those jewels, madame, are all you 'ave of your illustrious past, and I will not 'ave you sell them, not while I have the power in me to prevent it," Jemmy said proudly. "You 'ave given me more than all the jewels in the world already. You 'ave given me myself, and you've done it with your years o' kindness and guidance and devotion—and, may I say it, madame?—your love as well," he muttered low.

"You may say it, Jemmy, and say it in a firm voice, too. I do love you as deeply as a woman may love a son. Now, will you please open the shutters of my bedroom windows and see that it is well lit? I shall show Enid some things that should interest her."

"Yes, madame," he said, and left us at once, disappearing through a door at the far right side of the room.

"My dear," she said, turning to me after he was gone, "I do love him and am proud of him, all the more so for knowing his background; for having seen him as a wild, wily, dirty young boy of the streets, and for having seen him come, with great effort, to be the strong, poised, intelligent young man that he is today. He speaks roughly by the standards you have been taught to accept, and he is of low, low birth compared to any man you have ever met, but he has been toughened by life and strengthened by experience. He is kind and good and has learned the wisdom of tolerance and has an understanding of others, bred of his own suffering. He is like tempered steel, and his friendship will stand the test of time."

"And Ambrose?" I asked. "Your *son* Ambrose," I said pointedly.

"He is not my son—and I think you know it."

"Your stepson, then?" I conceded.

"There is nothing to be done for Ambrose. He is chaff, even as Jemmy is wheat."

"A cold thing to say, madame."

"Enid, my husband, Hugo De'Ath, loved his first wife and baby son. He gave them everything, but then his wife died. Ambrose was not yet four. He—"

"Pray spare yourself, madame. Mr. Ottermole has told me of Ambrose—of the . . . the thing that he did on the night his mother died," I said, placing my hand on hers to comfort her and stay her from retelling such a painful tale. She nodded slowly.

"The boy was already seven when I came to know him. I tried, after I married his father, to be everything that a kind and well-meaning stepmother should be to a motherless child, but he was already marked by madness.

"He spent long hours in the crypts below the abbey—Jemmy has shown them to you, I think?—and affected mourning clothes from the time he first took over his own management. He collected skulls and *memento mori* with every cent of his allowance. And, of course, the unfortunate coincidence of his name being so similar to the English word 'death' only served to fire his obsession. Hugo's forebears took the name De'Ath from the little town of Ath from which they came. It was once a part of France, but is now considered Belgian, I believe. One never knows anymore, does one? The map of Europe has changed so in my lifetime that I can hardly read a map anymore."

She waved her hand as if impatient with her own digression. "Ah, that is neither here nor there. Hugo sent him away to school, but it did no good. The influence of boys his own age did nothing to change the morbidity of his interests and his nature. Ambrose even came to deny the fact of his real mother's death entirely, insisting that I was in truth his own natural parent. We tired of trying to make him see reason and so I eventually gave in and have played the part of his real mother ever since. Since I have no love for him at all, it has been a particularly difficult role to play and one compounded by his resentment of my interest in and affection for Jemmy.

"It was when he was seventeen that he first began to sleep in a coffin. He used to dose himself with laudanum as well, to reproduce a semblance of death, I presume. Later on, he drugged a young woman and slept with her in a coffin surrounded by candles. There might have been a scandal, but Hugo, with the help of Mr. Ottermole's late father, was able to prevent it. The girl and her family were helped to emigrate, I believe. At any rate, we realized that he had gone back, in his madness, to the night of his mother's death and was reliving it over and over again. We were helpless to stop him or make him see reason. In that one thing, he was beyond reason, although he behaved fairly normally in other aspects of his life." She paused to reflect for a moment, looking drained and sad at her memories of what she had been through over the years for the sake of her loyalties. A look of pain crossed her lovely old face, and she went on with her story.

"When Hugo was on his deathbed, I promised him that I would care for Ambrose as best I could for as long as it was necessary. That was in 1830, and I have managed to keep that promise for all these years. In 1833, Jemmy came to me with Ambrose, drugged and near to death, and with the tale of having found him in a low hovel, nearly robbed and left for dead by an old prostitute. I was at my wit's end, and having no way to control such midnight excursions on my own, I hired the boy to watch out for Ambrose—to be a bodyguard in effect. I could no longer hope to stop his escapades, for he was of age, but I could at least protect him from harming himself or others.

"After some years, Ambrose's mania abated somewhat, or the outward manifestations appeared to anyway, and he became obsessed with what he called thanatology. He had changed the name of this house from Abbey De'Ath to Thanatos Abbey upon the occasion of my husband's death, and now he became intent on making this a center of learning where he would prove the existence of a life beyond the grave. Part of the reason for this sudden interest in the scholarship of the 'hereafter,' if you will, was that I had suffered a fall and was ill for some time afterward. The thought of my possible demise seemed to drive him near to the brink. Jemmy thinks, and I agree, that even though he refuses to remember his mother's death, he fears my death as a revival of the original occurrence. My death may indeed drive him insane beyond all return to reason. Since that time, he has sought to prove that when I—or anyone—dies, they can return or at least wait on the other side to be reunited with their loved ones. It is a deep need with him to believe in this, though he is too intelligent to be fooled by trickery of the sort that we use to help him with your aunt."

She sighed and sipped some water poured from a carafe. "We traveled in Europe, where he collected books on death, dying, spirits, the occult, and allied subjects. He enlarged his already extensive collection of *memento mori* and macabre *objets d'art;* by all this extravagance he virtually beggared his father's estate. I could only watch in horror. I had no legal power or even moral influence over him. I spent more and more of my own time caring for Jemmy and helping him with his own life, helping him to make of himself the man that I knew he could be. . . . He became my companion, my friend, and my joy.

"And this is my reward." She smiled, holding out a hand toward Jemmy Burkers as he returned from her private apartment. "Is he not a fine, handsome young man?"

He took her hand and smiled. "I've got a fire going and the chill is off, madame."

I looked at him carefully as he spoke. He stood to his full middle height, broad of back and shoulders, his dark head bowed to Madame De'Ath with deferential respect, his dark eyes alight with warmth and admiration of this old lady he both loved and served. There was a look of such tender kindness on his rawboned face that I could not help but agree with her assessment.

"Why, yes, Madame De'Ath, he is very handsome." And I truly meant it. His features were not fine and angular like a gentleman's, but then they were not cold and stiff like a gentleman's either—nor so haughty. His was a face that mirrored his feelings and his passions, the life he had led and the strength and force of his inner being.

Unlike Ambrose, he was real. He wore no mask, hid his soul in no armor, his feelings in no madness. I saw more and more of what it was in him that Madame De'Ath loved so much.

"Come, it is a chilly evening with nothing to do till the dinner hour, so I shall play at jewels with you both," Madame De'Ath exclaimed, taking me by the hand in that friendly and informal manner of hers and leading me to the door of her boudoir, which place I had not ever seen. Jemmy walked behind us, and as he did, an odd sensation passed over me. I could feel the very warmth of him against my back, though he was at least two feet away. I could feel the warmth of his gaze on me as well, and though it disconcerted me no end, I found that I really rather liked the feeling.

"And here, my dear Enid, is my secret lair." She smiled, bringing me into the boudoir, furnished in old, classic French furniture of *le style étrusque*, popularized in the 1780's and rather austere and simple of design compared to the Baroque pieces in the salon and dining hall, relying on rich mahogany wood and burnished gilt surfaces, ancient Greek and Etruscan motifs in ormolu. These motifs were winged griffins, patterns of palm and acanthus leaves, claw-footed furniture legs, and the like. Dominating this room was Madame's canopied "campaign" bed of burnished giltwood decorated with "Greek" vases of inlaid ivory and ebony.

The predominating colors of the room and its hangings were pale blue and ecru with accent touches of black. "Come look at this, Enid," Jemmy said as Madame De'Ath withdrew her hand from my arm and took a seat by the fireplace, leaving me free to make my own inspection with Jemmy as my guide.

He led me by the hand to a painting on the wall opposite Madame's campaign bed. It was the portrait of a very young and beautiful woman, fine and noble of feature, with wide, frank dark eyes that were soft and alive and lustrous with life. Only an artist inspired by the perfection of nature's art could have so well captured the reality of those living eyes—the eyes of the Clotilde du Roc that had been—the eyes of the Henriette De'Ath that was!

The hair was dark gold, curly, and dressed in the manner of the 1780's—soft masses of hair about the brow and temples, rolls of long curls hanging down the neck and along the curve of the shoulder. Ropes of pearls and pale aquamarines were entwined in those darkly golden tresses, hung from her ears and from around her long graceful neck. The bodice of her softly sensuous blue satin gown was tight and low, exposing the youthful beauty of the full white bosom, the tininess of the waist and the perfection of her form. Her long, slender hands were delicately posed, pink shells of nails and bejeweled fingers gracfully arched.

It was the portrait of a great beauty, the portait of an age as well, and it embodied all that Clotilde du Roc had been—youthful, poised, brazenly sensual, forward, and honest in her frank gaze out of the canvas into the viewer's own eyes; head held high and proud, back straight and strong, her personality forceful and her elegance undeniable.

I looked from the painted woman on the canvas upon the wall to the living lady in the chair by the fireplace. They were the same. Fifty-five or perhaps sixty years divided them, the one from the other, yet they were the same. The poise was more relaxed now, second nature now; the elegance less studied, the beauty seasoned and even deepened in a way by great age, and the wide, challenging eyes tempered by greater wisdom and deeper sorrows; by what had been seen of life in the intervening decades, but nevertheless it was unmistakably the same face. The face of a princess aged into the majesty of a queen.

"It is truly a wonderful portrait," I said at last.

"It is Clotilde du Roc *exactly* as she was," Madame said simply but with pleasure in her voice, and pride. "Never was a portrait more like." She herself liked that beauty on the wall. Who could blame her? "It was painted in 1790 when I was twenty-one, and it was a birthday gift from the Marquis de Lafayette, under whose protection I was at the time. Revolution was already in the wind then, of course."

"My God," I exclaimed. "Lafayette. Why, madame, you were *there*, you saw so much. Why, the Revolution must have happened in a veritable whirlwind all about you."

"I was there. I saw what there was to see." She shrugged in that small Gallic gesture of hers. No wonder there was so much to this woman. In her lifetime she had seen it all—the rise and fall of men and of kingdoms, of queens and cardinals and nobles of every sort. She had seen the great and the lowly, and they were all one to her.

"Jemmy," she said, "the little box," and with that he went to a small, very lovely mahogany and ormolu coffer set on a stand of four long, slender legs delicately fashioned to represent the legs and hooves of an antelope. Lifting it carefully, he set it before her chair. From a small chatelaine at her waist she pulled a bronze key and opened the lock on the front of the coffer, lifting the lid to reveal a tray of beautiful jewels, the amethysts and pearls set in silver that she had worn the night of the séance. Slipping a catch in the wood, she opened a secret door behind which was a large golden box lined in crimson velvet. From within its depths twinkled a mass of bloodred rubies and a heap of lustrous, satiny white pearls of great size.

She lifted this treasure out of its box with great care and pleasure, her eyes warming to the beauty of the object even as did my own. "I am not a Catholic, but this gift of the Cardinal de Rohan— de la Cressonière mentions it, does she not?—means much to me nevertheless. It is a rosary of fifteen decades of perfectly matched pearls. The *Paters* and *Glorias* are rubies and the preface is of rubies and pearls as well. The crucifix is of pavé rubies and the Christ figure is done in the finest medieval enamel work—champlevé, I believe it is called." She held the long rope of pearls and rubies to the light, enjoying the effect of luster and blood which held us all rather spellbound. "The cardinal knew, of course, that I was a Huguenot, and he gave me this as a gift because it had once belonged to the evil Catherine de Medicis. It was at her instigation that the persecution of my French Huguenot ancestors began on St. Bartholemew's Day in 1572.

"He had an ironic sense of humor, or at least he did under my influence, for I made him feel young and devilish, and he thought it fitting that one of the humble descendants of the victims of her persecution should one day own Catherine's personal rosary. He was a good enough man, kindly disposed to me and to most others, was de Rohan, and he died sadly, in exile—which is another story." She sighed resignedly and handed the treasure into my fingers for my closer inspection.

"It is exquisite," I said as I admired its workmanship and compelling beauty. "I love rubies and pearls. They seem meant to be worn together."

"The gossips of Paris made much of a cardinal of France giving such a gift to his mistress. We just laughed, the two of us, and enjoyed the joke. I took to counting my beads as if in divine meditation while out for my afternoon carriage ride, and he would scold me for a brazen, mischievous minx, his tongue in his cheek all the while. He was not a bad man at all. I really rather liked him," she reflected, eyes trained on some long-ago sight in some long-gone day.

"Now," she went on abruptly, coming back from the days of the old Cardinal de Rohan, "*this* will one day be Jemmy's. I have offered it to him many times, but he always refuses it, though he occasionally placates me by wearing it during our private suppers together. Nevertheless, one day it will be his." She smiled and handed from the depths of a black velvet box a mass of blazing diamonds, which proved to be, upon closer observation, a large and very old-fashioned closed-case pocket watch of rose-cut diamonds set *en pavé*. With it was a long waistcoat chain of wide, flat links, each of which was literally encrusted with more pavé diamonds. Cupped in the hands or run through the fingers like water, that mass of fiery, multi-faceted stones leaped and gleamed and blazed like fire and ice, as if by a miracle they had been captured from nature and translated by the arts of man into something possible to touch and hold and keep forever.

"This watch and chain belonged to Alessandro di Cagliostro himself. He claimed to have had it as a gift from the mysterious and supposedly immortal Comte St. Germain, but this I doubt. It smacks too much of his charlatanry to be more than just a romantic story. I came by this watch because among the last things he was able to do from his prison cell in Italy was to instruct Lorenza that before she retired into her convent to live out the rest of her days as a penitent, she was to give me this watch and chain as a token of his affection and appreciation of my loyalty to them in their hours of disgrace and trial.

"He died horribly, after years in prison. I was able to do nothing for him. The Italian authorities were implacable. Lorenza lived to be a very old lady, counting her beads and lamenting the sinful life she had led with Cagliostro, not because she *had*, but because those narrow, evil-minded sisters of her convent persecuted her with hatred and envy and guilt.

"I went to see her once, but could not bear the sight of what she had allowed them to make of her. After that, selfishly and for my own sake, my own peace of mind, I never went back. I sent her gifts of linen and food and medicines, and many letters of love and comfort, but I could never bear to look on her again. It was cowardly of me, but I could not bear the sight of her after what she had been.

"Many of the pieces of furniture that you have seen here, some of the jewels that I shall show you, were once theirs—those things that they were able to salvage and save from being confiscated by the authorities of the various countries that hounded them once they fell from favor with the gullible courts of Europe. Ah, how sad it was!

"The rest, the bulk, in fact, are mine, gifts from admirers and lovers, or those who sought in vain to be my lovers—a saucy and a venal wench I was in those days." She laughed tolerantly at the memory of her not-so-nice self. "There are, too, many love tokens from my dear love, my husband Hugo, who though not a rich man by any means, was ever a generous one."

She looked long and hard at the glittering watch and chain in her hand. Thrusting it away from her with a gesture of appeal, she suddenly cried, "Wear it, Jemmy. I insist upon it," and Jemmy Burkers slipped the end of the chain through a button of his striped servant's vest and the watch into his pocket. It would have become him better had he not worn the livery of a menial, but I saw that this mattered not to the old woman who loved him. Her eyes lit in delight at the sight of him wearing her old friend's treasure.

For a long while she amused us with the opening of box after box, chest after chest, until the carpet before the fireplace between her chair and the settee upon which I sat was literally paved with glittering gems—necklaces and bracelets, chatelaines and stomachers, parures and demi-parures, earrings and rings galore—all of magnificent beauty and artistry and of great worth. There were pearls by the yard, and rubies, emeralds, amethysts, canary diamonds and white ones, sapphires and peridots and garnets, the very aquamarines and pearls that she had worn to sit for her portrait, every type and color and shape of stone and gem imaginable—and in every setting, whether gold or silver or iron or gilt bronze. The profusion of beauty and dazzling array spread before me on that floor was the stuff of dreams, beggaring the imagination. A fortune in jewels!

"I would gladly give any of it to him if he would sell it for us to go to America, but he will not hear of it," she said, looking up at Jemmy in mock annoyance.

"These things are hers, Enid; they embody her whole life and history," Jemmy said, turning to me to explain, and then looking once more to Madame De'Ath. "Every jewel of this collection has a story to it, and I will not have you give up one stone of them on my account, madame," Jemmy said quietly, his voice strong and firm.

"Well, I for one have no such scruples, *ma mère*," Ambrose said all at once, his sudden appearance causing us all to look up and exclaim in surprise. He had crept up on us without warning, and we had been totally unaware of his presence until he spoke.

He walked up to us and stood beside me, one bony hand gripping my shoulder like a vise as he looked down his long, angular nose at the wealth of treasure scattered across the carpet at his feet. Jemmy, who had been on his knees on the carpet beside Madame De'Ath, scrambled to his own feet with an oath. The chain of Comte Alessandro di Cagliostro's watch blazed like fire across his waistcoat as he moved.

"Don't you knock, Ambrose?" he snarled.

"All paste, you have told me for years. All paste, *ma mère*, but these are not paste," he said, snatching Catherine de Medicis' pearl-and-ruby rosary from my hands and holding them to the light. "These are quite genuine, I think, and very, very fine," he appraised them coolly, his face sneering and contemptuous with controlled anger. "And that watch you're sporting, Jemmy. That blazes far too spectacularly to be paste. Why, is *he* wearing it, *ma mère*? Why is it not mine?" He sounded petulant and in deadly earnest in his wrath.

"Because, Ambrose, it is mine," the old woman said simply, and I sensed a tension in the air that I did not like or quite fully understand. It was as if these two, Madame De'Ath and Jemmy, were on their guard against danger.

"Have you not bestowed a gift on my bride yet? Ought you not give her a gem for having married me? A wedding gift?"

I blushed in embarrassment to be used by him in such a transparent manner. It was shameful.

"Are you not gift enough for any bride, Ambrose, my son?" She fenced with his own words.

He laughed nervously. "Hah, yes, yes, quite right. I had not thought of that." He paused. "It should be so, but is it? I think my bride has other interests than her husband. I begin to think she prefers a coarser class of man."

Careful, Ambrose, I thought as I watched a deadly, white-hot light creep into Jemmy's dark eyes.

"Tell me, Jemmy, since when have the master's mother and wife become part of the perks of a servant's office? I don't care if you sell the tallow ends and rendered fat from the kitchen, but when you steal a man's—"

"Jemmy," Madame De'Ath said urgently, placing one bejeweled old hand on his arm to restrain him. Clearly had she not, he would have come to blows with Ambrose right then and there. I could not have blamed him, for Ambrose's whole tone and implication was too insulting to hear with equanimity. I had no doubt that had any other person dared to say so much, Jemmy would have torn the man apart. Only the fact that it was Ambrose De'Ath who spoke and that they were in the presence of Madame De'Ath restrained him.

"Ambrose," he said coldly, "men have died for lesser insults than those which you 'ave just scattered across this room at all of us 'ere. It is only because you are a poor, sick madman with nothing inside you ta 'old you up but air, that keeps me from breakin' you inta pieces like so much kindlin'."

"Very brave words, but I did not come here to argue with the help. I have come straight from Miss Tregaron's room with news—good news. I have exacted a promise from her that if her brother Llewellyn manifests himself again on Friday next, she will endow my thanatology foundation with a grant of"—and here he hesitated for added dramatic effect—"of twenty-five thousand pounds in cash at once, and another equal sum, by a codicil to her will, at her own death."

"Wonderful," Madame De'Ath remarked.

"That's quite a sum, Ambrose," Jemmy said, his face dark with perplexity.

"She is sending for a lawyer. Everything shall be drawn up quite properly," Ambrose said in a funny tone, his eyes sweeping over the jewel-strewn carpet constantly, the gems at his feet a constant magnet to his eyes.

"What have you to say, Enid?" he asked.

"It is a goodly portion of her personal fortune, I should think," I murmured reflectively. There was far more yet, however, for while her private fortune might be that amount or somewhat more, she must still have the income at least from the bulk of Uncle Llewellyn's estate, which amounted to many times fifty thousand pounds. If he played his cards right, Ambrose had more yet to gain, though I did not say as much. In fact, I sat quite still and said not a word.

" 'Ow is she givin' it to you, Ambrose?"

"As an endowment. We shall journey to London together and arrange for the setting up of the foundation as soon as she is satisfied about the success of our efforts." There was something strange in his tone. I could not put my finger on it, but I knew that I did not trust him.

"*We?*" Madame De'Ath repeated.

"Augusta Tregaron and I."

"And 'ow do we come into it, Ambrose? 'Ow do your partners come into this foundation?" Jemmy asked quietly, with suspicion in his dark eyes.

"Oh, I shall think of something—once I get my money. Perhaps I shall pay you all a sum as research assistants, or under some such guise as that. Anyway, it hardly matters now," he said airily. "Besides, you are all rich enough as it is, if you can afford to spend your afternoon fondling a fortune in baubles. What's a few paltry thousand compared to these pretties?" he asked snidely, sweeping his hand over the gem-covered carpet. "I shall see you all at dinner, I expect. See the wine you serve is properly chilled, Jemmy, like a good manservant, eh?" And with that he left as abruptly and as unceremoniously as he had arrived.

"I 'ate that man," Jemmy seethed after Ambrose was out of earshot.

"Pity him rather," Madame De'Ath replied with a shake of her head.

"If 'e were a cur wi' a broken leg, I could pity 'im, but 'e's no cur, madame. 'E's not so good as a cur."

"There is something that I must discuss with you, madame, Jemmy," I said once Ambrose was away, steeling myself to broach at last the subject of my visit with Osric Ottermole and the matters that had transpired. I had been procrastinating all afternoon, enjoying rather our long and pleasant "afternoon of the jewels," but Ambrose's interruption had set the stage too well. I could not longer avoid the issue, although I made one small digression still. "Before I begin, one question."

"Yes, my dear?" Madame De'Ath prompted.

"I understand Ambrose's delusions and his sick obsessions now. I know that the seeds were sown in his earliest childhood. I know that he has been extravagant and willful and that this land and the abbey are entailed upon a cousin in the event—very likely, I may say—that Ambrose dies without male issue, but why, with all this wealth at your disposal," I said, waving my hand over the gems at my feet and at the fabulous old furniture and possessions of the boudoir in which we sat and, by implication, in the rooms beyond, "why do you indulge in trickery and charlatanry for an old woman's money?"

Jemmy growled in his loyalty to her, but Madame De'Ath silenced him with a look, choosing to reply herself to my question. She seemed to take no umbrage at my impertinence.

"Enid, my dear, your question is quite justified. The answer is a long one—both simple and complex at once. First, because I loved Hugo De'Ath with a deep and contented affection, I stand as well as I can by his son, but personally, I have come to loathe Ambrose De'Ath. Had I not made a promise to his father, I should have left long ago and Jemmy with me. But now it is too late and we cannot simply go—partly because Ambrose is so much deeper into his madness and obsession and partly because of a simple lack of cash. You see wealth here, yes, but I can show you no money, no private bank drafts or investments—no income at all of my own. Ambrose has, by beggaring his father's estate, ruined my income as well."

"I can understand that, but it still does not explain—"

"Hear me out, Enid." The old woman fingered absently a large emerald ring, green as a cat's eye in the dark. "In the past two years or so, Ambrose has pestered me into conducting séances, badgered me into card readings, evenings of automatic writing and the like—all 'tricks of the trade,' so to speak, that I had learned at the hands of Mesmer and Cagliostro; tricks by which they had cheated the foolish *noblesse de Paris* and enriched themselves and their companions in crime—such as my humble self, for instance.

"I was not always, in my youth, the good person that I try now to be. I had been the mistress of many men, partly to learn their secrets and pass them on to my clever Cagliostro, who used those secrets in séances and 'religious rites' and in his experiments in animal magnetism and spirit reading. I had delighted in my part in all these things and it was a pleasure to regale Jemmy with examples of our tricks by the hour. Ambrose knew some of the stories of my past life and talents, too, but over the years he had come to look upon them, not as tricks and games to be played upon fools, but as real powers of which I, alone amongst women, was possessed."

She shook her head at the thought. "Last year, he brought a couple whom he had met in London to visit the abbey, and after much pleading, prevailed upon me to conduct a séance for them in order to try to contact their dead son. Ambrose was bent on reaching beyond the 'veil,' as the Reverend Pond calls it, and proving that life exists after death.

"With Jemmy's help, I went through the storerooms where

many of Cagliostro's effects, left to me when he made his final, hasty departure from London, had been kept since my marriage to Hugo. We were able to salvage enough of his equipment and order enough chemicals and oddments to set up the séance room and the trick room below it. We showed it to Ambrose, insisting that he realize it was all a fake, but while he said he knew it was all a sham, we suspected that he was actually humoring us. He believes that even though our séances are fakery, yet the real spirits *will* get through; that ultimately it is all *real*!"

She sighed. "Jemmy, you go on. All this talk tires me."

"We put on a damned good show, Enid," he said with a certain glow of pride in his eyes as he spoke. "Quite good enough to make that old couple 'appy, which was all we 'ad intended really. They, quite unexpectedly I may say, rewarded ol' Ambrose wi' a considerable sum o' money and returned to London singin' our praises to the Ponds, who 'ad just newly come from America wi' news o' spirit rappin' and other such nonsense. It's evidently some new craze over there—a sort o' pseudoreligious mania what started in New York State as a result o' some hysterical young female by the name o' Fox banging on a table. Whatever!" He dismissed the whole silly story with a chopping gesture of his broad, strong hand.

"Ambrose approached me," Madame De'Ath continued then "about conducting séances and magnetic sittings on a regular basis, with the hope of getting an income from some wealthy persons in order to run the abbey and set up his foundation."

"This foundation, by the way," Jemmy broke in, " 'as been 'is mad ambition for some years now, an' 'e's been pesterin' Madame for 'er jewels for years over it."

"And I would not give them," Madame De'Ath said indignantly. "I love Jemmy and would give them to him gladly to further his desires to seek his fortune in America, but for Ambrose's madness? Not a farthing! The difference between the two men is that Jemmy has his pride and would rather make his way by his wits before taking a sou from me, but Ambrose would rob me blind if he dared—and beggar me for his thanatology. Only his deep fear of my disapproval and of my leaving him prevents him from trying.

"And it is true, as Jemmy says, that he pestered me for my jewels. Finally I lied and told him that the real ones had been sold long ago and all that remained were the paste copies with which I played at being wealthy, like some senile old lady living on the memories of her past glory.

"Until today he believed me, or at least dared not say otherwise to my face. Well, never mind that. It is too late now. Back to the way of things." She sighed again. This afternoon was hard on her. Ambrose's presence had truly spoiled our mood.

"When Ambrose asked me to help him to conduct séances for money, I looked upon the offer as a possible way out for us all and as a last fling at using the talents of my youth as well. A sort of swan song, you might say. And so I made a compact with him that if he should find *one* likely subject for us, that he and Jemmy would investigate and learn as much as possible to help in our deceptions, and that when that was done, I would conduct a series of 'experiments' to convince the . . . the *prey*, if you like, of an afterlife. Whatever money we were able to realize was to be divided amongst the three of us.

"My object in agreeing to this plan, unknown to Ambrose, was to help Jemmy gain the stake he needs to go to America. Later on, I was able to think of my own plans as well. Now, I shall go to America with him," she said with a delighted smile at the prospect of such an adventure.

"*You*, go to the United States, madame? I . . . At . . . at *your* age?" I blurted out rather rudely, I fear.

She laughed lightly. "And why not? What's the odds where I die? And I have never been to America. They say it is a wonder, that place!"

"Indeed," I concurred.

"Well," she continued her story after that surprising revelation, "Ambrose read your uncle's obituary, realized that he had known the man slightly and therefore had an entrée with your family, and that the man was very rich. We gerry-rigged an automatic-writing session in front of the most gullible witnesses imaginable, postdated the papers to fit the night of your Uncle Llewellyn's demise—and the rest you know," she finished with an eloquent shrug of her shoulders.

"With the proceeds of this relatively harmless and amusing piece of knavery, Jemmy and I shall take leave for America and Ambrose shall found his thanatological society. We shall all live happily ever after," she concluded with a delighted clap of her hands which annoyed me no end. It was all too pat.

"Dare you risk leaving him?" I asked. "What of your promised duty to him?"

"What more duty do I owe him now, my dear? He is over forty, he shall have money enough after this last séance to indulge his obsession to his heart's content and—most fortunate of all—he has a lively young wife to care for him and see to his needs from now on. My duty to my stepson virtually ended, Enid, on the day that Ambrose De'Ath took unto himself a *wife*."

"Enid, Enid, please wait," Jemmy called after me as I fled from the boudoir of Henriette De'Ath in a fit of trembling fury and anger and rage.

"Wife to Ambrose De'Ath! Corpse to Ambrose De'Ath, she means. That's why she's been so nice to me. I've freed her from this prison. She doesn't care if I've killed a dozen parents, so long as I take that animated corpse off her hands. Well, hell and damnation to Ambrose De'Ath," I shouted, turning on Jemmy like a wild thing as he pursued me through the salon.

"Enid, calm yourself. She . . . she didn't mean it," he said, trying to placate me. "Not the way it sounded."

"She didn't mean it? Why, of course she meant it—by all that's holy, under any other circumstances and with any other man, she'd be quite right. But not with Ambrose De'Ath. I will not be chained to that madman, do you hear?"

"I 'ear, girl, an' I don't want you chained to 'im either," Jemmy said quietly. I only half heard him at the time, so hot was my wrath.

"I will not be chained to him! No, not for a minute beyond the time it takes me to pack my boxes after my share of these ill-gotten gains is in my hands—that is, if it *ever is* in my hands."

"What do you mean by that? You'll get your share. We all will, in spite of what Ambrose implied this afternoon. That was all bluff."

"Oh, yes, Jemmy, honor amongst thieves, I know, but that is not at all what I meant," I shouted, still in a towering passion over Madame De'Ath's remark. Ambrose's wife! God, I could not bear the thought.

"Why?" came a cool, dispassionate voice that cut through the fury of my anger like a knife. "Why, Enid, should my remark about being Ambrose's wife disturb you so?" It was the voice of my mother-in-law, speaking from the door of her bedchamber.

"Because, madame, being married to your son is an insupportable prospect for me. I married him out of need of a champion, and he is no champion; out of need of a provider, and he cannot provide; out of need of a lover, and he cannot love.

"I am struggling with the troubles of my past, for I wish to be well and healthy of mind. Instead, I find myself chained to my husband's madness, his coldness, his isolating scholarship that admits of no love or companionship to be shared. I may have murdered once—I don't know—but I do know that I am not mad and I do not wish to be married to a madman. I shall stay until I can go, but I will not stay long."

"Neither, my dear, will Ambrose," she said softly.

"What do you mean by that?"

"As I have said, his madness grows upon him. It cannot be long before the brittle glass of his sanity shatters. I say this not in hope, my child, but in sorrow. It is true nevertheless."

"And am I then to wait?"

"It would be a kindness." She shrugged.

"And if it is not to be long, as you think, why do *you* not wait—as a kindness?"

"I have been kind too long already—and I have less time, I think, than you, my dear?"

I had no answer to that.

Jemmy had been silent during this exchange, toying thoughtfully with the large figured cards on Madame De'Ath's inlaid marquetry table.

"Enough, ladies, of all this quibbling. Enid, you said something rather pointed just now about *if* our ill-gotten gains, as you put it, ever get into your hands. What were you goin' on about, if not trust amongst us?"

"I said earlier that I had something rather serious to discuss with you both. Well, here it is for good and all.

"Your—nay, *our*—trickery is exposed. The spirit band will be meeting—if it meets at all, that is—for the very last time on Friday next."

# 15

# HEADLONG DOWN
# THE PATH

"Say, then, my peace is made."

"That shalt thou know hereafter."
—*Shakespeare*

Alas! my everlasting peace
Is broken into pieces.
—*Thomas Hood*

Ambrose sat in his study, his long, bony fingers passing back and forth over the lines of the pages in an old parchment-bound book, yellowed with age and broken of spine from much use.

I stood regarding him for some moments through the half-open door of his study before I took courage and knocked. I watched with a strange, detached kind of curiosity this man who was my husband; this man that I knew and yet did not know.

His past, the things that made him what he was, I could not help. No one could. His obsession was beyond all control, his madness too deep to reach or cure, his coldness and austerity of emotion far too repellant to my own newly reemerging nature of feeling and sensibility and need, for me to be of any real service.

I had been cold too long myself; had hidden too long my own past torments, to my soul's detriment, and now I wanted none of coldness and misery any longer. I wanted laughter and health of mind and sunlight in my life.

I watched him intently, fascinated, as if seeing him for the first time; that skull-like head and slender, bony frame, strung like a marionette on fragile strings. Mr. Ottermole had warned me that this man, this husband of mine, was far gone. Madame De'Ath as well had said it would not be long. And now, as I watched him, I saw how right they were. There was about him the very look of death, the smell of death. I knew it, sensing it with much the same visceral feeling that an animal has when it instinctively knows its prey is wounded unto death; when it hangs back, preternaturally patient, awaiting the end, awaiting its coming meal. I shivered. It was an ugly thought.

Madame De'Ath was right. It would not be long, and when, standing in that chilly, dreadful hall, I came to realize that fact for myself, an overwhelming sense of pity and sorrow overcame the detachment that I had felt heretofore in all my dealings with Ambrose De'Ath, and I found myself wanting to reach out to him and comfort him in the crisis that I sensed—nay, knew—must come.

I knocked at last.

"Ambrose, may I enter?"

"If you wish, Enid," he said, scarcely bothering to look at me.

"Do I disturb your studies?"

"I let nothing disturb my studies. Your momentary visit shall not break the train of my thought, I assure you."

"I am glad to hear it."

I paused, feeling awkward and unwelcome; not knowing how to begin; what, even, to say.

He stared at me unblinking, his bony fingers drumming an impatient tattoo on the edge of his desk, his thin white lips pursed disapprovingly; his pale, taut skin stretched over the knife-edged sharpness of his long, narrow nose, giving his face the illusion of blue-white translucence. He looked already dead, God help him! That wave of pity overcame once more the utter revulsion of my feelings.

"Ambrose, I do not wish us to be bad friends."

"Oh," he remarked noncommittally.

"You are my husband, after all, and I—"

"I was under the impression that you preferred my servant."

"Jemmy is not your servant, and I have none but friendly and business dealings with him, just as you do yourself, I may add. We are all partners, remember?" I answered tartly, although I had not wished to lose control of my emotions.

"You blush prettily, my dear, at the very mention of his name, and defend him well. He seems to have a similar concern for you. What else can I think but that you are lovers?" He spoke with a matter-of-fact detachment that was infuriating.

"We are not lovers."

"No? Well, no matter. I do not give it long before you are. You seem to share in common with my mother an absolute fascination for that lowborn lout."

"Ambrose," I said, ignoring his insults, "I came to make peace with you and tell you that I stand by my concern for you, my duty to you as a wife. I want to help you."

"I don't need your help. I have work to do. You will only disturb it."

"Can I not help it perhaps?" I asked softly. "Share in it?"

"It is my business and none of yours. Thanatology and the foundation are my concern. You are to keep out of it. I do not need you."

No, he surely did not.

"Nor *want* you," he spat at me maliciously.

"Why did you marry me?" I asked flatly, all life gone from my tone.

"That again?" he sneered.

"Yes, that again, Ambrose. Why?"

"I wish I knew. Lord, I wish I knew, but I don't know, and frankly, I don't much care," he retorted cruelly—more cruelly and coldly than he had ever spoken to me before.

"Can you not even guess?" I prompted him, as a sudden flash of intuition—painful—stabbed through my heart at his words.

He relented slightly, actually taking a moment to think. "I . . . perhaps . . . perhaps I thought you were . . ." He stopped, his mouth shutting tight, the thin lips taut across his set face. "Never mind what I thought," he said, and turned his back to me, bending his head to the open book on the desk before him.

"You thought I was a murderess when you married me, didn't you? And now you are not so sure," I murmured behind him. He hunched more tightly over his ancient text, ignoring me, yet by the set of his shoulders I knew that he had heard; heard and flinched at the hearing. He *did* want me to be a murderess—a wanton killer. He was angry now he realized that I might not be what he thought I was.

"Well"—I sighed sadly—"I have tried. God knows, I have tried, but you have long ago dug your own grave, Ambrose, and soon you must lie in it. I cannot save you from it, husband, but I'll be damned if I choose to lie in it with you. Good-bye."

I turned and left him, closing the door behind me softly for good and all. Wife or not, married or not, I would not live with Ambrose De'Ath; I would not stay at Thanatos Abbey. I *could* stay at Thanatos Abbey.

Yet there I was, still trapped, and every day a nightmare; every night a hell.

I could not sleep but that I dreamed, and I could not dream but that the dreams turned frightful in their intensity—images of graveyards and coffins and tall black candles, jagged shards of mirror reflecting old, debauched French cardinals in scarlet taffeta and draped with jewels. Bloodred rosaries and naked, painted damsels, beguiling in the licentiousness of their gyrations; fat, sensual Cagliostro and beauteous, remote Lorenza, and the lurid forms of blue-white corpses robbed of their grave clothes and sold to the anatomists like so much meat. Ambrose and Jemmy in the stews of London; Madame De'Ath as she had been in youth, laughing at me from the window of an old French stagecoach, her painted face a mask, her jeweled hands like claws. In short, all was madness when I slept, and all was tension when I awoke.

I felt like a living butterfly, struggling to be free, yet pinned forever to the killing board.

So, too, Augusta Tregaron.

As if sensing something threatening and frightful in the highly charged atmosphere of the old abbey, she moved like a nervous caged bird, hardly ever leaving her rooms at all save to take an afternoon carriage ride out along the high road that wound along the cliffs above that grim, isolated place. She did not seek the distractions of the town, however, for never once did she venture toward Wadebridge, always taking instead the turning that led westward out where nothing lay but broad meadows and barren cliffs, gorse and ancient hedgerows, windswept and bent to the very ground by time and the elements. It was a spare land, and a spare woman that rode out into its wilds.

Once, out of whatever perverse motive I know not, she asked me to accompany her on one of these drives. In some similar perversity of mind, I agreed.

We rolled away from the doors of the abbey with a blinding spring sun forcing itself like a wakening eye out of a pearl-gray ceiling of ocean mists, to drench the spare, treeless spring green land with color. As ever, there was the stark contrast of green turf and damp, gray stone—the stone of the abbey walls and of the massive, grotesque, lichen-covered outcroppings that reared like old bones right through the thin skin of the earth itself. And there was the black, of course; the ever-present funereal black of Ambrose's carriage and horses, his liveried driver and footman, and Aunt Augusta herself, naturally, in her own never-changing dark weeds.

She was as black as the crows that scuttled about on the meadows as we passed, and her voice was as harsh and sharp as well; her eyes every bit as cold and penetrating as theirs.

I sat facing her, my back to the horses, and watched her withered, white old face intently. How strange it was to sit with her like that and not hate her; how strange that I pitied her rather, seeing with some illumination of understanding the emptiness and loneliness of her long, drab, unfulfilling life.

Half an orphan she had been at seven, acting almost as a mother to her younger half brothers from the age of ten, and because of them, whether by choice or not, she had made no life of her own—married no husband, borne no children, loved none but those three brothers, each of whom had betrayed her in his turn by growing up, growing away, and by wanting to marry.

What had she ever had but them? What if she had possessed the baby of them, Rhys, to such distraction as to drive him ultimately to a suicide's grave? What if she had compelled my father, Morgan, to live in Wales with his young family in order to try to escape her domination? What if she had forced my Uncle Llewellyn into a long and secret engagement before his marriage, and eventually done his wife to death with her harassing and scolding? What had it all availed her?

What did it avail her now, so old and lonely and bitter that she even invited the company of the niece she had hated and reviled and tormented for all these nearly fourteen years past? There was nothing in her to admire or respect or love, but oh, how I could pity her that blasted, wasted life, empty now of all emotion save fear and hatred and utter malice, just as once it had brimmed with a sick and possessive thing that had passed for a love of sorts. I looked into that parched white face and saw suddenly how close she was to death—and how afraid.

No, I could not disabuse her of her slight, pathetic comfort. Never mind the money, though I sorely needed my share of it and hoped that if it was indeed to be had, that I should have it. Even that was not really important, however. I could not rob her of the last shred of hope that these silly séances, futile though they be, would give her. Let her go to her grave believing, if she could, that Llewellyn Tregaron waited with open arms to conduct her to some heavenly reward.

No cruelty she had perpetrated upon me or mine was so very great that I had not borne it and survived it. I would not be as cruel as she. I would not rob her of her hope—not now, not ever.

"You have said nothing, Enid, yet your eyes are busy. I think you have been reflecting deep and long," the old woman said suddenly, breaking in upon my reveries.

"I was thinking, Aunt Augusta, that we have come far together."

"Is it time already to turn back then?" she asked, looking about her as if to see what place in the road we had reached.

"I meant in span of years, Aunt, not length of miles," I answered with a weary smile.

"You grow sentimental perhaps?"

"Perhaps," I agreed, something within the depths of me warming slightly. I wanted to reach out to her suddenly, in my newly realized pity for her sad and worthless life. I wanted to be kind.

"Well, *you* may do as you wish, Enid, but *I* have naught to do with sentiment. I shall never forget . . . nor forgive." She looked away from me, out over the spare, uncompromising landscape through which we rode.

I smiled ironically at the sad humor of it all. "No, Aunt," I answered her at last, "I would not even expect it of you." How close, how very close I had just come to reaching out; to touching her.

Well, I sighed to myself, it is not me. At least it is not me. As it is with Ambrose, so it is with her; *she* will not be touched.

Neither of them, it seemed, would be—or could be— touched. I turned my thoughts instead to the events of the previous evening.

It was then that I had broken to Jemmy and Madame De'Ath the facts of my conversation with the Ottermoles and Lucas Pond. I had spared them no detail of the talk and had expected that they would react with some worry or anger, especially directed at me, since it was my curiosity that had revived general interest in the memoirs of the duchesse and thus revealed Madame's penchant for charlatanry. On the contrary, however, they had taken my revelations with a surprising equanimity despite my telling them of all the words that had passed amongst the Ottermoles, Lucas Pond, and myself, ending with Mr. Ottermole's pointed suggestion that someone speak to him before the coming séance which was scheduled for Friday next.

They, neither of them, had seemed overly concerned. Jemmy was ready that very night to take horse and ride into Wadebridge for a confrontation. Madame De'Ath had stayed his brusque and impetuous enthusiasm for that task with a wave of those graceful and eloquent hands of hers.

"No," she had stated with finality. "This is a situation, Jemmy, that calls for finesse. Osric Ottermole is an upright and moral man, yet one of surprising wisdom and sophistication for a man of his provincial background. Moreover, I have always known that he is a romantic, as some of his remarks about me to Enid confirm. No, you, dearest boy, however much you may wish to deal with him on my behalf, are not the one to do it."

"Then Enid, madame?" he asked, looking toward me doubtfully. I felt a sudden surge of panic. Too much rested on satisfying Osric Ottermole's sensibilities for me to feel up to the task. Surely Jemmy was the one to do it.

"Of course not Enid." Madame De'Ath smiled. "She has let her curiosity bring us to this pass, the naughty child, but though she put us in the soup, she is not the one to ladle us out. Moreover, one does not send a girl out on a woman's job," she said with a certain catty pride.

"Who, then?" Jemmy asked naively. I already knew, of course.

"Why, me, naturally," she said with a small moue and a shrug of her shoulders.

"Are you going to send for Mr. Ottermole, then?" I asked.

"No, children, I think the mountain more likely to crumble to our will if Muhammad"—and there she bowed her head as if to indicate her humble self—"journeys to the mountain rather than asking the mountain to journey to Muhammad, n'est-ce pas?" she asked with a wicked gleam in her eye.

"Mais oui," Jemmy and I had replied mischievously, he with a deep, deferential bow and I with a graceful curtsy.

And so, for the only time since I had known her, Madame De'Ath made preparations to leave the precincts of Thanatos Abbey. It had all the earmarks of a momentous event.

A rider had been dispatched that very evening with a note

requesting an interview with Osric Ottermole on the following afternoon (which was a Sunday) and suggesting that Madame De'Ath would be delighted to visit the Ottermole manse, the charms of which she had not enjoyed for far too many years.

The wording of this missive was inordinately discreet, yet, reading between the lines, Mr. Ottermole would realize that she wished to discuss the urgent matter at hand. Moreover, the implication could hardly be lost on him that a great honor was being bestowed, for the aged *grande dame* of Thanatos Abbey rarely journeyed beyond the boundaries of her son's estate.

Not only could he not refuse the interview, but he would be in the position of acting as host to one whose very presence in his home was a signal honor. In short, Madame De'Ath began the game with her fair share of the "ace cards."

I had not seen my mother-in-law off upon her Sunday-afternoon journey to the "mountain," owing to my accompanying Aunt Augusta on her own ride into the countryside, of which I have already made mention, but I did chance to be in the front hall after storming from Ambrose's study when she returned from her visit.

I had scarcely made out the distant rumble of carriage wheels upon the high road above the abbey when Jemmy Burkers came tearing into the hall from the servants' wing.

"Enid, she's back." He hurled that announcement at me as he slipped his coat on over his striped servant's waistcoat, buttoned it, and dashed past me to the front doors.

He pulled them open just as the carriage came to a rumbling, swaying halt before the abbey steps. The footman leaped down from behind, opened the door, and pulled the steps into position for Madame De'Ath to alight.

She was a pleasure to look upon as she was handed down from the closed carriage, and I could not help but think how she must have conquered the susceptible Mr. Ottermole with her charms, even as she conquered me. She wore a deep mouse-gray velvet traveling costume and fitted jacket, cut, as were all her clothes, in the old French style. Upon her curly, caracul-gray wig was perched at a rakish angle a delightful gray velvet miniature of a gentleman's hunting top hat. Its sole accent was a wide gray grosgrain band ornamented with a small, dazzling brooch of rose-cut diamonds set in dark silver in the form of a cluster of flowers that quivered *en trem-*

*blant* upon their stalks with every move of her graceful head.

The larger brooch upon her jacket, the bracelets and rings she wore, and the earrings peeping from out of the curly ringlets at her ears were all of the same old, dark silver and brilliant rose-cut diamonds, set as flowers on stalks that trembled in constant, blazing motion with her every move. They gave the enchanting illusion, those diamonds in silver against her gray velvet garb, of ice flowers growing like magical talismans from a field of soft gray moss.

But as alive with crystalline fires as were those lovely jewels, no living fire could match the fire of Madame De'Ath's wonderful old eyes. She was flushed with the rosy glow of youth; it showed even from beneath the old-fashioned pallor of her antique, white-lead-painted face. Her carmine lips were pursed in self-satisfaction and her eyes danced in delight and mischief. I had no doubt, looking at her, of the success of her mission.

"Jemmy," she said with a kindly smile and an order meant more for the ears of the other servants present than because it needed to be said, "see to the lighting of candles and tend the fire in my salon. I shall be along shortly."

"Very good, madame." He bowed deferentially and with a significant gleam in his eye. I had no doubt that all those things had been seen to already. He left us at once and I watched him go with a strange feeling in me. Perhaps Ambrose knew me better than I knew myself.

"Now, my dear," Madame De'Ath said, turning to me and taking my arm with a confidential manner and a look of some affection, "you have nothing to worry about; not a thing to fear. All is well, and if anything, I am rather glad the kitten has escaped from the bag, so to speak."

"Mr. Ottermole will not stand in the way of our plan, then?" I asked as we walked slowly up the corridor to her apartment.

"Oh, that," she said with a wave of her gray-gloved hand, "he understands. I have put it to him plainly and he sees that it is a once-to-be-done venture, not a habit we have got into, of cheating gullible old folk of their money. I explained that last year we had no larcenous motive when we held séances with the old couple over their son dead in India; that one thing led to another and that it was their totally spontaneous generosity that decided us to try one deliberate coup of a similar nature."

"And?"

"And we are agreed with you, who know your aunt best,

after all, that it is too far along to turn back without risking harm to the old lady, your aunt, and, dear," she said more gently, "to poor Ambrose as well, who sinks more deeply all the time into his obsession with thanatology. We are agreed that, just as he can no longer admit his mother died and that I am merely his stepmother, so he is fast coming to the point—has reached it perhaps already—where he can no longer admit of the trickery used by us in the séances, and the preposterousness of contact with spirits from beyond the grave." She patted my hand reassuringly.

"You set the stage well enough, by your honesty in the face of their discoveries, for me to make them understand and allow—if not condone—our last séance." I sighed in relief at that intelligence from her. Thank God, in spite of me, all was yet well.

We had reached the New Hall by then, and Jemmy welcomed us with much animation, hanging on her every word as Madame De'Ath repeated to him, behind the privacy of her closed doors, what she had confided to me just moments earlier.

She removed her hat and tossed it upon a settee, throwing her jacket and gloves aside with a similar gesture of airy nonchalance. "What fun we have had all afternoon. He is a charming man, as I have always known, of course, but oh, how I wish I had not been so reserved all these years. What a delight it was to regale him with tales of the old days. He has read so much that it is almost as if he knew the same people and of the same events as I. My, we have had a jolly time," she exclaimed with satisfaction, and dropped down into her chair like a tired but happy young woman rather than an elderly and frail octogenarian.

"Would it be safe to say, madame, that you charmed the bloody pants right off o' 'im?" Jemmy asked with mischievous, if inelegant, humor.

"Well, Jemmy," she retorted with a devilish smile and a roll of her eloquent eyes, "I did not have to go *quite that far*, but in a manner of speaking, yes." We all laughed at her small innuendo.

"Thank heavens." I sighed in relief. "I did not say as much to you, but really, I felt quite terrible about having opened this Pandora's box in the first place, and being the reason that you have had to visit Mr. Ottermole in the second."

"My child, pray think no more of it. No harm has been done, Mr. Ottermole and I are faster friends than ever, and I have even managed to gain an interesting new insight into the mind of that seemingly dull boy Lucas Pond. I suspect that he shall go far."

"Do you? How interesting. I think I rather agree. Did you find him at all difficult, madame?"

"No, not really. He seems to respect Osric Ottermole mightily, and allowed himself to be guided by him, which I think was wise on the boy's part. He is a circumspect fellow and no romantic, to be sure. One must appeal to his practical side, but that offered no more difficulty than I had expected from all that you had said of him last night. He is shrewd, unlike his father. I wonder where he gets it from?"

"Well, not 'is mother." Jemmy laughed, but I wondered about that.

"And now, children, I shall shoo you out, for it has been a long, exciting day for me, and although I do not often admit it, I am not so young as once I was, and I need my rest."

We all arose, began to part, she toward her bedroom door and Jemmy and I toward the outer hallway.

"Jemmy," she called after us, "I shall want only a very light supper tonight, and some chocolate, I think. Serve it to me here by the fire," she added, nodding toward the fireplace along the wall between us. "And do not worry, for it will all be over soon. We are well on our way toward our success of next Friday evening."

"Indeed we are, madame," Jemmy agreed, "but I shall be quite glad when it is all far be'ind us."

"And so shall I," I added with conviction.

"La," she said with a smile, "do not be impatient, children. Friday night shall come soon enough. Events are hurtling headlong." She laughed lightly, disappearing into her boudoir as she spoke.

Headlong! "Hurtling headlong," she had said, and God alone knew how right she was. We were all, though we knew it not, hurtling headlong down the primrose path to nightmare.

And if now, after the passage of many years, I can still swear to the nervous tension that had been building in me all the week and which I felt on a particular Thursday night so long ago as palpably as I now feel my heart beating in my breast as I sit to my little desk and write this narrative, why, who can say that this is mere hindsight? Who can say but that on that Thursday night in one long-ago April, I did not feel in the very fiber of my being the first warning of that coming storm, hurtling headlong over our heads, about to break around us and change all our lives for great good or terrible ill, depending on our several destinies? Who can say?

"All is in readiness for the morrow, my dear?" Madame De'Ath asked Jemmy as he entered the New Hall on that fateful Thursday evening to join the two of us for dinner.

"It is, madame," he reassured her with a smile as he bowed and kissed her upraised hand. And then, taking my hand in his and touching it to his warm lips: "You look lovely tonight, Enid."

I gazed into his face with a pang in my heart that I hardly understood. It was so strong; so brutally handsome; no pretty face, but one that had been buffeted by life and mirrored a man of character, able to endure—for himself and for those about whom he cared. It was the face of a wily warrior—a Ulysses, a Hephaestus, a wise Nestor someday to be.

I broke my gaze from the face by main force, and catching Madame De'Ath's smile of amusement, I blushed scarlet to the roots of my hair.

"Do not be embarrassed, Enid," she said amiably. "There is much to see in that handsome dear face of his. I am glad to see you know it."

"I know it, madame."

"*Bien*! Jemmy," she said, "you look quite fit and splendid tonight, in your evening kit." And indeed he did, with his formal white waistcoat and black onyx studs upon his shirt-front, for Jemmy Burkers' figure, so strong and lithe and muscular, was far more suited to well-tailored evening dress than to the demeaning livery that his usual pose in the household demanded. "Do you not agree, Enid?" she asked pointedly.

"I do indeed, madame," and again I blushed.

"And you, dear child, in your lovely and defiant scarlet velvet—the velvet of that dreadful tribunal night, I believe—you look especially beautiful tonight. But," she said, cocking her head thoughtfully, "a trifle too austere, for you wear no jewels."

"Perhaps my mood is austere tonight, madame," I replied, for in truth I did feel rather subdued and tense despite the calmness of the past afternoon and the pleasant dinner which we were about to share.

"Nonsense," she exclaimed. "No more of austerity in this house amongst my little family. This is a night to be gay. The way is clear, the séance is planned and set up. I can growl in Welsh like a true Tregaron, and we shall have made a coup by this time tomorrow." With that happy thought, she pulled a key from a little gold chatelaine at the waist of her amber satin gown.

As she did, I watched her in fascinated pleasure; her evenings parure of jewels was of huge amber-colored topazes set in heavy gold collets which were joined by chains of gold, draped *en esclavage* about her long neck. The bracelets and rines and earrings of the parure were set similarly.

The darkly golden hair of her high, elaborate wig, which I supposed must closely approximate the natural hair color of her youth, was bound in amber satin ribbons and set with topaz hair ornaments in great profusion. As always with her, she looked dramatic, but on that particular night she was most bizarre and bright as well, a fantastic, living ghost out of another age. She was gay, in a light and playful mood that fateful Thursday evening.

It was a mood vastly at odds with my own. A sense of dread was growing in me, like a spreading fever within the very depths of me, though I fought it tooth and nail.

"Jemmy," she was saying, "take this key, please, and fetch both the Cagliostro watch and the Medici rosary." He made a move to protest, but she stayed him with a wagging finger. "Uh-uh, we are in a gay mood tonight and shall play at being very grand. Do as I say."

Jemmy disappeared into her boudoir with the little key, and Madame De'Ath, turning to me, changed her tone and demeanor with surprising abruptness. "All right, now, Enid, what is it that troubles you so? You are edgy and nervous as a cat, although you do attempt to conceal it."

"I do not quite know, madame. I don't know how to describe my feelings."

"Try, child," she urged gently. "Feelings are most important. I think people pay far too little attention to feelings—their own and others'."

I smiled wanly. "Yes, madame, I think I can agree with you wholeheartedly on that." I paused then, groping for words. "Do you know how it is when a storm approaches; how restive and high-strung one sometimes feels?"

"*Oui*! I was a farmgirl, remember? The very cattle in their stalls grow restless; horses whinny and kick; chickens behave more stupidly than ever; and cats run about like mad things."

"And people, too," I interjected. "People like myself seem especially keen to the changes in the atmosphere, keen to the sense of building oppression that pervades the air. The sky—the very air itself—turns a strange, still, yellowish-gray, and my nerves quiver within me and my mood grows tense with apprehension."

"Yes, I know the very feeling, and I see its effect on you right now." She nodded thoughtfully, looking at me with penetrating eyes. "But, Enid, there is no storm approaching. They are clear, the skies."

"I know, madame. The storm is not outside, you see. I have fought it all the week long, madame, and generally won out, but it threatens now to overwhelm me entirely. Something is in the air of this house tonight—something so palpable and terrible that it has all the aspects of a haunting."

Jemmy came back just then, intruding on the building tenseness of my mood and breaking it for the nonce, for which I was very grateful. He stopped dead in his progress when he saw my face.

"It is all right, Jemmy," Madame De'Ath assured him. "Bring my trinkets here," and she laughed at her own small joke, for we all knew that the jewel boxes that Jemmy carried so gingerly in his hands contained some of the most valuable "trinkets" wrought by the hands of man out of the arts of nature.

"Now, look at this," she exclaimed with all the aplomb of a conjurer, and dangled the huge pavé diamond watch and chain of Comte Alessandro di Cagliostro before our distracted eyes. "Fire and ice captured in one glittering handful of treasure. How exciting are the beauties of a jewel. Mesmer would have used such a trinket as this to entrance and bedazzle his patients, as he called them, waving it back and forth before their eyes thusly," and she leaned forward toward me, swinging that blindingly beautiful watch case before my face by its long, sparkling chain. "See how relaxing it is to watch, my dear? Follow the light with your eyes. See how easy it is to become lost in the depths of the jewel and lose all the tensions that are in you? Lose them in the jewels, my dear," her soft voice urged, fading so that I could hardly hear her any longer.

I grew frightened and shook my head as if to clear away the cobwebs, pulling my eyes from the bewitching beauty of the diamonds.

" 'Mesmerizing,' they have come to call it," she said. "His trickery is even now become a part of our language. Do you feel more relaxed, my dear?" she asked sympathetically.

"Why, yes, madame, I think I do," I agreed with her in surprise. She went on blithely with her conversation.

"But Cagliostro! He had a method far more subtle for the

use of such a bauble as this. He would not deign to dangle this before his subjects like a carrot before the nose of a stupid donkey. He was far more cunning than that. He put it where it belonged, in the waistcoat over his comfortably rotund stomach, and forgot it was there. Let others notice it and be impressed by it and be dazzled by its rarity. To him, it was just another of his many possessions. He would absently ask the time, and then, laughing as if embarrassed by his own absentmindedness, reach for his infinitely beautiful diamond watch as others in the company, anxious to oblige him, reached for their lesser ones at the very same moment.

"How, they would ask themselves, could such a man be a charlatan? He was too wealthy, too detached from the common herd, too fine and grand a man to have to resort to cheating or chicanery.

"Money attracts money, and so by having a large and nonchalantly displayed show of seemingly vast—virtually endless—wealth, he attracted to himself far more money than he ever could have got by being humble. It is a rule of thumb that I have always adhered to myself, after seeing how well it worked for him. My jewels have multiplied like bread cast upon the waters that cometh back a hundredfold, or something like that anyway. I never did read all of that book. Anyway, my point is that had I cried poor, poor I would surely have remained, *n'est-ce pas?*" We nodded in agreement of a sort.

"But," she went on, "wearing one man's gift of a topaz parure led the next to show off his greater wealth or generosity or more ardent devotion by giving me pearls, the next to bestow emeralds, and the next, diamonds. You see?" She waggled the watch in the air before us. We nodded again in unison, two disciples at her feet, so to speak, learning the lessons once taught to her by no less a devotee of venality than Cagliostro. Amazing!

"Jemmy, put it on and play my clever Cagliostro for me."

"I cannot with grace refuse." He smiled and hooked the diamond-studded chain into a buttonhole of his waistcoat, dropping the watch into his pocket. It only served to enhance the splendor of his already prepossessing figure.

"*Magnifique*," Madame De'Ath breathed, clasping her hands together in delight. Then, turning her attention to me: "Now, my dear, stand up and face me," she ordered with humorous severity.

I did, and she stood then herself, facing me with an appraising look at the cut of my gown. "Like this, I think," she said at last, and taking Catherine de Medicis' long pearl-and-ruby rosary from its velvet nest, she lifted it over my head and wound it around my neck several times in order to form a choker about my throat. Then, pinning the pearls to the center of my corsage at that point where they came together to form the circlet of the rosary itself, she took the ruby crucifix and affixed it to my waist in such a manner that the long chain of the preamble, consisting of alternating groupings of rubies and small Baroque pearls hung loose from the center of my bodice to the left side of my waist.

She stood back then and surveyed my appearance with a critical eye. "Elegant," she exclaimed at last. "Red has never been my color, so I have never worn it on scarlet, but the effect of pearls and rubies against your dark red velvet is most attractive and dramatic. See in the mirror how lovely you look."

I walked toward one of the many giltwood-framed mirrors in Madame's salon and contemplated my image with no little satisfaction. The warm iridescent glow of those literally hundreds of pearls interspersed, between the decades of the rosary, with ruby *Paters* and *Glorias* was utterly breathtaking; the magnificent crucifix of pavé rubies and enamelwork completely arresting. I liked what I saw very much indeed, and stood posing and modeling before the mirror in delight, watching the effect of red fire and white pearl as I moved.

"I am no Catholic and cannot guarantee the efficacy of wearing those holy beads, my dear, as a salve to your soul, but as an enhancement to your already considerable attractions, they are most effective indeed," she called lightly down the room to where I stood. "Would you not agree, Jemmy?"

"I would, madame, I would," he concurred with feeling, his dancing black eyes feasting on me in a way that I both welcomed and feared. Ambrose was right. Jemmy Burkers did have the power to make me blush. I came back down the room to resume my seat across from Madame De'Ath. Jemmy handed me a glass of our usual preprandial sherry and we each raised our little cut-crystal glass in toast.

"To our pleasant evening ahead," Jemmy said in a tone not quite convincing; suggestive of a troubled soul and not an easy one. We each sipped at the sweet, warm wine.

"I am aware, Jemmy, that our little Enid here is not herself tonight, but I did not think that you were troubled as well," Madame said, prompting him to speak.

"I was not, madame, until I sensed Enid's mood. If she is troubled, why, then, it troubles me."

"That is well," she said with a small moue of satisfaction. "Speak, Enid." And I did, my heart warmed that these two, and perhaps Jemmy especially, were concerned with my feelings and sensitive to them as well. This was a new thing in my life, and a secret joy to my lonely heart.

"I . . . it has been building for some time now. I have mentioned before that haunted feeling that washes over me like a wave whenever I am in the hallway between my rooms and those of my aunt. Well, this week it has grown worse; far, far worse. It is as if an atmosphere, palpable enough to touch or smell or see, were building up in that place . . . and in me. I can at times, though I fight it manfully, feel an oppression mounting in me that threatens to burst me into fragments, I swear, and I . . . I am afraid."

"Jemmy has spoken to me of this feeling that overwhelms you in that corridor by those doors. He thinks that it is something—a reminder, perhaps—of something that you knew a long time ago. Some thing or place from your past," Madam De'Ath suggested gently, tactfully.

Something in me grew frightened and panicky at her words, gentle as they were. I resisted them. "No . . . no, never mind my past. I . . ." All at once I was crying, the tears rolling down my cheeks in droplets as big as the pearls of the rosary that I wore, splashing onto the wide red velvet corsage at my bosom and from thence down onto my skirt, where they twinkled even as brightly as the ruby crucifix in my lap. Jemmy rushed to my side, sitting next to me on the settee and taking me gently into his arms so that my head rested on his broad shoulder as if upon a pillow. Now his black dinner jacket caught my dropping tears.

"I am afraid, Jemmy," I sobbed. "Something dreadful is about to happen. I can feel it to my soul's very core." He said nothing but held me close as if he would take into himself all the pain and fear in my body. How grateful I was of his strength and his silent comfort. "It is as I have said before, madame. That feeling one gets when the light turns grayish-yellow and the storm clouds gather and the air is charged with electricity as yet unleashed and lightning bolts as yet unhurled. There is a storm coming to this house—a terrible storm—and when it breaks . . ." I dissolved once more into tears, and Jemmy held me close against him, kissing me gently on my temple and brow.

"And when it breaks, my dear child, we shall all run for cover," she said thoughtfully, her eyes trained on the large marquetry table in the center of the room; that table at which

I had first caught sight of Madame Henriette De'Ath; the table across which she was wont, upon occasion, to lay those large, strangely figured cards of hers.

There was a knocking at the outer door just then. My mother-in-law's concentration broke and she came back to herself at once. "Sit up, you two," she instructed, "our dinner has arrived," and with that we two pulled away, somewhat embarrassed by our unconscious intimacy, and Madame De'Ath called a command for the servants to enter with our dinner.

We dined à trois at one end of the long mirrored table in the glass dining room, only one of the three chandeliers overhead lighted and the far end lost in a mellow, crystalline gloom. Since we were served by a butler and waiters, we had no chance to speak further of the troublousness of mind that had threatened to overwhelm me earlier—which was just as well.

The simple mundane act of eating served to calm my overwrought nerves somewhat, and the excellent wines that accompanied each course in turn did much to lift my spirits and lighten my mood. The final aid to the renewal of my spirits was Madame De'Ath herself, who regaled us, Jemmy and me, with more tales of her adventures in the long-gone fashionable world of old France.

It was only at the end of our meal that I recognized that most of her marvelous gaiety and charm during the dinner hour had been a pose and a sham, for it was then, as we arose from the table at last, that I saw the mask drop and an expression of perplexed concern pass over her lovely, majestic old face. She, too, had become infected by the mounting tension in that house, or if she sensed it not herself, she at least gave serious concern to my own dark mood.

"Children," she said after the servants had removed the remains of our meal and shut the outer doors of the New Hall behind them in their wake, "I shall ask you to amuse yourselves at reading or solitaire awhile. I must excuse myself in order to make some calculations."

"As you wish, madame," Jemmy said deferentially. He turned to a shelf and pulled out a recent work of Mr. Dickens, while I, too restless to read or sit, wandered about the room examining once more the vast and distracting array of bibelots and curios that I never tired of marveling over. However, out of the corner of my eye as I wandered, I could see my mother-in-law at her table, and I came to watch her with care and ultimately with undisguised fascination.

She sat rigid and upright at that lovely table, removing from a hidden compartment somewhere on its underside a pair of boxes, one of gilded ivory and the other of silvered ivory. From each she took a thick pack of large cards, formed of the thinnest wafers of old yellowed ivory and bearing on their faces those strange figures, the likes of which I had never seen before coming to Thanatos Abbey. Like the boxes that contained them, the backs of one set were of silver and the other of gold. Save for that distinction and the fact that the silver-backed pile was the thicker of the two, they were otherwise similar, bearing on their faces an array of strange and mystical figures: devils, death's heads, suns, moons, magicians, and all manner of other strange symbols, the meanings of which then escaped me entirely and which even now I only vaguely understand.

Those cards which Madame De'Ath used that night—*played at* would be too light a phrase to use—were called the tarot, the fifty-six silvered cards (which she did not use) being those of the four suits of the minor arcana: Cups, Pentacles, Wands, and Swords. The gilded ivory cards were those of the major arcana, consisting of twenty-two *atutti* cards—the trumps or *tarots*.

She set the minor arcana aside and carefully placed in consecutive order the numbered trumps of the major arcana by which she meant to practice her divination—for divination it was she meant to do with those cards, even as surely as a priestess of ancient times might once have done with the entrails of a dove.

I watched as she shuffled those stiff, slightly warped, quite ancient ivory boards, and held my breath almost fearfully as she thrice cut that gilded deck. Jemmy's eyes wandered from the pages of his book momentarily and snapped back with a slight glint of anxiety mirrored in them.

Then, just as she cut that deck slowly, for the third time, there came a sudden sharp, single rap of bony knuckles on the outer door. A look of high-strung, almost fearful satisfaction passed over her normally placid old face, and she nodded slightly toward the door as if in affirmation of what she had expected. "Enter," she called out firmly.

I watched with amazement. It was uncanny. She had *known* there would be a visitor, but by her face I saw that she had not been sure just who the visitor would be. Now, as Ambrose entered and walked stiffly down the room toward her, I knew that she remained silent, awaiting his own first words.

"Ah, the tarot, *ma mère!*" he exclaimed with haughty good cheer. "Tell me, shall I have my way with the old lady, and will the outcome be as I expect?" he asked patronizingly and with a smug sneer passing across his cold features. His mother flinched, and a shudder went through her ancient frame. She seemed suddenly very old and almost shrunken since Ambrose's entry and, more particularly, since his light and mocking question.

"Have some sherry, Ambrose, and leave me to my auguries," she ordered him, her eyes intent upon the gilded backs of the ten cards that she now laid out, one by one, across the top of the desk in two straight ranks of five and five, setting them down ever so slowly and carefully, positioning them with almost overpunctilious perfection. I sensed that she feared what it was she would find when she turned each of those magical cards over, each in its turn.

I knew not what they meant, though even to this day I can see them in my mind's eye, turned over one by one and slowly, carefully contemplated by Henriette De'Ath. First came the fourth card, called Emperor, followed by the tenth, called Wheel of Fortune; the twentieth, called Judgment; the unnumbered card called Fool; and last in that top row, the fourteenth card, called Temperance.

She stopped there for a long moment, surveying those five upturned cards before she began to reveal the last five, ranged beneath them. Of those, the first was the eighteenth numbered trump, called Moon, and then the seventh, called Chariot; the ninth, called Hermit, followed by the fifteenth, called Devil, and lastly, after a long, chilling pause, she overturned the last of the ten cards, number sixteen, which was called the Tower of Destruction.

I had come around the far side of the room and was standing behind her as she sat to those cards. I saw them dealt and studied; saw her breathe a deep sigh and shrink farther into herself, bending over that table like a shriveled old sibyl; watched as, with one swift, clawlike motion of her bejeweled old fingers, she swept those ten cards into a disordered heap and shuffled them back into the remaining cards of the gold-backed major arcana. She made no move at all to confirm her auguries by a further use of the other, silvered deck of the minor arcana. *What she had seen had been enough already.*

Jemmy caught my eye just then, and I saw that he, too,

had seen her swift obscuring of the tarot reading, although from where he sat he could not have seen the cards themselves. Nothing boded well. The tension in that room, especially now that Ambrose had joined us, was nearly unbearable, yet Ambrose himself remained calm and serene, like the great eye of a storm around which all the tempest swirls.

"You have set things up, Jemmy?" he asked with that same air of condescension he had used toward his mother. I hated it.

"I have, Ambrose," Jemmy answered with a nod of his dark head, his eyes remaining on the book before him in his lap.

Madame De'Ath, whether out of a nervous desire to keep her hands busy or by deliberate desire, had begun to set the gilded tarot deck in order again, starting with the unnumbered Fool and upward through the final card, number twenty-one, called World. Slowly, having turned the reordered deck facedown, she began to shuffle them, watching neither Ambrose nor Jemmy nor even the cards themselves. Rather, her gaze seemed fixed then upon the hall doors at the far end of the room, which she viewed full-on from where she sat.

I looked that way myself, to focus on that dimly realized double door, its outlines nearly lost in the golden aura of the multitudes of candles in that long salon of Madame De'Ath. I could not be certain then, though now, of course, I know for a fact, but it seemed from the angle at which I viewed it that the door was ever so slightly ajar, as if Ambrose had not bothered to close it properly behind him when he entered. It was only a vague impression, and I gave it but passing thought, turning my attention rather to the slow verbal sparring between Ambrose and Jemmy, during which Madame De'Ath kept up a steady, purposeful, rhythmic shuffling of those gilded ivory cards with her large, dark eyes staring fixedly ahead of her into the candlelit gloom of that eerie room.

"You have spent the day, I take it, in putting your trumpery spooks of painted scrim in order, have you?" Ambrose snapped maliciously.

"You may put it that way, if it pleases you, Ambrose," Jemmy conceded evenly, his attention still ostensibly on Mr. Dickens.

"If it pleases me? Hah! It pleases me to laugh, it pleases me," he rasped with a high-strung, nervous guffaw. He was no longer the calm eye of the storm. He, too, was caught in the swirl of the tempest, victimized by the building mood of terror and tension in the atmosphere of that dreadful house.

"You may go to all the trouble you like, Jemmy, with glowing smoke and phosphorescent paint, cackling like a demented hen into a hollow speaking tube or pushing buttons and pulling stops like a Sunday-morning organist, but it is all quite useless."

"Is it?"

"Useless as an old man's privates." Ambrose smirked in an uncharacteristic use of crudity that indicated to me as much as anything else how close he was to snapping. "Useless as trying to see the future in those cards," he added, gesturing toward his mother with an almost fearful gleam in his cold eyes.

"Then why are we holding the séance, Ambrose?" I asked softly, but even so, still rather startled at the sound of my own voice as I spoke.

"Because, my own bonnie bride," he retorted mockingly, as if he explained himself to an idiot child, "the séance is not useless; only your precious preparations for it are trumpery nonsense. We need no painted images of Llewellyn Tregaron, nor photographic lantern slides on smoke.

"The séance is real. Last week, his tobacco—no trickery of mine, as you all thought, but real—burned in that room because he wanted it to. He was there amongst us—and he will be again tomorrow. I have spent all this week researching such olfactory manifestations as we witnessed on Friday last.

"They are not uncommon, and they are generally a prelude to more dramatic and more positive manifestations of spiritual presence." He spoke with intensity then, trying to convince me with the force of his own belief. Naturally he could not, and his foolishness, unfortunately, only served to rile me.

"Are you saying, Ambrose, that Uncle Llewellyn, in his spiritual form, may still indulge the habits—nay, vices—of this world? He may still smoke his pipe? From what otherworldly tobacconist is he able now to purchase his favorite blend, and with what specie of currency does he pay his bill? Tell me, Ambrose, for I want to know.

"If my favorite milliner in London dies before me, may I look forward, upon my own demise, to the pleasure of wearing her latest other-worldly chapeaux in the afterlife? Or if I die first, must I put up with the inferior creations of other, less-talented, but already established ghostly milliners, until my own goes to her reward? Answer me that, Ambrose, for if, by all that's holy, Llewellyn Tregaron may come back as a good whiff of pipe tobacco, I may fancy a desire to come back as the latest Paris bonnet." I was hot by then, my nerves quivering down my arms, my temper near to a boil. Injudicious it may have been, but I could not hear his madness and accept with good grace his haughty condescension to us. It was too much.

And then I saw that even as I had been speaking, Jemmy, in a similar mood to my own, had quite calmly and unobtrusively been doing something very odd, his whole manner belying totally the force of the bombshell which his simple act was about to precipitate about our heads. It was not really an odd thing he did, and surely it was a simple thing, but one of the deepest import, as it turned out.

He had merely reached into the drawer of a table near which he was seated, pulled out a white clay pipe and a small paper twist of tobacco. He proceeded to stuff the bowl with the tobacco. He replaced the twist in the drawer, placed the pipe between his teeth, and lit a lucifer to it. All this while Ambrose, unmindful, harangued at me, berating me for my levity in the face of the spirit world and what lay beyond the veil. I listened only halfheartedly, most of my attention drawn, as a snake is drawn to sinuous music, by that small, homely act of Jemmy's in simply preparing and lighting a common clay pipe.

In seconds the scent of Uncle Llewellyn's tobacco pervaded the air around us. Ambrose bolted upright from the settee by the fireplace and whirled, looking about him in the empty air until his eye at last caught Jemmy, still seated, his eyes upon his book, his leg crossed casually, as he smoked that fateful pipe with all the relaxed demeanor of a satisfied publican.

He cocked a mocking eye at Ambrose's expression of utmost dismay and asked in the broadest cockney accent imaginable, "Care fer a puff o' me pipe, mate? It's a fine and rare ol' blend, this. Got it orf o' a bloke wot croaked."

Ambrose stood staring down at Jemmy Burkers' smug, mocking face. He was too stunned to move, to speak; even to curse, which is what I think he would have liked to do.

The atmosphere then was virtually unbearable; the silence so stunning as to drive one nearly mad. And then, out of that demonic silence, the small clicking sound of Madame Henriette De'Ath cutting the gilded tarot cards of the major arcana; cutting them once, cutting them twice . . .

And then the doors to the corridor flew open, flinging wide with their knobs crashing into the painted paneling of the salon, jarring the crystal drops on the wall sconces, rattling bibelots on their tables and shattering our taut nerves like so much breaking glass.

Ambrose shrieked in shrill alarm; Jemmy turned, knocking over a sherry glass as he did; and I found my stomach knot with such abruptness that it seemed I had been struck.

From the shadowy corridor beyond those wide-flung doors stepped the black-clad, funereal figure of Augusta Tregaron.

"Villains," she whispered in a malevolent hiss, "do you think I am such a fool as all that? Do you think that you shall get the best of me?"

Madame De'Ath cut the deck for the third time.

# 16

# THE TOWER TOPPLES

O! that a man might know
The end of this day's business, ere it come;
But it sufficeth that the day will end,
And then the end is known.

Caesar: The ides of March are come.
Soothsayer: Ay, Caesar; but not gone.
—*Shakespeare*

I do not know what more it was that Augusta Tregaron said just then. She came down the length of the room like a virago, her voice one long, croaking shriek of invective. She attacked us all by turns, inveighing against us with such ferocity that even Jemmy was stunned to inaction. He sat with that devilish pipe growing cold in his white-knuckled grasp.

Ambrose stood like a tall, bare tree that is lashed by a storm, leaning stiffly backward from her harangue as if bent by the steady force of a blowing gale.

Madame De'Ath, hunched over her cards, gave no sign that she heard aught of what was being said, her eyes instead trained upon the gilded backs of the ten tarot trumps, newly dealt, that lay ranked before her on the tabletop. And then she began the slow, contemplative overturning of those inscrutable cards, one by one, with all the mystic aura of an ancient Delphic oracle about her. I watched transfixed, looking down over her left shoulder, seeing each card in turn, unable to interpret the meaning save by inference, by the flinching and tensing or easing of Madame De'Ath's suddenly shrunken old body.

The first card was numbered eighteen, called Moon. The last four cards in the row were Wheel of Fortune, Judgment, Fool, and Temperance—the same four cards that had appeared, and in the same positions, earlier, upon Ambrose's entry into the salon. The sixth card was number fifteen, called Devil; the next, number eight, called Strength; the next, number seven, called Chariot, followed by number seventeen, called Star. She paused long over the last gilt-backed ivory card before she turned it over. The amber stones of the rings twinkled on her bent old fingers, which arched like claws, hovering over that last, fateful card as if loath to reveal its terrible, inevitable secret. And so intent was I upon its revelation that even the sounds of my aunt yet raging in the shrill unabated fury of her hysteria could not distract my eye from that last turning of that last card.

Slowly, my mother-in-law reached out, grasped at it, flipped it over, dropping it as if it were a poisonous toad. It was the same card that had been revealed before, when Ambrose was the subject of the augury—it was the Tower of Destruction.

Again that sudden sweeping of those ivory boards into a heap of disarray!

"Madame?" I whispered, reaching out my hand to touch her shoulder just then. She seemed so shriveled, so frail, tiny, and dried-up; suddenly too small for the clothes she wore, her high wig all at once too large to fit her bent old head, wobbling slightly as if it threatened to topple from her aged skull. Even the rings on her fingers seemed to turn and rattle against each other as if they belonged on a larger, stronger pair of hands. She was so drained and depleted of all her usually considerable strength and power that I actually feared for her well-being.

"I am quite all right, child," she answered, her old head bent to that heap of ivory cards, malevolent and terrible in the strange power of their fascination. "You are quite right. The storm has come."

"Remember what you said; that we must run for cover?" I replied, perhaps to comfort her, so vulnerable did she seem, and so fearfully frail and old. Perhaps also to comfort myself, for I did not want to lose her and I had never seen her so weak and depleted as this. Till that moment, Madame De'Ath had seemed virtually immortal to me, as if she had always been, and always would be. Now I saw the crumbling edges of her mortality and was momentarily frightened by it. I touched her again for reassurance, and in touching her I came to realize how much I loved that magnificent and strange old lady. It was a rare moment in my life, and to this day stands out with a kind of diamond-hard, crystal clarity in my memory. Her next words broke the spell of that tiny moment, and the reality of the present came crashing in around me once more.

"For some, child, there will be no running. Only wait, only watch, only listen," she admonished softly, placing a finger to her painted lips. Her eyes left the cards for the first time, fixing on the drama that had been playing before us all the while, unheeded.

"You sought to fool me, to cheat me, but it is *you* who are cheated, Ambrose De'Ath, *you*," my aunt was shrieking in a kind of hysterical cawing, like that of some frenzied, hunted bird. She was waving a set of documents. They hung open and unfolded, long, heavy sheets of foolscap, the lines of their folds bending and crackling as she waved them to and fro in his marble-pale, marble-cold face. Even from where I stood I could see that each page was crowded with tightly written lines of the old-fashioned copperplate script still favored by lawyers. From the blank back of the outer page dangled long, fluttering ends of the ribbons to which would be affixed the heavy globs of sealing wax intended to close the documents off from prying eyes.

"You see these papers, Ambrose?" she shrieked, waving them up into his drained, ashen cadaver's face. "They are all ready to be signed and witnessed. They bestow upon you twenty-five thousand pounds at once—*at once,* do you hear? This very night that sum would have been legally yours, to be deposited to your account in London by my solicitors at the earliest possible moment. "And *this*," she said, a mad gleam in her furious black eyes, "*this* is a codicil to my will, granting another fifty thousand to you upon my death."

Ambrose started visibly at that revelation, looking suddenly as if he would faint. "Fifty thousand." I saw his lips silently form the words, his eyes virtually glazing at the prospect of such a sum, now lost to him forever.

"See, see," she taunted, riffling the documents in his dead white face with a kind of mad, defiant triumph in her whole aspect. "I came here to this room tonight to find you and to have your mother or your servant and my niece witness the signing of these papers in your presence for all to see. I was not even going to wait until the morrow after the séance. I was so sure, so firm in my conviction, that I was going to make this gift to you tonight. Tonight, Ambrose, because I trusted you, trusted you and believed in you. I even believed that my bitter and skeptical niece Enid had been convinced as well. *Her* conviction, so artfully reluctant after such long and strong resistance, was the final proof I needed—*and I did believe!*"

Then, having reminded herself of my presence by her references to me, she wheeled away from Ambrose and turned instead on me, hurling her invective in my direction. I stood my ground, facing her rather numbly but, I hoped, with my wits yet somewhere about my person and ready, if needed, to be called upon.

"You," she cried, pointing an accusing finger into my cold and rigidly masked face. Beside me, Madame de'Ath, to keep her old fingers busy perhaps, had reordered the tarot cards and placed them in a pile before her. "You Enid, have betrayed me more than all the others."

"Have I?" I asked mildly, and moved by what mad impulse I know not—perhaps to keep my own fingers busy—I swept the stack of cards from the tabletop and began, with slow deliberation, to shuffle the stiff, slippery ivory boards as I stood my ground, to face my Aunt Augusta's continuing tirade.

"If ever, in these past few weeks since the night of that tribunal, as you all call it, I have even for a single moment doubted your guilt, relented for one single second in my utter conviction that my brother's innocent blood is on your guilty hands, Enid Tregaron, why, then, this night proves me to have been a doubting, sentimental old fool," she snarled, her small black eyes bright with menace, hot with her denunciation of me; all her vindicated belief in my utter vileness glowing triumphantly, her long hatred of me mirrored with new ferocity in her expression as she accused me. Such a face as she thrust into mine belonged on the head of the dread Medusa herself.

But I did not flinch before her wrath. I did not, in fact, once take my eyes from hers, yet somehow managed, unseeing, to set the shuffled deck upon the table at my side and cut the cards once, twice, and finally a third time, leaving the stack whole and neat before Madame De'Ath.

"Deal for me, please, Madame my mother-in-law. We are in the center of such a storm right now as I have sensed all day was coming. Deal for me what follows the passing of my own particular storm."

"No, child," Madame De'Ath whispered in admonishment.

"Enid, do not play at the tarot. It is not wise," Jemmy called to me across the room, calmly but firmly.

"I have shuffled and cut the cards three times, as seems to be the ritual. I have asked my question and I await an answer. Deal, madame, for I am not afraid—and I am *not* playing."

"*Mais oui.*" She nodded, giving in to the force of my desire and placing the first card down upon its face, the velvety gilded back a blank that hid the mystery beneath.

"Enid, you villain, you murderess, you shall not destroy me," my aunt hissed at me as I watched the laying out of those fateful cards.

"I have no desire to destroy you, but the seeds are sown. Mr. Ottermole remarked the other day that the seeds of the present are ever rooted in the past. A mindlessly simple statement, but true nonetheless. You have sown long ago the seeds that you reap the fruits of this night, Aunt Augusta, and pity it may be to say it, yet say it I must! 'As ye sow, so shall ye reap.'"

"Oh, you are hard, Enid, you are hard," she muttered, her head turning from side to side mechanically, her eyes steadily on mine.

"And if I am, what better teacher could I have had than you?"

"You quote the word of God, you irreligious, sinful girl. Since when have you dared to quote Scripture? And how dare you," she shrieked suddenly as she noticed for the first time the sacred beads that I wore as a necklace, "how dare you wear a rosary in such a fashion? It is blasphemy." She pursed her lips in disapproval, more indignant now than ever; aghast at what she noticed now as if she took it for some new sample of my brazen and evil character—murderess, plotter, and now blasphemer as well.

I shrugged. "Since when are you turned papist, Aunt, to be so shocked by such a small thing?" I was playing at words with her now, breaking the force of her passion, scattering the strength of her fury with my own coolness. It was an old trick between us, and one that I was quite good at from long years of bitter fencing.

By now the cards were dealt, all ten of them, and one by one they were overturned and I saw before me the representation of my own immediate destiny: first, the Chariot, Wheel of Fortune, the Sun, the Devil, and, fifth in the top row, the Tower of Destruction. I drew in my breath in fear.

Madame De'Ath placed a bejeweled finger on that

threatening card of ill omen. "The influence *now passing*, child."

I nodded in relief. It was well.

The first card of the second row came up. "The influence that will soon come to bear." It was the card called World. I nodded again, sensing somehow that it too was well.

Judgment followed; then Strength, which pleased me, for when it appeared I noticed that Madame De'Ath was more herself again, taller in her chair, higher of head, her fingers surer as they overturned the cards. The next was Moon, and the last card—the card of culmination—bore the image of the High Priestess.

"*Bien,*" she whispered under her breath, but by then her assurance was not needed. I understood, if not in detail, at least in essence the implication of those cards. It only confirmed the inner strength and sense of well-being that was gradually taking over my spirits.

"You will get nothing," my aunt was shrilling, suddenly aware that I had stolen her thunder and endeavoring to get it back by turning her wrath on poor Ambrose again. "No, not one farthing shall you get of my money—any of you—not one single coin, and I shall be out of this house at first light tomorrow. Do you hear, Ambrose De'Ath? At first light."

Ambrose said not a word.

"This for you, Ambrose De'Ath," she railed, tearing at the thick sheets of foolscap in her hands, "and for your mad old mother—gaudy, vile, eccentric old witch." She pulled again at the resisting sheets of thick paper, which crackled and tore reluctantly in her weak, old woman's grasp. "Be damned to your lowborn, thieving villain of a servant—if servant he be—and most of all, most of all, may you be damned to hell, you murderess, you spiller of your own blood, you betrayer of your own poor aunt. Most of all, may you be damned, Enid Tregaron."

With that she thrust her arms to their fullest length, and hurling those crumpled tatters of document in a great arc around the room, scattered their jigsaw pieces in such a manner that they struck us all one by one as they flew from her hands and hurled through the air like confetti. She fled then, wordlessly and in a cold, blind fury, back through the open doors, and I knew that she meant to pack her boxes and be out of Thanatos Abbey at first light even as she had threatened. I had seen her like that before upon occasion. It was Augusta Tregaron at her strongest and most defiant; at her most powerful. In that way, at least, we were something alike. I had much that same sort of power myself at times and could use it even as she. How strange it was, that moment! I found myself really rather liking her—admiring her. She had been entirely right in her every word and act. We *had* sought to cheat her. And she *had* discovered it. I was almost proud of her at that moment, and closer to her in spirit just then than I had ever felt in my life. I think that I even smiled at her figure retreating through the doorway.

For some few seconds no one said a word, and then I spoke, in a strange, distant voice that hardly sounded like my own. "She was in the hallway all the while," I said flatly. "Ambrose left the doors ajar when he entered. She heard our every word. She heard it all. She smelled the tobacco."

"It had to happen. It was . . ."

"In the cards, madame?" I asked, finishing my mother-in-law's thought in a low whisper.

"It was." She nodded simply. She, too, I could see, was numb and spent from what had just passed. Only Jemmy seemed in some possession of his wits. He sat, the cold pipe still in his grasp, looking with alert, thoughtful eyes at Ambrose.

Ambrose! He had said nothing through all of this; not one word that I could remember. He still stood rooted to the floor by the settee from which he had bolted upon first scenting Uncle Llewellyn's pipe tobacco rising in the still air of the salon. He had not moved except to sway as if wind-whipped by Aunt Augusta's raging in all the time that had since elapsed. Suddenly all our eyes were upon him. His own were fixed on the wide-flung doors through which Augusta Tregaron had just fled.

And then he started to babble—at first incoherently and then with more clarity. "No, no, no, she doesn't understand. She must not; she cannot turn back now. I need her. *I must have the money.*"

He turned and bent low, not seeing us, I think, and scrambled after the torn fragments of the documents that she had strewn about the room in her fury. "Where are they? I must have them all. She'll see reason. She'll mend them and she'll sign," he mumbled, his eyes stark in his skull's face, the pulses in his temples throbbing to the insane rhythm of his reeling words. He ranged all around us as if we were merely articles of furniture, picking up the scattered pieces of foolscap from floor and table and settee, smoothing them clumsily in his hands as he found them. At last he had them all.

"You shall see," he cried, "you shall see. I shall make her

understand," and with that he fled after her, the scraps clutched in his bony hands, ribbons aflutter, and a look of fearful, demonic agony in his madman's eyes. The terror of it all was that he had not spoken any of those words to us, but only to himself, so deep into his final madness had he been plunged. It was as if we no longer existed for him. Only he existed at that moment—he and Augusta Tregaron—he and Augusta Tregaron and Augusta Tregaron's money.

Jemmy leaped up and faced Madame De'Ath, his hands against the edge of her table, his body arched across it toward her. "The cards, madame? I could not see from where I sat. The last cards of each of them, what?"

"The Tower, Jemmy, the Tower."

He looked down at the cards of my own tarot, spying the dreaded Tower amongst them, and uttered an inarticulate cry.

"No, it is in the position of passing influences, Jemmy," she declared with great emphasis. "She will weather it."

He looked down again at the deck. "They both had the Tower?"

She nodded solemnly. "The benevolent influences are passing for both of them. They share the Moon and the Devil as well," she added significantly. "Enid has sensed it all along, Jemmy, and she is right. There is a storm around us in this house tonight. Tonight that storm breaks, the tower topples—and the earth will shake."

Her old voice sounded hollow and echoing, far away to my ears as I listened. I was numb entirely now, save for my stomach, which was knotted with a dull, constant ache, and my feet, which felt like lumps of ice in my little red velvet slippers.

Somewhere far, far away, down the labyrinthine corridors of Thanatos Abbey; somewhere down the long labyrinthine corridors of my mind, I heard the shouting: Ambrose's deep, cold voice, shrill now with desperation—or was it another voice, long stilled, deep and booming with an uncontrolled fury that paralyzed me even now?

And then the faint, strident retors of Augusta Tregaron carrying down those long corridors to my keenly listening ears, or was it rather the high sweet pleadings of another, gentler voice, long hushed by death? I could not tell. I only heard and knew that I must run.

"No," I heard myself cry out in a rising shriek, "I cannot let it happen. I cannot. No, no, no . . ." I sang in a nightmare litany, running like a madwoman down the long halls of the abbey, my scarlet velvet skirts held up before me lest they check my headlong pace, the heavy weight of that ruby crucifix thumping like a second heart against the bodice of my dress as I ran pell-mell toward the violent sounds of argument and accusation that issued from the corridors somewhere far ahead—far ahead of me? Or long, long behind?

It had happened once before and I had failed. I had not been able to stop it, for it had been too, too late.

But tonight I would not fail. Tonight I would save her.

"I'm coming, Mama, I'm coming. I won't let him hurt you this time. Mama, Mama, it's all right. I'm here." The voice was screaming now, the words coming in searing, throat-wrenching gasps as she sped down the long halls of Thanatos Abbey—or was it another house long ago and far away? It was the voice of a child, a thirteen-year-old girl child—the voice of the Enid Tregaron that once had been, running; running to help her mama, who was screaming in fear and fighting for her life even as her own beloved husband turned on her, first beating her with his fists and then plunging at her with that damnable knife.

There was no cook this time, running up from belowstairs in her long, patched night shift and robe and cap to meet with a knife blade in the chest. Janet was not there this time, staggering from Mama's bedroom door with her white-clad breast all bloodied, her reddened hands groping for support along the corridor wall. There were no steps now either for Papa to catch her at the head of, plunging the knife again and again into that broad, fat old woman's back of hers until she spat great gouts of blood from out her mouth, losing her grip on the banister, falling slowly over and over till she landed softly, like a great, fat bolster at the bottom.

No, there was none of that this time. This time, there was only Enid, running in her bloodred dress, shrilling and calling out in alarm, "No, Papa, no. Don't hurt Mama, don't hurt Mama. Please stop it, stop. She's my mama; don't hurt my mama," over and over and over until the long stone corridors echoed with that pathetic litany as once they had echoed, ages earlier, with the Latin chants of ancient monks long since moldering in the crypts below the abbey chapel.

They rounded that last turning together, both of them; the Enid that was and the Enid that had been. The shrieking, pleading voice belonged to the other, the child Enid; the fear and the terror and the mounting nausea belonged to them both.

The atmosphere of that last, dreaded stretch of hallway

was no vague imagining now; no subtle, suggestive hinting at nightmares past or nightmares yet to come. This was it! It was now! A wall of horrors as thick as fog and as dense as molasses. They waded through it as if in slow time, those two frightened, brave, lonely, struggling Enids, girl and woman, lashed together by the common bond of soul and body and experience.

The last few feet, the open door, the furious sound of anger and blows and struggle; of pleading and terror and rage. There was no plunging of a knife this time, gripped in a strong man's bloody hand; no tiny sewing scissors raised in futile, pathetic defense, but still it was the same struggle, the same scene of horrors past, horrors relived.

The old woman lay back against the rumpled counterpane of her narrow bed, forced thus against her feeble struggles by the greater strength of the man who grappled with her in his mindless rage. Pieces of foolscap, torn and wrinkled, lay scattered like snow across the Turkey carpet and the bed itself.

"You must sign. You must, do you hear?" the man's voice shrilled desperately. "You don't know what you're doing. It was *they* who wanted to cheat you, not I. Sign, sign, for God's sake, sign." His long bony fingers were about her frail old neck.

From the old woman's mouth came the guttural, inarticulate cries of strangulation and terror. Her eyes rolled, bulging horribly from their sockets with the pressure of his viselike grip as he pressed and pressed and pressed upon her scrawny, wrinkled old throat.

"Sign, I say," he shrieked again, throttling her as she struggled against his grip. "Sign, damn you."

The old woman's rolling eyes fixed suddenly on the girl in the doorway and lighted with a newborn hope.

The girl in the scarlet velvet gown paused only a second, though to the old woman it must have seemed a yawning eternity, and then she ran up behind the man—what man? her husband? her father?—who attacked—whom?—her mother? her aunt?

"Papa, no," she cried. "Papa, no. Leave Mama be. No, no," she wailed, clinging to his arms like a wild thing, trying to pull him away by main force, though what availed the force of a child—and a girl child at that—against the force of a man? He let go the old woman's neck for a moment, only long enough to fling off him the lightweight body of the wife who sought to stop him. He would not be stopped.

"Enid, save me." The old, cracked voice croaked like a broken thing, pleading and desperate.

"Papa, Papa, I have to *kill* you," came the despairing little-girl cry of the Enid-who-once-had-been. "I have to kill you, Papa. I have to save my mama," and with that the Enid-that-now-was snatched up the nearest thing to hand—a tall brass candlestick—and, unmindful of the falling candle, the scorching flame and spattering wax, she raised the heavy stick high over her head and sent it crashing down upon the back and shoulder of the man who struggled with the woman on the bed.

She would have kept on raining blow after blow, screaming "No, Papa, no, I have to kill you, Papa, I have to kill you," endlessly, had it not been for the strong hand that gripped her wrist from behind, wrestling the candlestick from her grasp and flinging both it and her aside in order to pull the man—Ambrose De'Ath—in order to pull the body of Ambrose De'Ath from off the prostrate, strangled form of Augusta Tregaron.

"*Enid*," Jemmy shouted firmly, commandingly, "*Enid*, look to your aunt. Ambrose is strong as an ox in his insanity an' I'm 'aving job enough to restrain 'im."

"Yes, Jemmy, yes." I gasped, my words coming in painful, breathless gulps from my raw throat. For the first time in minutes I knew once more who I was—and what I must do.

I turned to the rumpled bed; Aunt Augusta's bed—no one else's bed—in the small guest bedroom of Thanatos Abbey—no other bedroom of any other house—and looked to the old woman, who was simply my aunt and no other, closer, dearly beloved relation of mine. She lay on her back across the bed, her face ashen white now, though just moments earlier it had been taking on the bluish-purple tinge of death by strangulation. Her eyes were still bulging, bloodshot, and terrible to see, from bruised, blue-rimmed sockets. She made no sound but a small, childlike whimpering that issued from her mouth as sounds issue from the mouth of a skilled ventriloquist—without movement—and a trickle of blood and spittle ran down her chin. Her breathing was barely discernible. She was not dead, but I knew, seeing her condition, that it could not be long.

With more sorrow than I knew I could ever muster for that bitter old woman; with more pity than I dreamt was in me toward her, I lifted her in my arms and laid her in the bed, drawing the covers over her to keep her warm. She was as light as a child and so frail and bony to my touch that I might have been handling the delicate, hollow-boned body of a broken bird. I fixed the pillows beneath her head, loosened the tight, high collar of her black dress about the bruised and battered thinness of her scrawny old neck.

Her breathing deepened slightly and rattled in her throat, her exhaled breath fetid with blood and spittle and bile. I drew back involuntarily, assaulted by the stench, wanting suddenly to run from it—run from it in an unreasoning and almost mindless dread—and then I remembered.

It had been just such a stench—blood and vomit and other matter, voided in death—that had filled my mama's room on that night so long ago, that night I finally remembered after so many long, unknowing years, the night on which she was killed; that had filled the halls as old Janet, the cook, fled from my father's attack to try to reach safety and help. It was the same stench that had come from my father's broken skull and scattered brains as I beat at him in that poor, desperate, futile attempt to save my mama from the furious, death-dealing blows of his fists and the knife.

Ignoring the stench and forcing from my mind the unutterably painful memories that it evoked, I worked now to try to save my aunt, chaffing her wrists to warm the blood, bathing her face with soothing rosewater brought to me just then by Madame De'Ath's own hands.

"Enid, I am leaving Bess with you," she whispered as I laved the blood and spittle from Aunt Augusta's face. I nodded. "I have sent the coachman for a doctor—and for Mr. Ottermole," she added significantly.

Again I nodded, not taking my eyes from my labors even for an instant, for long streams of tears ran freely from my eyes and I kept my head averted lest they be seen.

"Jemmy has had a deal of trouble with Ambrose. He is raving now—a lunatic—and powerful in his madness. The footman has helped to restrain him in his study and they have dosed him with laudanum, but they are not sure what effect it will have on him in his present condition." She paused.

"Go on," I prompted her as I lifted my aunt against my shoulder and began to unbutton the back of her dress, hearing her labored breathing in my ear with a kind of benumbed detachment as I worked.

"They have bound him to the sofa in his study, and the laudanum has calmed him somewhat, but I think I should be with him, dear. He is calling for his mother—for me—and I must go to him shortly. Can you manage here with only a maid? Bess is a good girl, I think, and cool enough of head, if she is needed. I would rather not rouse anyone else unless I have to. The fewer who witness all this, the better, I think." She was being so gentle, so careful in her manner of speaking to me, as if I myself were poised on a brink and she worried for me. I felt I must reassure her.

"I can manage, madame. Thank you," I muttered, the words bubbling in my throat as I fought back my tears. "Please go now to Ambrose for me. I can be of no service to him, for he does not need or want me, but he does need you. Your place is with him, just as mine is here with my aunt."

*"Oui, ma chérie."* She sighed and turned away toward the door.

"Madame," I called after her softly in the small, broken voice of a child, "I know now what happened all those years ago. I killed my papa. He was hurting Mama and I tried to stop him. I didn't want to, but . . ." The tears came, blocking my throat, and I could not speak further.

"Yes, my dear, I know. Jemmy thought that that is what must have happened as soon as he heard the details of the murders and how the bodies were found. He pieced it together from what you told us on the night of the tribunal, and he knew, even more surely than I, who, overprudently perhaps, chose to reserve my judgment, that you were no murderess."

"But I did kill . . ."

"You only did what you had to do, child. That is all." Her calm voice sounded soothingly across the room, the mellow warmth of it stroking my pain and doubt as a mother's gentle hand soothes her child's fevered brow. "Bess is waiting in the corridor. I shall send her to you now."


"Enid, do not leave me," Aunt Augusta croaked from the depths of her bruised and broken throat. Her strength was feeble, yet she managed to grasp my wrist with the white old claw that rested on the coverlet by her side.

"I am here, Aunt. I have been by your side throughout the night."

"All night?" she asked, her eyes rolling with a kind of fearful gleam toward the window.

"All night," I reassured her softly. "It is now just nearing dawn. The first light must soon be showing in the east, I imagine."

"It will soon, ma'am," Bess concurred. She had slipped out of a light doze at the sound of our voices, and leaning from her chair near the window, pulled the curtain aside and looked out toward the eastern horizon.

"Shall I open the curtains for you, Aunt?"

"No, no," she whispered urgently, tightening her grasp on my wrist. "Send the girl away," she pleaded. "I must speak."

"You are too weak yet. Rest. Try to sleep again to regain your strength," I urged her gently. "We shall talk later."

"Send her—" she croaked in exasperation.

"Very well," I broke in, lest she upset herself needlessly. "Bess, please leave us for a time. Take the chair and sit in the hall. I shall call if I need you, do you hear?"

"Yes, ma'am."

Aunt Augusta waited till the girl had left, her anxious eyes following the maid's retreating figure impatiently until the door closed behind her.

"Enid, that night—all those years ago, that night . . ."

I stiffened. Would she even now, so near her own death, torment me yet?

"Yes? What of it? Do you choose even now to gloat over me? You were right after all. I am a murderess. I did not know it then, I swear, but I do know it now. And so, it is true, I killed your brother." And then, all my stiffness and reserve in the face of her words broke down once more. "Oh, Aunt, I killed my papa, I *did* kill Papa." The tears spilled from my eyes and dropped upon our hands, locked in a grip of mutual despair and need for the very first time in all our long and bitter years together.

"Can you ever find it in your heart to forgive me, Enid?" she croaked in that terrible, broken voice.

"Forgive you?" I cried in surprise. "Forgive *you?*" Why, all your accusations over the years have proved true, your hatred of me is vindicated, and yet you ask *my* forgiveness?" I was too amazed to think clearly or to understand her meaning.

"You had to do it, child. I can see that now. Tonight, I saw through your reactions—you were not *here*, you were *there*. I . . . I thought you killed them all, killed Morgan, but it was he who . . . You were trying to save *her*"—and even after all those years she did not like to say my mother's name—"just as you have saved me tonight."

She understood. She actually understood. "Yes, Aunt." I nodded. "I know now that is the way it was. I remember now."

"*I* drove him to the fights that they had, didn't I, Enid? I drove Morgan and your mother apart, didn't I?"

"Yes, Aunt, you did," I agreed with pitiless honesty.

"I drove them all away," she whispered, a glazed, faraway look in her eye as if she saw, with sudden new understanding, down the long tunnel of her years to the wrongs of her blighted, selfish life.

"Yes, Aunt, I am afraid you did. All of them—and me, as well, who might have loved you, perhaps, had you ever let me." The words came spontaneously, unexpected even by me, and with them, hot tears as well.

"That is true," she whispered, seeing into my face with a deep, stark stare. In those seconds she saw me for the very first time, I think, in all the years that she had known me. She saw what was, and what might have been, and it was pitiable to watch.

"Enid, forgive me," she pleaded out of a depth of realization that I saw welling in her and that I could not deny or rebuff.

"Aunt Augusta, I forgive you all, all—if you will forgive my cruelties to you as well. We have both been guilty in this."

She nodded feebly, clutching at my hand.

I gripped hers in return. "Our peace is made," I whispered.

She smiled a feeble smile of irony. "You always said, Enid, that we make our own hell right here on earth, and I look at my life from the last edge of it and I see you were right."

Tears filled her old eyes. "It might have been nice in that house for the three of us—good between us all those years. I might have helped you."

"Yes, Aunt, you might have helped—and I might, in turn, have been some comfort and consolation to you, as well. The best that I can do now is be here with you this moment," and as I said those words, my eyes flooded with burning, stinging tears once more and I could not speak.

"I told Ambrose that I should leave by first light—and see, the first light comes and I am leaving," she croaked hoarsely, and her eyes filled with fear, her hand gripping mine like the feeble talons of a dying bird.

"Enid, I am afraid," she whispered.

I put my arm about her shoulders and cradled her against me. "Do not be afraid, Aunt," I whispered. "There is nothing to fear. No hell; there is only forgiveness now, and rest and peace at last."

She clung to me for a moment like a frail, frightened child. "Forgiveness and peace," she said slowly, dreamily, and with a little shudder sank lifeless against my breast. I held her still, for one long, quiet, thoughtful moment. "Say then our peace is made," I said, snatching the words from somewhere in my memory in a sort of valedictory to the old woman lifeless in my arms.

I laid her gently back against the pillows and closed her eyes and pulled the coverlet smooth across her shoulders and looked down at her with a kind of exhausted, benumbed sense of pity and sorrow. Her face was calm. It looked as if, in those last few moments of her life, some peace had finally come to her bitter old soul, and I was glad of that. I could not have begrudged her the small comfort she had wrested from the last minutes of her long, bitter life. The deep sorrow—for both of us—was that it had been so brief a time, mere seconds in a lifetime of selfishness and hatred.

I walked to the window and looked toward the barren meadows of the bleak eastern horizon. She had been right. She did leave Thanatos Abbey at the first light of the dawn.

"Peace, Augusta Tregaron," I whispered to the blue-green dawn. "Peace and rest and freedom from bitterness and sorrow and regret. Most of all from regret."

There was no more that I could do there, and so I left, closing the door behind me on her cooling, lifeless body. Bess, the maid, rose sleepy-eyed from her chair as I came out.

"Ma'am?"

"My aunt has died, Bess. There is no more to be done. I think it would be quite all right if I were to dismiss you now," I said, my whole body suddenly weak with fatigue and spent emotions.

"Not just yet, Bess. Your mistress needs you now." Jemmy's softly whispering voice carried down the corridor from the doorway of Ambrose's rooms. He disappeared from sight as fast as he had appeared, and after we had waited a minute or two, he came out again, carrying Madame De'Ath unconscious in his arms.

Bess started, and I cried out in a hoarse whisper, "Oh, Jemmy, no . . ."

"Shhh, she's only fallen asleep sittin' wi' Ambrose," he said *sotto voce* as he carried her gently down the hallway toward us. He glanced toward my aunt's closed door and then at me questioningly.

"She's gone. Just a few minutes ago. In my arms."

"I'm sorry, Enid," he said simply as I walked beside him. Bess had gone on ahead to make way for us and to turn down Madame De'Ath's bed.

"So am I, Jemmy, so am I."

"I thought you would be when the time came. I didn't think you were as 'ard, girl, as you claimed to be," he answered.

"You're right, Jemmy. I'm not. I'm not hard at all. I'm too soft, too easily hurt, and I hide my hurt behind a wall."

"Enid?"

"Yes, Jemmy?"

"When this is all over—and it soon will be, really—I want you to 'ave learned something from it."

"What's that?"

"That . . . that I won't 'urt you, an' that *I* want no walls between us, do you 'ear?"

"I . . . I hear."

"And?"

"Let everything be over first, Jemmy. Please?"

He nodded, and our attention was drawn then to Madame De'Ath, who stirred sleepily in Jemmy's arms as he carried her through the salon toward her boudoir.

"Shhh, madame. I'm takin' you to your bed. Bess'll 'elp you to retire."

"Oh, Jemmy, yes," she mumbled sleepily, "but I should be with Ambrose," she added in mild protest.

"Tom is wi' 'im, and as soon as I've stowed you away safe, Enid an' I'll go back an' sit wi' 'im. The doctor and Ottermole should be 'ere before long as well."

"Enid," Madame De'Ath asked as Jemmy placed her gently on her own bed in her own beautiful boudoir, "your aunt?"

"She is gone, madame. She . . . she . . . We made it up at the last. She realized what must have happened that night— the night . . . She asked *my* forgiveness."

"And did you give it, child?"

"Of course, and asked hers as well. I could not let her die alone—not alone in body or in spirit." And again tears of sentiment welled in my tired, aching eyes.

"*Bien*. It was well done, child. The best end that could be to a long, long enmity. You could do no more, I think." She sighed sleepily, and with a last "good night" and an order from Jemmy to lock the shutters and doors as a precaution, we left the old Madame De'Ath to Bess's careful ministrations.

"Oh, Jemmy"—I yawned as we left the salon—"I am so very tired."

"Sleep, then," he urged. "I can carry on."

"No, there is Ambrose yet. I should be with him now."
And we hurried back through the dark corridors of Thanatos Abbey with only the frail morning light of a wan sunrise illuminating our way.

In our absence, all hell had broken loose in Ambrose's study. Tom, the footman, lay unconscious by the chair in which Jemmy had left him sitting guard over his prisoner, and the silken drapery cords with which Ambrose had been bound to his couch lay in a knotted, shredded heap on the carpet. One of the very legs of the couch had been wrenched from its pegged socket by the force of Ambrose's furious struggle to free himself from his bonds. Furniture and the macabre *memento mori* of his study—skulls, bones, figurines, and curios—lay everywhere in scattered disarray.

The single casement window of the room was smashed wide open, its lock broken and the leaded frames twisted as if by the force of a brute. Outside on the lawn, a chair lay on its side amidst fragments of broken glass.

Jemmy brought the footman around with much ungentle slapping of the face and calling of his name. "Tom, Tom, fer Christ's sake, wake, man. What 'appened? Where the devil 'as 'e got to?" Slowly the man came around, moaning and mumbling out of a bruised and swollen mouth. His eye was blackening visibly before our gaze. Ambrose—gaunt as a skeleton—had become a berserk in his frenzy, possessed with the strength of a demon.

"Here," I said, bringing a bowl of water from the nightstand in Ambrose's dressing room next to the study and starting to lave the man's head with a cold compress.

"Thank you, ma'am," he said in some embarrassment, and taking the cloth from me, held it to his own head. I had forgot his place, but he had not. Jemmy looked across at me with a funny smile.

No, Jemmy, I thought as I looked at his expression, I am no longer the snobbish, class-conscious bitch you once thought I was. I have unbent; I have learned to reach out a bit since coming here to the abbey; since knowing you and Madame De'Ath and little Arabella. When all this was over I would have to find the proper time and the proper way to thank them—but not now.

"'Ave any idea where 'e's got to, Tom?" Jemmy repeated.

"No, Mr. Burkers, I don't. We struggled something fierce. He struck me a smart blow on the head with that skull there," he said, nodding toward a medieval wooden presentment of a death's head, "and I think I heard the window breaking as I passed out. That's all I know."

Jemmy turned his head toward the window. " 'E can't 'ave got far, not on foot an' there's been no stirring of 'orses in the stables since I sent the coachman into Wadebridge." He turned again to Tom. "Can you make it to your room all right?"

"Yes, sir, I think so."

"Good man. See you 'ave someone rouse the other men first if they're yet abed, an' 'ave them dress at the double. Tell them I want them to meet me by the stables in a quarter of an hour to 'elp search for the master. Do you 'ear?"

"Yes, sir. I can make it."

"Good! Then see you rest. You've 'ad enough for one night." The man stumbled to his feet with not much assistance needed and left the study.

"Enid, I'm going out after Ambrose. Maybe I can track 'im. You go to your rooms and lock the doors be'ind you. I don't think 'e'd attack you, but I'd rather be safe than sorry, do you 'ear?"

"And the shutters too, as in Madame's room?" I asked, feeling the urgency in his tone and hearing it echoed in my own.

"It wouldn't 'urt," he said with a glint in his eyes that did nothing to allay my concern. We both knew Ambrose was totally insane now, and being insane, might be capable of anything.

He crossed to the shattered casement and started to climb through it, reminding me by his actions of a night not terribly long before when he had come to me in such a way. He must have thought of it too, for he stopped and turned toward me again, giving me a warm and tender smile.

"You're 'olding up well through all this, girl. I'm proud of you."

"Jemmy," I cried, rushing across the littered, book-lined room toward him, "Jemmy, please take care. Do not let him hurt you," and I threw my arms around his neck impulsively, unthinking and uncaring of any propriety. I just wanted desperately to hold him and not to lose him.

" 'E won't hurt *me*, girl, not at all," and with that he took me in his arms and kissed me as no man—no man ever—had kissed me before. It was a kiss of such feeling and such passion as I had not known a woman could feel, and I clung to him, returning that kiss with a passion and abandon that matched his own, and with such surrender as I had never yielded up before in all my life.

One long deep, knowing look between us and he was gone, slipping out through the broken window with a slight tearing of cloth and the tinkling of falling shards of glass.

I watched him stalk out across the wet greensward, looking for traces of Ambrose's footsteps in the dew, and as I watched, I prayed for his safe return—for, of all the things I had come in recent days to know, and of all the things I had come in recent days to feel, the surest thing that I knew and felt was that I loved Jemmy Burkers, loved him and desired him as well.

I did not obey Jemmy's order to go at once to my rooms. I was far too spent and tired to move, and so I sank instead upon the couch there in Ambrose's study and stretched to my full length, letting out an exhausted sigh of relief at the sheer pleasure of being able to rest my weary bones at last.

Bones! My God, what bones there were in that room, and skulls and sculptured presentments of death in every form imaginable. I lay there in my exhaustion and let my eyes—too tired even to close—range around the shelf-lined walls of that ghastly room. It was mostly books one saw, and mostly old, old books at that; parchment-bound and crumbling, stained by time and scarred by use. His desk was piled with them, and so was the floor surrounding it, but on every surface not yielded to a book or a manuscript or folio of some sort, there was a skull or little bronze skeleton figure or leering devil or bone or some other grim reminder of our inevitable mortality.

The grimmest reminder of all, of course, lay in the next room; in Ambrose De'Ath's bedroom. Slowly, almost idly, my eyes wandered with listless curiosity toward the half-open door to that terrible sanctuary, and I found myself remembering the first time I had ever seen that room.

I thought back to how angry Jemmy Burkers had been at my marriage to Ambrose, and how he had reviled me because he thought that I had known all along of Ambrose's sick delusions and had married him in spite of them—perhaps even shared his horrible perversion with him for the sake of catching myself a supposedly wealthy husband. I remembered how he had come, during our heated exchange, to realize that I did not know of my husband's preferred sleeping arrangements and how he had dragged me down the hall from my own rooms to these; how he had unlocked that dreadful door and thrust me before him into that horrible morgue of a room.

"After you, Mrs. De'Ath," he had said mockingly, laughing a wicked, ugly laugh that made me hate him then and fear him as well. How odd that, for now I loved that same man—and feared *for* him.

I cast my mind back to what I had seen in that room on that first day—black-draped walls and carpet of black as well. Black candles in gilt-bronze sconces; four tall thick black candles set like four sentinels around a low, black-draped bier, and on that bier a large, wide coffin, the ebony wood polished to the sheen of patent leather, as hard and cold as onyx, with its lining of soft white satin, the delicately smock-worked pillow, the coverlet of white satin, quilted and comfortable as the coverlet in a baby's crib.

Jemmy had thrust me before him into that room, forcing me to see the dreadful place; forcing me to see for the first time the secret life of the man that I had married so foolishly, so precipitately. I had married Ambrose De'Ath to escape the hell of my narrow, bitter life in Park Lane, and by doing so, I had merely traded one hell for another.

A chill of dread went through me as I looked back in time to the remembrance of that room and that coffin—so stark with its hard black wood and soft white satin. My eyes, listless and burning with fatigue and swollen with the many tears I had shed through that long, exhausting night, wandered through the half-open door again, to that ominous black-draped bedroom and that long, shiny black box on its black-draped bier, flanked by its black candles.

Black! All black. My eyes saw nothing but that endless blackness; black upon black upon . . .

Where was that stark contast that I remembered so vividly, that I could conjure up so readily in my mind's eye? That sharp contrast of white against the black, the satin lining against the ebony wood?

Again that knotted feeling in the pit of my stomach.

There was no stark contrast of black and white, no ebony and satin in my sight, because, unlike the other time I had seen that dreadful coffin, *this time the coffin was closed*.

I sat up at once, calling Jemmy's name, but too long a time had elapsed. Jemmy was out upon his fruitless search, directing the servants of Thanatos Abbey in a reeling, senseless hunt for their master.

Oh, yes, it was a senseless hunt! I knew that well. I stood up slowly, unsteady on my feet, my eyes, unblinking, trained straight ahead of me through Ambrose De'Ath's half-open bedroom door, and walked, rather as one walks in one's sleep I think, across the study and into the dreaded cell itself.

The polished ebony of the coffin was hard and smooth as onyx, the bronze handles along the sides cold to my idle, stroking fingers as I circled the box like one in a daze. The handles moved slightly under my hands, tapping lightly against the wood as I touched them.

Ebony! It must be heavy, I thought almost dreamily as I gazed at the blackness of the wooden top of that long, grim house of death. I slipped the fingers of my two hands under the rounded lip of the edge of the lid. There was just enough room to get a grip; just enough strength left in me to lift that lid and swing it open on its oiled bronze hinges.

There was just enough courage left in me to take one glance at the congested, blue-white face—swollen with suffocation—that was the face of my husband, the face of Ambrose De'Ath, the face of *the late Ambrose De'Ath*.

There was just enough courage left for that sight and that realization before I fell swooning to the black carpet at the foot of Ambrose's bier.

They found me not long after, I am told, but I, of course, remember none of that.

It was a long, long time before I remembered anything at all.

They called it "brain fever," for want, I suspect, of any more sure and certain diagnosis. They only knew that I was fevered and delirious, raving one moment, calm and nearly lucid the next. The doctors gave me up in despair, shaking their solemn heads and advising Madame De'Ath and Jemmy to expect the worst.

But those two never expected the worst—and especially not of me. They knew, better than all the doctors in Cornwall, that the fever that raged like a storm through my trembling body and overwrought mind would work itself out and pass and that I would be whole again.

To that end, Arabella Ottermole came to live at Thanatos Abbey for a time, caring for me with Madame De'Ath and Jemmy by turns so that no matter what time of the day or night, one of them was ever at my side, cooling my fevered brow, nourishing me with rich broths and strong tea, talking endlessly and soothingly to calm my troubled mind with kind and gentle words of encouragement only half-heard, only half-understood if heard or understood at all. They never flagged in their devotion, and to that devotion I perhaps owe my sanity if not my very life itself.

Lucas Pond came often, more I think for the company of his Arabella than for my comfort, but nevertheless I remember waking occasionally from my strange and fevered stupor to find the boy—more man than boy with each passing day it seemed—sitting by my side, reading aloud from some light, pleasant book or other in his monotonous, twanging, somehow comforting American drawl. Arabella would be at the end of the bed, nearest the window, working at her needlepoint or some Berlin-worked beading, a small, contented smile upon her face as she listened to his voice.

If I stirred, she would be at my side at once, whispering softly, touching my brow with gentle fingers, sending Lucas to fetch Jemmy or my mother-in-law. They would gather then, all of them, and Jemmy would speak to me, his eyes earnest, fighting back the tears, gripping my hand too tight for comfort in his sometime fear of actually losing me.

I would, in those fleeting, dreamlike moments, try to tell him that I was fighting, that he would not lose me, that I would not die, but words failed, strength failed, and my mind would slip once more into the abyss of terror—of memories too harrowing to grasp, sights too awful to see, fears too dreadful to realize.

I would rave then, unmindful of the loving, caring souls about me; unaware of the warm spring sun turning the bleak Cornish coast into a place of stark, majestic beauty; unaware of the daily masses of flowers with which Jemmy personally bedecked my room, or of the fresh, pure air that wafted through my open window and caressed me with its healing, scented charms.

And then one day it happened.

I awoke, as if from one long dreadful night of tormenting dreams, and found that that night of mine had been full six weeks long. The sun was streaming in at the window, and in its light I saw Jemmy clearly for the first time in weeks. He stood half-turned from he, his dark eyes looking far out across the cliffs to the waters of the channel beyond, and tears were streaming down his cheeks. His lips were moving slowly, though no sound came forth, and I knew that he was praying—and that his prayers were for me.

"Jemmy," I whispered, "Jemmy, it's all right. I've come through. I'm back."

He turned and looked at me, uncertainly at first, and then quite hard for one long moment before he came quickly to my bedside, taking me in his arms and holding on for dear life. He knew that it was true. This time it was no semiconscious rousing of a fevered brain. This time it was *me*, and I had come back at last; had won through the long raging storm of my past nightmares and was myself again—my true self; the self that I should always have been.

"Thank God," he whispered over and over, kissing my face with a gentle rain of kisses, caressing me hungrily in his joy at my recovery from the long ordeal of my delirium.

It was many weeks yet before I was strong again, and in that time I gradually learned of all that had passed during my illness.

On that fateful night when Ambrose and my aunt had died, Mr. Ottermole had been the first to discover me, still unconscious at the foot of Ambrose's bier, and to find Ambrose dead within the black box that Mr. Ottermole himself had sold to his friend. It was he who summoned Jemmy back from his fruitless search of the grounds and broke the news of my condition.

Amongst them—Jemmy, Madame De'Ath, Osric Ottermole, and the doctor whom he had brought with him from Wadebridge (and who was the local coroner as well)—they had conspired to keep private the true happenings at the abbey on that awful night, my aunt's death being ruled a natural one and the fact of Ambrose's evident suicide being buried under the all-inclusive term of "death by misadventure," and it was well that it was so. Had there been a deeper inquest into the events of that night, a dreadful scandal would otherwise have ensued and the name of Tregaron, already infamous in the annals of unsolved crimes, would have been dragged again through the mud and across the pages of the more sensational newspapers. It was enough to have learned, in one terrible night of horrors, the true secret of that murderous night that had haunted my life for fourteen years—and of my own desperate act of murder, however innocently enacted—but to have had it all spread out in the press for all to gape at might have proved too much for me. Mercifully, thanks to the efforts of friends too kind to ever repay sufficiently, I was spared a second such ordeal in my troubled life.

And so, whilst I raved in my bed of death and murder and all the horrors that I saw in my delirium, they had buried my aunt and my husband side by side in the graveyard behind the church in Wadebridge. There is a certain irony in that, I think, because those two poor souls, each fascinated by death in their own mad way, and each drawn to me like a magnet in the unconscious supposition that I was, as a wanton killer, some living personification of their fear—some death-dealing focus for their madness—found, rather, that I had no relationship to death at all, save as a victim of ugly circumstance. I had only wanted life and happiness and sunlight, however long I had been trapped in the dark corners of death and murder that had haunted my life for so long. So then, myself aside, their true direction, from virtually the moment that they met, had been one long, unavoidable collision course, with their mutual destinies bound—not so much because of me as in spite of me—to end in their deaths.

And now, their greatest common fear and fascination met, their date with death accomplished, it is fitting that they lie side by side forever, having found in each other the very culmination of the terrible thing they sought and dreaded and wanted all their sick lives long.

But enough of death.

As I lay resting, recovering gradually from my illness and resolving, by dint of many quiet talks with the patient, loving Jemmy and the wise, experienced Madame De'Ath, all the many turmoils and guilts of my past, all about me in that house I could hear the hitherto unfamiliar sounds of movement and of packing, of hurrying feet and excited voices—in short, the very sounds of life that had been so long missing from Thanatos Abbey. Every stick of Madame's furniture, her every treasure, was being inventoried, packed, and crated with utmost care for the long journey ahead. Lawyers came and went, and amidst much hustle and bustle of anticipation, Ambrose's cousin, Hubert De'Ath, the heir to Thanatos Abbey, visited to survey his property and make plans for his occupancy.

Despite our fears that he might make some difficulties about the delay in our removal from his domain, which owed to my illness and the monumental job of packing Madame's possessions, Hubert De'Ath turned out to be a most kindly and accommodating man, very agreeable in his manner and person, with a merry wife and thirteen (!) rollicking children. He had been rather strapped for funds, as one might imagine by the size of his family, and positively doted on the property he had inherited; hated Ambrose's furniture and *memento mori* with a passion that equaled our own, and made immediate plans to sell them at the earliest possible moment and invest the money in the land, turning the abbey (which he also planned to rename) into a jolly home for his family, which by the silhouette of his wife, gave promise of still further enlargement, and a working farm as well, much as it had been in its heyday as a monastery.

In short, there was an aura of goodwill and happiness over the whole of the doings in the abbey as spring progressed. I could not, of course, be a part of the general activity, owing to my convalescence, but I did manage to be of some help to Arabella in the sewing of her wedding dress, which was of ivory satin and trimmed with her mother's wedding lace. Her father had engaged a London dressmaker, and the two of them would visit my rooms on many an afternoon during that May and we would work and laugh and help the bride-to-be with her trousseau, to which Madame De'Ath made many generous contributions in the form of lace and linens and fine cloth of rarest beauty.

Mr. Ottermole was the proudest of men, happy in his daughter's happiness, well satisfied with his prospective son-in-law, Lucas, who took to the family business with that same stolid but effective acuity of mind that had surprised us all one by one in our turn as we had come to know him. The dear little man, on one of his many visits to me, confided how pleased he was with Lucas and that he planned, upon the arrival of the first grandchild, to make his son-in-law a partner in the firm, perhaps even expanding the business to Portsmouth eventually.

I remember even now how I smiled at his enthusiastic optimism and at the prospect of fat, yellow little Mr. Osric Ottermole a proud grandsire. And, true to his word, as of mid-1852, the wording on the bronze plaque beside the door of Mr. Ottermole's business came to read:

OTTERMOLE AND POND
UNDERTAKERS & COMPLETE
FUNERAL FURNISHERS
ESTABLISHED 1815

In fact, for several successive years thereafter, a number of boy and girl children made their appearance by turns, some being small and round of stature, others tall and broad, but each bearing the unmistakable stamp of their mother's good nature and their father's somewhat charmless but unquestioned astuteness of mind.

At the latest letter from that estimable matron Mrs. Arabella Ottermole Pond, the family firm is well established in several south-of-England cities, Mr. Ottermole has relinquished the running of the business to his son-in-law in exchange for the more rewarding pleasures of fishing expeditions with his grandchildren, and Lucas, of whom she is very proud, is eyeing London hungrily as a new field of funereal endeavor, the death of the late, somewhat overly lamented prince consort having created in England a veritable fashion—dare I say *passion*—for funerals and the products attendant thereon.

In short, the fruits of the Ottermole-Pond wedding, conducted with so much joy and homely, country style in late June of 1850, have ripened well and still give great and much-deserved happiness to all concerned.

The elder Ponds, Reverend Enoch and Mrs. Peggy, still utterly convinced of the veracity of "spirit rapping," have long since returned to America, where they preach the gospel of "spiritualism" as it is now popularly called, and are currently involved in forming a "psychical society" of some sort for the further "scientific study" of "spirit phenomena"—a direct descendant of poor Ambrose's idea of a thanatological foundation and one of many such that have since sprung into being. Poor Ambrose indeed! He was not right, I think, in his mad delusions and obsessive quest for proof of a life after death, but as it turns out, he certainly was not alone in his obsession either—simply ahead of his time.

And that leaves three—Madame Henriette De'Ath, Jemmy Burkers, and myself. What of us?

We packed, we collected together what money we had amongst us—my own inheritance was yet to come, not being mine, you may remember, until my thirtieth birthday—and after attending Arabella's wedding to Lucas Pond, we set off for Portsmouth to find a ship and set sail for the more hopeful shores of America.

It was a whole new life that we sought; one where Jemmy might be free of the hidebound class distinctions that held him down in England, where I might forget my past and the notoriety ever threatening to revive the scandalous Tregaron murders, and where Madame De'Ath might be free, after years of duty to her stepson, to see new sights and charm new people with her magnetic powers and her unusual charms.

The America of the 1850's was quite a place; full of new-rich yokels with too much money and not enough sophistication, ripe for the machinations of a P. T. Barnum and the host of lesser rogues and scoundrels (our humble selves cheerfully no longer numbered amongst them!) who followed in his wake, making their fortunes from the gullibility of the rich and restless masses on that burgeoning, teeming young continent.

There has always been some question as to whether the aforementioned Mr. Barnum has ever actually said "There's a sucker born every minute" (he has refused to be pinned down on the matter, although I have pressed him about it often), but there is no question that whoever did say it was absolutely right, as our subsequent observations of America have proved.

We have, the three of us, moved in the finest of New York, Philadelphia, St. Louis, and, more recently, San Francisco society, quiet and modest in our own ostentatiously bejeweled and lavishly costumed way—a direct use of Cagliostro's philosophy, remember?—and by doing so, we have reaped ourselves a pleasant and honest little fortune from the generous hands of others, for we have, over the years, established several thriving and luxuriously extravagant hotels in the major cities of this mad, striving new country. The Du Roc in New York, the Burkett in Philadelphia, the Tregaron House in St. Louis, and, more recently, the Huguenot in San Francisco are justly celebrated for the elaborate elegance of their decors, the perfection of their service, the magnificent cuisine of their fine restaurants, and not least, the superiority of their gaming rooms.

We live well, numbering the elite of America's strange mélange of celebrities and politicians and actresses and society figures amongst our countless acquaintances, and, more important, we laugh a very great deal. Our pasts are all behind us, where they are best left, our present circumstances are a delight, and the future remains where it should be— ahead of us, somewhat mysterious, but always a challenge to be enjoyed and savored or braved with courage as circumstances will warrant.

Madame De'Ath is very, very old now, and if not as strong of body as once she was, even yet she remains our strong and guiding force of mind and heart, for her spirit never flags— and will not, I think, even at the last, which cannot, we fear, be long in coming. But for now, we have her with us still, loving her dearly and cherishing her well. Needless to say, she is something of a wonder to those who meet her; a rare and exotic bird flourishing amongst all these American "pigeons," as Jemmy is wont to remark with a devilish grin on his handsome face.

And as for Jemmy and me?

He laughs as I ask, and says to say that he is quite content and that I am the perfect mate to his ambitious endeavors and damnably good in bed! Well, whilst I may not be *perfect*, I *do* try!

And what do *I* say?

Why, simply that he is a perfect lover—and that he is almost as perfect a mate as he is a lover. Now, what lady could ask for more than that?

I have set before you life and death,
blessing and cursing: therefore choose life,
that both thou and thy seed may live.
*Deuteronomy 30:19*